The Ghost and Dr. Monroe

Andi stepped out of the tub and quickly dried off. Wrapping the thick white towel around her, she inspected the room. How many times had she envisioned this place? Hundreds of thousands. Even her dreams didn't match up.

Except for the mysterious man she thought she'd seen dressed as a medieval knight twelve years before. She remembered his rugged, handsome face, his long, dark hair, and the most intriguing shade of blue eyes she'd ever seen. He'd been rough, demanding, yet kind enough to offer his assistance. Why he hadn't physically helped her, instead of barking orders at her from the steps below, still baffled her. And had her hand literally fallen through him? No. She refused to believe it. She'd just been scared.

His voice, very deep and raspy, had shaken her to the bone. She remembered her knight as being huge, with wide shoulders and muscles, all covered in chain mail.

"Boy, talk about a realistic vision." With the palm of her hand, she wiped the fogged moisture from the mirror and shook her head. "Dr. Monroe, you ~~riously need to get a life."

Spirited Away

CINDY MILES

A SIGNET ECLIPSE BOOK

SIGNET ECLIPSE
Published by New American Library, a division of
Penguin Group (USA) Inc., 375 Hudson Street,
New York, New York 10014, USA
Penguin Group (Canada), 90 Eglinton Avenue East, Suite 700, Toronto,
Ontario M4P 2Y3, Canada (a division of Pearson Penguin Canada Inc.)
Penguin Books Ltd., 80 Strand, London WC2R 0RL, England
Penguin Ireland, 25 St. Stephen's Green, Dublin 2,
Ireland (a division of Penguin Books Ltd.)
Penguin Group (Australia), 250 Camberwell Road, Camberwell, Victoria 3124,
Australia (a division of Pearson Australia Group Pty. Ltd.)
Penguin Books India Pvt. Ltd., 11 Community Centre, Panchsheel Park,
New Delhi - 110 017, India
Penguin Group (NZ), 67 Apollo Drive, Mairangi Bay,
Auckland 1311, New Zealand (a division of Pearson New Zealand Ltd.)
Penguin Books (South Africa) (Pty.) Ltd., 24 Sturdee Avenue,
Rosebank, Johannesburg 2196, South Africa

Penguin Books Ltd., Registered Offices:
80 Strand, London WC2R 0RL, England

First published by Signet Eclipse, an imprint of New American Library,
a division of Penguin Group (USA) Inc.

First Printing, May 2007
10 9 8 7 6 5 4 3 2 1

For my husband, Brian, and my kids, Kyle and Tyler, for being such a wonderful family and the greatest part of my life.

For my grandma, Frances Harden. She's no longer with me, but man, she'd have gotten a kick out of this!

For my mom, Dale Nease, who has believed in me from the very first day I mentioned writing a book.

For my dad, Ray Nease, who taught me all about self-promotion at a young age. (Remember all those flyers, Dad?)

For my sisters, Sheri Dotson, Tracy Pierce, and Nikki Nixon. All stunning women whom I'm proud to call best friends.

For my brother-in-law, Jerry Dotson, the cutest Miami-Dade fireman at the station and a real hero (can I have that ride in the ladder truck now, please?), and my other brothers-in-law, Will Nixon and Jordan Pierce, who are both adorable knuckleheads.

For my Harden Family, who gave me the best childhood ever, and my Sumrall/Morris/Palmer Family, whom I'm so glad to have in my life.

For Hank Heller, my wacky cousin who shared many crazy adventures with me (beebees *do* hurt!).

Finally, for my aunt Dona Denmark, a fine writer in her own right whose true love affair with her husband, John, for nearly sixty years inspires me every single day.

ACKNOWLEDGMENTS

So many terrific people have cheered me on, nudged me forward, and made this book take form and become a reality. For the following, I owe my sincere gratitude:

Jenny Bent, a phenomenal agent who saw my potential and believed in me and my stories.

Holly Henderson-Root, for her enthusiasm and encouragement from the very start.

Laura Cifelli, for her expert guidance, quick eye, and editorial savvy.

Jolie Mathis, a sensational author, for her undying loyalty as a true friend, her sweet, funny spirit, and for all the fabulous brainstorming.

Cynthia Reese, for her unflagging support and sound advice, and for Babette de Jongh and the ladies at Romancinghistory, all superb critique partners and super writers.

Shay Chesser and Linda Davis, for trudging across many a misty moor and ruinous castle, just so I could "get the true feel of it" for my stories. (*Sheildaig! Sheildaig!*)

Cathy Hendrix, for being my very first reader and super support system.

Julie Johnson Blake, my best childhood pal with whom I share so many wonderful memories (THE OTHER! JAWS! SLEEPOVER!).

Betsy Kane, Molly Hammond, Evaline Chapman, Michelle Green, Olga Fogam, Amy Bailey, Valerie Morton, and the rest of the gang on PCU at St. Joseph's Hospital in Savannah, Georgia, for their inexhaustible support and friendship.

Michelle Hall, Robyn Edenfield, Loretta Kirby, and their families for their love and support.

All the folks at EGRMC in Statesboro, Georgia, who rallied my spirits and elbowed me to "write another book."

The Northumbria Police in England, for answering my endless questions regarding all things British and forensic.

Sue-Ellen Welfonder and Julie Kenner, for taking time out of their hectic schedule to read my book.

Leah Brown and Virginia Farmer, both excellent writers and my first critique partners who taught me so much.

Finally, to those superb writers before me who never cease to inspire: Charles Dickens, Washington Irving, Jane Austen, Lynn Kurland, and Erin Hart.

Thank you all for helping make my dreams come true!

Prologue

Dreadmoor Keep, 1292
Northern England

Tristan cracked open an eye. He shook his head and peered through the hazy light. Slowly, he stood.

A single torch flame cast shadows across a floor littered with broken shell and rock. Stripped of his mail, he felt the chilling damp that clung to the air and seeped into his bare skin. He moved forward, but cold shackles held his wrists. With effort, he threw himself hard against the iron fetters. The chains held fast. Panting, he gathered what strength remained and grunted, pushing all of his weight against the bindings.

Blood pounded behind his eyes, his vision blurred. Rough stone wall caught his weight as he fell back, spent. His head hammered and his stomach rolled. The stench in the dank chamber threatened to make him lose what little remained in his stomach. He'd know that rancid smell anywhere.

'Twas his own bloody dungeon.

A soft groan came from the corner. Squinting, he made out the slumped form of his youngest knight. Beside him, his captain. Both were tethered to the wall.

"Jason?" His voice cracked through the silence. "Kail? Answer me." Neither made a sound.

"Come forth!" Tristan's bellowing command echoed off the stone walls. A warm stream trickled down his face and caught on his lip. The bitter taste of blood clung to his tongue and he spat it out. God's teeth, he would kill whoever did this with his bare hands!

"Ah, the notorious Dragonhawk." The calm, smooth voice scolded from the darkness. "Such a temper. It seems to favor your family. Loud, disgusting heathens, the lot of you. No doubt your mother's Scottish barbarian blood." A man emerged from the concealing shadows. "Whatever shall I do with you?"

The blood drained from Tristan's face, a knot formed in the pit of his stomach. The breath lodged in his lungs, choking him as he stared, disbelieving, at his foster father. "Erik, what is this?" He pulled at his restraints. "Remove these shackles!"

"Nay, my bound giant. I do believe I have you"—he inclined his head toward Jason and Kail—"and them, exactly where I want you." Erik de Sabre reached for the scabbard strapped to his side and produced a sword—polished, gleaming, and lethal.

A sapphire stone in the hilt winked its apology at Tristan.

'Twas his own sword.

His body shook with rage. "What is the meaning of this? Erik!" He threw himself at his foster father. "Erik!"

De Sabre closed his eyes and swayed. A soft, murmured chant rolled from his tongue.

Tristan stared in disbelief. A curse? "What has befallen you? Are you mad?" He bucked hard against his bindings. "Erik, cease!" God's teeth, had he killed his men?

Erik de Sabre continued his chant, the strange words falling fast, slow, fast. Then with a jerk, he looked up. "I've waited years for this moment, de Barre. I gave you and those other scrawny lads twelve years of my life. I taught you everything." His eyes blazed. "I *made* you, Dragonhawk. Then you . . . killed my boy. And you and your pitiful knights shall pay." He lifted the sword, eyes fixed on the stone. "I have carefully practiced the verse taught to me. It will bind you, Tristan de Barre, to Dreadmoor Keep for eternity. Never to sleep, nor eat."

He stroked his beard and turned, sinister eyes fixed, unblinking. "Never to draw your blade, nor ride a horse. Never again to taste the flesh of a woman, nor have her bear your children. A most perfect plan, indeed. Do you not agree?"

Confusion mixed with hatred and churned low in his stomach as Tristan met de Sabre's cold stare. How could this be? His own foster father. "Christ, Erik. This is about Christopher? Damnation, we tried our best to save him!" He couldn't believe what he was hearing, or seeing. "You were like a father to me—to all of us!"

A brief flicker sparked in Erik's eyes, but was quickly extinguished. "You'll never know the pain I suffered when my only child was murdered, and whilst in your care, high and powerful Dragonhawk. 'Tis unfathomable. But you'll certainly know the pain of death, as will your men. Along with an eternity of misery."

Tristan growled and stretched his iron fetters taut. "I don't believe in curses."

One corner of de Sabre's mouth lifted. "Ah, but you will. How does it feel, Dreadmoor, to know you are about to draw your last breath?" One eyebrow lifted. "And in the dungeon of your very own keep?" He took one step closer, just out of Tristan's reach. "I do wish your beloved family could see you now. Bound, like a mad beast, begging, frothing at the mouth—"

Tristan lunged, but the chains snatched him back. Enraged, he pitched forward again, straining against the manacles. His roar filled the dank chamber as he cursed in his grandfather's French-Norman tongue. "You're wrong, Erik! Your son's death was an accident, and you damn well know it! Don't do this, or you will die by my hands. I vow it!"

De Sabre's quiet laugh filled the chamber. "I think not."

Tristan held de Sabre's unholy gaze as his foster father hefted the sword. Gritting his teeth, Tristan hissed as the cold steel of his own blade slid between his ribs. Erik's face grew dark as he pushed the sword deeper.

He lowered his mouth to Tristan's ear. "If you're wondering where your mighty knights are, don't. I've called for them. They're rushing here at this very moment." He gave the sword a push. "They'll be here to watch you die. . . ."

Tristan sucked in an agonized breath. Pain ripped through his body but he forced his eyes to remain on the man he once trusted with his life, a man whose mind was maddened from the loss of his son. His words gasped from his lips. "I—will—not—yield."

De Sabre twisted the blade. "Aye. You will."

The chamber shifted and Tristan's vision blurred, shapes and planes faded, losing their color, their rigidness, settling into distorted figures, shadows . . . and then darkness.

Chapter 1

"You want me to do *what*?" Dr. Andi Monroe wiped the rain from her eyes and stared, disbelieving, at her boss. "You're kidding, right? A joke?" She pushed the hood of her weatherproofs from her head and pointed at the five-by-five-meter-square area of mucky earth. "You want me to pack up? We've only been on this for three days, Kirk. We've still hours of recording to do, photographs, soil samples, and screening—and Jamie's just getting started with the GPS unit—"

A gust of wind whipped in from the moors and caught the corner of the rough canvas tarp. The stake anchoring it jostled loose and a sail of wet cloth slapped her face. "Oh, crap." Grabbing the flapping material, Andi fell to her knees, then pulled the small mallet from her tool belt and secured the tarp before it exposed the dirt-stained humerus and skull remains nestled in the spongy black soil. "Kirk, this is not the time for jokes. You know how excited I am about this find."

Kirk Grey, British-born with a clipped accent, squatted beside her and leveled his gaze with hers. He grinned through the drizzle. "Dragonhawk."

A breath escaped her lips. She blinked. "What?"

Kirk's gray eyes crinkled at the corners. "Terrance Daughtry just rang my mobile. It appears last night's storm turned over a massive oak, centuries old, right in the Dragonhawk's lair." His smile widened. "A body of bones entwined in its roots." He feigned an exaggerated yawn. "What appears to be a rather large hoard of medieval weaponry accompanies the remains—I don't know all the details. Besides, I wasn't sure if you'd be interested, being so engrossed in this dig as you are, so I told him we'd have to get back—"

Andi laughed and flung herself into her mentor's arms. "Oh my God! Yes! Of course I'm interested! You know how long I've wanted Dreadmoor Castle!" She pulled back and searched his face. "When?"

"Tonight. But there's a catch, I'm afraid."

Narrowing her eyes, she rose, then stepped back and cocked her head. "What is it?"

Kirk shrugged and stood. "You'll be excavating the site for the rest of the summer." One eyebrow lifted. "Alone."

She suppressed a snort. "Another joke, right?"

He shook his head. "I fear I'm speaking the truth of it. Dreadmoor's a terrible eccentric, from what I hear. He doesn't want a throng of people traipsing over his land. Very private, that one. According to Daughtry, Dreadmoor hadn't planned on even reporting the incident. Seems, though, his curiosity got the better of him." Kirk rubbed his chin. "After Daughtry came out to investigate, Dreadmoor made it clear this project would be kept quiet. No museums, no Heritage Center involvement. So he's agreed to only one forensic archaeologist for the remainder of the summer." A smile curved his lips. "You."

She turned and surveyed the Grey Archaeological Research team, busying themselves in their bright orange and yellow GAR weatherproofs under the steady pelting of rain. She shouldn't just leave them. Some of them, the volunteers, were first-year students. They were relying on her.

They'd been called to the remote moors of Northumberland where a pair of hill walkers had discovered skeletal remains. They were excited about it. She hated quitting a job. *Loathed it.* "But what about—"

Kirk pulled Andi under the tarp. Tapping her on the nose, he then pushed a strand of wet hair from her eyes. "I'll take over as site manager here. I know, it's been a while since I've gotten my hands dirty. Besides, you've done nothing but bore me with tales of yearning for that desolate heap of rocks, not to mention the tiresome tale of that scourge Dragonhawk. You'll just continue to do so if you don't get this dig out of your system." He raised an eyebrow. "Unless you don't think you can handle it alone?"

Excavating alone, without even one little intern. Was she crazy? *Yes, Monroe, you are.*

She grinned. *Dreadmoor Keep.* Situated on an ancient shelf of rock overlooking the blustery North Sea, the thirteenth-century hold had a haunted, mysterious past. Fifteen knights, the original Lord Dreadmoor, a.k.a. Dragonhawk, included, vanished from the keep in 1292. No trace of them had ever been found. It was as though they'd never existed.

The memory of the majestic keep took her breath away. It had been years since she'd first crept onto the castle grounds—how old had she been? Eighteen? What a little daredevil she'd been. But she'd never forgotten it—had never forgotten *him.* A strange experience, one she wasn't too sure had even happened. *Obsession* didn't quite sum it up.

A massive man, dressed in thirteenth-century chain mail, had appeared out of nowhere. He'd saved her from falling through a hole in the crumbling steps of the kirk. *She'd reached . . . her hand had fallen right through him.*

Like a faded image on an old projector movie, he'd been there . . . but hadn't been there. She'd caught herself, screamed, and he'd been there again, talking her down from the jagged stone hole. When she'd reached the bottom, he had vanished. She'd chalked the mishap up to an overactive teenage imagination. Youthful drama. Yet, her scientific thought process aside, she couldn't help but wonder sometimes . . . *Had he been one of the missing knights?*

She'd gotten into big trouble with the dean of forensics. But it'd been worth it. Never would she forget that day, or those piercing sapphire eyes. . . .

"Dr. Monroe?"

Andi met Kirk's steady gaze. A striking man of fifty-eight, he kept his salt-and-pepper gray hair clipped as close as his trademark pencil-thin goatee. Andi felt as though she'd known him forever—practically had. He'd been not only the dean of forensics, but also like a father to her, and the closest thing she'd ever had to family. An implanted Brit from Canterbury, he'd groomed her through all of her college years into the respected forensic archaeologist she was today. And he'd just offered her the chance of a lifetime.

"I take it *yes* is the official answer? I need to ring Daughtry, posthaste. No patience, that one."

Dreadmoor Keep. The legend of Dragonhawk and his private order of knights—gone without a trace of their physical existence. And now a body of bones and a hoard of medieval weapons turn up on Dreadmoor's land. *Could it be?*

She'd longed to return, but being that it was private property, GAR had never been given an invitation. Until now. Shoving her hands into her pockets, she grinned. "Absolutely. You tell Daughtry I'll be there yesterday."

"We're nearing the castle grounds, missy. Best ye get your belongings together," Gibbs, the cabdriver, said.

"We're already there?"

"Aye, 'tis but a few more miles ahead."

She glanced out the window. Black and gray clouds twisted and churned overhead. Great. Another storm, and it looked like a big one. Storm or not, she couldn't wait to see Dreadmoor again. Even if it meant excavating the site alone.

A familiar feeling of anticipation knotted her stomach, just like the first time she'd laid eyes on the hauntingly beautiful keep. No guard had been at the gate, and it hadn't taken much maneuvering to sneak in from the shore side. Adrenaline had flushed through her veins with each new discovery. The dark corners, the rough old stones, and the ancient church near the cliffs—what a thrill! Now only minutes separated her from the castle—not to mention the fascinating find last night's storm had unearthed. What if the medieval weapons truly were clues to the castle's mysterious past? She couldn't wait to grid the area and get to work.

Andi pressed her nose against the cool glass of the window. Just south of Northumberland, she admired the quaint little seaside townships hugging the North Sea coastline. Beautiful stone cottages and old cemeteries flashed by. Although there was still daylight, the stores were all closed, their lights turned off. This time of year, the skies didn't darken until well after eleven p.m. A thick mist crept in from the sea, settling over the green landscape and slipping through the weathered, dark stone buildings like a silvery blanket. It gave the place a ghostly glow. A shiver scurried through her. She could barely stand the wait.

Gibbs shot her a lopsided grin through the rearview mirror. "You're that American archaeologist, ain't ye? Truth be told, we all thought ye was a gent."

We? It'd been less than a day since she'd accepted the job, and the whole village knew about it? "I'm kind of used to the name-gender mix-up. Happens all the time." She smiled at Gibbs in his mirror. "And yes, I'm an American."

"Figured as much. Well. Best ye watch yer step, girlie." His eyebrows lifted. "Strange things have been known to go on round that old spooky pile o' rubble."

Andi's thoughts rushed back to her own weird experience and Dreadmoor's unexplained past. "What kind of strange things?"

Gibbs shrugged, his bushy gray eyebrows disappearing under the bill of his cap. "Battle cries. Fierce ones, too. They can be heard all the way round to the village, on a good day. I even once heard a terrible thundering, like horse hooves pounding." He glanced back at the road ahead. "I got paid an extra fifty pounds just to pick ye up and drive ye out here, ye know. No one else would do it."

Andi stared back at the old cabby and raised an eyebrow. They were no more than two or three miles from the village. "What's there to be afraid of at Dreadmoor?"

Gibbs ignored her and pointed a long, bony finger. "Get your bags ready, missy, 'cause I ain't staying long."

Andi looked up, surprised to find the castle perched high on the cliff ahead. Her breath caught in her throat. It was just as wonderful as it had been twelve years before. "Aren't you going to drive me through the gates?"

"Nope." He turned onto the gravel path leading up to the outer barbican. "Jameson's the butler. He'll help you, once inside. A bit daft, that one, as were his ancestors before him, to work in that haunted heap. And there'll be young Will, the guard at the drawbridge. He just don't know any better. But that's as far as I go."

Andi stifled her own concern. "All right, then. No problem." She gathered her pack and site kit. Gibbs pulled up near the outer barbican and came to a halt. *Barely.*

"Okay, missy. Here ye go." The cabby's eyes darted back and forth across the castle grounds. Did he expect the ghost of Dragonhawk to jump out at any moment and run him through? Or was it all hype? England was full of ghost stories, and nearly every castle had one or two. Green Lady. White Lady. Lady in Gray. None, she thought, as fascinating as Dragonhawk and his missing knights.

What, then, had she seen all those years ago?

"Ye heed my warning, girlie," Gibbs said. "Watch yourself."

"Don't worry. I will." Andi cast the driver a smile and jumped out of the cab. She grabbed her bags and tools from the trunk and stepped back just in time. Gibbs pulled away as soon as her bags cleared the back end.

The car rambled down the cliff's path. With a shake of her head she faced the aged stone building and drew in a satisfied breath.

The barbican. In medieval days it would have housed several heavily armed and mailed guards. Hopefully, the present owner would be eccentric enough to at least house one, and maybe that one would help her lug her bags to the great hall. As she trudged closer, bags in tow, a man stepped out from the thick-stoned entranceway.

Without the first trace of a welcoming smile, the guard held his hand up. "Stop right there, miss."

The young man wore a solid navy blue uniform—like the constables she'd met on the moors. She smiled and shrugged her pack. "Hello. I believe I'm expected?"

"Nay, miss." He shook his dark head to reaffirm his *nay*. "I've no lass on my roster." He cast her a stern look. "I'll call your driver back. This is not a touring castle."

"No, wait." Andi hurried forward as the guard stepped back into the barbican. "Does your roster include a Dr. Monroe?"

The guard didn't even spare a look at the clipboard he held. "I'm afraid that is none of your concern, miss. Now. Himself doesn't take kindly to mishaps. So if you would step to the side and wait for your cabby—"

"Wait—I am Dr. Monroe." Andi flipped open a side pocket on her backpack and dug for her Grey Archaeological Research Institute ID badge. Normally, the confusion wouldn't bother her so much. But she ached, was tired, and had a gnawing sense of uncertainty that she'd like to have the owner of Dreadmoor alleviate—ASAP.

A booming clap of thunder made her jump. Fat, heavy raindrops fell, one by one, and plopped on top of her head. *Great.* She flashed the guard her badge. "I am Dr. Andi Monroe—Andrea, actually, a she, not a he." She threw him a pleading look. "Please, let me in."

Chapter 2

Please, let me in.

Tristan's head snapped up. A woman at the outer barbican? By the saints! He'd been waiting in anticipation for Dr. Monroe's arrival, and by the devil's horns something was amiss at the gates. He stormed out of his solar, down the long, winding stone steps to the kitchens where Jameson busied himself preparing the evening fare.

"Jameson, what in bloody hell is going on at the barbican?" His shout echoed through the larder. "We are expecting Dr. Monroe at any moment."

Jameson, unmoved by his bark, lifted the lid from a pot on the stove, stirred its contents a time or two, then replaced the top. Folding the dish towel into a perfect rectangle, he set it aside and looked up. "I believe," he said, his tone bored, "Dr. Monroe has arrived."

"Do you have sealing wax in your ears, old man? I said there's a woman wailing at my gates!"

Jameson flicked a piece of lint from his jacket. "I know." He looked up, stone-faced.

It took only a moment before Tristan grasped what Jameson had so eloquently pulled off. "Are you telling me, you old meddling busybody, that Dr. Monroe is—"

"Dr. Andrea Monroe." The corners of his mouth twitched. "My lord."

"Saints' coats!" Tristan threw his hands up, paced a time or two, then stopped and glared at his steward. "You know how I feel about wenches in my hall. Why was I not informed of this sooner?"

"Dr. Monroe is by no means a 'wench.' Besides, it never came up, my lord."

"Cease the 'my lord' nonsense, Jameson. You kept it from me a-purpose!"

"As you wish, young master Tristan."

Tristan rolled his eyes heavenward. "If I could throttle you, old man, I would do so straightaway."

Jameson didn't even flinch. "Of course you would, my lord."

Tristan raked a hand through his hair and closed his eyes, pinching the bridge of his nose. A moment passed before he slowly opened them and glared at his man. "Why is Dr. Monroe wailing so?" A loud crack of thunder sounded across the castle grounds and rumbled the walls of the keep. He lifted one eyebrow.

Jameson instantly paled. "Oh dear." He hurried across the room and lifted the phone off its cradle on the wall.

"I suppose Will has no inkling Dr. Monroe is a woman?"

"Nay, he does not."

With one last lordly glare, Tristan turned and stormed off. He walked right through the kitchen wall. He heard Jameson mutter a faint retort. *This will be a most interesting summer, indeed.*

Tristan grumbled to himself. The humorous lilt in his steward's voice more than annoyed him. *Mortals.* He banked the comment to memory. He would deal with the meddler later.

At the outer barbican, Tristan remained invisible and watched as his guard argued with their new guest in the pouring rain. *Bloody bones, man, move out of the way!* The damned buffoon blocked his view. Frustrated, Tristan drew closer, standing to the right of Dr. Monroe. Quite a fetching wench, even soaked to the bone. She had her face turned from him, waving her arms about, brandishing a small piece of parchment about and arguing her professional status with Dreadmoor's barbican guard. Saints, if she would be still and look his way.

Then she did.

Tristan's mouth dropped open. It couldn't be. By

God's blessed bones, if he'd had a heart that beat within a live body it would surely have ceased at that very moment. He stared, not trusting his eyes.

It was *her*. The gangly-legged wench from—how long ago? He'd lost count. He recognized her, though, immediately. She flicked the rain from her eyes, tucked her wet hair behind her ears, and continued to argue. Aye, 'twas truly the same lass as before, only no longer gangly.

Rain ran down her bare arms, her newfangled hose soaked and clinging to her long, shapely legs. A thin tunic formed to her breasts, then flattened against her stomach. His mouth went dry. Nay, 'twasn't possible. Dead men didn't lust.

He suddenly had a craving for a large tankard of ale.

He was going to kill Jameson for this.

Dr. Andi Monroe reared back her soaked and booted foot, then soundly kicked poor Will in the shin. She pushed by the barbican guard and through the gates with the swiftness of a seasoned warrior.

By all of the merciful saints above, she'd gained his castle. And with naught but a swift kick!

Tristan watched the stiff, retreating back of Andrea Monroe as she stormed his keep, armed with no other weapons save her lethal foot and razor-sharp tongue. How the lads would roar when they found out.

He materialized before Will, crossed his arms over his chest, and glared.

After a startled gasp Will lowered his head. "I'm sorry, my lord."

"Hmm." Tristan disappeared into the pounding rain. He would not miss the well-deserved dressing-down his wily old steward was about to receive.

For the first time in over seven hundred years, he had something to look forward to.

Jameson quickly dialed the outer barbican and waited for the guard to pick up. "Yes, Will? Please cease your harassment of Dr. Monroe and allow her to pass. And be a good lad and assist her with her luggage."

Will grunted. "I can't, Jameson. She's already passed. As did Himself."

A loud clap of thunder boomed in the background. "Oh dear." He set the phone back in its cradle and grabbed an umbrella from the coat closet. His Lordship was not going to like this one bit. He hurried through the kitchens to the great hall, skidded to a halt, and threw open the door. His mouth dropped open.

Dr. Monroe stood on the steps, drenched to the bone.

Jameson quickly composed himself. "Oh, my dear girl. I do so apologize for this inconvenience." He grabbed what appeared to be the heaviest bag. Gently grasping her elbow, he pulled her inside.

"You must be Jameson."

He followed her gaze down to a rather large puddle on the floor at her feet. She looked back up and dropped her rucksack on the floor. It landed with a heavy *thud*, followed by a squishy *splat*.

"Everyone seems a little . . . surprised to find that I'm a woman." Her eyes narrowed and she tapped a sodden hiking boot, awaiting his answer. "Know anything about it?"

"Dr. Monroe, allow me to retrieve a dry towel for you."

"Oh no, you don't. Is there a reason you kept my gender a secret?"

Jameson felt his face blush. "My lady, I assure you—"

"Everyone thought I was a man. Even the cabbie thought I was a man. Under usual circumstances, it's no problem, my being mistaken for a man." She frowned. "But you knew. The Northumberland coroner told you."

Jameson's eyebrows shot up in surprise at the not-so-unexpected sight of His Lordship, who materialized behind Dr. Monroe, a wicked smile upon his face. Jameson knew the young lord was enjoying himself, and at his expense.

Dr. Monroe turned to look behind her. Himself quickly disappeared, the white of his teeth the very last thing to go.

"I extend my most gracious apologies, Doctor." Jameson gave her a low, proper bow. "I truly did not think the lack of information would be so bothersome." He drew the most solemn expression he could muster and met the young colonist's gaze, awaiting her forgiveness. As he'd hoped, it came right away.

"Well, no harm done, I suppose." She took a deep breath and smiled. "I apologize. I'm usually not so cranky. I guess I'm just exhausted." She glanced around, then met his gaze. "So. When do I get to meet the lord of Dreadmoor?"

"My lady." Jameson produced a dry towel and gave it as a peace offering. "Wrap this about you and let us be off to your chambers, shall we? His Lordship would no doubt be passing irritated if I allowed you to catch your death." He placed the towel in her hands and gently pulled on her elbow. "Come now, Dr. Monroe."

Andi accepted the towel from Dreadmoor's steward. The steward with, apparently, only one name. "Thanks, Jameson." She wiped her face and hands, and squeezed some of the water from her hair. "About Lord Dreadmoor?"

Jameson gave a solemn look. "I apologize, Dr. Monroe. Himself is indisposed at the moment. I will show you to your chambers where you can unpack and freshen up."

Hmmm. Too busy to greet her. Oh well. Maybe he was old and sickly and had to remain in bed. Kirk had described him as eccentric. Since she didn't want to be rude and ask, she settled for seeking him out later. Eventually, they needed to talk.

"Oh. Jameson. I've got to do one thing before I clean up." She squatted, unzipped her site bag, and pulled out the jacket to her rubber weatherproofs and a lantern. She pushed her arms into the coat. "I need to check the cutaway. Something I'm a little retentive about." Exchanging the wet hikers for her tall, waterproof Wellingtons, she gave him a reassuring smile. "I just want to make sure it's properly covered."

Jameson nodded. "Of course. 'Tis located in the far end of the bailey. I'll call Will from the gatehouse to assist you."

Setting her site bag off to the side, she stood, fitted her tool belt around her waist, and zipped her coat. She waved Jameson's offer aside. "No, that's okay. I know where the bailey is, and this will only take a few minutes."

A puzzled look flashed across his stoic features, then quickly disappeared. "Then I shall accompany you. If you'll give me but a moment to—"

Andi shook her head. "No, really. It's all right, Jameson. I won't be long. I just want to make sure everything is secure." She grabbed her soaked boots and waited.

With a wary gaze, he nodded. "Very well, Dr. Monroe." He led her back to the door and threw a switch on the wall. "Mind the grounds as you walk. It's quite murky out this eve and these outdoor lamps don't quite reach the bailey."

Andi flipped on her torch and pointed the wide beam across the ground. Had it been a clear day, the late-evening light would still be bright. As it was, the heavy mist and blackened sky dimmed the light to near darkness. *Eerie.* She set her hikers on the stone steps to dry. "Thanks, Jameson. And don't worry. I'll be careful." Pulling up the hood of her weatherproofs, she then headed once more out into the drizzle.

Wet, spongy turf squished under her Wellingtons as she made her way across the castle grounds. The heavy scent of sea life permeated the moist air, and the North Sea waves crashed against the rock base that served as Dreadmoor's foundation. God, she couldn't wait until morning so she could see everything in bright light. The place tagged a spot deep within her, unexplainable, powerful—an insatiable craving she'd experienced since the first encounter. The legend of Dragonhawk pulled at her, too.

Sweeping her torchlight left to right, she made out the silhouette of the old kirk through the mist, where it nestled near the cliffs, along with a few other outbuildings.

She knew, though, that Dreadmoor had a six-foot stone wall encircling the property. Had it been to keep enemies out, or keep those within prisoner? She'd read everything she could about the castle—what little there was in print—and filled in the blanks with what she knew of medieval history. But she couldn't wait to get firsthand information from the present lord.

If, that is, he ever showed up.

A crisp wind brushed her cheek and she paused. Turning in a slow circle, she swept the lantern light in an arc and stared into the dark, thick blanket of mist slipping over the bailey. "Who's there?" No response. "Hello?"

Hairs bristled on her arms and she drew a deep breath. Another circle, this time faster, but the light landed on nothing unusual. Deciding to walk the strange feeling off, she headed for the oak.

There, a few meters ahead and to the right, a large tarp covered what Andi knew to be the uprooted end of a large oak tree—along with the remains and hoard of armor. With hurried steps, she crossed the distance and stopped at the corner of the canvas.

She shot a quick glance over her shoulder. "What?" Her heart slammed against her ribs, thumping the same erratic rhythm as the adrenaline rushing through her veins. Hadn't someone just spoken? Pointing her torch, she peered into the gray mist, following its beam to the end of the shaft. "Is someone there?" Again, no answer.

With a deep breath, she turned back to her task. Following the line of canvas, she knelt and made sure each corner was knotted and secured over the stakes. The last one jiggled. She lifted the mallet from her belt and knocked the head of the spike into the ground until it sat flush with the soil.

With a yelp, she jumped and turned. "What? Who's there?" A chill came over her, the sensation turning her insides frosty. The fine hairs at the nape of her neck stood rigid and a burning lump formed in her throat. Moving as fast as her Wellingtons would allow, she rounded the tarp and, finding it secure, took off, slipping across the sodden soil, back to the keep, her torch beam bobbing through the thick, murky haze.

The sudden urgency disappeared as soon as she stepped into the glaring outside light implanted into the stone face of the castle. Andi didn't stop running until her hand rested on the iron knob of the front door. Pushing open the heavy oak, she turned and looked over her shoulder, expecting to find something, or someone.

She found nothing.

Jameson greeted her, his brows pulled close in a frown. "Dr. Monroe? Is there something amiss?"

Andi stepped into the great hall and closed the massive door behind her. After a few gulps of air, she caught her breath. "It felt like . . ." She reached down to unlace her Wellingtons. "I thought someone was out there." She shook her head and took a deep breath. "I . . . could've sworn I heard someone speak. It sounded so real." She gave a nervous laugh. "Crazy, huh?"

Jameson frowned. "What did you hear, lady?"

Peeling off her weatherproofs, she met Jameson's questioning gaze. "Save them."

Jameson's eyebrows shot up. Anger flashed in his eyes but disappeared so fast, Andi wasn't sure it had happened. Then he smiled.

"I'm sure it was only the wind, Dr. Monroe. Very brisk off the North Sea, you know. I assure you the grounds are quite private and secure." He placed an age-spotted hand on her shoulder. "You've nothing to fear in this place, lady. I swear it."

God, now she felt like an idiot. Of course she didn't have anything to fear. All those tales of missing knights and see-through knights in chain mail with no bodily substance and skeletons clinging to tree roots had her imagining things. "Thanks, Jameson. I guess it was my imagination working overtime. I truly appreciate the opportunity to work this find. It means a great deal to me."

He nodded his gray head. "I'm so glad that it does. Now. Shall I assist with your baggage whilst we venture above? No doubt you'll want to rid yourself of those sopping garments?"

Andi smiled and shouldered her site bag. "Absolutely. Lead the way."

For the first time since entering Dreadmoor's great hall she looked—really looked—at her surroundings. A smile pulled at her lips as she took in the room.

Bold stone walls and exposed wooden beams, just as it would have been in the thirteenth century, made up the interior of Dreadmoor Castle. Tapestries that appeared to be centuries old adorned a good amount of wall space. A monolithic fireplace took up the space of an entire wall. Medieval torches—finely crafted replicas, anyway—situated in their cradles cast a dim glow over the enormous room. Very impressive, to say the least, and just as she'd dreamed it would be.

"This place is perfect." She didn't miss a thing as she allowed Jameson to pull her through the great hall toward a massive staircase leading to the chambers above.

They passed an immense tapestry, and she stopped for a short look. The color had faded, but someone had done a wonderful job of keeping it preserved. Such tiny stitches! The scene depicted two knights at tournament, their lances lethally pointed at one another while their magnificent chargers raced forward. A large flag waved in the background, a mystical beast with its head thrown back, roaring. *Dragonhawk.*

"Dr. Monroe?"

"I'm coming." She turned and followed Jameson up the stairs, down a long, shadowy corridor until they reached another set of steps.

"The tower chamber, Dr. Monroe." He indicated their direction with a slight nod.

Andi's skin prickled. She couldn't believe her good fortune. "The tower chamber?"

"Yes, now if you'll step with utmost care . . ."

Jameson's words trailed behind her. Excitement bubbled as she mounted the darkened stairs and rushed ahead into the darkness.

"Colonists."

"I heard that," she said. A single door stood open at the landing. Pitch-blackness poured out. "Hey, Jameson, where are the—"

Lights from the tower chamber flickered on. Andi turned to look behind her. Jameson took the remaining two steps as he approached her room. She turned back to her chambers. She hadn't bumped into any switches. Jameson must've hit one in the hall. With a shrug she walked into her room, then pulled up short. She could do nothing but stare, openmouthed, and hope with all her might she didn't drool and loll her tongue.

"This is so great . . ." More tapestries, similar to the ones in the great hall, draped the rounded stone wall, each depicting a knight either at battle or at tournament, the figures stitched to perfection. A huge, four-poster curtained bed sat in the center of the room, the heavy velvet a lush, dark burgundy. The fireplace, which took up the breadth of the wall directly in front of the bed, had a large, wooden, medieval shield in use as a hearth screen.

She set her site kit on the floor and walked to the shield. She skimmed her hands over the aged wood and steel straps. It measured at least six inches thick and was painted yellow, with a black and green mystical creature rampant in the center. The animal, whose origin Andi didn't recognize, had a sapphire-colored eye. She turned and smiled at Jameson, her waterlogged state forgotten.

"Dragonhawk's crest, right? Is this dated?" She fingered the creature.

"Yes, my lady." The old steward beamed, unable to hide the pride in his voice. He cleared his throat. "Thirteenth century, I do believe." He glanced around the room, then walked across the hardwood floor to a small door. "The lavatory, Dr. Monroe." He took a step inside, pulled back the curtain on the tub, then stepped back out. "Everything you need should be here." Jameson gave her a somber look. "I do apologize for tonight's events, Dr. Monroe. I hope these facilities suit you."

Andi reassured him with a pat on the shoulder. "Jame-

son, I'm used to staying in a tent during an excavation."
She looked around the room and felt another ping of
excitement. "This is way more than I expected. And
don't worry. I'm quite used to the he/she mix-up. And
no excuse for myself—I'm sorry for being rude earlier."
She gave a lopsided grin. "I suppose I should check on
the guard at the front gate. I sort of . . . pushed my
way through."

"Not to worry, my lady. Will is a sturdy lad. He'll be
fine." Jameson gave Andi a low bow, then stood and
straightened his already-straight suit coat. "Have your
bath and then hasten down to the kitchens for a late
supper." Turning on his heel, he walked out of the chambers, pulling the heavy oak door behind him.

Andi looked around the room and shook her head.
Walking over to the window, she threw open the sturdy
wooden shutter. While she'd expected the tangy balm of
fresh air, she was instead met with double-paned glass.
Funny—while a good portion of the castle had been
modernized, a greater portion hadn't. It fascinated her.
She flipped the twin latches at the bottom and shoved
the glass up.

The rain had slowed to a light sprinkle, and a moist-
ened, mid-June sea breeze wafted in. The briny air
washed over her, comforted her. What good fortune she
had, being selected for such a fantastic job. *Thanks, Kirk.*
Had it not been for his connections with the coroner,
another private firm might have been chosen.

Smiling to herself, she grabbed some dry clothes from
her bag, along with her toiletries, and stepped into the
bathroom. God, this was great! She could hardly wait to
get started. After the initial inspection of the site in the
morning, she'd get a lift into the village and start with a
verbal investigation. She wanted to know more about the
legend of the missing knights before laying out the grid.
There was a great chance the two could be connected.

Her stomach rumbled—loud. The pack of digestives
pilfered from the mess tent in Northumberland had long
ago worn off. She was starving. *Ooh, fish 'n' chips.* A
craving to visit one of the chip shops in the village

tweaked her stomach. Steaming batter-fried haddock, a heap of fried chips smothered in vinegar and brown sauce all wrapped up in thick, white paper . . . yum.

With a spring in her step she set to her task, anxious to meet Jameson in the kitchens and, not only eat, but ask a few questions about the lords of Dreadmoor, past and present—

"What?" Andi peered around the doorjamb. Hadn't someone just spoken? "Hello?" Her gaze crossed the empty chamber. With a shake of her head, she ducked back into the doorway. On second thought, she flipped the lock.

Either she was going crazy, or she'd just heard another whisper. It was the same message from earlier.

Save them.

Chapter 3

Tristan materialized in front of his man at the bottom step in the great hall. Jameson, damn his arse, gave him a deep, scolding frown.

One gray eyebrow lifted. "Have you nothing better to do with Dr. Monroe than use her as sport?"

Tristan crossed his arms over his chest. "What?"

"Dr. Monroe. She came running in from the fallen oak, scared out of her wits. She said someone spoke to her in the bailey, but no one was about. I would like to know who . . . and why. She's here to help—and by your bidding."

Tristan scowled. "I don't know what you're talking about, old man. I had nothing to do with it. She just began turning and asking aloud 'What? Who's there?' I thought mayhap she'd seen me. Finally, she bolted. After I made sure she was at the door, I went to question the others."

Jameson's gray brows furrowed. "And had one of them done the teasing?"

Tristan shook his head. "Nay. The lads all denied it."

The blood drained from Jameson's face. "If you didn't do it, sir, nor the others, then who did?"

Tristan crossed the great hall to the hearth and stared into the burning embers. "I vow I don't know. She said someone spoke to her?"

"That is what she said."

Tristan cocked his head. "And what did the voice say?"

"Save them."

Save them? What by the devil's horns did that mean? He hadn't heard a voice, and he'd been right behind her, every step of the way. "I did follow her out. She shouldn't go alone. But I vow I didn't speak a word aloud." He thought a moment. "She was rather edgy. I knew she was afraid, but by the devil, I couldn't see what of." He met his butler's worried gaze. "Is she settled now?"

"I believe she is, my lord."

"Well, it's a bloody good thing I switched on the lamps in her chambers, since you didn't bother to. She could've fallen in the dark." He rubbed his jaw. "What is she doing now?"

"I believe she is bathing, my lord."

He cleared his throat. "Of course she is. She was soaked to the bloody bone. Now, we've another issue at hand. There is a small change in plans as to Dr. Monroe meeting me."

Jameson raised one gray eyebrow. "How's that?"

Tristan began to pace. Pacing always did seem to help him ponder. With a quick wave of his hand, he created the dying embers to instantly blaze. "I cannot allow Dr. Monroe to see me."

Jameson inclined his head. "And why, pray tell, is that?"

Tristan stopped and stared. "You know good and true, old man, that I did not want strangers traipsing over my land. I'm a private sort." He raked a hand through his hair. "If only that storm hadn't turned over the bloody tree." He leveled his gaze to his manservant. "I certainly didn't want any bothersome females to have to worry over. And now I have one for the saints only know how long."

"That, my young lord, is a most lame excuse. Besides, you yourself said you'd like to find out more about the bones and armor."

He paused. "Aye, true. 'Tis baffling." He let out an exasperated breath. "We've met once before, I'm afraid."

Jameson blinked. "Come again?"

"The wench. I've, er, well." He coughed. "We've met."

"When, exactly?"

Tristan paused. "Right after your Margaret passed." Saints, how it pained him to remember that sweet woman. Jameson's beloved wife had worked her way into Tristan's heart and taken root, and he mourned greatly for her. Yet another reminder of how useless it was to allow his heart to grow close to a mortal. 'Twould lead to nothing more than an eternity of pain.

Jameson's expression softened at the mention of his Margaret. "I was gone but for a fortnight, sir. I had no idea you'd gained such trouble in such a short time."

"I know." Tristan shook his head. "She was a lovely thing, even back then, although a bit gaunt. She came rambling onto Dreadmoor's lands, eyes wide with wonder, and then came up from the shore side as if she had no fear of the place, or what may lurk here." He shrugged. " 'Twas after that we hired our first barbican guard."

Jameson cleared his throat. "I see. Strange, you've never bothered to inform me of this little adventure before."

"Be you quiet, Jameson. As it goes, the silly lass decided to enter the kirk—no doubt to simply explore. The next instant, the stone steps caught her eye."

"Those steps are quite treacherous, my lord."

Tristan frowned. "I know that. 'Twasn't as though I invited her in. But in she went anyway, of her own accord." He waved his hand in the air. "Then her foot went through a crumbling step and she nearly fell. There she was, stuck and flailing about, with no one around . . . save my bloody, useless self."

"How—"

"I followed her from the barbican, and had even attempted to frighten her off with a few crisp gusts of wind. But the wench was determined." He looked at Jameson and shrugged. "I had no choice but to appear before her and talk her out of the situation. She was nigh onto breaking her skinny neck." Pinching the bridge of his nose, he shook his head. "If only that were the whole of it." He peered at Jameson. "She made a grab for me, and before I could retreat, she . . ." He closed his eyes. "Her hand fell through me."

"Oh dear. This does change things a bit."

"Aye." Tristan paced in front of the fire, his hands clasped behind his back. He stopped and whirled around. "I've got it. Tell her I've come down with the ague, and I mustn't see anyone in my weakened condition." He walked over to the fireplace and extinguished the flame with another flick of his wrist. "The small room at the end of the corridor will be suitable, I suppose. You can tell her that is my chamber, and it is not to be entered at any cost—physician's orders. My solar is to be kept locked at all times, for I doubt these past years have been long enough to douse her curiosity." Tristan came to stand in front of Jameson once more. "Got it?"

" 'Tis a broom closet, my lord."

Tristan frowned. "I know that. She, on the other hand, does not."

" 'Twould be a simple excursion to the west tower for her to find your solar."

"Aye, and 'twill be your duty to make sure she does not." Tristan drew a deep breath. "I do not want her meddling in any other aspect of my business, save what she was hired for. I've no idea whose bones are lying about my bailey, but mayhap we'll recognize the weapons. Other than that, I've no interest in her. I've had privacy for over seven centuries. I prefer it that way. Besides, the lads are already restless. They don't relish having to hide whilst she is about. Nor do I."

Jameson shook his head. "I do not think you will be able to fool Dr. Monroe. She seems quite bright, my lord. But . . ."

Tristan frowned. "But what?"

"I don't know, sir, but I think you should consider changing your attire befitting to a modern-day young lord and face her directly, as planned." He brushed his cuff. "You look as average as I, you know. 'Tis only you have no substance."

Tristan grimaced. "I need no reminder of that, Jameson."

"I'm sorry, sir. No disrespect intended. Only stating the facts." His wise gaze met Tristan's. "She was a young girl before, and you appeared in your mail. Certainly, she'll think you a different sort, dressed in modern-day clothing."

Tristan walked to the hearth. "I just don't know, man. What if I bumble through a wall and she sees I'm not, well, *of the living*?" He shook his head. Not that it'd stopped him from getting close to her before. "Let me think on the matter. I shall let you know on the morrow."

Jameson headed for the larder. "Very well, my lord, but don't ponder it overmuch. She's asked on your whereabouts more than once. Quite anxious, that one. Now, I'm off to the kitchen. Dr. Monroe will be down shortly for her supper, and I don't want her to have to wait." With that he strode away.

"You're taken with her, old man."

Jameson didn't even bother to turn around. "I most certainly am, my lord."

Tristan glowered at his steward's retreating back, frowned a good, lordly frown, and then disappeared through the wall.

Jameson had it aright. Things were about to become quite interesting at Dreadmoor Keep.

Andi stepped out of the tub and quickly dried off. Wrapping the thick, white towel around her, she inspected the room. How many times had she envisioned this place, about what it would be like on the inside? Hundreds of thousands. Even her dreams didn't match up.

Except for the mysterious man she thought she'd seen dressed as a medieval knight twelve years before. She remembered his rugged, handsome face, his long, dark hair and the most intriguing shade of blue eyes she'd ever seen. He'd been rough, demanding, yet kind enough to offer his assistance. Why he hadn't physically helped her, instead of barking orders at her from the steps below, still baffled her. And had her hand literally fallen through him? No. She refused to believe it. She'd just been scared.

A smile pulled at her mouth as she recalled his words. His voice, very deep and raspy, had shaken her to the bone. God, she could still hear it echo in her mind. *Now, if you'll reach with your left hand, there, and grasp for that stone—aye, like that. Well done. Now pull yourself up. . . .* She remembered her knight as being mammoth, with wide shoulders and chunky biceps, all covered in chain mail. "Boy, talk about a realistic vision." With the palm of her hand, she wiped the fogged moisture from the mirror and shook her head. "Dr. Monroe, you seriously need to get a life."

A life—unlike the poor soul wrapped around the thick roots of the oak tree out in the bailey. What had happened? And why had the body been buried with a bundle of armor? Hopefully, after a forensic inspection, the photos, and a few field tests, she'd be able to determine the gender and approximate age of the skeleton—which, given that the tree itself rivaled close to seven hundred years old, so must the remains be at least that many years. After gridding the area, then placing several cuts in the soil, she could begin sifting. Perhaps she'd find coin, pottery shards—maybe one of the weapons found would have an identifying mark. A peek into the past sat right at her fingertips. *God, I love my work.*

And could this one body be tied in with the missing fifteen from 1292? So many questions brewed in her mind. If only Kirk could be here to assist. He'd agreed to meet her in Berwick for dinner in two weeks to discuss her findings, but she'd phone him tomorrow after the first set of tests. Maybe she could even convince Dreadmoor to allow Kirk to help her on the first day of bone removal. On second thought, she'd call him first thing in the morning. That is, if he didn't phone her first. He had no patience. Hopefully, she'd have a decent report to offer.

She'd start with Jameson at dinner. If Dreadmoor made himself available tonight, she could speak with him, as well. Then, first thing tomorrow morning, she'd inspect the area. After that, she'd head into the village. Townspeople always had a stow of information. Even if it came in the form of lore and legend, usually there were hidden truths in the verbals.

Lord Dreadmoor would be her first choice. A perusal of the castle library, if there was one, would be heaven. At this point, a few old xeroxed copies of documents shoved into a shoe box would make her happy. Anything.

Hanging up the towel, she quickly dressed in a pair of faded jeans, a clean tank top, and sneakers, then pulled her wet hair into a ponytail. Satisfied, she stepped out into the passageway.

Tristan fell into step behind the young woman, remaining in his invisible state. She took long, graceful steps as she made her way down the corridor. A small pinch of guilt nagged at him for staring at her hose-clad legs and curvy bottom. It had only been for a fraction of a second longer than he should have. Saints, what a breathtaking woman.

She trotted down the steps to the main passageway. Without warning, she stiffened, came to a halt, and spun around. Unbeknownst to her, she stared right at him for a moment, not more than a foot away. Her nose twitched and she sniffed the air, reminding him of an inquisitive hare. Then she shrugged and continued on.

"Too many ghost stories, Andrea," she said. "There is no chain-mailed Dragonhawk, no missing knights lurking around, and you know it. Shake it off. Don't get all spooked-out on me now. Get a grip. Scientist. Remember? Smart. *Veeerry* logical."

Unable to help it, Tristan grinned at her self-encouraging words. Such a charming lass.

As they entered the kitchens a powerfully good smell

must have hit her square in the nose, for her stomach rumbled—loudly. Jameson stood at the table, his back stiff, with a folded dish towel draped across his forearm. He nodded and pulled out a chair. Remaining invisible, Tristan walked around to the side of the table where he stood and watched.

"I trust you're hungry, my lady?" Jameson asked.

She flashed Jameson a smile. It nearly knocked Tristan to his knees with the beauty of it. *Ah, to be on the receiving end of such a gift. . . .*

"Starved. It smells wonderful."

"I'm sure it does. Now, if you'll have a seat I shall be with you in a moment." Jameson turned and headed for the stove.

Dr. Monroe sat down and shook her head. "You remind me of someone."

Jameson spared her a slight glance, then turned back to the stove. "Oh?"

Tristan frowned. Who did Jameson remind her of?

Saints, another smile. Then she snapped her fingers. "I've got it!"

"You've got what, lady?"

She beamed. "I know who you remind me of. Batman's butler, Alfred. Don't you think so?"

Alfred? Batman? Tristan ran the names through his memory. Who were they? And what sire in his right mind would name his child *Batman*? Pitiful, he thought.

"Yes, my lady. I'm quite certain that I do." With a loaded tray of food he walked over and placed it in front of her. He turned to leave.

"Jameson, I've got a few questions for you. If you could spare a moment?" She gave him a challenging glare, daring him to walk off.

He, of course, did not. "What can I help you with, Dr. Monroe?"

She swallowed a mouthful of crusty bread, followed by a sip of water, then looked him in the eye. "First, where is the lord of Dreadmoor? Is he going to be available at all?"

Tristan could no longer stand by like an idle dolt.

Jameson wasn't one to lie, and he didn't want the poor man to slip. Moving behind Andi, Tristan materialized, then crossed his arms over his chest. Jameson swallowed his yelp, his Adam's apple bobbing with the effort. Tristan flashed him a grin, then placed two fingers over his lips, cautioning his steward to gain control and be silent.

"Well, my lady, unfortunately Himself had some rather urgent business to tend to this eve. I'm sure he'll be available on the morrow." Jameson tried his best to look grave, hands clasped in front of him.

She studied him for what seemed like minutes, then nodded. "That would be great. There are several things I'd like to discuss before the excavation process begins, concerning the history of the castle and grounds." Andi took another sip of her water. "What may seem like minor details could hold a completely different meaning when investigating such a find as what's in your bailey."

Jameson patted her on the shoulder. "I do know quite a bit of the history myself. My family has worked Dreadmoor for centuries. In fact, my son, Thomas, is away at culinary school, readying to take over in my stead."

Her lips closed over a spoonful of stew. She briefly wondered where Jameson's wife was. So far, the only people she'd met were Jameson and Will, the barbican guard.

Nodding, Andi wiped the corner of her mouth, then smiled at Jameson. "Actually, I do have a few questions regarding the disappearance of Dragonhawk and his knights. Is there anything you can tell me about them? Different from the legend, that is."

A worried line creased Jameson's brow. "Very little, I'm afraid. 'Tis a blurry history verbally passed through the generations at best. Nothing documented officially, anyway. 'Tis why it's considered more lore than actual event." He straightened his coat. "Lord Dreadmoor—better known as Dragonhawk—was a legend throughout Scotland and England—even France. Still is, actually. Young mothers used his name to frighten their children into submission. Quite the warrior, that one. The others were his personal guard. His entire garrison, actually.

'Twas rumored he didn't employ many men. Or, rather, felt he didn't need them. 'Tis why there were naught but fourteen."

Dr. Monroe rubbed her brow. "Fourteen men plus Dreadmoor himself made fifteen. Not a large number, considering the size of the castle."

"The first lord thought 'twas guarded appropriately. He never traveled with more than five or six men, to his father and mother's dismay, I'm afraid." He shrugged a thin shoulder. "So the story goes."

"What happened?"

Jameson solemnly shook his head. "I'm not at all certain, my lady. No one is. But there have been whispers of murder and mayhem throughout the centuries, although I've never been one to speculate." He lifted his gaze. " 'Tis best if you question the likes to Himself. On the morrow."

An unsatisfied look crossed her lovely features, but she nodded. "I will. Thanks for your help. But if you think of anything else, let me know."

Jameson gave Dreadmoor's new guest a low bow. "As you wish, Dr. Monroe."

Tristan met his steward's gaze and, with a nod of approval, disappeared.

Andi kicked off her sneakers and flopped back onto the bed. "Ugh, I'm stuffed." She undid the top two buttons of her jeans and let out a sigh of relief, staring at the ceiling in complete amazement. Old, thick wooden rafters stretched from one end of the room to the other. She followed the beams to the open window, then across the wall to the breathtaking tapestry of the jousting knights. Rolling off the bed, she padded across the wooden floor to get a closer look. A very small but fascinating detail caught her eye. She peered at the tiny stitches.

One of the knights, dressed in chain mail and wearing a black surcoat, carried a shield with the same exact rampant black and green creature as the shield propped up against the fireplace. She knelt in front of the ancient piece of armor. Sitting cross-legged on the floor, she pulled it onto her lap.

The two shields were identical. The creature, unlike anything she'd ever seen before, appeared to be half hawk, half . . . dragon. *Of course!* "Dragonhawk." It had the most incredible blue eye. Lethal. Captivating. Powerful.

She studied the artifact, so carefully preserved. "A dragon warrior." In all her studies, never had she encountered another creature like it. No doubt it had probably intimidated more than one man in battle. With caution, she touched the dings and notches embedded in the wood. *The marks of previous battles fought . . .*

A shiver of excitement ran through her. "Could it have belonged to the first lord of Dreadmoor?"

"Aye. . . ."

Andi jumped and nearly dropped the shield. "Who's there?" She looked around but found nothing. No one. A chill grabbed her.

Who had just whispered?

With caution, she eased the shield back into place, crossed the chamber, and cracked open the door. The darkened hall stood empty. She waited, but after a few seconds, she closed the door and shrugged. Her imagination was getting the best of her.

The shield once more caught her eye. She'd have to ask Jameson—and hopefully *Himself*—more about it. It completely intrigued her. With a stretch and a yawn, she crossed the room to her bags. Digging through her belongings, she found her boxer shorts and tossed them onto the curtained bed. With a decision to unpack in the morning, she started to slip down her jeans and change when a sudden wind whipped through the room. The shutters slammed shut. She jumped in spite of herself, her heart slamming against her ribs.

The lights on the wall extinguished, throwing the room in pitch-blackness. "Oh, great." Easing her way across the floor, she made for the desk on the other side of the room. Her foot struck an object in the middle of the floor. She stumbled and went sprawling onto her backside.

Stunned by the tumble, she sat in the dark for only a moment. Then, just as quickly as they'd extinguished, the lamps flickered back on. Andi looked down. She'd tripped over her sneakers.

"Good going, Monroe." With a shake of her head at her own foolishness, she picked up her shoes and set them under the bed. She drew a long, deep, cleansing breath. "I hope the old crusty battle-ax of Dreadmoor is available tomorrow. There are so many things I want to know." After brushing her teeth, she slipped into her boxers and sought comfort on the soft, feathery-down mattress.

Tristan materialized in the corner of the room and stared at Dr. Andrea Monroe. By the devil's pointed teeth, he'd nearly lost his composure when she'd started to remove her garb. As if he had expected anything less of her, being in her own chambers. "Bloody dolt."

"Excuse me?" A soft whisper rose from behind the curtains.

He squeezed his eyes shut. What a big mouth he possessed. He had only wanted to watch the woman for but a moment or two, just to see what mischief she combined. But he had become so caught up in her exploration of his shield he'd not realized the wench would soon disrobe and make ready for bed.

He crept closer. Professors of archaeology were not supposed to be fetching young maids with beautiful hazel eyes. They were supposed to be corpulent little men with balding heads and ill-fitting, brownish garments. God's bones, what a headache.

The corners of his mouth lifted a fragment. She'd called him a "crusty old battle-ax." She was, if anything, quite amusing.

A slight snore escaped from under the bedcovers, causing Tristan to take a closer look. The moon chose that moment to peek out from behind the clouds, bathing the room in a soft glow. He leaned over and studied her features. Chestnut hair fanned across the pillow, her smooth and creamy skin flawless. A small nose tipped slightly upward. Full lips, parted and relaxed, appeared soft, delicate. Lashes the color of her hair brushed her cheek as she slept, and on closer inspection Tristan could see the pulse tap at the base of her throat. *Damnation, what a lovely creature.* The woman snored again, then made a smacking noise. He almost gave way to a smile.

Instead, he frowned. The woman had seen him before and would no doubt remember the incident. Could he pull off Jameson's plan to conjure himself into a modern-day lord? Mayhap. It would only be for a couple of months whilst the girl excavated the bailey. Aye, he'd do it.

Saints, to be alive to help. Who, by the forked tail of the devil, was entwined within the roots of that oak? And what of the armor? He'd yet to lay eyes on the discovery, save the bones. Dirt covered the rest of the find; only a few shards of metal showed through the thick, midnight turf. Mayhap he'd recognize something? Neither his nor the lads' weapons had ever been found. Should he dare to hope?

He glanced down at the sleeping form in what was once his own bed. She'd find the answers, he felt sure of it. Excitement pitched the tone of her voice every time she spoke of the find. It had been a good decision to choose her.

Pinching the bridge of his nose, he turned to leave. Christ, he was tired, weary, and sick of roaming. He felt sure an answer lay hidden within Dreadmoor. Or was that wishfulness? If only they could remember. An answer, perhaps, would put himself and the lads to rest. With that gloomy thought in mind Tristan disappeared, his mood more foul, if possible, than before.

Tristan shifted what would have been considerable weight, cracked his neck as he would have in life, then waited a moment more before his patience, quite thin to begin with, deserted him. Entering the kitchen, he crossed his arms over his chest and scowled. "Well? How do I look?"

Jameson turned from the stove and lifted one eyebrow. "You look most modern, sir." The other brow followed. "And very much alive. I must say, I'm impressed." He cocked his head. "And where did you get such a fashion idea? The tele?"

Tristan glanced down at his conjured-up garments. A snug-fitting black tunic, soft bluish hose similar to those Dr. Monroe wore, and ankle-high leather boots. Jeans and hikers, he'd been told. Not a bad fit. "Young Jason gave me aid in the task, and I daresay he was quite pleased with himself once finished. I don't fancy going without my blade and mail, even if it is just an illusion." He shoved his hands into his pockets. "Think you she will believe, Jameson? I vow I'm no good at lying. Nor do I fancy breaking the code."

"You look quite convincing, my lord. And there's no need to fret yourself about the code. This is a delicate matter, and one you can not avoid. Mayhap you can eventually tell her the truth?"

"Tell her the truth? Are you mad? She's a scientist. A mortal. *A woman.* She will not believe."

Jameson inclined his head. "I believe. Miss Kate believes, as does her daughter and young grandson, Heath. Will believes, too. Last time I checked, we were all mortals, as well. My lord."

"Will you cut the 'my lord'? By the saints, 'tis driving me senseless." He leaned against his desk and pondered the task. "I plan on having as little interaction with her as possible, Jameson. None of this sits well with me. But you're right. It must be done." Rising, he made for the door. "I shall meet her after breakfast in the morn. Eight thirty sharp."

Jameson turned back to his stirring. "Very well, young Tristan."

Tristan shook his head and disappeared.

Andi stretched, relishing the warmth on her skin by the low-burning fire in the hearth.

She bolted upright and looked around. *I didn't light a fire last night. . . .*

Swinging her legs over the side of the bed she rose and rubbed her bare arms. *Maybe Jameson lit the fireplace.* She did remember being chilly during the night. Her bad habit of rolling into a fetal ball instead of seeking warmth from the covers, which were usually either under her or bunched at the end of the bed, had caused her to wake up freezing her buns off more than once.

Crossing the floor to the small fire, she turned her backside to the flames and rubbed. She looked around while her derriere warmed. Her gaze landed on the shield, now propped up against the opposite wall, out of reach from the flames. She was fascinated by it.

After warming herself, she made her bed and got ready for the day. Finally unpacking her suitcase, she put her clothes in the large, wooden trunk in the corner, then pulled on her Washington State T-shirt and a pair of jeans. As she was clasping the last two buttons on her 501s, a soft rap sounded at her door. She walked over barefoot and opened it.

A smiling young boy stood on the other side, proudly displaying his missing front tooth. "My lady, I've come to fetch you for breakfast."

She grinned at the boy. "Why, thank you," she replied, adopting his formal manner. "May I ask your name?"

"Heath, my lady." He drew up to his full height of, oh, probably four feet.

"Well, Heath, give me a minute to put on my sneakers and I'll be right with you." She crossed the room, dug a pair of socks out of the trunk, then sat on the lid while she put on her shoes. She looked at the boy, who still stood, smiling at her. "Do you live here?"

"Oh, nay. I come here Mondays and Thursdays with me grandmum and helps her with the cleanin'." His smile widened. "I get money, too."

Andi crossed her arms over her chest and raised her eyebrows. "How's the pay?"

The boy's grin widened. "Quite good." He held out a small hand. "Me grandmum's away today, though, running errands for Jameson. Mrs. Dawson's taking her place. Ready?"

Andi laughed and crossed the room. "You bet. I'm starved." With that they left the room.

She had to trot to keep up with Heath as they made their way down the long corridor to the steps. They reached the landing at the bottom and crossed the great hall, where an older woman swept embers from the massive fireplace. Heath grabbed Andi's hand and pulled her to the woman, who stopped her chore as they approached.

"Mrs. Dawson, here's the bone lady I told you about!" Heath jumped up and down in place.

A hesitant smile crossed the woman's face; then she clucked. "Heath, love, stop pullin' on the woman so!" She turned to Andi. "Forgive him, lady. He's an excitable sort."

Andi gave the older woman a warm smile. "No problem." She stuck out her hand. "I'm Andi."

The woman ignored her offered hand, but instead leaned in to whisper, "Lady, if you know what's good for you, you'll leave this place." She cast a skeptical glance around the room before meeting Andi's gaze. " 'Tis haunted."

Heath's eyes twinkled. "Aye, she has the right of it, to be sure."

Andi stared at the two with raised eyebrows. "Haunted? I doubt that."

"Nay, 'tis true!" Heath tugged on her arm. "By the dreadful and fierce knight, Dragonhawk, lady. All gruesome and bloody guts, he is. And he will lop off your head whilst you sleep—he or one of his gruesome guardsmen."

She glanced at Mrs. Dawson, who bobbed her wiry, gray head with as much enthusiasm as he did.

Andi smiled. "I'd love to know more about the missing garrison. Can you tell me anything—"

"Whist!" The older woman's eyes rounded and she crossed herself. "They'll hear you, girl. Keep yer voice down." She glanced around. " 'Tis why I don't come here often. Bloody spirits."

"I'm sorry," Andi whispered, fighting back a grin.

Maybe she could question the woman at her home, where she'd be more inclined to speak out loud. She'd ask Jameson later where the woman lived.

Satisfied their warning had been taken to its fullest, the old woman nodded her approval and returned to the sweeping. "Hurry and take the lady to the kitchens, love," she said. "Then return straightaway and help me finish, so we can be gone."

Heath grinned his gap-toothed grin and grabbed Andi by the hand. "C'mon, then. Let's go!"

In order to keep from being pulled down and dragged across the great hall, Andi ran alongside Heath, where they skidded to a halt just inside the kitchen. Heath drew in a large breath and yelled, "Jam-e-son, I've got her!"

Jameson stepped from out of the pantry with a disapproving look. "Yes, Master Heath, I see that you do. But you must remember, a gentleman does not bellow thusly."

"Yes, Jameson." He turned and smiled up at Andi, his voice lowered. "I've got to go help Mrs. Dawson, lady. Will you be here next Monday?"

She grinned and bent down to the boy's level. "If I don't get my head lopped off in my sleep."

Heath's smile widened. "Best you cross yourself, then. Like this." He crossed himself, winked, and fast as lightning, ran from the kitchen without another word.

A faint, deep chuckle erupted from the room. Andi glanced up at Jameson. From the dour look on his face the humorous sound couldn't have come from him. She looked around the kitchen. Empty, save for Jameson and herself. She turned her gaze on Dreadmoor's steward. "Did you just laugh?"

"I never laugh, my lady." His back stiffened. "Now, would you care to have your porridge?"

"I must be hearing things." Shaking her head, she gave Jameson a wistful smile. "I don't suppose you have any Pop-Tarts?"

"Dr. Monroe, I doubt you'll find such an atrocious excuse for a meal in all of England. Porridge?"

Andi nearly burst out laughing. "Sure. Porridge is fine."

He nodded and placed before Andi a steaming bowl of creamy oatmeal, along with several pieces of wheat toast. He followed with a large mug of hot tea.

"Thanks." Her stomach growled from the aroma. "It looks great."

"I'm sure it does."

Andi reached for the bowl of brown sugar on the table and dumped three heaping spoonfuls into the porridge. She followed it with cream. It earned her a blistering look from Jameson.

He cleared his throat. "Lord Dreadmoor has finished his business and is quite anxious to meet with you, Dr. Monroe."

Andi took a sip of tea and nodded. "Perfect. I was hoping to meet with him before starting the examination of skeletal remains this morning." She took a slice of wheat toast, slathered it with raspberry jam, and took a bite, followed by another sip of tea. "I'd like to call a cab and ride into town later this afternoon. Do you suppose Gibbs would come back out? I'll pay him extra."

Almost a smile, but not quite. "I'll be glad to take you in myself. I've a bit of shopping to do for the larder."

"I don't want to be any trouble, Jameson."

"No bother at all, my lady. Let's say, five-ish?"

"I'll be ready. Oh, and one more thing. I'd like to have Dr. Grey assist me with the first inspection of the bones, if it's okay?"

Jameson gave a nod. "I'm sure you'd be better to ask Himself. He's a private sort, you know."

"So I've heard," she said under her breath.

She finished her bowl of porridge and drained her teacup. "What time do you expect His Lordship to get up this morning?"

The corner of Jameson's mouth twitched. "If you're finished, he's awaiting you now, Dr. Monroe." He walked to the doors leading to the great hall. "Shall we?"

Andi wiped her mouth and followed Jameson with enthusiasm. "Lead the way, Jameson." *Time to face the crusty old battle-ax.*

Chapter 4

Andi followed Jameson across the great hall and up the wide, stone steps leading to the second floor. They made their way through the *bowels of the castle*, as Jameson had put it. They'd be meeting in the solar. She was more than ready to begin her work.

At the end of the corridor they turned left, then wound their way across the keep. The lanterns cast a luminous glow to the ancient stone walls. A few more tapestries hung here and there, but were scarcer on what Jameson called the west side of the castle.

Finally coming to a dead end, Jameson stopped, pulled open a door, and held it open for Andi. She stepped in, her sneakers squeaking on the circular stone stairs as she began the climb. One lantern, perched way above them, lit the stairwell.

Andi peered into the dimness. Shadows flickered against the walls, giving a completely wonderful medieval effect. At the end of the steps stood another door. She waited for Jameson to enter and announce her. It surprised her to find her heart pounded a little faster than usual. Maybe she should have dressed more appropriate? After all, she was about to meet an English lord. *Too late now, Monroe.*

Jameson glanced at Andi, raised an eyebrow, then pushed open the heavy wooden door. He stepped in first and cleared his throat. "Lord Dreadmoor," he announced, "Dr. Monroe is here to speak with you."

Andi peered into the room over Jameson's narrow shoulder.

"Send her in and close the door."

She jumped. Jameson didn't even flinch. "As you wish, my lord." Jameson led Andi into the room, then turned and left her alone. With *him*.

Her breath hitched in her throat as Lord Dreadmoor rose from his place behind a massive oak desk.

Some battle-ax.

Andi swallowed—hard. Good Lord, she wasn't usually so nervous when meeting new people. The battle-ax didn't look or sound at all like, well, an old battle-ax.

Virile. Healthy. Massive. Lordly. *Mouthwateringly gorgeous.* Not at all like the wheezing old eccentric geezer she'd conjured in her mind. The black T-shirt barely fit shoulder to shoulder, stretching taut against massive chunks of muscle. Hips snuggled within a pair of worn and comfortable-looking jeans, his long, dark hair tied back—nope, not a battle-ax. His deep, raspy voice sounded like a strange combination of Britain's English and, if her years of studying medieval languages were correct, French-Norman. That odd combination of accents suddenly interrupted her thoughts.

"Dr. Monroe?"

Inwardly, she cringed. *How unprofessional, Andrea. Come on, now. No ogling.* Stepping closer to the polished desk, she smiled. "Yes. I apologize. You're . . . not what I expected." She extended her hand and met his gaze. "It's very nice to meet—"

Lord Dreadmoor retracted and shoved his hands in his pockets.

Andi gasped, and she felt her face blanch. She'd know those eyes anywhere. "Oh my God. It's *you*."

A look of surprise crossed his features, then quickly disappeared. "Have a seat, Dr. Monroe." He motioned with a large hand, thick veins roping up an arm bulging with muscle. He cleared his throat. "Forgive me if I don't remember. Have we met before?"

God, he acted as though she had the plague. Why had he not taken her hand? How embarrassing.

Had she mistaken? Unable to help herself, she chanced a look into those sapphire eyes, rimmed with thick, sooty lashes. He definitely wasn't wearing chain mail. Yet, he looked similar. But that incident with the knight *couldn't* have happened. It was absurd. It'd all been her juvenile imagination.

With a slight laugh, she shook her head and lowered herself into the soft, leather chair. "No, I suppose not. I apologize, Lord Dreadmoor. It's just that you look like someone I've met before."

He sat, and then his gaze shifted to the pen in his fingers. "You must be mistaken, Dr. Monroe, for I vow I would have banked the occasion to memory." Lifting his eyes level to hers, he sat down and made a steeple with his fingers. "First, let me say I hope your venture to the bones last night didn't prove too fearful. Jameson said you'd had a fright?"

It sounded sillier coming from someone else's lips. "I think I let my imagination run away with me a little. It was dark, misty, and I was out there alone. I'm fine. Honest."

He stared, as if not believing, then nodded. "Very well. Now, about the matter at hand? I'm a busy man."

God, she'd die from humiliation before she left this solar. "Of course. I'm actually very excited about the find and more than ready to get started." She tucked her hair behind her ears. "Have you any documents or ledgers regarding the castle's inhabitants? Its history? A blueprint perhaps?"

Tristan smothered a grin. He couldn't believe the wench wasn't the least bit fearful. Not that he wanted to scare her, but anyone else, save Jameson, would be near to bolting, had he used that tone of voice. She hadn't budged. Instead, she'd launched into a thread of excited questions—ones he wasn't truly prepared to answer. At least he'd managed to make a convincing modern-day lord. Even the illusionary pen he held betwixt his fingers looked real. He hoped.

"Lord Dreadmoor?"

Tristan thought for a moment. How much did he want

this tenacious young woman to know of his past? 'Twould come to no good end, for a certainty. Truth be told, he enjoyed her wry humor and boldness more than he would be willing to admit to anyone. What harm could come of her seeing the plans? They had been well protected over the years, thanks to his sire.

Gage de Barre had been insistent his younger brother, Tristan's uncle Christopher, take over the running of Dreadmoor after Tristan's murder, so he'd been told later on. Uncle Christopher had carefully preserved the parchment under leaded glass and placed it in Dreadmoor's vault. It told nothing more than the complete layout of the castle. *Let the woman have a look at it.*

He nodded. "Aye, there are the original parchments. I have faith you will handle them with utmost care, Dr. Monroe. 'Tis the only set I have, and 'tis very dear to me."

Her lovely mouth dropped open. "Oh my gosh . . . you have the originals? I assure you, Lord Dreadmoor—"

"By the saints, woman. Do not call me that again. It annoys me fiercely."

Andi stifled a sigh. She couldn't have told him her full name at that point, so entranced by the deep, slightly graveled voice. Plain-out *sexy* didn't even begin to describe it. Strange how she heard it more inside her head than, say, in the room. Downright nerve-racking. *You're a scientist, Monroe. A scholar. Here on a job. Digging up bones and armor. Remember? Get a grip.*

Nonetheless, a dead woman wouldn't be able to resist even a slight swoon, what with that uniquely blended, slightly medievalish accent. Where on earth had he acquired it? Actually, she didn't care where he'd acquired it, as long as he kept on talking to her.

"Lady! Have you heard a word I've spoken?"

Andi jumped, embarrassed. Where, and more to the point, why, had her thoughts rambled? Wow, so unlike her. Good thing he couldn't read minds.

She cleared her throat. "Yes, of course. Calling you Lord Dreadmoor annoys you. So what should I call you?"

"Tristan will do. Now, what else do you need of me today? I grow weary of all this speech and I've important business to tend to."

Tristan. The name certainly fit the voice. Andi tucked her hair behind her ear and continued. "Do you know of any disputes, whether real or lore, that might give a clue as to the owners of the hoard? Any murders or disappearances—any hint as to who might have been buried under that oak? I mean, the oak itself is pretty amazing. Over seven hundred years old—one of the oldest and largest I've ever seen. The girth is over ten meters wide." She rubbed her brow. "What about notable battles? Witch burnings, maybe?"

One, dark eyebrow lifted. " 'Tis a thirteenth-century castle, lass. Battles, swords, bloodshed, head-lopping, jousts . . . aye, disputes aplenty occurred. No witch burnings to my knowledge. 'Twas the way of life, although I did manage to keep a peaceful way of sorts here at Dreadmoor."

Andi blinked. "Excuse me?"

A brief look of surprise flashed his features, then disappeared. "I said, they did manage to keep a peaceful way of life here. 'Tis why the castle remains intact."

Now she was hearing things. Hadn't he said *I*?

After a moment's silence he cleared his throat. "What do you really want to ask me, Dr. Monroe?"

She smiled. "Anything you have to offer would be of great help, of course. But I have to admit, I do have a curiosity surrounding the legend of Dragonhawk and his missing knights. It's fascinating. Is there anything you can tell me about it?"

He studied her, an intense observation she felt clear to her bones. "Nothing in writing, nothing official. Nothing that has been found, anyway. 'Tis a verbal legend passed down through the centuries."

She leaned forward. "That's what Jameson said. I'd love to hear it."

A slight hesitation, only for a moment, and then his look, if possible, grew more intense. "First"—he shifted in his chair—"I would have your name, if you please."

"Andi."

"Nay. Not your nickname. Your full, given name at birth. Your Christian name."

Andi gulped. His voice washed over her like a heavy sea mist, escaping to land from a turbulent storm. *Oh God,* her inner voice groaned. From scientist to sappy poet? *Puh-leez.* Her interns would have a field day with that.

She cleared her throat, making sure she wouldn't crack as she spoke. "Andrea Kinley Monroe." She lifted a shoulder. "At least, that's what they tell me."

He stared, apparently awaiting more.

"Who's interviewing who here, anyway?" she asked, smiling.

"Humor me. Then I'll answer your questions."

"Deal. I was adopted by a sweet older woman named Mary Monroe. I called her Aunt Mary. She died several years ago." She shrugged. "I had a typical Catholic school upbringing, then college."

He frowned. "You've no family, then?"

She nodded. "Only my mentor, Kirk Grey."

"The owner of the research institute who sent you?"

"Yes. He's been like a father to me. He taught medieval history at St. Catherine's School when I was in tenth grade, and sort of took me under his wing when I showed such a great interest in the subject. He was my professor in college, as well. After that, I came to work for GAR Institute." Shaking her head, she smiled. "I would never have come this far, had it not been for him. He is the one who told me about Dreadmoor and its legends. Got me completely hooked on the place."

A slight frown, then a nod. "Aye. Well, they are fortunate to have you, from what I hear. Jameson says you've quite a name for yourself in your field."

"Thanks. Now, what can you tell me about the legend? You know I've already been warned by Mrs. Dawson—"

Before she could finish her sentence, Tristan abruptly stood. "Unfortunately, I've no more time for you this morn. I'm late as it is. Mayhap on the morrow?"

Wow. Talk about fast-changing gears. One minute, he

was asking her questions, the next he was booting her out on her ear. She glanced down at her watch, pretending the dismissal didn't sting. "Would you look at the time? I've got to run anyway. I need to inspect the cutaway and take photos before obtaining samples. In other words, a ton of work to do." She rose and this time, didn't offer Tristan a hand. "I appreciate your time, Lord—"

"Tristan."

She smiled. "Tristan. Can I meet with you later and hear your version of the legend of Dragonhawk and his knights?"

He inclined his head. "Aye. Until then, Andrea."

Dear God, the way he said her name made her knees wobble. "Yes, until later," she answered. With that she quickly left the chambers, pulling the heavy door closed behind her.

Before he saw her drool.

Andrea Kinley Monroe. Tristan stood and walked over to the wooden shutters. With a flick of his wrist the wind banged them open. Although he could not feel the air, his unobstructed view of the sea calmed him immediately.

Merciful saints above, he'd enjoyed talking with the wench. 'Twas as though he spoke with her as he would have in life; as though he were not a spirit. Worse yet, he had agreed to meet later with her.

A comforting image of himself, soundly bashing his head against the battlements for his stupidity, came to mind. His wits had fled. The important thing at present was solving the bloody mystery of the hoard and bones, so he could get on as before.

He thought of his existence—of endless days and nights, of continuous waking hours, of growing close to someone, only to watch them grow old and die. 'Twas a lonely life a ghost led. Weary didn't even begin to describe it.

But damnation, she intrigued him. Would that he were a live man . . .

Tristan pushed off the sill. Nay, he would not doom

himself with another heartache, not this time. He'd not allowed himself a mortal friend in hundreds of years, save Jameson and his wife, Margaret. 'Twas more than he could stand.

Christ, how he missed that sweet woman, Margaret. The grief he'd experienced when she'd passed away pained him to this day. And he knew the same pain would engulf him when Jameson's time to leave this world came. 'Twas bad enough, he'd already started thinking fondly of Miss Kate and that whelp Heath who came to clean twice a week. He had a suspicion Jameson was sweet on Miss Kate, as he became a bumbling fool any time the woman was about.

Tristan blew out a gusty sigh. He had watched Jameson grow from an infant to the impossibly arrogant man-servant he presented now. In the same manner, he'd watched Jameson's own son, Thomas, grow to the young man he was today. And although he would not admit it to either, he loved them dearly. And one day Jameson would die, as would Thomas—they'd all die, leaving Tristan alone. Again.

Aye. He was finished growing close to mortals.

"Tristan?"

Tristan jumped at the sound of his captain's voice. "What do you want, Kail?"

Kail appeared, stood with legs wide apart, and crossed his meaty arms over his chest. "By the saints, man, you look comely."

Tristan frowned. "Shut you up, fool. 'Tis for the lady's benefit. Naught more."

Kail grinned and walked a slow, perusing, annoying circle around him. "Hmm. No doubt."

Following the dolt with his eyes, Tristan all but growled. "Is there a purpose for your intrusion, Kail? Or are you here simply to irritate me?"

The big, burly knight had the decency to look hurt. "Me? Irritate?" Kail stopped. The corner of his mouth lifted into a crooked smile, one eyebrow shooting skyward. "Never. The lads and I, well, we're interested, is all."

Tristan narrowed his eyes. "In what?"

"Her."

"What of her?" Tristan walked to the window and stared at the whitecaps dotting the North Sea. "I've already told you. She's here to investigate the bones and weapons. She'll be here for . . . a while. Then she'll be gone."

"How long? A sennight, mayhap? A fortnight?"

Exasperation pulled Tristan's mouth into a tight line. He sighed. "Three. Mayhap four."

"Ah, quite a spell, then." Kail moved to stand next to him, shoulder to shoulder, staring out the window. "Mayhap she can help, Tristan. I sense something about her, and I vow I cannot put a finger to it. But 'tis strong."

Tristan focused on the waves. "I don't know."

"The lads feel it as well. They're a might restless."

Turning his head, he pegged Kail with a hard stare. "They are not to approach her, Kail. And it will be your bloody duty to remind them of such. Saints, the girl just arrived." He pinched the bridge of his nose. "And I need to think on the matter. Is that understood?"

A grin spread across his captain's face. An annoying, victorious grin. "Aye. Completely understood." With that he clapped Tristan on the shoulder, turned, then stopped at the door. "Remove that dour look on your face by this eve. Rugby tonight, little lad. The quarter finals replay. Leinster versus Tigers." He grinned. "Should be good." With that, he disappeared through the door.

Moving back to the window, Tristan leaned a shoulder against the frame and stared out. What if Kail had it aright? Mayhap the lass could help. On the other hand, they could have a stroke of luck and his sword lay within the hoard found below the oak.

Running a hand across his jaw, he drew a deep breath and let it slide back out between his teeth. He liked the damned girl. More than liked having speech with her, and by the saint's robes, she was passing lovely. In the end, it could lead to nothing but disaster. And he damn well bloody knew it.

Mayhap he should leave well enough alone and leave her to communicate with Jameson if she needed more information. The old man knew as much as he—nearly, anyway. She would excavate the site and maybe give him a clue as to who'd been buried under that oak, and whose weapons were buried alongside him. Then, by the bones of all weary saints, he'd get his life back. Rather, his un-life. Such as it was.

He paused as a thought struck him. Mayhap the hoard and bones had not been buried beneath that oak? Instead, could the oak have been planted upon them? 'Twas something to ponder. If only there weren't chunks of his memory missing. 'Twould truly be something, if Andrea could help.

Such help would no doubt lead to fondness for the wench. And that, he'd decided, just couldn't be.

Tristan disappeared through the wall. He aimed his course for his steward, to make sure Dr. Andrea Kinley Monroe did not seek him further. Then he'd find her, have a bit of speech with her, to satisfy her curiousness regarding Dragonhawk and his men, and that would definitively be that. No more. She could do her work without his presence. Besides, he had a rugby match to watch tonight.

A frown tightened his mouth, his mood much fouler than before.

And if he did not make haste he would surely do something absurd. Witless. Daft, even.

Such as change his mind.

Chapter 5

Andi stepped out of the main hall and into the morning sunlight. After leaving Tristan's solar, she'd stopped off in her room to gather her site kit and tool belt, exchanged her sneakers for the Wellingtons, pulled on her weatherproofs, and made for the cutaway. Although she was excited about what her efforts this morning at the site might find, her thoughts—the more girly ones—wandered back to Lord Dreadmoor.

Tristan.

Never had she met someone who'd taken her so off guard—enough to make her act like a blathering dingbat. Twice he'd had to draw her attention back to the conversation. But she couldn't help it. Tristan of Dreadmoor made her breath escape. . . .

With her soles squishing through the sodden soil, she shook her head to ward off *that* foolishness and covered the courtyard to the bailey. As soon as it came into view, she pulled up short. It was an amazing site. The ancient branches of a partially upturned oak tree stood up like bristles as it lay on its side, sunbeams filtering through the long, crooked arms. A large canvas tarp tented the base and roots. She remembered the tree from before, when she'd sneaked onto the Dreadmoor estate. It'd stood in the bailey like a giant, its massive branches gnarled and reaching, protecting. She remembered running past it when . . .

When she'd run screaming from the chain-mailed knight. The one who'd looked a lot like Tristan.

But that hadn't really happened. It couldn't have.

Sad, now, that after so many years, so many centuries, the majestic tree lay on its side, lifeless.

Just like the bones entwined within the roots.

Setting her site kit aside, Andi knelt at each stake and released the tarp. Massive hunks of sod clung to the tree's origins, the scent of fresh-turned earth and rotting vegetation mixing with the ever-present salty sea air.

There, nestled within the intricate root system, lay the soil-stained bones, coughed up by the storm and bound by . . . something. Dark—almost black—and thick, it appeared to be a separate root, or vine, entwined with the skeletal remains. A hole, several meters deep, rested beneath the tree. Squatting down, she peered into the dark mouth of the cutaway—too dark to make anything out. She pulled a torch from her tool belt and pointed the beam of light into the hole.

Save him.

The faded whisper caused Andi's spine to stiffen. Oh no. Not again. Slowly, she turned and peered over her shoulder.

Tristan walked toward her, only a few meters away. Too far to have been the speaker, his voice too male.

Find me.

Andi stood, her eyes darting first left, then right. No one about—just her and Tristan. She wasn't imagining that whisper, and it wasn't the wind. An icy shiver crept through her as she watched the big man grow closer.

Tristan.

The voice had said *save him*, and when she looked, the handsome lord was the only one around. *Wait, Monroe. Did you just say the voice?*

God, she sounded like an idiot, even to her own ears. But it wasn't just a voice. It was . . . she shuddered at the thought.

A presence.

What was wrong with the wench? Her face had gone pale, and she looked as though she searched for something. Or someone.

He knew he risked his guise by approaching her, but he preferred to be in control of their meetings—which is exactly what he'd told Jameson would happen from here on out. Besides, damn his own self, his interest steadfastly grew in not only the mysterious and unfortunate bones of the unknown buried in his bailey, but in the one researching those bones. Whether he liked it or not.

Unable to stop himself, he drank in the sight of her. Small hands with slender fingers smoothed her dark hair behind her ears. She tried to look as though nothing was amiss, but he knew better. The look of fright on her features was unmistakable.

Striding up to her, he stopped a safe distance away. He prayed she wouldn't reach for him again. Saints' souls, what a disaster that would be. Before he could say a word, she spoke.

"Did you just say something?"

Tristan frowned. "Nay, you haven't given me such a chance."

Her eyes narrowed as she studied him; then she lifted her shoulder in a slight shrug. "I didn't think I'd see you again until this evening." She turned and waved a hand at the uprooted tree. "I've just removed the tarp and was about to take the initial notes and photos. I'd like my boss to assist me when I remove the bones, if that's okay?"

He gave a good, lordly nod. "So long as you finish your task as agreed upon. Alone." Truly, he didn't want any more strangers traipsing across his estate than need be.

He pondered her earlier reaction. What had baffled her so? Did his visage appear odd? 'Twasn't as though she could see through him. Even in sunlight, he appeared as alive as any mortal, or so Jameson had said. Could she have heard another voice? When he'd questioned the lads, none laid claim to the deed. So who? Devil's hooves, he didn't want to seem inadequate.

Deciding to turn the subject until he could find out more, he pointed to the overturned oak. "Explain to me the order in which your tasks will proceed. I want to make sure your duties go accordingly while on Dread-moor land. Then, if you've any further questions for me, you may ask them now."

"Okay. First, the photos."

She discarded the brightly colored waterproof cloak, laid it aside, and crouched down, pointing to the bones and the surrounding soil. The tunic she wore rose above her waist, exposing the small of her back, the slight bones of her spine raising her smooth skin. Damnation. *Focus on her words, dolt, not her body.*

"I want to get as much on the digital as possible before touching anything. Once the area is disturbed, especially once the bones are removed, all facts and evidence are destroyed." Shielding her eyes from the sun, she gave him another smile. "That's why it's so important to get it down right from the start. I can't miss one little detail, or it's lost. Forever."

Tristan stared at the tenacious woman, squatted down in the black muck with her knee-high waterproof boots on, *enjoying herself.* By the blade, he shouldn't be here. Leave her alone and let her be, he'd told himself. He'd had business to tend to this morn, 'twas true enough. Having used a portion of the ghastly amount of gold he'd accumulated before his death, not to mention that of his uncles—secured through the years by the thrifty Jameson family—he had procured a trustworthy solicitor and had several lucrative investment properties throughout the south of England, which not only kept his bank account more than plentiful, but paid the taxes on the castle and managed the running of it. Without a doubt, the best course of action should have been to leave Dr. Monroe to the digging of the bones.

But nay. He'd watched her take her leave from his solar, then found himself staring whilst she worked. He'd hurried through his phone meeting with Mr. Adams, his solicitor, and had sought her out. He'd regret it later, he knew. But for now, he wanted to know more.

He felt . . . drawn to her.

"Tristan?"

Damn. Crossing his arms across his chest, he frowned.

"I'm glad to see my coin has not been wasted." He peered over her head into the gaping hole. "And what do you expect to find after fetching all the bones out?"

Andi rose and walked toward a canvas bag on the ground. She unzipped it and lifted a camera. "Well, although not my primary profession, I do have a background in forensic anthropology. It won't be a fast procedure. There are 206 bones in the adult skeleton. I'll be able to tell you whether the bones are male or female, if the right bones are available. I may be able to tell how long they've been in the ground, which, since they're rooted under this tree, I'd estimate at least six or seven hundred years, maybe more. And how old the person was. At least, an approximation." She unscrewed the cover protecting the lens. "After the photos are taken and I've made a record of how everything is laid out, I'll slowly collect the remains and send them to a friend of mine—a pathologist. He'll do more extensive examinations on the bones while I excavate the rest of the site here."

Tristan nodded, hoping he appeared more interested in her work than how fetching she looked in the modern trews snugged against her bottom. He swallowed. "Good. I expect you'll do a thorough job."

She gave him a half grin. "I always do." Then she turned and began snapping photos.

Hmmm. A saucy wench. He rather liked that. He liked her confidence and determination, as well. It nearly gave him the courage to trust her.

Saints, would that he could.

"Does this mean you won't be meeting with me this evening?"

Go on, Dreadmoor. Answer her. He looked into round, hazel eyes, widened with expectation. Waiting for an answer. Wanting to meet with him tonight. Where was his bloody strength? The more he met with her, the more he wanted to meet with her again. And again. Besides, what about the quarter finals? Of course he couldn't meet with her.

Damn his arse.

"Aye. Mayhap for a short spell. I am very busy. You can always confer with Jameson. He knows a great deal regarding the castle's history."

She nodded. "I don't want to be a nuisance. But the more you have to offer, the more I'll have to offer." Turning, she began taking more photos.

Now. What was he to say to that? Not what he wished. He cleared his throat. "Yes, well. I'll do what I can. In the meanwhile, I've Dreadmoor business to attend to." Which he didn't, but that was a fact she need not be aware of. Before she could answer, he turned and made for his very unimportant Dreadmoor business.

A cool breeze brushed Andi's cheek as she walked through the kitchen's double doors. "I forgot to ask you this morning. Did you light my fireplace last night, Jameson?" She glanced at her watch. Three thirty. She'd been surveying and recording for six hours.

The aging butler spared her a glance. "Yes, my lady, I'm afraid I did take the liberty of doing the like. 'Tis a dreadfully drafty place, the castle. Even in the summer months, the north of England is a tempestuous place." He cleared his throat and raised an eyebrow. "I take it you made headway with your tasks this morn?"

She crossed the floor and sat down at the kitchen table. "I did, actually. All the photos have been taken of the remains and area, and I began the recording. I've got to note every grain of dirt, every rock, and every misplaced bit of tree bark surrounding the exposed soil."

Jameson raised one gray eyebrow. "I see you've been busy. But you mustn't make a habit of missing tea, Dr. Monroe. You're passing thin as it is."

As if in response, her stomach growled. "I guess I got busy and forgot." She smoothed the tablecloth before her. "Lord Dreadmoor came out and viewed the area."

The other eyebrow shot up. "Did he, now? Were you able to gain any more information regarding the Dragonhawk legend? I daresay if anyone would know, 'twould be Himself."

Andi shrugged. "I think I annoyed Himself, actually.

Although he halfheartedly agrees to meet with me for information, he seems to do it with reluctance. I did find out he has the original plans of the castle, which I've been given permission to examine. I didn't have time to ask him about the shield in my chambers, though."

"Ah, well, I can enlighten you somewhat." Jameson placed a plate before her. "I do hope you like egg and dill salad with mayonnaise on wheat?"

She nodded. "Absolutely. Thanks." Lifting the packed sandwich, she took a bite. *Yum.*

"Of course. Now. 'Twas the original Dreadmoor's war shield, passed down from the centuries. Quite a sturdy piece of armor. You can feel the battle notches carved in the wood."

Wiping the corner of her mouth with a white linen napkin, she met his gaze. "The original Dreadmoor—that would be the infamous Dragonhawk, right? I discovered that fascinating detail earlier, but I'll be sure and ask him about the rest this evening."

Jameson cleared his throat. "I daresay you must have made quite an impression on him."

Andi took a sip of tea, placed the mug down, and eyed the steward. She crossed her arms over her chest. He knew something, and she wanted to know what. "Okay, Jameson. Give it up." She rapped her fingertips on the tabletop, awaiting his answer.

Jameson slowly turned. The bored expression on his face gave nothing away. "Give what up, my lady?"

Andi raised an eyebrow. "He is not a typical English lord—not what I expected at all." She pinned him with a stare. "Himself. I want to know about *him*—and why he doesn't want to talk to me."

The corners of Jameson's mouth twitched, just a bit. He straightened his already straightened jacket. "Yes, of course. Lord Dreadmoor—"

"Oh no. His name is Tristan." She smiled. "Tristan *what*?"

The collar of Jameson's coat rustled, as if a breeze had caught it. He stiffened again, then went on.

Weird. She hadn't felt a breeze. Maybe the kitchen vent had rushed a pocket of air near him.

"Tristan de Barre, my lady."

Andi crossed one leg under her rear end and propped her chin in the palm of her hand. Whoa. De Barre. What a sexy name. Man oh man. "Go on. I want the scoop. The skinny. Details, man."

Jameson straightened himself and walked to the pantry. "I daresay 'tis much like gossip, if you ask me."

"I didn't. Proceed."

"Ahem."

Andi looked around the room. She saw no one but the steward. "Was that you?"

Jameson cleared his throat, then coughed several times. "Aye. Allergies." He confirmed that with another bout of throat-clearing, followed by a few sniffles.

She narrowed her eyes at the butler. "Hmm." Finishing her sandwich, she drained her mug of tea, stood, and pushed the heavy oak chair under the table. Her brows furrowed together. "If you won't give up the information I want, then I'll just have to ask Tristan myself. Tonight." She smoothed her hair behind her ears. "Now, are we still on for a trip to the village?"

"Well, old man, you've done it now. You'd best answer the lady."

Jameson, used to years of having been sneaked up on, didn't even grace Tristan with a jump. "Of a certainty, my lady." Jameson lifted his chin. "I'll be ready to leave promptly at five."

Andi grinned. "Great. I'll just clean up a bit and change my clothes." With that she turned and nearly bounced out of the larder.

As soon as she was out of sight, Tristan materialized, his mirth now gone. He turned a brooding scowl on his man.

"Yes, my lord?"

Tristan's brows rutted as he crossed his arms over his chest. "That woman is not to return to my solar—tonight, nor in the morn."

"But you invited her to have speech with you this eve."

"I don't care. Fix it."

Jameson inclined his gray head. "I take it the meeting did not go as you'd hoped?"

"Nay, it bloody well did not. God's bones, the wench is infuriating. Passing nosy. She wants to know too much regarding the legendary Dragonhawk. I just won't have it."

"What could she possibly have done to foul your humor so?" Jameson blinked, flicking something off his shirtsleeve. "She is quite polite."

"She is too bold, for one, and 'tis just the beginning." He paced behind Jameson. "She has haughty ways, which explains why you've taken to her." He stopped to stare down at the stone floor. "She is intriguing. Beautiful. Witty. Tenacious beyond belief." He looked up at Jameson. "And she thinks me a live man."

"Did she remember you?"

"Aye." Tristan rubbed his chin. "But I convinced her 'twas not me she'd seen all those years ago." He hardened his stare once more. "I do not wish to speak with her again."

"My lord, if you will." Jameson inclined his head. "I'm quite sure Dr. Monroe meant no harm. She is rather enthusiastic regarding her work and the legend surrounding Dreadmoor. Allow her to at least speak with you this eve." He raised an eyebrow. "Besides, you've already agreed to do so. I do believe she is only interested in the history, but in case you haven't noticed, she is quite persistent. More likely than not, she'll continue to pursue you until she is satisfied."

"Persistent hardly describes her," Tristan muttered as he walked away, then turned back to glare at his steward. "I will see her tonight, answer her ridiculous questions, and then tell her I'm off on a business trip and won't return until her work is complete."

"You're no good at lying, my lord. 'Tis dishonorable to break the code. You said so yourself."

Tristan glowered and drew within an inch of his man's

nose. "Blast the bloody code. The code was written before women became so . . . independent. After tonight, it will be up to you to keep her away from me." He drew up to his full height and cracked his neck—or at least conjured up the effect. 'Twas a habit he'd retained through the centuries that he couldn't seem to break. "Do not cross me on this, Jameson. I vow you'll regret it." With that, he vanished.

Jameson folded the dish towel he'd had in his hand and placed it neatly on the marbled counter. He heaved a great, weary sigh, one well deserved, to his notion.

"I shall do my best, my lord." He knew Tristan would hear him.

Poor young de Barre.

Against his ghostly will he'd become enamored by the charming young colonist. And in no less than a day's worth of time.

For a moment, Jameson allowed the past to surface, and memories of the day he'd seen his Margaret for the very first time flooded his thoughts. She'd been so lovely in her pale yellow frock and white skirt. His heart had been lost immediately the moment she'd smiled.

Jameson shook his head. Saints be with the young knight.

Chapter 6

Tristan stormed toward the battlements. "Jason!"

"Aye, sir?"

Turning, his young squire materialized at his side, struggling to keep pace. "Right. There you are. I want you to go to the village and await Jameson and Dr. Monroe. They'll be arriving within the hour."

With a hand resting on the hilt of his sword, Jason jogged a few steps to match Tristan's long stride. "Aye. And is there anything in particular you wish me to do once there, my lord?"

Tristan stopped at the battlements and turned to answer Jason. "Aye. Practice how not to call me lord. You know it annoys me fiercely."

Jason's mouth twitched with a smothered grin. "Aye. Beg pardon. Consider it done."

Tristan cleared his throat. "She's going there to nose around the villagers. Our infamous legend has her interest piqued and she is on a mission to inquire about it further. I only want to make sure she receives the correct lore. You know how some of those old birds cluck."

Jason grinned, then nodded. "Aye, I know it well. I shall return posthaste." He began to vanish.

"Jason!"

The young squire materialized. "Aye?"

Tristan narrowed his gaze. "Do not approach the lass. I know you lads have been talking about her. There is no need to give her any cause to suspect what is here."

Jason shifted his weight and kicked at a rock. Ah, the

little devil. He'd had something planned after all. Tristan could tell by the expression on his face. How well he knew his men.

Tristan leaned closer. "Am I heard clearly, boy?"

Jason nodded. "Aye. Ye are."

"Good." Tristan made for the pair of men at the far end of the battlements. "Find me as soon as you return."

Jameson pulled the Range Rover into the Safe Way and turned off the ignition. "Here we are, Dr. Monroe. I trust you can find your way around with the map I provided. 'Tis a small village. You shouldn't have any trouble at all."

"Great. I appreciate it, Jameson." She pocketed the hand-drawn map and stepped out of the Rover. Easy enough to remember, she thought. The town formed a small horseshoe, the bend hugging the sea path. Shading her eyes from the descending sun, she chose her direction. "I'll meet you back here, say, in an hour?"

Jameson closed his door and pressed the autolock. Pulling the bill of his soft hat down, he nodded once. "Very well, my lady. I shall be ready."

With a wave, she smiled at Dreadmoor's butler and headed up the concrete footpath. What a great little town, she thought. A bakery, a fishmonger, and oh, thank God—a chip shop. After popping in to see how late they stayed open, she continued on the path toward a small row of B&Bs. Bright red geraniums bloomed in window planters, each small yard boasting a typical English garden of mums, blooms of white and blue hydrangea, and a variety of tall, colorful foxglove. Pansies filled large hanging wire baskets.

Stopping at the last cottage, Andi noticed a small, faded, hand-painted sign flapping with each passing breeze. KATE'S B&B. VACANCY. Jameson knew the proprietor and had directed her there first. Pushing open the black iron gate, she walked to the front door and rapped with the knocker. When no one answered, she rapped once more.

"I don't believe Miss Kate is home, my lady."

Andi turned to find a smiling young man standing on the footpath. Funny, she hadn't noticed him before. He must have walked up behind her.

Pushing her hair behind her ear, she gave him a smile. "I guess you're right. She's not answering my knock. I suppose I'll have to come back later."

Making her way out the gate, she closed it behind her. Eyeing the passerby, she nodded. "Thanks."

"Is there something I could help you with?"

Tall, lanky, and handsome, the auburn-haired youth wore a crisp white T-shirt, a pair of faded jeans, and worn-looking hiking boots. His hair was long yet neatly collected at the back of his neck. He looked no more than seventeen. The warm grin he gave her spread from one ear to the other. How could she refuse?

"Well, actually, yes, maybe you can. I'm doing research at the castle and was hoping to get a little input from the locals. Do you know the history?"

"Aye, lady. I do. I've a penchant for history meself. What do you wish to know?"

They continued around the horseshoe footpath, toward the shops and Safe Way. "The original Lord Dreadmoor, for starters. Dragonhawk. What do you know of him and his missing knights?"

He grinned. "Aye, the Dragonhawk. Passing fierce, that one. 'Tis said he was a massive brute—well over six feet. A mighty warrior, nigh unto unbeatable with the blade. The best jouster in all of England and Scotland." He glanced down and met her gaze. "He and his men were a secret order of knights, bound together by fealty to Dreadmoor. 'Tis said his men had such loyalty, they would follow him anywhere—even into death." He nodded. "A great lord, truth be told." He winked. "And from what I hear, his lads were a fair lot of warriors, as well."

Andi listened to the strange accent—much like Tristan's. English, yes, but mixed with something . . . older. How strange, she'd never heard it before coming to Dreadmoor.

They completed the horseshoe and rounded the footpath. When they reached the chip shop she stopped and faced him. Odd. He spoke as though he knew the first lord personally. "Do you know what happened to him?"

The young man's smile faded. "You mean the legend? Everyone knows a bit of it, I'd warrant. 'Tis a tale which has been told through the centuries, passed from sire to son. Lord Dreadmoor, his knight squire, whom I've heard was quite a fearsome lad, Dreadmoor's captain, and twelve men disappeared without a trace. It's rumored they were murdered, but no one knows how or why. Some fear witchery may have been involved." He glanced at the chip shop's open door. "If you're ordering, you may want to do so now. The chippy is about to close."

"Oh, right. Give me a minute." Andi stepped into the small shop and up to the counter. A tall, wiry balding man of about fifty gave her a grin. "Haddock and chips, miss?"

Andi nodded. "Two, please. And lots of vinegar and brown sauce on one." The other she'd gotten for Jameson.

The man nodded. "Right."

She turned toward the young man. Wow. She hadn't even gotten his name. "Would you like something?"

The Adam's apple at his throat bobbed and he licked his lips. "I thank ye, but nay."

"Excuse me, miss?"

Andi turned back to the chip shop owner. A puzzled look stretched across his sea-weathered features. He glanced over her shoulder, then back to her.

Andi smiled. "Oh, he doesn't want anything."

The chippy owner shook his head and stared. "Who?"

Andi turned and glanced out of the shop door. Her newfound friend had disappeared.

"Here you go, miss. That'll be six pounds, twenty pence."

Andi paid the man and accepted the steaming fish and chips, wrapped in thick, white wax paper. "Thanks. By the way, do you happen to know the young man I was talking to? I didn't get his name."

The chippy owner shook his head. "Miss, there's been no one here but you."

"No." Andi smiled and jerked a thumb toward the door. "There was a young man waiting for me outside. Just a second ago."

The look on his face grew more puzzled, his brows drawing together in deep concentration. He scratched the crown of his head. "I'm sorry, miss. No one's passed my shop, save you, in over an hour."

A few minutes later, she stood at the Rover, awaiting Jameson. She'd briefly spoken to the fishmonger and the baker, and a cashier in Safe Way even had a moment to spare. She'd learned nothing more than what the mysterious young man had told her.

She watched Jameson cross the small parking lot pushing a loaded trolley of groceries from Safe Way. Stopping at the trunk, he gave a quick assessment, then raised one gray eyebrow.

"Is there something amiss, lady? Beg pardon, but you don't look well."

"No, I'm fine." She hated to lie, but worse, she hated to admit out loud what sounded ridiculous in her mind.

She'd just imagined an entire conversation with someone who didn't exist.

"I see you couldn't resist the chippy. Too much of that batter isn't good for you."

Forcing a smile, Andi helped Jameson unload the cart. "I know, but it smelled so good." She held out the waxed bundle. "I got you one, too."

His lip twitched. "Excellent. Thank you." Hefting a gallon of milk, he gave her a skeptical look. "I take it you didn't find the information you were seeking?"

She shook her head. "Miss Kate wasn't home. Maybe I'll try her later on in the week. I did talk to a few people, and they gave me a little bit of information."

He nodded and closed the trunk. "A fine idea, that. Any time you need to take the Rover in, you may do so." He glanced in the direction of the B&Bs. "I, er, could ring Miss Kate and perhaps invite her to tea? Then you could question her to your heart's content."

Andi studied Jameson. His face reddened, just a bit. Interesting. Maybe he was sweet on the B&B owner.

She smiled. "Thanks, Jameson. That would be great." Finished, they started back to Dreadmoor.

Come.

Andi jumped, her heart pounding. Was she going crazy? Glancing at her watch, she pushed the indigo button. *Seven.* Wasn't it too early for anyone to be about?

You're making excuses, Monroe. You know you're hearing a voice. Go on. Admit it. You're a nut.

"No." She stared at the laptop screen and at the week's worth of data she'd logged the night before, ignoring her annoying, inner voice. It was just the atmosphere of a dark, thirteenth-century castle making her imagination run away, just like it had all those years ago. Something about Dreadmoor did that to her, but she wouldn't give in to it this time. Pulling out her notebook, she began to log more of the dig.

Follow me.

A cool breeze, barely even there, brushed her cheek, feeling more like icy fingers grazing her skin. Snapping her laptop closed, she jumped up. "Okay. Who are you? Why are you doing this to me?" A glance behind the curtain proved empty. Nothing under the bed. The shower stall was empty. Even the lamp was free of microphones or bugs of any kind.

This way.

An invisible breath of air lifted the pages of an open book resting on a phone table near the door to her chambers. When she didn't move, several more followed.

"This is crazy." Andi slipped on her sneakers and crossed the room. On tiptoes, she slipped out into the corridor.

As gently as she could, she pulled the door to her room closed. She felt foolish for sneaking around the castle at the crack of dawn. What if she ran into Jameson, or worse, Tristan? How would she explain herself?

As if urging her to follow, another crisp waft of chilled air swiped the back of her neck. Almost pushing her.

Moving down the passageway, Andi made her way to the steps and down to the great hall. Once there, she stopped, unsure where to go.

A wispy stream of mist rose and swirled before her, as though someone invisible had just puffed a lungful of cigarette smoke from their lips. It drifted across the great hall, then disappeared through the crack of a lone, narrow door.

A lump formed in her throat. It figured.

The dungeon.

What was she doing? To tell anyone of this would make her look like a big, fat idiot. It was bad enough she thought it herself. With a quick glance around the hall, she ran to the door leading down to the dungeon, pushed it open, and slipped inside.

The mist had disappeared. She wanted to disappear, too. With small movements, she crept down the steps. The room felt positively creepy, cool, and reeked of . . . something. No wonder Heath and Mrs. Dawson crossed themselves so much, although Andi often wondered if the boy did it just to pick on her. Quickly, she made the sign on her chest. What could it hurt?

The roughened walls boasted of stone and mortar, the floor hard-packed dirt. Damp and dark, the torches on the walls flickered the only available light. Actual torches, not lanterns. Were they kept lit all the time, or had someone just set them to flame?

She wiped her palms on her pj bottoms and slowly walked the room as her mind rambled. Why had she been led here? Men had probably died in this dank place. If she'd been superstitious, which she definitely was not, it would easily make her give way to a severe case of the shivers. Lucky for her, she had her wits about her. Sort of.

"Lady?" A small voice called from the top of the circular stone steps. "Are you down there?"

Andi jumped and stifled a scream. God, it was only Heath. She'd forgotten it was already Thursday, and later this afternoon she and Miss Kate were to have tea. With a final glance around, she made her way to the steps. "Yes, I'm here."

"How come?"

A smile touched her mouth as she watched his little head peek around the corner. Wasting no time, she reached the top and closed the dungeon door.

Heath's small nose wrinkled. "Whatcha doin' down there?"

Andi lifted one shoulder. "Just . . . looking around."

"But it's the dungeon." He glanced around, then whispered behind a cupped hand, "*He* might be down there."

Lowering herself to his height, she narrowed her eyes. "He who?"

"Dragonhawk, lady. With his bloody sword."

"Ah, Dr. Monroe. I see young Heath has found you."

Andi turned to find Jameson crossing the hall. "Are you up for a spot of tea and porridge this morning, or would you prefer something cooked?"

God, how she wanted to confide in him. Better yet, how she'd love to tell Tristan de Barre about the very real spirit he had wafting around in his castle. With a smile, she nodded. "Porridge would be great, Jameson. I'll just run upstairs and change."

He took in her pajamas, shrugged, then made for the kitchen.

"I'll see you later, Dr. Monroe. Me grandmum is waitin'." Heath made a big production of crossing himself before he sped from the hall and out the front door.

Strange, Jameson hadn't even questioned why she'd been lurking about the dungeon in her jammies. Well, all the better for now, she supposed. Not only did she have an incredible amount of real work to do involving the bones and armor in the bailey, but she had to gather the courage to ask Lord Dreadmoor if she could excavate his dungeon. She'd be meeting with him before having tea with Miss Kate, so if she was going to gather courage, she'd better do it fast.

Something was in that dungeon. And she wasn't leaving until she found out what.

Or, more likely, *who*.

Damnation, how he wished the wench would hurry up. He'd nearly paced himself senseless waiting for her arrival to his solar. The lads had kept him busy the earlier part of the day, although he had snuck out a few times to watch her work. He must be truly witless. He'd made an attempt to stay away from her as much as possible. 'Twasn't an easy task. She bloody well fascinated him.

Jameson, damn his arse, had told him 'twas voyeurism, watching from his invisible state. So be it. It wasn't as if he could help it.

Something perplexed her, though, and by the saints, he wanted to know what it was. More than once he'd watched her look over her shoulder. And twice she'd talked aloud. *What do you want from me?* she'd asked under her breath. Hell. He'd almost answered. Until he realized it wasn't him she spoke to.

A light rap sounded against the oak door. Drawing a deep breath, he cleared his throat. "Aye. 'Tis open."

The door cracked and Andrea peeked her head inside. She smiled. "Hi. Can I come in?"

Saints, if she didn't stop smiling at him so, he would go mad. He muttered under his breath and made a show of shuffling illusionary papers on his desk. "Of course you can. You're late."

"Right." She slipped in, closed the door, and made her way to the chair facing him. She sat, eyes fixed on his.

Bloody bones, what a distraction. She wore a sleeveless tunic of sorts and a pair of those fetching modern hose. Good thing he'd positioned himself behind the desk, or she'd witness him bumble around like the fool he knew himself to be.

Where was his infamous willpower, anyway? He'd vowed not to have much doings with her, and yet for a solid week, he'd met with her nearly every night to discuss her work. *Liar. You meet with her because you're passing fond of her.*

"Tell me about the ghost who resides in your hall, Tristan," Andi said.

He almost toppled over in his seat. "I do not see where that has anything to do with what you've been hired for, Dr. Monroe."

"Oh."

Dolt. "What I mean is there couldn't possibly be any information from those childish tales that would aid you in your excavation."

"I was just curious," she said. "I was lured to work in a medieval castle that's rumored to be haunted, and yet I wasn't told."

"Would you have still come?"

Andi laughed. "Of course I would have. I don't believe in ghosts."

Tristan squelched the urge to laugh himself. If only she knew. "I see."

She gave him one of those smiles again. "Now, about this ghost?"

Devil's toes, the wench had spirit. He wondered if she knew just how many ghosts she spoke of. Better to not encourage her, though. "You are a professor of archaeology, am I correct?"

She paused before answering. "Yes, you know I am."

"Excellent. If I desire someone to oust the spirits from my home, I'll ring another, say, a paranormalist, who is more qualified."

Soft, hazel eyes narrowed as she leaned forward. "I'm more qualified than you could possibly imagine."

Tristan laughed. Damn, she grew bolder by the second. "What mean you?"

A flash of emotion crossed her features, a fleeting hesitation, a wavering of thought? Something, or someone, had terrified her. She warred with whatever it was, and damnation, he was determined to coerce it out of her.

He leaned back in his chair. "Does this have anything to do with your fright from your first night here?"

Averting her gaze, she sighed. "No. Everything's okay." Again, she set her eyes to his. "But I would like to know about Dragonhawk and his knights. You've yet to give me the full story."

Tristan rubbed his chin, searched her eyes. "Andrea, if something is amiss, you must tell me at once. I will not allow a guest of Dreadmoor to feel threatened." He leaned toward her, careful to keep a safe distance away. "I can see it in your eyes, woman. What terrifies you so?"

Twice, her lips parted as though to speak. Lips he had a bloody difficult time not staring at. For a moment, he watched her wage a silent battle, brows furrowed, breathing becoming more rapid. Finally, her teeth clamped against her lips and she shook her head.

"It's nothing. Really, Tristan. Just my imagination." She smiled. "You know. An old castle, filled with old, interesting tales. All of which I'd love to know about."

Stubborn wench. He returned her brave stare with one he knew revealed disbelief. She ignored the challenge and lifted her chin.

"The more you can tell me about the history, even if it's legend and lore, the more I can tell you about the poor soul wrapped around those oak roots in your bailey."

Saucy, stubborn wench.

If she wouldn't concede, he'd simply have to continue following her. The lads had all denied having anything to do with the mishap. Soon, he would get to the bottom of it. Another ghost, indeed.

Inclining his head, he rose and moved to the two large chairs near the hearth, where the fire he'd started earlier glowed with red embers. "Very well. Why don't you have a seat here? For I daresay this is quite a lengthy tale."

"Thanks." She moved to one of the chairs and sat down. "You have the most unusual accent. Where are you from? De Barre is French, isn't it? Yet, you don't sound French. What about Scottish? It definitely sounds like you have a little brogue thrown in."

Tristan frowned and moved to the chair opposite hers. "What has that got to do with your work?"

"Absolutely nothing. Are you from England?"

He saw her shake her head.

"I just can't seem to piece it together."

"You, my lady, are naught but a nosy wench." Tristan sighed. What would it hurt to tell her a few minor details of his life before, well, his un-life? She would never know the whole of it anyway. Once she concluded her job she would be on her way, leaving him in peace.

"Well?"

Tristan cleared his throat. "I was indeed born in Scotland. My mother was a Highland lass, very bold of tongue and very lovely. Terrible character traits for a woman, I can assure you."

Memories assaulted him anew. His wee mother, hands on hips with her head thrown back, giving his father—who was three times her size—a devil of a tongue-lashing for muddying up her freshly laid rushes. He wouldn't have wanted her any other way but bold.

"And your father?" The curiousness in her voice edged with excitement as she leaned her chin on her fist and watched him closely.

He squelched the urge to squirm.

"Aye, my sire. He was born of a Scottish mother and a French-Norman sire." Gage de Barre had been a giant of a man, whose skill as a knight had been known in several countries. Damnation, he missed them so.

"Well, that explains it." Her voice had grown soft.

"What mean you?" Tristan said. He leaned forward, elbows resting on knees.

"It explains your unusual accent." She paused a moment, then continued. "I didn't think the term French-Norman, let alone sire, was used anymore."

Oy, Dreadmoor. Mayhap those modern slang terms Jason wanted to teach weren't such a bad thing after all. "Aye, well, 'tis just a family . . . tradition, I suppose. Sort of a habit."

She nodded. "Forgive me, but you speak as though your parents are no longer living."

"They are not."

"Oh. I'm sorry."

"Aye, 'twas a long time ago."

After a moment's silence, she spoke. "About the disappearance of the knights? I can't tell you how intrigued I am with it."

Tristan nodded. "No need to. 'Tis quite revealed by your incessant questions."

Her lips twitched. He found it immensely tolerable.

"Well, allow me to tell you the tale. 'Twas the year of our Lord, 1292. Lord Dreadmoor, who is rumored to have been quite a fierce sort, his squire, captain, and six of Dreadmoor's personal knights were on their way home from a cousin's wedding celebration. 'Tis said the lord was taken unawares and murdered. The others soon followed as—"

"As he only kept the castle guarded with a few men," she finished. "But even though that was a small number of men to sentry a castle, it's quite a number of men to have all disappeared without a trace. Quite a large number to kill off." She leaned forward and quirked a brow. "So, what happened to them? Why would anyone want an entire garrison killed, their bodies hidden?" Her brows furrowed. "Was it for money? No doubt Lord Dreadmoor had to have been quite wealthy."

Saints, he wanted to tell her more. He wanted to tell her everything. Yet he didn't. Couldn't, without her knowing his real identity. Couldn't let her know 'twas because he'd allowed his foster father's only son to be killed. Instead, he offered speculation. "Mayhap 'twas the castle itself? 'Tis a grand one."

She all but rolled her eyes. "If that were the case, a de Barre wouldn't still have ownership. No. It had to be something else." She slid out of her chair and skirted behind him, idled up next to the window. "What was so special about the knights? About the feared Dragonhawk himself? Did they hold a secret, I wonder?"

Tristan studied her as she stared out the window. Smoke all but rose from the top of her head as the wheels of her mind went round, trying to figure out the legend of Dreadmoor. Against his better judgment, he rose and came to stand a safe distance behind her. "Are you a detective as well, lady?"

She lifted a narrow shoulder and continued to stare out the window. Should he venture into asking her more personal questions? 'Twas absurd for him to want to know more, and yet he found himself wanting just that, bloody fool that he was. "And what of you, Andrea Kinley Monroe? From where do you hail?"

"Virginia."

Tristan grunted. "And what drew you to do the work you seem to love so?"

A soft laugh escaped her, and she turned to face him. "I've been fascinated by medieval history ever since I was a little kid, and I guess I never outgrew it."

Tristan's heart slammed against his ribs. At least, so it felt. Christ, the woman was beyond beautiful, and it took more strength than he'd conjured in centuries to keep from reaching out and touching her. Instead, he cleared his throat and gave a good cough. "Knights and dragons and the sort, no doubt?"

She nodded. "Yes, I suppose so."

Tristan, having lost all wits, moved closer. "Might you enlighten me on the nature of this knight? Is he someone you know?"

Softly arched brows pulled together in a mock frown. "This *really* has nothing to do with your find, now, does it?"

"An ancient hoard of medieval weapons. A legendary knight. One cannot be spoken of without the other, lady. They go hand in hand."

"You got me there," she said.

"Aye, I know. And I can feel your mirth from here, woman. Now make haste with your paltry tale, for I've not the patience nor the stomach to sit here all night with you." *Lying dolt.* He'd sit here all bloody century with her, truth be told. But he'd never let her know such drivel. "Now begin."

"Yes, sir. And no, I don't know him—only in my imagination, I guess. He's enormous—a giant," she said. "Very strong, probably from years of swinging a sword. To protect his lady's honor, you see."

Tristan scowled. Had she somehow met his uncle Killian? "Go on."

With the tip of her finger, she rubbed the steamed breath from the window. "He has long, dark hair, past his shoulders, and the most amazing pair of blue eyes. He's very strong and well over six foot and a half."

His uncle Killian was six foot and a half. *The bloody whoreson.* Tristan pulled his brows into a deep frown.

"He wears an armor of chain mail. It creaks when he moves. That fascinates me for some reason."

"Yes, well." He moved to his desk, resting a hip on its surface. "I suppose those are the imaginings of a foolish girl, eh?"

She ignored him. "Funny thing is, I've seen him before. In life."

Tristan's mood fouled, although he couldn't exactly fathom why. "Have you now? Where?" 'Twould be better to find out so he could at least haunt the buffoon. If he'd been alive and capable he'd soundly throttle the bloody idiot.

"I sort of saw him here, at Dreadmoor."

Tristan gulped.

"About twelve years ago."

He gulped again.

"At least I thought I had. At the kirk. I kind of snuck onto the grounds. He . . . sort of saved me."

Merciful saints above. *He* was Andi's knight. Bloody hell.

A soft laugh escaped her, and then she turned and moved toward him. "Funny thing is, I thought it was you." She faced him straight on, her eyes holding his. "When I first arrived, that is. But of course, I was mistaken. You said as much yourself."

Neither moved, neither spoke. Their gazes remained fastened for several moments. Christ, how he wanted to kiss her.

Saints, the girl was making him daft.

"I suppose I'd better—oh!"

Tristan jumped back just as Andi's foot caught the claw of his desk. She sprawled forward, and had he not moved, she would've continued to fall straight through him.

As it was, she fell to the floor.

And just as fast as she went down, she jumped back up. Saints, her poor cheeks were blazing.

"What is wrong with you?" she asked, smoothing her tunic. "You'd rather let me fall on my face than reach out a hand to help me?" Turning, she made for the door. "I've got notes to log, tea with Miss Kate, and a busy day tomorrow. Bones to collect. Thanks for the information."

He could do nothing, save let her storm from his solar.

For the life, or unlife, of him, he couldn't recall ever feeling more like an idiot.

Chapter 7

Andi fumed as she stomped back to her room. How humiliating. Not only did the big oaf fling himself away from danger as she plummeted toward him before she smacked into the floor, but he didn't even bother to apologize. Didn't even extend a hand to help her up—not that she needed it. Didn't even try to stop her when she left his solar.

She was exasperated with herself. Why was she trying to make friends with a stuffy English lord who apparently thought a little too much of himself? Twice, he'd pulled away from touching her, horror written all over his face, as though the thought of his royal hide scraping skin with a lowly, pock-marred serf such as herself sickened him. As if she'd actually *let* him touch her. Please. The man was *gorgeous*. She was aching for him to touch her. Actually, she'd wanted him to kiss her. Badly.

As if that would ever happen.

Moments later, Andi greeted Heath's grandmother, Miss Kate, as everyone called her, in the great hall for tea.

Kate MacDougall, an attractive Scottish woman in her early sixties with straight, shoulder-length gray hair she wore neatly pulled together at the nape of her neck, rose from her chair and smiled. "Afternoon, Dr. Monroe. I hope you don't mind Heath here playing by the hearth while we chat. He fancies lying about in the great hall." She grinned at her grandson, whose missing-tooth smile beamed back. "The lad likes to pretend he's lord of Dreadmoor."

Andi grinned at the boy. "I don't mind a bit."

Jameson bustled into the hall, carrying a tray laden with fresh-baked cookies, a large, steaming pot of tea, cream, sugar, and four cups, spoons, four small plates, and a silver set of tongs. He placed the tray on a solid oak table situated between the chairs, and glanced at Miss Kate. "You're looking quite well this afternoon. Tea?" His cheeks reddened.

Not surprisingly, Kate's blushed, as well, and she giggled. "Thank you, Edgar. I'd love some."

Andi nearly choked as she stifled a laugh. *Edgar?*

Jameson shot Andi a look, then hurried through the filling of all cups. Heath joined them, and everyone set about with sugar, cream, and cookies, which were beyond heavenly.

After a few moments of idle chatting, Andi spoke to Kate. "Can you tell me anything of the legend?"

Kate, Heath, and Jameson shared a look, and then Kate smiled. "I was born in the Dark Isles of the Highlands, lass, and I've heard stories ever since I was a wee girl." She set down her plate of cookies and wiped her mouth with a napkin. "What do you know so far?"

"Well," Andi started, "I've been told Dragonhawk and his knights disappeared after returning from a wedding celebration. No bodies, no armor—and that witchcraft could have been involved."

Kate nodded. "All hearsay, mind you, but 'tis the same story. No one knows why, or how so many fierce men could have been subdued. Their families never heard from them again—so the legend goes."

Heath chimed in. "I heard from me best mate at school that fairies came and took them back to their hollows underground." His face screwed up. "But that sounds like it was made up by a girl. No way would the Dragonhawk be taken by a fairy!"

Andi smiled. "I wholeheartedly agree."

"A witch, perhaps?" Kate said. " 'Twas a lot of evil in those days, and witchery wasn't uncommon."

Andi shrugged. "Even if witchcraft were involved, that wouldn't explain why there were no bodies."

Kate leaned forward. "Witchery can be a powerful evil, lass. Don't dismiss it so thoroughly."

Andi glanced at Heath, who crossed himself.

Jameson, who'd remained uncommonly quiet, rose. "I daresay all you'll find is lore and legend, Dr. Monroe. 'Twas many a century ago, you know. Not much detail, other than business of the church, was recorded. Rather, recorded and preserved. In a desolate area such as Dreadmoor, 'tis highly unlikely anything was written down."

Andi stood and tried to wrap her brain around the illogical aspects of witchcraft. She smiled. "Forgive me, but I just don't believe in witchcraft or ghosts. It's just not in my nature. Something more solid had to have been the cause of death for such a large group of virile medieval warriors."

Jameson's mouth twitched. Kate's eyes sparkled. Heath downright grinned. Had they all lost their minds?

Then their eyes all averted to some point behind her. Andi turned to find the lord of Dreadmoor himself, standing with hands shoved into the pockets of his nicely packaged faded jeans. A dark blue Henley pulled at the muscles bunched in his arms and chest, and Andi had to check for drool on her chin.

Sexy hardly described him.

"Virile, you say?" Tristan lifted one dark brow. "Since it is my ancestor we speak of, I can assure you *that* bit of legend is true."

Muffled though it was, Andi heard Kate's giggle.

"My lord, you've just missed tea," Jameson said. "Can I prepare you a tray?"

"Nay, man, but thank you all the same. I'm off. Business, you see." Tristan gave a low bow. "Ladies. Master Heath."

With that, Tristan de Barre left the hall.

Under his breath, Heath muttered, "He's cool."

Andi watched Tristan go, her insides tingling. Good Lord, he was . . . cool.

"Right. Come along, Heath. We've got a bit of baking to do for our guests this eve." Kate met Andi's gaze.

"High season for tourists, you see. Lots to do." She smiled. "If you ever tire of this drafty place, come for a visit, won't you? I love a bit of girl talk here and there."

"And you can meet my mum," Heath added. "She likes girl talk, too, I bet."

Andi smiled. "Absolutely, I'd love to. Thank you for the offer."

Kate turned and gave Jameson a smile. "Lovely tea as always, Edgar."

Jameson gave a low bow. "Lovely company as always, Miss Kate. Come, Master Heath. I'll show you and your grandmum out."

Andi waved them good-bye and plopped down onto the overstuffed chair. Grabbing the last cookie, she nibbled and waited for Jameson to return. Her thoughts turned to their previous conversation as she chewed.

Witchcraft and ghosts. While fascinating to hear the tales and lore, it simply didn't make sense, and it certainly didn't add up. Yet, she'd heard that voice, had seen that waft of mist . . .

"I see you've cleaned the cookie tray," Jameson said behind her. "Quite an appetite you have."

Andi rose from the chair and smiled. "I can't help it. Those cookies are delicious."

"I'm sure they are," Jameson said.

Together, Andi and Jameson cleared the tea setting and loaded the dishwasher. While muttering under his breath that it just didn't sit well with him for her to be doing house chores, he allowed her to help put the great hall chairs to rights and tidy up.

When they were finished, Andi headed to her room. "I think I'll go over my notes for a while," she said.

"I'll announce when dinner is ready," Jameson said.

As she passed by, Andi gave Jameson a wide smile and a wink. "That'll be lovely, *Edgar*."

Edgar Jameson's face turned bright red. "I'm sure it will be, my lady."

After a couple of hours spent poring over her site log, Andi stretched and decided to walk around the castle. Powering down her laptop, she slipped out of the cham-

ber and started up the corridor. Long, winding passage-
ways ran this way and that, and Andi lost track of the
way she'd come.

Suddenly, she pulled to a stop. She listened, turning
her head to find the sound floating up the passageway.

It came from the opposite direction. A TV, perhaps?
Loud. Male voices. Several of them. Funny, she thought
she was the only one at Dreadmoor, besides Tristan
and Jameson.

Moving back down the corridor, she passed several
doors before seeing a light flicker under the one at the
end. The sound of several excited rowdy males drifted
out. Carefully, she pushed the door open, just a fraction,
ready to peek inside.

"My lady?"

Jameson's voice made her jump, knocking her head
against the door frame. Rubbing it, she felt her face grow
hot with embarrassment. "Oh. Hi." She inclined her
head. "I thought I heard a party going on."

Jameson cleared his throat, speaking louder than normal. "Nay, my lady. There isn't a party going on this
time of eve, here, in this corner chamber."

What was up with him? Cocking her head to the side,
she turned and pushed the door open.

No rowdy males. Nobody at all. Only a big-screened
TV against one wall, a large fireplace taking up the space
of another, an overstuffed leather sofa and love seat, and
a few footstools. A rugby game blared from the TV.

Shrugging her shoulder, she backed out of the room
and slid a glance at Jameson. "Sorry. It must've been
the game I heard."

Jameson nodded. "Indeed. Master Tristan must have
left the tele running. Are you ready for supper?"

After a delicious meal of pot roast and vegetables,
Andi helped Jameson clear the dishes.

"Shall I walk you to your room?" he asked.

She shook her head and headed up the corridor. "No,
that's okay. The food was great, thank you. See you in
the morning."

"Good eve to you, Dr. Monroe."

Once to her room, she shut the door behind her and leaned against the cool wood. A long, exasperated sigh escaped her lips as she thought of the day's events.

Nosing around the castle, sneaking a peek into a room she had no business sneaking a peek into . . .

And there was Tristan. He'd set her on edge earlier. Beyond handsome—mouthwatering, to be exact. And very, very much like the man she'd *thought* she'd seen so long ago. Then she thought of how he'd jumped back in his solar and allowed her to fall on her rump without even trying to help.

But that man, the one dressed like a knight, had at least feared for her safety. Had tried to help her. Lord Tristan de Barre of Dreadmoor had simply faked to the left, allowing her to plunge to his hard, old floor.

The sharp blast of her mobile snapped her from gloomy thoughts of Dreadmoor. Pushing off the door, she crossed the room and read the illuminated face. *Kirk.*

Flipping the cover, she sighed with relief. "Hey, you. What's up?"

Her mentor's deep voice sounded from the other end of the line. "Bored without you, of course. How is it at the dark and gloomy Dreadmoor castle? Run into any bloodcurdling spirits yet?"

Kirk had pulled a string or two to get her here. No way would she let him think for a minute she was upset about something. "It's fantastic, actually. Dark? Yes. Gloomy? Definitely. But absolutely fantastic. You should see this room. Gorgeous doesn't even begin to describe it."

"Making much progress?"

Kicking off her sneakers, she padded over to the window seat in the alcove, plopped down, and stared out into the faded evening. "A lot of progress, actually. I've taken all the photos, logged the site, and sent the soil and bone fragment samples that had been flung to the side to Terrance Daughtry. Tomorrow, I begin to remove the remains. And guess what? Dreadmoor said you can be here for it."

"You're kidding?"

Andi grinned. "I would never kid. I was just about to call you myself and beg you to come. I'm sorry it's taken so long with the logging and pictures, but without an intern—"

"I know, I know. Not to worry, then. I'll be out straightaway in the morning, say eightish?"

"Absolutely," Andi said.

"That's my girl. Have you inspected any of the weaponry?"

"Not yet. It's a bit further to the right and under the root system and remains. I'll have to collect the bones first, then have a team hired to cut and drag the oak away. It's enormous—the trunk is ten meters wide. I can barely see a slip of metal through the dirt, though, but that's all." She pressed her nose to the glass. "Why?"

"Pah. Just wondering, love. I'm rather interested in the hoard."

Stretching her legs, she turned on her back and propped her stockinged feet in the sill. "How's the team doing?"

"Quite green and demanding, and I wouldn't think of leaving them for a moment." He chuckled. "I have to keep my eyes glued to them every second. But they'll enjoy a day off tomorrow, whilst I come out and give you a hand."

"I can't wait," she said.

"Right. Get some rest, girl. We'll have a big day tomorrow."

They rang off, and Andi grinned. Unearthing the remains would be interesting. Tiring, with just the two of them, but at least Tristan had given her the okay to have Kirk give her a hand.

A wave of exhaustion washed over her, and her eyes began to droop. Too tired to move to the bed, Andi set the mobile on the floor, turned on her side, and closed her eyes.

Tristan rested his hand on the hilt of his sword and watched Andrea in slumber. Saints, she was passing lovely. A thick strand of dark hair draped over her brow, and soft, full lips parted as deep, even breaths slipped past. Her folded hands cushioned her cheek like a pillow. More than passing lovely.

She was *beautiful*.

And she thought him a big, horse's arse.

Damnation, he'd felt like one earlier. The look on her face as he'd jumped back, allowing her to fall, would forever be emblazoned on his sorry memory. He deserved it, no doubt.

He should never have allowed her to come.

But, he thought as he studied her, she *was* here. Here to help unearth the unknown being in his bailey. And hopefully, to find out more about the weapons—

With a jerk, Andi sat straight up and gasped, her hand covering her heart. "Please! What do you want from me?"

Tristan quickly glanced down at himself. He'd not materialized. On a closer look, he noticed she wasn't even looking in his direction.

She shook her head. "No. They're going to think I'm crazy. I . . . I can't do this."

Tristan scanned the room. Who was she talking to? By all the saints' blood, *was* she daft? Christ, the poor lass.

Uttering a weary sigh, Andrea rose from the window seat, slipped on her shoes, and walked right past Tristan. Crossing to the door, she eased silently out into the corridor, closing the heavy oak behind her.

Only a scant moment passed before Tristan walked through the door and followed. Down the corridor, the steps, across the great hall, Andi finally stopped at the entrance to the dungeon. Glancing around, she opened the door and stepped inside. Tristan followed.

Once inside, he saw the beam of light from her torch sweep the floor as she descended. He hadn't seen her pick one up from her chamber. Where had she gotten it from? He watched, amazed, as she crept down the spiraling steps and crossed the dungeon floor, stopping in the center.

"Okay, I'm here. Now what?" she asked.

He took in the darkened chamber. Saints, how he hated the place. Who was she talking to?

Scanning the crumbled mortar walls with the beam of her torch, Andi slowly made a circle until she'd gone full round. Then she swept the floor. "I just don't know what you—oh, wow."

Dropping to her knees, she dug the hard-packed dirt away with the butt of her torch. Turning it over and anchoring it with her chin, she stared at the illuminated spot, brushing it with her hand, then leaning over and gently blowing. "Whoa. No way."

In the glow of the flashlight, Tristan watched Andi, mesmerized. Damnation, she was indeed engrossed in the task at hand. What in bloody hell had she found on the floor of his dungeon? He crept a bit closer, bent over at the waist, rested his hands on his thighs, and peered over her shoulder at the brushed area.

Bleeding saints. It couldn't be.

"Hello? Are you still here?" she asked. A few minutes of silence passed, then, "Hello?" With a shake of her head, she glanced back down. "No freaking way."

By the devil, he couldn't believe his eyes. Then, before he could step out of the way, Andi stood and whirled around.

And walked right through him.

She froze, back stiff, breathing rapid. After a moment, she moved up the stairs and quit the dungeon, latching the heavy door behind her.

With a flick of his wrist, torches on the wall blazed and flickered. Tracing his previous steps, he knelt over the place Andrea had unearthed.

"Saints, I hate this foul place. Well, what have you there?"

Tristan looked up. First Kail appeared, followed by Jason. Within seconds, the rest of the Dragonhawk garrison had gathered around the freshly turned dirt. He shook his head. "See for yourself." Turning his head, he met each man's stare. "I gather none of you are responsible for luring the lady in here, aye?"

A unison of mumbled nays sounded in the chamber.

Kail squatted down beside Tristan and peered at the overturned earth. "Christ, Tristan. 'Tis a bit of mail."

"Aye. And Dr. Monroe was led here by someone. I did not see, nor hear, but it happened all the same." He glanced at his captain. "If a spirit is the culprit, then why can't we see or hear it?"

"And why would it show itself only to the lady?" Jason asked. "If 'tis a piece of mail, then why not show it to one of us?"

"Mayhap because she's a woman?"

Tristan turned to the knight. "That is something to think on, Sir Richard." He shook his head. " 'Tis useless information if we cannot see or hear the spirit." Looking back at the links of steel mail, he squinted his eyes. "I wonder what else she'll dig up." Rising up, he addressed the garrison of men. "We shall all be on watch from here on out. Jason, I want you at the lady's door during her sleeping hours. If she pokes one little foot out of her chamber, I want to know about it."

Jason nodded once. "Aye, my lord. Consider it done."

"The rest of you will simply watch her during the day, invisible, of course. But allow her privacy." Tristan met each man's eye as they answered. They were incomparable to any others, his knights. They'd warred together, squired together, and they'd all been fostered together. Not once had they failed him. As they wouldn't now.

Turning, he moved to the stairs.

"Where are you off to, my lord?" Sir Richard asked.

Tristan stopped and inclined his head. "This foul place reeks and I'm ready to be done with it. Besides, I've got a lady to watch over."

Snickers rumbled behind him as he quit the dungeon.

Chapter 8

After hours of tossing and turning, Andi checked the time on her wristwatch once more. *Five fifty-five.* Jeez, it seemed as though the night had dragged by, one painful second at a time. She could stand it no longer. Besides, Kirk would be at the site by eight and she didn't want to waste any time. Slipping out of bed, she washed her face, brushed her teeth, and pulled on a pair of khakis, a white tank top, and a light blue sweater, slipped on her Crocs, then left the room.

Awake or not, Lord Dreadmoor would make the time to speak to her about the strange things going on right under his nose. And her plan to do something about it.

She'd marked her limit and could take no more. If someone was playing jokes on her, it would stop. Had to stop. Now.

Farther along the hazy corridor she went, courage in hand, until she arrived at Tristan's door. Lifting her hand, she paused, knuckles hovering over the solid oak. Should she? Shouldn't she? Should? Shouldn't? Ugh.

"By the saints, Andrea, open the door. I vow I can hear your breathing through the wood. Come in."

The sound of Tristan's deep voice washed over her, caused her breath to hitch, and she swallowed at least twice before opening the door.

She almost wished she hadn't.

He was bare to the waist, and his hair hung in dark tousled hanks past his shoulders, resting against chunks of a rock-muscled chest. A pair of deep maroon draw-string pants hung low on his hips. . . .

"Oh, I'm sorry. . . ." Andi blinked, unable to stop herself from staring, then resisted the urge to rub the disbelief from her eyes. "Why," she said, pointing to his hip, "are you wearing that?"

Sapphire-blue eyes widened when Tristan glanced down at the sword strapped to his side. A flash of annoyance followed by a quick recovery settled across his features. He lifted one dark eyebrow and crossed his arms over his chest.

"A bit of a workout before starting the day." He cocked his handsome head to one side, studying her from toe to eyebrow. "Why? Is there aught amiss at this early hour, Andrea?"

Whew, the heat in the room crept up her neck and she squelched the urge to fan herself. "As a matter of fact, yes, there is aught amiss." She made her eyes focus on his face and not the washboard abs.

Crossing the room, he waved her to the chair, then leaned a hip against the desk. "Well, Dr. Monroe, by all means tell me about it."

Ooh, the way he said her name, spearing her with such hot looks, staring at her mouth—he made it very difficult to concentrate. Attraction sizzled and snapped in the room. He knew it, and he knew *she* knew it. *Grr.*

Lowering herself into the overstuffed leather chair, she drew a deep breath and met his fiery stare with a hot one of her own. No way would she allow him to get the best of her.

"By the by, you look passing lovely this morn. If I may be so bold."

Grr.

She wondered if her neck was as red as it felt. "Thank you. Now, I know this is going to sound really strange, but here goes." Another deep breath. "Remember the first night I was here?"

A slow smile spread across his face, deep dimples pitting his five o'clock–shadowed cheeks. "Oh, aye. Of a certainty, how could I forget?"

Ignore, ignore, ignore. "I was frightened out in the bailey by"—she lifted her shoulder—"something. Or someone. And twice since. I don't know how it's being done, unless." She hesitated for a second as he watched her. "Unless you've a ghost in your hall."

Tristan rubbed his jaw. "A ghost in my hall, you say? There's been rumors aplenty for centuries, so it's nothing new, I assure you. Why do you think a ghost has approached you?"

God, it sounded even more stupid when said aloud—especially coming out of someone else's mouth. "It's nothing I can see. It's more of a . . . feeling. A presence, maybe." She shook her head and rubbed her brow. "I sound completely nuts. I'm a scientist. I don't believe in ghosts or the presence of one." She stared him down. "But I do believe there's something in your dungeon worth checking out. I'll work after dark each evening, when I'm finished with the cutaway in the bailey." She leaned forward. "It won't interfere with what you've hired me to do, I promise." She sighed. "Please, allow me to excavate your dungeon? I've felt something, a pull, to this place ever since I was a teenager. I promise to put everything back to rights, and I swear I'll reveal my findings only to you."

A muscle flinched at his jaw. His brows pulled together as he studied her with such a thorough intenseness she nearly squirmed in her seat. Finally, he rubbed his jaw and nodded. "I see no harm in allowing you this extra activity. But tell me, what do you think you'll find in my dungeon?"

"Well," she began, "I sort of already found something." She gave him a wan smile. "I was led down there by . . . let's call it a sixth sense."

Again with the intense stare, this one longer than the last. "You may begin with your promised revealing of information, posthaste."

"Fair enough." She rose from her chair and moved toward him. In a flash, he placed himself behind and at the other end of the desk.

Andi frowned. "I don't bite, you know. I've even had all my shots."

Gone was the smoky look his face held earlier, replaced now by a look of complete boredom. "I don't know what you mean by that, but get on with your findings, if you would." He checked the clock on his desk. "I've an appointment to ready myself for."

Wow. Talk about changing gears. One minute the look he gave dripped with lust. The next, total disinterest. *That's not why you're here, Andrea Kinley Monroe. Forget him, just do the job.*

Ugh, why was her inner voice always right?

She nodded. "Just below the surface of the dirt I discovered what I believe to be a few links of steel-gauged chain mail. I can't tell the age, of course, but there's bound to be more down there." She glanced at her watch. "I'll send for the rest of my equipment—a generator and GPS unit. I . . ." She paused and pushed her hair behind her ear. "Thank you for allowing me this opportunity. It means a lot to me." She stared in silence for a moment before turning for the door.

"Until later, Andrea."

At the door she turned, nodded, then left the chamber.

Once Andrea's footsteps disappeared down the corridor, Tristan flung himself into the chair. He rubbed his brow with thumb and forefinger, then closed his eyes. Saints, he couldn't take much more. . . .

"You look like hell, de Barre. What ails the fierce and powerful Dragonhawk this fine morn?"

Tristan cracked open one eye and stared at his captain. "Kail, you horse's arse. What think you ails me?"

"I daresay, sir, if you'll forgive my boldness. But you're not yourself when around the lady." Jason materialized and added. "You're passing . . . stodgy. My lord."

Tristan threw his young knight a glare. "If you know what's good for you, pup, you'll mind that cocksure tongue of yours."

Jason pressed his lips together, then nodded. "Of course. Cocksure tongue being minded, posthaste. Sir."

Kail walked over and leaned against the desk. "I don't see why you're so dismal. The lass seems passing agreeable. Being right honest, I'd say."

"Of course you'd say. You're not the one who has to sit and lie for scores of minutes at a time. You're not the one who has to pretend to be someone you're not."

"You didn't lie, my lord. Not once," Jason said. " 'Twas only minutes earlier, before the lady showed up, when you and I were dueling with the blades." He smiled. " 'Tis a workout of sorts, methinks."

"Methinks 'tis not the lying our Lord Dreadmoor is worried about," said Kail. He grinned and leaned forward, tapping Tristan on the head. " 'Tis being in close quarters with Lady Andi." He winked at Jason. "Aye?"

Jason raised one eyebrow. "Mayhap."

Tristan jumped from his seat and stormed past the two annoying men. "I didn't lie about an appointment, either. Meet me in the lists, the both of you." With a flick of his wrist, he conjured up his normal attire of chain mail. "I've a mind to work off my frustrations on you two dolts."

He disappeared, the sound of Kail's and Jason's laughter booming in his head, a frown tightening his face.

Stodgy, indeed.

What annoyed him fiercely was the fact that they were both right.

After a quick breakfast, Andi changed and geared up for the day. That was by far the easy part. The hard part was going to be to get that vision of a bare-bodied Tristan, complete with sword strapped to hip, and that glorious hair hanging wild around his broad shoulders, out of her head long enough to concentrate on unearthing the remains in the bailey.

Good luck, her inner voice taunted.

Dimples. Had she mentioned the man had dimples?

Andi didn't think she'd sounded more ridiculous in her entire life. Thank God no one knew but her own self.

When she reached the bailey, Kirk was already there, waiting. The grin on his face spread ear to ear. They shared this excitement, and she felt indebted to him for her path in life. He'd led her as a teen, and now worked side by side with her as an adult.

He rubbed his hands together. "Right. Let's get on it, shall we?"

Together, they got to work.

After several moments of studying the area, Kirk wiped his brow. "Quite bizarre, I'll say. It's as though the roots wormed their way throughout the skeleton and scattered them on purpose." He knelt in the overturned soil and looked up. "I'll retrieve, you bag. Then we'll switch." He grinned. "Not sure my old knees can stand it for too long."

Kirk paused over the first bone. "Nothing's been touched, right?"

Andi leaned forward. "No. I'm the only one who's been here and I did all the logging without touching anything—except the bone fragment that had been knocked loose and flung near the surface."

Kirk nodded. "Right." He leaned forward and, very carefully, lifted the first, and most obvious.

The head.

With both hands supporting each side of the skull, Kirk gasped. "Damn me, but this is weird." He glanced over his shoulder. "This chap met a grisly end. Could be a pickax made this hole in his head." He shook his head. "And there's a bloody vine wrapped about the skull." With sure hands, he removed the vine. "A yew garrote . . ." He stopped his movement. He didn't budge, just . . . held the remains and stared.

Andi noticed his breathing becoming more rapid, his hands beginning to shake. "Kirk? What's wrong?" When he didn't answer, she spoke louder. "Kirk?"

He didn't even flinch.

Just as Andi was about to lower herself into the grid, Kirk drew a long, exaggerated breath.

"Kirk? What's wrong with you?" she asked again, worried. "Let me help—"

"No. I'm . . . feeling a bit ill." He set the skull back in the spongy black soil, rose from the grid, and stood. He turned in a circle, as though slowly taking in the Dreadmoor estate.

Andi placed a hand on his arm. "Kirk?"

He didn't answer. Instead, he walked to the perimeter of the grid, bent over at the waist, and vomited.

"God, Kirk," Andi said. "You should leave. Maybe you ate something that didn't set well in your stomach?"

He lifted his gaze, watery and red. "Aye. Mayhap so."

Even his voice sounded strange. "I'll call you a cab, okay? Don't worry about all this." She indicated the area with a wave of her hand. "I can handle it. Don't even give it a second thought. You need to rest."

Within fifteen minutes, Andi settled her mentor into a cab and watched them pull away from the barbican. Too bad, she thought. Kirk had been so excited to work the initial removal.

"He'll be fine, lady," Will, the barbican guard, said. "More likely than not, he's gotten hold of a bit of poor meat. A few more times of emptying his belly, and some rest, and he'll be good as new."

Andi smiled at the guard. "Thanks, Will. I hope you're right."

With that, she turned and headed back to the grid.

Chapter 9

Andi wiped the sweat from her brow and stretched her aching back. She'd been at the cutaway for nearly nine hours straight. Retrieval was a tedious task, especially when doing it alone. Yet the satisfying sense of accomplishment always overwhelmed her when doing a project like Dreadmoor. Well, no other project had ever come *close* in comparison to Dreadmoor, she thought.

But to find ancient bones and relics always fascinated her, got her blood sizzling. No one understood. Kirk, maybe. But it was akin to sifting through history one small bit at a time, or like reading a mystery novel and having the plot unfold one thin layer by one thin layer until all layers lay before you. Exposed. Ready to be gone through. Poor Kirk. He would have totally enjoyed himself.

She'd been more than a little disappointed when Tristan hadn't shown up today. Not that he'd agreed to— he could be quite elusive at times. But she thought he might drop by the site. *No, Monroe. You wished he might*, her inner voice chided. How that voice annoyed her.

With several bones retrieved and bagged, Andi felt she'd done a thorough job for the day. And although the remains had been disseminated and scattered within the tree's root system, now exposed aboveground, a few had remained unearthed and entombed in the damp, black soil. None of the others, she'd noticed, had been secured with the yew vine, as the skull had been. She wondered if it'd been a ceremonial burial. That's something she'd definitely have to check into.

She'd been troweling for close to most of the day, and her back and knees were killing her. Deciding to cover the site and get a bite to eat before starting on the dungeon, Andi secured the tarp and collected the bagged bones. Maybe by next week she'd have made enough progress to start retrieving the weapons, and maybe something to identify who the body actually belonged to. And, more importantly, how the poor soul died. She could almost bet that thin yew vine coiled around the head had something to do with it.

Beware.

Small hairs on her neck stiffened at the now-familiar whisper. Although she knew it'd be useless, she turned slowly, to see if anyone was about.

There wasn't.

Still, she acknowledged the voice. "Beware of who?"

Only the crash of waves at the base of Dreadmoor echoed on the breeze. *Figures.*

Scanning the bailey, she took in the sight of Dreadmoor. Thick, gnarled oak trees shot up from the ground, centuries old, their leaves rustling with each brisk wind. The sun had broken through the clouds, shooting golden beams of light between the branches. The castle stood majestic, gallant against the whitecapped North Sea. How breathtaking the place was. To her, anyway.

To someone else, long, long ago, it'd become a grave.

"La-dy? Are you still down there?"

"Yes, Heath," she called, grinning to herself. What a cute kid. "Still in one piece, too." Heath had crossed himself a dozen times or more before entering the dungeon earlier, but he'd then jumped the stairs two at a time, all the way down.

She looked up in time to see the young boy, followed by Jameson, carrying a small cardboard box of her tools. The hard part had been getting the generator down the steps. But at least they'd managed it.

"Where shall we put these, Dr. Monroe?" Jameson looked about the room with distaste.

Andi hurried over and took the burden from his arms. "Thanks, Jameson. You're a lifesaver."

"No doubt." His dry tone cracked her up. "Does this conclude our labors for the day?"

She grinned. "For now."

"Hmm." He gazed at her with a critical eye. "I vow you have a lot of work ahead of you, young lady, what with the bailey project and the dungeon. I will be upstairs, preparing the evening meal, should you need me." With that, he turned and walked away.

"What about me, lady?" Heath held out a small box. "What's all this stuff, anyway?"

"They're my digging tools," she explained, "used for unearthing old relics and treasures."

"Crikey!" He looked about him quickly, as though attempting to thwart any unwanted ghouls from knowing their plans. "And bones, too, I bet. Bloody bodies and limbs everywhere." His voice dropped to a whisper. "Can I come watch sometime? You might need someone to watch your back."

Andi looked down into Heath's wide blue eyes and smiled. "Sure, kiddo." She bent down lower, so that only he, not the ghouls, could hear. "Do you have a sword, perhaps? Something to defend us with?"

Heath's grin stretched wide. "You mean against the ghastly knight ghost? Against Dragonhawk?" He gave a nod. "Aye, lady, I'd do me best." He scratched his thatch of dark hair, then stood as tall as his four-foot frame would allow. "I promise nothing would harm you. I can yell loudly, if anything were to try and get you."

She smothered a grin. "You got a deal."

Heath turned and flew up the stone steps, but stopped halfway up and spun around. "Will you be all right down here, all by yourself?"

"You bet." Andi waved him on. "You'd better go before your grandma comes looking for you."

"Aye. See ya!" he said. He crossed himself again, then disappeared through the door, leaving Andi alone.

She walked over to the stack of boxes and placed the small one Heath had been carrying on top. She turned to face the generator. It'd been filled with gas, once they'd managed to get it down the steps, and was ready to go. She could hardly wait to get started.

Tristan watched from the shadows of the dungeon in his invisible state. He couldn't have torn himself away had he tried. Andi's hair, not much longer than her shoulders, glossed with a healthy, rich shine. The kind of tresses a man relished to touch, let slide through his fingers, rub against his skin. He frowned at that thought. Not just any man. *Him.* But that bloody well wasn't going to happen, not in his sorry state of existence.

He leaned back against the wall and continued to watch. The girl checked the gear and busied herself preparing her tools. The young lad Heath had been as taken by her as Jameson. Witless, the both of them. Maybe he would tell the youngster one day he need only cross himself but once, and not the scores of times he had done that day, although he was quite sure the boy did it just to jest at Andi.

He found himself amazed by her confidence, her intelligence. On her hands and knees, she crawled around on the damp and dirty floor of his dungeon, looking at something that interested her under the strange beast she had called generator. He might be over seven hundred years old, but he wasn't completely dim. More than once, he and his men had watched something other than rugby on the tele with Jameson. Tristan knew the beast would cast the entire chamber in light. Saints, but his brothers would've loved to see such.

Unable to help himself, Tristan continued to watch as Andi studied her items. She stood and moved from one thing to another, each with more interest than before. She bent over at the waist to pick up something she'd dropped, giving Tristan a full view of her backside. Damnation, but her hose fit considerably different than they had her first time at Dreadmoor. The wench had longer legs than any woman he'd ever seen. Long and slender, with the cutest little . . .

"Bloody dolt," Tristan muttered. What was he thinking?

Andi spun around. "Who's there?" She could have sworn someone had cursed. She looked over the entire chamber. Empty. Maybe that devil Heath was playing tricks on her. She crept over to the tallest stack of boxes and slowly peered around the side of it. No one. She turned, baffled. Now she heard things, spawned, no doubt, from Heath's stories about the "ghastly knight" who roamed the halls of Dreadmoor, rattling chains and lopping off heads. Along with her own ghostly encounter, of course. "Too many ghost tales, Andrea." Shaking her head, she went about her business.

She wondered if Tristan knew such yarns existed about his hall. He probably didn't care. If anything, it raised his ego-meter up a notch or two.

Just exactly who was the lord of Dreadmoor? She'd find out tonight. Hopefully.

With one last glance around, Andi knocked the dust from her knees, wiped her hands on her thighs, and headed up the steps. Just as she reached the top she turned and looked back down the way she had come.

And blinked.

She could've sworn she'd seen a knight in chain mail.

Tristan paced before the hearth, perplexed.

"Perhaps, my lord, you should have refrained from being, let's say, so charming to the young woman." Jameson covered a yawn.

"Charming? 'Twas naught but courtesy, which I sorely regret doing the like now. The wench wanted answers, and an endless stream of them, no less. I merely gave her a choice few."

"My lord Tristan," Jameson said. "I hardly would call giving her a small history of your family lineage, albeit vague, anything but courteous. If you'll excuse me for saying so." He flicked a bit of something from his sleeve.

Tristan stormed back and forth, arms crossed over his chest, frowning. "Nay, old man, I'll not excuse you aught." He knew Jameson was right, but he would be the last one to admit as much. He stopped and pointed an accusing finger. "I cannot continue speaking with her, Jameson. 'Tis too difficult to lie. I don't lie. Sooner or later she's going to see straight through that pitiful facade. You answer her questions from now on." With that he disappeared through the wall.

He heard Jameson sigh. "As you wish, my lord."

Had Tristan been alive and able, the thundering of his stomping down the corridor would have been loud enough to awaken the entire keep. He went through the motions, hoping he at least gave a good showing of it, even if only to himself. Involved in making such a good showing, he didn't notice the slender form trotting up the passageway until too late.

Andrea ran right through him.

She stopped in her tracks and sucked in a gasping breath. Just like before, she slowly turned to look behind her. She rubbed her arms vigorously with her hands as if a sudden chill had crept over her. After a moment she shook her head, then shrugged. Resuming her previous pace, she started back down the passageway.

Tristan stared as he watched her retreat down the corridor. He almost summoned the strength to ignore her, but by God's thumbnail, he just couldn't help himself. Damn his own arse.

He turned and followed her.

Down the long passageway and across the great hall, Tristan watched as she rushed along, fearless of any ghosts or ghouls who might be lingering close by, himself included. In truth, she seemed as excited as a child. Without hesitation she pushed the heavy oak door open and stepped inside. He thought she'd quit the dungeon for the eve. She hadn't even had supper. Tristan followed, intrigued.

*   *   *

Andi drew a deep breath as she entered the dungeon and pulled out her flashlight. Pointing the beam of light ahead, she descended the steps. "Jeez, it is so dark in here." She hadn't wanted to leave the lamps on continuously for fear that the generator would give out. It was an old model, but she didn't want to buy a new one any time soon.

A musty dampness filled the room. She could just imagine the dread and terror one may have felt when thrown down the steps into the pit of darkness.

A squeak erupted from the darkness as she made her way to the generator switch. She jumped, shuddering to think of the furry creature that noise had escaped from. Somehow, she didn't relish being on her belly in the dungeon while the castle rats used her back as a playground. Maybe Jameson had a cat? She'd ask him about it later.

The light beam finally landed on the lamp switch. Andi made her way to it and flipped it on. With a low purr the lamps flickered, casting a dim but workable glow within the eerie chamber.

A chill tingled her skin. She whirled and looked behind her. Nothing. No voice, no Dragonhawk—nothing. She shrugged and then crossed the room to the worktable she'd set up earlier.

Atop the table, carefully preserved between two panes of leaded glass, rested the original plans of the castle. Tristan had been very kind in allowing her the use of them for the project. What a rare treat to have them at her disposal. Original Dreadmoor blueprints! She'd pored over them nearly all night when he'd first given them to her.

A tickle crossed her nerve endings. She supposed she had Heath to blame for her spooky feelings—partially, anyway. All the talk of heads getting lopped off had her jumping at the least little thing. She scanned the chamber, and, as before, found it empty. Wiping her damp palms on her jeans, she grabbed a few brushes from her worktable and walked across the floor to the linked rings of steel embedded in the hard dirt.

Andi stretched, then lowered herself onto her belly and began the tedious chore of softly brushing the edges, followed by light, gentle blowing. Could there be an entire suit of mail?

Then she froze. Turned ice-cold, glacier-in-the-North-Atlantic frozen. Every hair on the back of her neck stood up. She stilled her brush and held her breath. *Something, or someone, was in the dungeon with her.* It couldn't be Jameson. After he'd begun preparations for the afternoon meal he'd excused himself, saying he needed to make a trip to the village market and take Heath home.

Slowly, she resumed her work, making small, wispy strokes with the brush. She didn't want whoever lingered in the room with her to notice she sensed them. With a deliberate, slow breath, she inhaled a breath and held it, lifting her gaze to eye-level of the dungeon floor.

Her eyes stretched as wide as the sockets would safely allow, and then she gulped.

An enormous man, dressed in knight's chain mail and bent over at the waist, watched her work. Neither she nor the man made a move; they didn't blink, breathe, or flinch.

Then he looked down at himself. "God's bones!"

"Whoa!" Andi yelled, much louder than she thought herself capable. She jumped up from her position on the floor and backed away, unable to tear her eyes from the vision before her. The knight ghost? Dragonhawk? She shook her head to rid herself of such a childish notion. She didn't believe in ghost knights. Right? Even if she had seen one herself before. Besides, he looked too real to be a ghost. Ghosts were soft, flimsy sheets of weightless matter, not substantial, real-life-looking men.

Then he spoke again.

"Cease your movement, lady, before you fall upon one of those sharp axes you have lying about and impale yourself."

Andi's head snapped up and she peered at the man. "Tristan?" She'd know that deep, raspy voice of his anywhere. "You scared the crap out of me! Why are you sneaking around in here? And dressed like that?" She brushed her hands off on her thighs and jumped from the pit, coming to stand in front of him. She looked up.

And gulped. Again.

Standing face-to-face with the man she'd already stood face-to-face with a dozen or more times, she suddenly realized something. Correct that. Several things.

Huge. Massive. Stunning blue eyes. Long, black hair. Sexy voice. Sexy *everything*.

He was the same man she'd seen twelve years ago.

The very same man she had dreamed of ever since.

Her knight.

Chapter 10

"It can't be." She stared at Tristan's big, booted feet. His legs, covered in hose, were long and thickly muscled. A mail hauberk hung to his thighs, covered by a black tunic. A mystical creature stared at her from its center. *The same creature from the shield in her room. Dragonhawk.* A sword hung low on his hips.

She continued to gawk, noticing his broad back and thick neck. His hair, dark and wavy, hung well below his shoulders. An authentic-looking mail coif rested in folds behind his head. Lifting her eyes, she saw a chiseled jaw tighten, making the muscles bunch. His jaw-length bangs hung in disarray across his face. Sapphire-blue eyes peered down at her as dark brows came together in a seriously annoyed frown.

He was just as magnificent as he had been before. Must be the uniform. . . .

That mind-boggling revelation struck her right between the eyes. It gave way to several unsettling thoughts. And who was she to allow such a revelation to remain idle? Besides, she was famous for blurting. "It *was* you all those years ago. Why did you lie?"

"Well, I—"

"And why is it you just let me flail about in that crumbling old kirk? I could have been killed!"

"Aye, but—"

"And why is it"—she took a step closer to Tristan—"you haven't changed one little bit—" She poked her finger at his chest as she spoke.

It went straight through him.

She snatched her hand back and held it against her chest. Her eyes widened. She stepped back, her breath difficult to catch. The blood rushed from her face.

Tristan stared at the woman, not believing what she had just done—and he'd allowed it to happen. She backed away from him, her mouth working fervently but with no intelligible words forming. *Try and calm her before she trips, dolt.* He took a step toward her and cleared his throat.

"Now, Andrea." He began again, softer this time. "You are overwrought, no doubt from all this bloody digging. Come sit you down here and we'll have speech."

Andi tried to speak but words would not come forth. She continued to back away, eyes wide and unblinking.

Tristan watched her mouth work, but even his unnatural hearing capabilities could not make sense of the words. He leaned a bit closer and strained his ears. "What say you, lady?"

Andi stared with glassy eyes and pointed at him. "Y-you're dressed in m-medieval chain mail. The knight. M-my knight. N-not a man. A g-g—" She shook as though a shiver coursed through her. "I—I d-don't believe in g-g-g . . ."

Her head lolled, seemingly bobbing on a neck with no bones to keep it straight. Her eyes rolled back and before he could move, she fell to the floor.

Tristan jumped to her side where she lay sprawled on his dungeon floor. "Damnation, she's fainted dead away." *Poor choice of words, de Barre, you idiot.* He kneeled beside her slumped form and studied her as best he could. He certainly hadn't cared for the way her eyes had wheeled. 'Twas unnerving, to say the least. Now, here he knelt, like the buffoon he knew himself to be, unable to help her in the least. *Again.* He stood and paced the floor in hopes of discovering some way to assist the girl. Jameson, damn his sorry arse, remained at the village grocer, so he would be of no use. He couldn't very well pull his one and only mortal man from the gatehouse. Saints, what a pitiful situation! He turned and walked back to Andi's huddled form on the floor. Bending down on his hands and knees, he did the only thing he could possibly do to help.

He bellowed.

And quite loudly, truth be told.

"Andrea! I vow if you do not pick yourself up from my dungeon floor you will be crawling with vermin in a matter of minutes!" He gave that time to sink through, but it didn't seem to work. He bellowed again. "Get up, wench!" He sat and waited, but nothing happened. "I've not the patience for this," he mumbled as he jumped up and began to pace. He crossed his arms over his chest and scowled. "By the saints, 'tis useless!" He lowered his head and paced some more.

"Damnation, Tristan! What did you do to her?" Kail shouted as he materialized.

"Christ, you don't want to know." Tristan glared at his captain, just to be glaring. "She poked her damned finger through me."

"Merde."

Tristan nodded. "Aye. My thought—several times over."

"My lord?" a voice called from the platform above.

Tristan glanced up in time to see Jameson blanch.

"What have you done?" The old man rushed down the stairs.

"I've no doubt deafened her with my bellowing. And before that I soundly thrashed her beyond an inch of her life, for digging up my dungeon. I'd planned on impaling her with my sword before you interrupted."

Jameson ignored Tristan's sarcasm. "Did she see you?"

Tristan sighed. "Worse."

"Oh dear." Jameson kneeled down to gently pat Andi's cheek.

"I vow I don't know how it came about. I suppose I became engrossed in watching her—"

Jameson glared. "I've warned you about voyeurism, my lord."

Tristan frowned. "You sorely test my mood, man. Just

rouse the woman and get her off the damned cold floor. 'Tis bloody drafty in here."

"I daresay you two had best go. For now," Jameson urged him quietly. "No doubt the poor thing is in terrible shock."

"Aye, no doubt. She jabbed her finger right through my bloody chest." Damnation, he should be the one patting Andi's cheek and trying to rouse her, not bloody Jameson! That fact made his mood fouler than before. "She's your baggage now, Jameson. I've not the stomach for this." With that he and Kail disappeared.

Andi slowly opened her eyes and blinked as she realized where she was. *The cold, hard, smelly dungeon floor.* Jameson's voice reached her ears, a frantic plea to get up.

"My lady." He patted her cheek. "You must wake up now. 'Tis too drafty and damp to be on the floor."

She sat, with his hand gently on her elbow, looked up into his usual stoic expression and blinked. "Jameson, what's going on?" She stood and glanced across the room. Empty, save her tools and generator. "Where'd he go?"

"Where did who go, Dr. Monroe?"

"Too late for that, Jameson." Andi peered into every corner, every nook of the dungeon. Taking a step forward, she turned and raked the room with her eyes. She laughed and shook her head. Inch by inch, she lowered herself back down to the floor. She rested her head in her hands. "I'm not crazy after all. Twelve years ago. It did happen. My . . . fingers went right through him."

"So I heard."

Several moments passed before she lifted her head and met his gaze. Her eyes watered. "It can't be. It's just not possible." She lowered her voice to a whisper and shook her head. "He's not real."

The tug of Jameson's hand on her elbow forced her to stand. "I'm afraid he's as real as you and I, my lady. Now come. We'll have a nice hot cup of tea together."

Andi allowed Jameson to lead her from the dungeon. At the top of the stairs, she pulled to a halt. "I think I just want to lie down for a while. I don't feel so good."

He inclined his head. "As you wish. I'll escort you to your chambers."

He did, and Andi felt grateful for his assistance. The door clicked shut and she stumbled to her bed. Throwing herself facedown on the feather mattress, she lay there for only a few moments. Then she got up, crossed the floor, threw the bolt, and crawled back in bed.

Tears rolled down her cheeks and dampened the pillow. How could any of this be happening? People died and were buried. Maybe there was a heaven, maybe not, but they certainly didn't turn into ghosts. They didn't remain on earth, dragging chains—or wearing chain mail. They didn't whisper commands, lead you about, warn you of things. They certainly weren't big, virile-looking knights with deep, real-sounding sexy voices, and they sure as hell didn't invite professional archaeologists to dig up centuries-old relics, or try to solve centuries-old mysteries.

Tristan was the infamous Dragonhawk.

Chapter 11

Andi found a steaming cup of tea pushed in front of her at the kitchen table, followed by the sugar bowl and creamer. She spooned in the brown raw sweetness, unaware of exactly how much she'd already dumped into the brew until Jameson cleared his throat. Loud.

"My lady?"

Andi frowned, then added one more spoonful. She took a sip, set the cup down, pulled her feet up into the chair, and tucked them neatly under her bottom. She'd had her night's rest, if you would call it that. Tossing and turning, she dreamed of fingers poking through mailed chests and swords lopping off heads—including her own—all night long. Well, she'd had enough. She was over the shock. What happened in the dungeon had really happened. What had happened in the kirk twelve years before had really happened. The whispering presence had happened. And by God, she wanted to get to the bottom of them all. No more games.

She glowered at the steward of Dreadmoor, who, whether by coincidence or not, wore a guilty look plastered to his face. "Okay, Jameson. Talk. And I mean it this time."

Jameson busily set about the kitchen, seeing to his work. Efficiently ignoring her.

"Jameson!"

He didn't even grace her with a jump—or a look. "My lady, 'tisn't befitting of a gentlewoman to bellow so."

Andi drummed her fingertips on the solid wood of the

oak table and ignored his reprimand. "No use in trying to distract me with all that proper English befitting gentlewoman crap, Jameson. I'm waiting for answers I more than deserve. And you have them."

Jameson turned and raised a white eyebrow. "My dear girl, 'tis best if you ask Himself the details. I vow he can tell the tale much better than myself."

She shook her head. "Nope. Won't do. Who is he?"

Jameson sighed. "He is as he told you before, lady. Tristan de Barre, formerly of Greykirk, lately of Dreadmoor." He walked over to her and placed a gentle hand on her shoulder. "Yes, he is the legendary Dragonhawk. But if you want the entire tale, you shall have to uncurl yourself from that most comfortable-looking position atop your feet and see to the deed yourself."

"He's dead, Jameson."

"Aye. And has been for quite some time."

Andi stood and drew in a deep breath. She could do this, couldn't she? She'd heard of psychic mediums, ESP, and many other unexplained phenomenons. Time travel had been studied extensively. None of it had been proven, no solid evidence, no proof she could sink her teeth into. Yet all of those things fascinated her. At least, the possibility of those things did.

Ghosts. Impossible, and yet she found herself believing it; *wanting* to believe it. God, she had no choice but to believe it. She knew what happened last night in the dungeon really did happen—not an illusion. Her freaking fingers had gone right through him! It went against all things logical. And she was all about logic. Had based her entire life on science and logic. And in a few short weeks, all her solid beliefs on life and the universe were thrown efficiently out the window. Good Lord, it was enough to give her a migraine. She rubbed her pounding temples, contemplating her next move.

She looked up at Jameson and threw him a grim smile. "I guess you're right. Besides, I'm a forensic archaeologist. I'm all about solving mysteries." She picked up her cup of tea and drained it in one gulp. "Where can I find him?"

"I'm quite sure he is on the battlements by now, lady,"
Jameson began, "but most likely 'twould not be a grand
idea to go there. He does possess an uncanny ability to
hear rather well, though. More likely than not he will
come to your voice, given his mood is sweet enough."
Jameson turned back to the stove. "Which I can assure
you, it is not."

"Thanks a lot." She shoved her hands in her pockets.
"Can he hurt me?"

Jameson shook his head. "Nay, child. He wouldn't,
even if he could. An honorable sort, that one."

Andi nodded. "I'll find him." She turned and walked
out of the kitchen, leaving Jameson to his duties.

Jameson turned, once he thought she wasn't looking,
and watched her go. "Good luck, my lady. You, no
doubt, shall need it."

Andi turned and stopped once she reached the great
hall, unable to decide just where to go. She tried not to
think too heavily on what she had to do, but it was an
impossible feat.

Tristan is a ghost. He's Dragonhawk. . . .

Breathe, Andrea Kinley, breathe. She needed lots and
lots of air. Drawing several deep breaths, she headed out
the main doors and out into the inner bailey, past the
gardens and stables, then into the outer bailey and past
the cutaway. Even that held no appeal to her right now.
From there she headed straight for the cliffs.

The wind blew fiercely from the sea, and she welcomed
it. She wrapped her arms around herself and looked to
the sky. The sun beat down from a cloudless canopy of
bright blue. A variety of sea birds called out to one another as waves rolled in to greet the sheer cliff rock
Dreadmoor rested upon. The sounds, the wind, and the
saltiness from the surrounding sea life soothed her, but
not nearly enough to rid her mind of the craziness that
had just coldcocked her.

Andi drew in another deep breath and exhaled it
through pursed lips. As a second thought, she drew in
several more, inhaling, exhaling . . . Now was just as

good a time as any, she supposed. Gathering her nerve, she cleared her throat. "Tristan?" she asked just above a whisper. "Can you hear me?"

Several seconds passed with no answer. A seagull screamed overhead. Waves crashed against the base of the cliffs.

"Aye."

She jumped. Slowly, she turned toward the deep voice behind her and her breath snagged in her throat. Tristan materialized before her, legs spread wide, his arms folded across his wide chest. Good Lord, the man towered over her. Her mouth went dry, as if she'd been chewing on a handful of cotton balls. Nervous? Apprehensive? *Try terrified.*

She looked down at the rocky ground, then over her shoulder to the sea. Moments passed before she turned back to him. He stood still, patiently waiting for whatever she was about to say. Dragging up what little courage she possessed, she drew closer to him and met him with a steady gaze. "Are you real?"

Tristan stared down at the woman. He could tell she wrestled herself from within, but there was naught he could do, save tell her what she wanted to know. "What think you?"

She stared at him, from his boots to the top of his head. "You look pretty real to me. You've . . . always looked real."

He chuckled softly. "From that gandering look I'll take that as a compliment, lady." He stepped a bit closer to stand beside her, and then looked out over the ocean. "How does it smell this day? I vow 'tis one of the simpler things that I miss."

"You can't smell?"

Tristan shook his head. "Nay. Nor can I touch. Or taste." He turned to face her. "But I can hear the slightest of mumblings, be they intelligible words." He shrugged. "And a few other unusual things. Now, about the smell?"

"Oh." She drew in a lungful of sea air and smiled. "Quite salty, actually."

"Ah, 'tis how I remembered, then." He nodded. "A most pleasant scent, indeed."

"Can you hurt me?"

Tristan glanced at her, then frowned. "I can do many things, Andrea, but harming a woman is not one I partake in." He inclined his head. "At least not on an empty stomach. Mine has been empty for over seven hundred years, so I vow you are more than safe. Besides, 'tis part of the code."

"The code?"

"Aye. The knight's code. Vows sworn to uphold. Protecting those weaker than one's self is among them."

"Oh." Andi stared out across the sea. "I remember you, you know." She looked up at him. "From before."

Tristan did not like how this was going at all. The way the girl looked at him—'twas almost too much for him to handle. He gruffly cleared his throat a time or two and looked away. "I gathered as much." Shifting only his eyes, he peered down at her.

Andi shook her head and continued to stare. "You're Dragonhawk."

A moment slipped by; then he answered. "Aye." More questions brewed in her eyes; he could see them. Some things, aye, she needed to know. But there were other things she did not. He hardened himself against her sweetness, her innocent inquisitiveness; steeled himself against *her*. Saints, but he could not afford to make a new friend. 'Twas just too painful. To gain another mortal friend meant heartache, and he most definitely did not need the like in his sorry state. What he needed was the bloody curse undone. But that was impossible.

"Do you remember me?"

He sighed and scrubbed his jaw with his hand. "Aye."

"I thought I had dreamed you up." She took another bold step forward, staring directly into his eyes. "But you're just as I remember." She rose on tiptoes and peered closely at his face. "I somehow missed that scar—"

"God's bones, wench!" he bellowed loud and stepped back. She would be the ruin of him, no doubt. "You came to Dreadmoor for a specific reason, and I vow 'twas not to inspect my visage thusly." He scowled as he leaned closer. "I suggest you perform your duties with haste, and if you feel you are not up to the task, I shall find another who is." He turned and began to fade. "Someone who remains out of my personal affairs." He strode from her, slowly disappearing with each step. "At least things can bloody return to normal around here." He faded completely.

Andi stared at the empty spot of ground. *Normal?* There was absolutely *nothing* normal about any of this. But he was right, of course—at least about her. She'd been hired to do a job and she would do it, no matter what strings were attached.

Even if those strings happened to be fastened to an arrogant but breathtaking ghostly knight whose legend still drifted off every pair of lips within four hundred miles.

She rubbed her arms as a sea wind tore over the cliff tops. She looked around at the castle and grounds, at the buildings still standing. The drawbridge was raised, as it would have been in medieval times, protecting those within the walls from any outside forces lurking that might be waiting for the right moment to attack and conquer. She felt protected here, and she had no logical reasons behind that feeling; she needed no protecting.

The moat, filled with water and lily pads, set a fairy-tale scene, along with a blooming English garden. The gray stone walls had withstood the harsh elements of nature, and for many centuries at that. The castle held a dreamlike aura—an impossible dream she had no desire to awaken from.

Dreadmoor's lord—tangible enough to talk to, look upon, feel at ease with, yet . . . She sighed as her practical, inner self took over, slapping her back to reality.

Reality. What a joke. Reality had long ago stepped out and deserted her, just like she'd been deserted as a child.

One thing was for real—the fact that Tristan wanted nothing to do with her. He wanted the use of her skills as a professional and nothing more. What did she expect?

With that dreary thought in mind, Andi turned and quit the bailey, seeking the safety of seclusion that had never let her down before. She'd complete her job and leave Dreadmoor and its lord. Dreams of solving centuries-old mysteries and befriending centuries-old knights were just too far out of her reach.

Chapter 12

Andi jerked awake. She blinked, unsure of the noise that had roused her. Thunder? No, closer than thunder. She opened her eyes fully as the thought took hold. It sounded like a train running wild across a gravel-studded track. The crack of wood splintering caused her to jump, followed by a lot of male shouting. She leaped out of bed, tangling herself in the bed curtains in the process, and flew to the window. She stood, gripping the cool stone of the sill, and searched with her eyes.

Said eyes suddenly found said noise.

Andi felt her mouth slide open as she stood in complete and utter fascination, unable to believe her eyes. A curse, worthy of any bar of soap supplied by her aunt Mary, slipped from her lips.

She threw the window open and stared, awed at the sight.

It just couldn't be.

But it was.

Without another thought she ran from the chambers in her stocking feet, dressed in nothing but T-shirt and boxers, along the passageway, down the stone steps, and out into the great hall. She skidded past Jameson, who threw her a disapproving look, then headed out the door. Around the bailey she ran, dodging as many rocks as she could with her unprotected soles, until she came to a teetering, abrupt halt.

Her heart nearly seized.

At the far end of the bailey lay the lists, something

she knew hadn't been there before. On each side of the field men stood in a line, dressed in chain mail, hose, swords by their sides. Squires ran here and there, seeing to their masters' needs.

Two knights faced one another, one in black at the far end of the lists, the other, on the opposite end, in yellow and red. The one in black was enormous, as was his destrier. The horse blew and snorted so loud Andi could almost feel it where she stood. She crept closer, unaware and uncaring as to her appearance. She knew she gaped but she didn't care.

The knights were about to joust!

Wait. *Knights?* Plural?

She slipped to a spot next to a huge and ferocious-looking man, who had to be all of seven feet tall. He had a terrible scar to his cheek, and he scowled down at Andi as she approached. After a series of grunts and scowls, he inconspicuously moved over for her to see. Who were these guys? And where had they all come from?

A sharp cry broke her thoughts as a man called for the two knights to begin. Andi's eyes remained glued to the knight in black, now thundering toward her. The ground quaked under her feet from the force of the gal-loping horses. With lances pointed at one another, the knights charged, head-on. A deafening crash broke the air, followed by splintering wood as the two jousters came together. The one in yellow and red went flying off his steed's back from the impact of the hit, landing with a thud in the dirt.

A rowdy round of cheers went up all around her. She glanced at all the men gathered. There had to be at least fifty chain-mailed guys surrounding her, and as she looked over the crowd she got an eerie feeling, one she knew she'd had before. She leaned toward the giant man beside her. "Who's the one in black?"

Her eyes widened as said knight in black thundered toward her. She shrieked as he came to a halt in a cloud of dust. The dead silence alerted her instincts, and she glanced around at the crowd. They all stared directly at *her.* She looked up at the knight who sat on his horse, towering over her. He pushed up his face guard and glared. The look in those sapphire-blue eyes froze her to the spot.

"Lucifer's tail, woman!" Tristan jumped from his horse. "What in the bloody fires of hell are you doing out here?" He looked down at her and his eyes sparked a dangerous gleam. They traveled, starting at her feet, and raked slowly upward. "Garbed like that?"

The familiar feeling of blood pounding behind his eyes had Tristan fuming. Was she truly dressed in such little cloth? The wench wore a tunic that did not even cover her entire midriff, and nearly every inch of those long legs lay exposed for all to see, save for the bit of plaid covering her bottom. By the saints, her navel showed! Truth be told, 'twas a sight he was grateful to behold, but his men certainly didn't need to be privileged to it. He scowled at her for good measure.

The girl had the grace to look down at herself, then around at the men staring at her. She crossed her arms over her chest, mumbled something about not sleeping in a bra—whatever that was—and stuck out her chin.

"The noise woke me up and I just wanted to see what was going on." She peered at the men, who now stood all about her with their eyes bugged out. "Who are these guys, anyway?" She shifted where she stood and waited for an answer. "Where did they all come from?"

Tristan followed her gaze and he frowned at his men. "I vow if your bloody eyes do not find something else to light upon besides the lady's bared limbs," he bellowed over the lists, "you will not have use for them again." He cast a treacherous glance over the crowd, then turned said glance back to Andi.

Andi watched in fascination as a muscle ticked in Tristan's jaw, the small vein at his forehead protruding. *He's a ghost,* she reminded herself, which brought her to her next realization. She leaned up on tiptoes and wagged her finger toward Tristan, beckoning him to draw closer to hear her words. He did as she asked, she looked around, and then she whispered behind a cupped hand,

"Do these guys know you're a, um, well . . ." She hesitated, not knowing just what to say. "*A ghost?*"

The deafening silence lasted all but a few seconds; then one man in the crowd snorted loudly. In one fierce explosion, the entire group of mailed men erupted into a raucous fit of laughter, with a few shrill catcall whistles and hoots to boot.

Andi slowly turned around, watching the men as some slapped one another on the shoulder. A few bent over at the waist, apparently trying to catch their breath, and others wiped tears from their eyes. She turned back to Tristan, ready to ask him what could possibly be so funny, but her breath caught just as quickly and naturally as it escaped her lungs.

Tristan was smiling at her.

Easily the most beautiful sight she'd ever seen on such a ferocious man. Brutally beautiful, he had a dimple in each cheek, a slight cleft in his chin, and his grin was wide and contagious. Unfortunately, though, she still had no idea what was so funny.

"Lads, cease!" Tristan tried to smother his mirth. "I enjoin you lecherous dolts to file past the lady Andrea," he said, "and greet her accordingly. Then my men begone and man your posts. You others, be back at daybreak, if you've the stomach for it."

Andi stood next to Tristan as the first man, the other jouster, came by, leading his mount. He passed by, nodded his head respectfully, and smiled. "Lady," he said, then walked on past.

And then faded into thin air. Along with the horse.

Tristan bent over, his lips close to her ear. "Close your gaping mouth, Andrea."

One by one the men filed past her, nodding and greeting her, then disappearing into the sunlight, one medieval knight right behind the other.

"Lady." A tall, balding man walked by. He smiled, revealing his missing front tooth.

"Lady." Another nodded as he passed, a grin splitting his boyish face in two.

"Lady."

"Lady."

Andi stared, her mind reeling. She couldn't believe it. They were all ghosts! But how could it be possible? Inconceivable. Right? Of course it was. She'd dealt with Tristan. Sort of. Her mind still reeled from the idea of his state of existence. But an entire keepful of medieval, knighted, chain-mailed ghosts? No way. It was crazy! And yet she'd just witnessed it. Hadn't she?

A giant headed her way. It was the same man she'd spoken to when she'd first walked onto the field. He stopped and leaned over, a wide grin breaking the scowl that had been there earlier.

"*Boo.*"

Andi squealed and nearly fell backward.

The remaining men erupted into another round of laughter, but Tristan's deep voice managed to get through to her.

"Steady, lady." Tristan shook his dark head and chuckled. "I vow if you swoon there's not a bloody soul here who can catch you." He looked at the man who'd just scared her and frowned. "Kail, you horse's arse, enough sport. Now begone." He waved a gloved hand in the air. "Don't forget. Ireland versus Wales tonight on the tele."

Kail grinned at Andi, then at Tristan. "Aye, my lord. Consider it done." Then, like all the rest, he vanished.

"Ireland versus Wales?" she asked.

Tristan nodded. "Aye. Rugby. A fine sport, indeed."

So. She *had* heard a roomful of rowdy guys watching a rugby game!

Andi stared as the last few disappeared, save one young man who, the closer he got, the more familiar he became.

As he stood before her, he ducked his head in a shy nod. "Good morn to you, lady. 'Tis wondrous having you about." He gave her a low bow. "My name is Jason, formerly of Corwick-on-the-Sea. I shall be ever so close by, should you need me."

"You're the guy I met in the village who ditched me at the chip shop."

"With regret, you are ever so right. I shall make it a point never to ditch you again."

"I thought I told you not to approach her," Tristan said with a frown.

Jason lifted a mailed shoulder. " 'Twas unavoidable, my lord." With a charming smile, he turned and disappeared into the hazy sunlight, leaving her alone with Tristan.

She looked about in disbelief, at the ground she stood on, at the lists. A long pole of wood ran the length of it, with dirt underneath. Yet there wasn't the first bit of splintered wood, not one horseshoe print. *Of course not, goof. Ghosts don't leave prints.*

She glanced skyward, noticing for the first time the bright and warm morning, how the sun shone, how the slightest of sea breezes softly blew through the bailey. She turned back to Tristan, who stared, watching her every move. At last, she found her voice. "I suppose this is one of the 'unusual things' you spoke of?"

"One of many."

Andi looked closely at the man before her. *Ghost*, she corrected herself silently.

Dragonhawk. He stood tall, a picture of power and masculinity, arrogance and confidence. His helmet was off now, his mail coif pushed back. His hair lay plastered to his head with sweat, the cords in his neck taut. The mail he wore in no way hid the heavy chunks of muscle in his arms and chest. Neither did the hose, for that matter. God, he looked so *real*.

Andi quickly caught herself before she drooled all over the lists. She looked up into Tristan's eyes—eyes that literally sparkled when he smiled.

"Are you quite through, lady?" A slow, sexy grin spread across his face. His dimples deepened. "Or shall I turn round for you, as well?"

Heat crept up her neck. Maybe she had drooled, and just didn't realize it. She checked her chin, just to be sure. "No, you don't have to turn around." Not that she'd mind. She shook her head and looked all around.

"This is all just a little hard to take in, I guess." She chanced another glance at Tristan. "Your fourteen knights—were they in that crowd?"

He nodded. "Aye. Kail, the big one, is my captain. Jason is my youngest, though a scrappy little lad."

Whoa. "Dragonhawk and his missing knights. Unfreaking-believable." She shook her head. "How is it that the others are all here?"

Tristan shrugged and shifted his weight. "How is it I'm here? They've all different reasons, I suppose. Most are here, I assume, because they left this world with unresolved matters. They cannot rest because of it. So they come here, pledge their fealty, such as it is, and in return I give them something familiar. A home."

"Is that why you're here? Because of unresolved matters?"

Tristan's brows pulled into a frown. "I wish it was as simple as unresolved matters." He looked down at the girl. He wanted to trust her, but 'twas more than just his secret. And by God's bones, he could barely concentrate, what with the very little she had on. Her long, shapely legs were smooth and flawless, clear up to the green and blue plaid trousers she wore. And damnation, but the sight of her navel nearly drove him daft. Her dark brown hair gleamed in the morning sun, and her brows, the same color as her hair, arched in a fine shape, indeed. Comely? Nay. Merciful saints above, she stole his breath.

The sorry thing was he just couldn't stay away from her. Even though he'd just warned her yesterday to keep to the business she was hired for, staying away from her just seemed impossible.

Damned, daft dolt he knew himself to be.

But that was exactly what he needed to do. *Stay away.*

He frowned a bit more, the best frown he could muster his pathetic self to perform. "Get you to the keep, lady, and clothe yourself." He glanced down at her feet. "I vow you'll catch your death out here with your hose pooled around your ankles." *Lovely, finely shaped ankles, I might add.*

"Are you coming with me?"

"Nay." Tristan frowned and replaced his helmet. "I am not. You've your duties to perform, as do I. Just because I'm a spirit doesn't mean I've nothing important to do. I've a castle to maintain." He turned abruptly and strode into the sunlight, promptly disappearing.

Andi frowned herself this time. She looked around the bailey; the very empty bailey—save the jousting field. It looked so damned real! She wanted to walk over to it, but her stockinged and shoeless condition stopped her in her tracks. She heaved a sigh as she turned and trudged back to the keep. "Must be nice to just . . . disappear every time you want to avoid something, Lord Dreadmoor. You just say your mind, then 'poof,' you fade into thin air." She waved her hand. "Me? I have to stand my ground, say my piece, then stick around for more. I stay until the bell rings. You? You take the easy way out."

He wanted nothing to do with her.

And she'd never been the type to be pushy.

Andi trotted back across the bailey and back into the keep, heading to her chambers to change. She had work to accomplish. Weapons to dig up.

And the faster she accomplished it, the faster she could pack her gear and leave Dreadmoor, before she found it a completely impossible task.

Chapter 13

"Perhaps if she knew the entire tale, my lord, she just may be able to help." Jameson looked over the rim of his reading glasses at Tristan. "I vow you've done a fine job indeed of avoiding Dr. Monroe lately. You've not spoken to her in a week. My lord."

Tristan glared at his old friend. "Be you quiet, Jameson. I cannot think thusly with you muttering." He leaned back against the marbled counter, raked a hand through his hair, and glanced at the beamed ceiling. Drawing a deep breath, he let it escape slowly. "Mayhap you have it aright." Tristan pushed off the counter and began to pace behind his steward. "After seven centuries, one cannot help but develop a loss of hope." He glanced at Jameson, who busied himself by stirring something in a large pot. "I'm weary, old man."

Jameson didn't spare him a glance. "You look quite healthy to me, my lord. Given your unusual circumstances, that is."

Tristan grinned. "You act as though you like me around."

Jameson didn't look up from his cooking. "You are passing tolerable."

Tristan laughed and shook his head. "I suppose I should tell her the tale after all. By God's robes, she has seen the entire garrison. A story of murder and witchery should not frighten the wench."

"You didn't exert yourself overmuch in hiding the garrison, Lord Dreadmoor."

Tristan raised an eyebrow. "You are a mouthy old busybody, Jameson. Stir you that stew and keep your bloody comments to yourself."

The corner of Jameson's mouth twitched. "As you wish, your Lordship."

Tristan disappeared through the wall. "Cease with the bloody lordship crap, Jameson," he called back. "I vow 'tis making me daft."

"I hope so. My lord."

Tristan could have sworn he'd heard the wily butler chuckle.

Andi struggled to keep her thoughts trained on her work—something completely foreign to her. She loved her work. Looked forward to it. In her own defense, it was a little hard to concentrate knowing she shared temporary residence with a garrison of ghosts led by the legendary Dragonhawk. Incredibly handsome. Charming, in a gruff sort of way. With dimples.

And very, very *dead*.

She wanted to talk to him in the worst kind of way, but to reduce herself to begging? Just to stay focused? Ridiculous. It had been a week since she'd seen him in the lists, and she hadn't gone after him, either. Or called to him. For whatever reasons he had, he certainly didn't want to be bothered by her.

It hurt. Why, she didn't know. She barely knew the guy. Just because she'd seen him as a teen, and then had dreamed of him ever since, didn't give her any right to feel all mushy about him.

Andi stretched her arms over her head, then her lower back. She eased down to her belly and resumed her work. But her thoughts, rebellious things that they were, seemed to wander in their own direction.

Maybe she simply did not appeal to him? She was fairly plain, in her opinion. She had long, gangly legs, a bit on the skinny side, and had been called dorky more than once in her life.

She blew softly on the soil-stained bone and continued to brush. Over the past several days, she'd collected eighteen bones within the five-by-five-meter square. Not bad, being a one-man team.

After the pelvic bone had been found she concluded that the skeletal remains definitely belonged to a man. She'd yet to speak to Tristan about it, since he'd made himself conveniently scarce over the last week.

Maybe it wouldn't matter to him? Either way, she could probably spend an entire year sifting through shovelfuls of Dreadmoor's soil and still not find all the missing pieces. Even if she did, what would it mean? That a man had been murdered in medieval England? Not exactly headline news. And yet, it fascinated her, made her want to know more. Who was the man? And what had he done to deserve such a grisly burial, including being bound about the head by a yew vine?

Tristan watched Andrea for several moments before materializing. Damn Jameson for convincing him 'twas the right thing—trusting her with Dreadmoor's secrets. Truth be told to no one, something about the woman stirred him: her mannerisms, her confidence and nerve, her complete unawareness of her beauty, and her intense dedication to her hired task. An innocent air hung about her that enchanted him. Tenacious? Aye, for a certainty. And damnation, the way she pushed her hair behind those finely shaped little ears surely would drive him more senseless than he already was.

He looked down at her whilst she wallowed about on her belly, diligently unearthing the bones. At least if he startled her, she wouldn't fall. He cleared his throat softly and began as gently as he could. "Lady Andrea?"

She jumped anyway, and her eye barely escaped being impaled by the end of her brush. She looked up from the excavation pit where she lay sprawled and glared at him. "You scared me."

"I vow I tried not to."

Andi turned her head back to her work and continued her brushing and blowing.

Ah, Tristan thought. *She's angry.* He supposed she had a right to be. Mayhap in time, she'd realize he'd avoided her for noble reasons. 'Twas misery, the knowing of someone only to lose them in the end. Torturous. "Have you found something of interest there?" He squatted down beside the pit.

With gloved hands, she gently lifted the bone, placed it in a see-through satchel of sorts, then set it aside. "The remains are those of a man, approximately between the ages of thirty and seventy. His skull had a hole in the side big enough to stick my hand through. It was wrapped in a yew vine, and actually, I believe the vine was probably wrapped around his neck, too. But as the root system grew, it maneuvered the skeleton. There was a loose sort of garrote hanging from the skull."

"Yew vine? Saints alive. 'Twas rumored in my day that witches used the vine of yew for many a reason." He cocked his head. "You can tell that, just by looking at an old bone?" She never ceased to amaze him.

"Yeah." Lifting herself out of the cutaway, she stepped out of her weatherproofs and laid them on a patch of grass. With a bold stare, she blew a loose strand of hair from her eyes. "Ever hear of a man being clobbered over the head here? Witches burned at the stake, perhaps?"

He frowned. "No. Not whilst I was alive, anyway."

She stared at him a moment. "Why are you here now? I thought you were too busy. Appointments and such. You told me just to do my job, remember?"

"Aye, but that busybody steward of mine advised me to speak with you."

He could have sworn he had seen her face fall. "I see." With a shrug, she began to gather the clear sacks containing the bones. Carefully laying them in a box, she lifted one back up for inspection. "This is a pelvic bone. Well, two parts to equal one. It was cracked in half." She pointed to a narrow area. "The female anatomy, especially after childbirth, tends to differ in this particular region than a male. It is noticeably wider, which is why I feel this is a male. I'd have to take a few measurements to be sure, though." She laid it back down and lifted another. "This is a femur bone." She touched the top of her leg. "From here, you can determine the approximate age range by how much the bone is worn down at the end, where it meets the socket of the hip. Since there appears to be a great deal of rub-marks—bone scraping bone due to lack of cartilage—my guess would be an older male, mid-sixties, maybe. There are porous traces, as well. Signs of arthritis."

"Damn. You are a tenacious wench, Dr. Monroe."

A smile tipped her mouth; then she turned and gathered her tools. "I know my bones, Lord Dreadmoor."

How utterly fascinating the woman was. Her eyes all but sparked flames whilst she was talking about the old bones. It gave him further cause to trust her with Dreadmoor's secrets. "I believe it would be of help to you if you were to know the tale of how this"—he waved his hand around—"came about."

Andi looked back up. "Do you mean it?"

If he'd had a heart in his ghostly shell it would surely have beaten him senseless at those simple, innocent words. And the look on her face? 'Twas nigh onto doing him in. "Aye, girl, I mean it. Now remove yourself from this unholy grave and let us have speech. I haven't the patience to wait for you all day."

She grinned. "Yes, you do." Turning, she stacked her tools into her pack, slung it over her shoulder, and hefted the box containing the bones. Quickly, she secured the tarp over the grid.

Cheeky wench. Raking a hand through his hair, he watched her gather her belongings. Damn his unlife. "Forgive my useless state. Never would I allow a maid to haul such a load."

The smile she cast him nearly brought him to his knees. "Thought I was a wench." Her grin widened. "Just kidding. I'm really used to it. Besides, I'm dying to hear your story." Her cheeks reddened. "Oops. Sorry."

Tristan fought a chuckle. "No doubt." He walked beside her, silence stretching between them, and he noticed how Andrea turned her head more than once to cast a sideways glance in his direction. Finally, she shook her head, causing her hair to bob like a horse's tail. It intrigued him. *She* intrigued him.

"This is just so fantastic. I find myself thinking about nothing else. It's"—she glanced at him—"you are amazing, and you go against everything I believe in."

"What mean you?"

"Well," she said, sidestepping a rock. "I investigate ancient bones and crypts, buried medieval treasures, old fortresses. And now"—her gaze drifted off—"I have to wonder if the bones I collect and send to the forensics lab belong to the ghost of someone standing right next to me."

He understood. How strange it all must be for her. "Aye. 'Twas odd for us, as well."

"God, I can only imagine." She mounted the steps and pushed open the great double doors.

With a frown, he followed her inside. How it chafed him to have her open doors. He should be the opener of the bloody doors.

Gently setting the box of bones against the wall, she slipped her pack off and turned around. "Dragonhawk and his legendary knights." She shook her head. "Unbelievable. You're really him."

With a nod, he gave her a low bow. "None other."

"Were you always a show-off, or is that a new development?" she said.

"You are passing cheeky, Dr. Monroe. Is that a new development?"

She gave a short laugh. "Claimed, and proud of it. Now, what's given you the change of heart to confide in me?"

"As Jameson so graciously pointed out, 'twould be beneficial to us both if you knew how I came to be in this . . ." He searched for words. "State of existence. Now, find yourself a seat by the hearth and prepare yourself, lady, for I vow 'twill be a tale unlike any other you've ever heard. And 'twill be a tale for your ears only."

*   *   *

Andi watched as flames from the hearth cast Tristan's features in shadows, making him look more real than he should. He'd told her it was an illusion he conjured, for her benefit. It unnerved her, gripped her, and squeezed with an amazing amount of strength. The knowledge that Tristan de Barre of Dreadmoor had been dead for more than seven hundred years—it refused to take root in her mind. She kept shaking her head, trying to make everything inside rattle and shift around until it all settled into place and made sense, but it just never happened. The more he spoke, the more that deep, graveled medieval accent washed over her, the more spellbound she became. A thirteenth-century knight, one who'd fought in battles, hacked at enemies with swords, had eaten out of bread trenchers. A phenomenon. An anomaly.

A miracle.

And she was here to witness it.

Pulling her legs under her bottom in the comfortable chair Jameson had dragged up next to the massive fireplace, she inclined her head. Tristan seemed nervous, unsure, as though he felt uncomfortable telling her the occurrences that placed him seven centuries into the future.

Nervous probably didn't even begin to describe it.

"You promised me a grand tale, Lord Dreadmoor." She grinned when he scowled at her for using his title. "I vow I've not the patience to wait on you all evening."

That won a chuckle from the big knight. Still, he continued to pace before her. "Aye. I'm stalling. 'Tis an uneasy thing of sorts, the telling of this." He turned a look on her and the corner of his mouth lifted in a slight smile. "And do not call me Lord Dreadmoor. It annoys me fiercely."

"I know. Proceed." She smiled. "Please."

He raked a hand through his long, dark hair. "Very well, you persistent wench." Drawing a deep breath, he started. " 'Twas the Year of our Lord, 1292." He shook his head. "So long ago, aye? Would it had been only my life snatched away." He paced, back and forth in front of the hearth, his face lined with memories. "Half of my garrison and I had just returned to Dreadmoor from the wedding of a cousin. We had caroused and drunk for three days solid, and I was passing less than my usual best, I can assure you. Someone must have knocked me senseless whilst I slept in my bed. When I came to I found myself shackled to the dungeon wall. My captain and young Jason lie slumped on the floor not far from me. They were near dead, if not already."

A flash of pain seized his features, and he scrubbed it away with a swipe of his big hand. At that moment, Andi's heart ached for him.

"My murderer taunted me and I vow I would have ripped him in twain with my bare hands, had I been able. The whoreson mumbled a chant of sorts, and I knew then 'twas a curse, although at the time I didn't believe in such."

Tristan turned and faced her. "The unholy look in his eye is one I can still see before me." He took two long strides and stood in front of her, towering over her as she sat, curled in her chair. "He ran me through with my own blade, Andrea. I stared him in the eye until I could no longer see. And it is that bloody sword I've long wished to have back in my possession. For . . . whatever reasons." He shook his head again. "But it seems 'tis never meant to be."

Andi stared up at the powerful man before her. A ghost, yes, but even in unlife, power radiated from him like a fierce electrical current. His profound stare caused her to shudder, and she fought the urge to squirm in her seat. She felt as though he could see clear through her skin, muscles, to her soul. "You were killed in the dungeon?"

"Aye."

"Oh my God." She glanced around. Centuries ago, Tristan was murdered in this very castle. *Unbelievable.* "You say the murderer showed himself. Was it someone you knew?"

Another glint of pain; then it vanished. "Aye. 'Twas my foster father, Erik de Sabre."

She nodded. "What happened to make him hate you so much?"

"I learned then that his son, only fourteen at the time, had slipped into the fray of a battle with an angry lot of thieves. The lad had followed us, wanting to join the Dragonhawk knights. He was killed, and Erik blamed us. It stunned me, to awaken in those chains, then to see him stand before me. He'd been like a father to me, to all of us."

"All?" she asked.

He nodded. "My knights all fostered under Erik. We trained together, fought together. That is how we all came to be."

That fact twirled around in her brain, processing. "But what does finding your sword have to do with any of this? And if you knew Erik was your killer, why didn't you just show yourself to your family and tell them?"

Tristan took a deep breath. "One question at a time, my impatient lady. I vow my head aches with the thought of the bombardment you'll no doubt hurl at me from here on out." He began to pace again. "Because, Andrea, the fool cursed me. I lay in something akin to what some believe purgatory may be like, for quite some time. A state of nothingness, blackness, never seeing, never hearing, never moving—yet conscious." He looked down at his hands, then back to Andi's face. " 'Twas torture. When I finally awoke, I found myself in the same rancid hole of a dungeon I'd died in. I remembered nothing except what had happened to me. Kail and Jason had awakened, as well. We soon realized over two hundred years had passed. And that we hadn't been the only ones who had suffered that night."

Andi slid forward in her seat. "The garrison."

He nodded. "Aye. The garrison. All twelve of them. In the dungeon with us."

She inclined her head. "Erik murdered them, too? How did one man kill so many?"

"The sneaky bastard used Tristan as bait and lured us all into this dank place."

Andi jumped and peered over the back of her chair. One by one, men in chain mail began to materialize. They slowly walked toward her and Tristan, forming a circle around the chair she occupied. Fourteen knighted warriors in all.

Tristan made the fifteenth.

The air drained from Andi's lungs in a long, silent sigh. The legendary Dragonhawk and his knights faced her. An incredible urge to sink into the cushions of her chair washed over her. She gave them a hesitant smile. "Um. Hello."

"Do not fear the lads, lady. They won't harm you."

Andi nodded without saying a word. She recognized most of them from the morning of the joust. Their expressions varied somewhat, but all revealed one common factor: immense inner strength.

"How did so many warriors fall victim to one solitary man?" she asked.

The one knight who'd spoken inclined his head. "Erik locked us in the dungeon. All of us."

"Aye," another said. "We knew naught of his deception and trusted him with our lives. Once we were all inside, trying to recover Tristan, he threw the bolt and locked us in. Bloody bastard."

"There was no one left to challenge him," a young knight said. "No one, save the cook and a few serving maids. They soon fled."

Tristan moved to stand next to Andi's chair. "Lady, these mannerless whoresons are Stephen, Richard, and the pup there is Gareth."

All three gave her a slight nod.

Tristan introduced the others, one by one. They studied her with interest, regarded her intensely, each giving a nod but remaining stoic and silent.

Tristan grinned. "I can see you're nigh onto bursting with questions, but I'll finish the tale and then you may barrage us."

She nodded, urging him to continue.

"The only soul around was an aging man named Alfred Jameson, and his family. According to the Jamesons, my sire hired them to remain at Dreadmoor. The keep had taken on a rather . . . perpetual marque of being haunted and plagued by witchery and evil. No one wanted to set up residence—no one even tried to lay siege." He winked at her. "A superstitious lot, we medievalists. But little did the Jamesons know that I, accompanied by fourteen others reputed to be dead for more than two centuries, would show up, demanding an audience. I daresay 'twas great sport."

Several of the knights chuckled.

"I knew there was a connection." Andi remembered accusing Jameson of looking like Batman's butler, Alfred. "You mean that was one of *our* Jameson's ancestors?"

"Aye, the very same. His family has worked here ever since. Alfred kindly showed me an odd missive which had been found by the first Jameson family. Although thinking it odd, they'd placed it in the vault with my uncle's copy of the plans of the keep, kept safe under a lead pane, and left it there. Then I had shown up. They gave it to me, posthaste."

She pulled closer to the edge of the chair. "What did it say?"

Tristan smiled. "I vow you've a curious bone, wench." His smile turned grave as he continued. The others were silent as he continued. "It read that I had, indeed, been cursed, and 'twould be my fate to roam Dreadmoor forever, as I deserved. It advised one more thing, which we've always found curious. It said *the Dragonhawk's eye will set you free.*"

Andi rose from her chair and wiped her palms on her thighs. "Damn. That just doesn't make a bit of sense. Dragonhawk's eye? What the hell does that mean?"

Tristan gave her a silent stare, then burst out laughing. The other knights chuckled, as well.

"You've a sharp tongue when angered, woman," Tristan said.

She smiled. "So I've been told." She peered at his hip. "Is that the sword?"

With a glance, he nodded. "Aye. Exactly."

"Amazing." She lifted her eyes. "What about your sword? You've never looked for it?"

"Over the centuries we tried. After so much looking,

we gave up, until our present-day Jameson. He got it in his youthful head that we should search anew. We, of course, being basically useless, and Jameson, well," he said with a gentle tone, "he searched aplenty with no success. And we could find no one else who would dare come to the wicked Dreadmoor Keep—not even Jameson's mates." He took one more step, bringing himself a foot away from where Andi stood. "Until you."

Andi stared up into the ghostly blue eyes of Tristan de Barre, then found it took every ounce of strength she possessed to stay upright. He looked at her in a way she had never experienced before, and although he'd said he couldn't touch, she swore she felt every inch of his six-and-a-half-foot frame as he stood over her.

His dark hair hung loose below his shoulders, and the width of his chest blocked anything behind him. His arms were long and muscular, his legs heavy and corded. Powerful thighs strained the hose he wore, and she could have sworn she'd heard his mail groan as he shifted. She looked down at his ungloved hands, fascinated by the thick, roping veins that crossed the tops and disappeared beneath the sleeves of his hauberk. Only his deep, soothing voice, laced with an edge she hadn't noticed until now, dragged her from the daydream she drowned in.

"Andrea."

She slowly looked up. The other knights had vanished, leaving her alone with Tristan. An intense pressure gradually built in her lungs as she made a hollow attempt at a normal breath. She watched his eyes, so dark now they nearly appeared gray, and she continued to watch as they dropped from her own eyes to her mouth.

"You look so real." She hadn't meant to whisper, but her voice lost all strength. She froze, unable to tear her gaze from his. Her insides tingled and her mouth went dry.

"Phone call for Dr. Monroe."

Andi jumped at least a good three inches and stifled a squeak. Jameson sounded like a train conductor. She blinked when the corner of Tristan's mouth lifted, his unwavering gaze more than unnerving her. "Who is it?"

Her voice came out as a croak. Tristan's mouth lifted a bit higher.

"Your employer, Kirk Grey."

Andi scooted sideways and backed away from Tristan, unable to look away. "I'm coming."

"Lady?"

She met his stare. "Yes?"

"I must ask you to keep this tale to yourself. Although there are rumors aplenty of our existence, it has remained lore for over seven centuries." His eyes bored into hers. "We prefer it to remain thusly."

She nodded. "I won't tell a soul." Backing away, she had a difficult time tearing her gaze from his. "Will I see you later?"

Tristan's smile widened, forcing both dimples to grace his cheeks. "I vow I haven't the strength to say you nay."

Andi grinned and passed through the door Jameson held open for her.

Tristan glanced at his steward, who pointedly raised his gray eyebrows, then cast a lazy smile before following Andrea through the doorway.

Tristan bellowed out a laugh and shook his head. "Bothersome old man."

"So. She knows the tale." Kail, his captain, stepped forward. The others reappeared. "Now what?"

"And what of the presence she spoke of in the past? What is that all about?" Richard asked.

Tristan looked at his men. "I don't know. She hasn't mentioned it today. Mayhap the presence has disappeared?"

Kail shook his head. "Nay. Ghosts don't disappear. They're always about, for some odd reason or another. And they usually don't hide."

"Aye, so why haven't we been privy to this one?" Jason asked as he came to stand beside Tristan. "We're spirits. It seems passing ridiculous that we couldn't see another like us."

The men grumbled an agreement to Jason's concern. He didn't blame them. So many years had passed, so many changes had occurred—yet century after century, they'd remained in their ghostly form with no end in sight, no peace to look forward to. They wanted to know more about Dreadmoor's newest guest.

But not nearly as much as he.

He stifled a snort. What a softhearted dolt he'd become.

Chapter 14

"How do you feel? I've tried to call but your mobile went to voice mail," Andi said.

"I feel fine. Have you investigated the weaponry yet?"

She felt the sting from Kirk's unusually harsh tone. "Well, no. I've just completed bagging and tagging the remains. There were several still unearthed that I had to excavate. I've got them boxed and ready to transport—"

"Will you be getting to them soon, then? You've been there nearly a month now," he interrupted.

She frowned. "Kirk, what's wrong?"

The line went silent for a moment, and then he sighed. "I'm sorry, love. I'm just anxious, is all. Quite a hoard, that one. I'm dying to get my hands on it."

Somehow, that didn't make her feel any better. "Don't forget, I'm subcontracting a job usually performed by an entire team. There are 206 bones in a human body. I've got to recover as many as possible before making an attempt to recover the hoard." It was like getting scolded by a father for something you hadn't done. What in the world was wrong with him? He'd never acted like this before.

"Of course you are, sweet. Forgive me. I guess my own team is getting under my skin." He chuckled. "Not used to getting my hands dirty, you know."

Andi smiled. "I know. It'll be okay. Really." She glanced up as Tristan walked through the kitchen door and gave her a lopsided grin. Unavoidably, her breath hitched at the sight. Would she ever get used to it?

"What's the matter?" Kirk asked on the line. "Who's there with you?"

Andi blinked at the accusing tone, so unlike the easygoing Kirk she knew. "Lord Dreadmoor, and you can drop the attitude. I really don't appreciate it."

Kirk sighed into the receiver. "I apologize. I'm just . . . edgy."

"Hmmm." She glanced at Tristan, who watched her closely. "I'll get to work on the hoard first thing in the morning."

"Right. We'll plan to meet in town next week. By then, you should have recovered some of the weapons. Bring whatever you unearth for me to inspect. I swear, I cannot wait." He paused. "Will you be in the mood for a nice dinner? Or shall you remain in this cranky state?"

"I'm not cranky. How about seven, next week?" she asked.

"Perfect. But ring me if you come across anything sooner." The line went dead as Kirk hung up.

Andi blinked and clicked off the cordless. She wasn't sure if he still suffered a sickness from last week at the grid, or if he was just having a hard time with the students. Either way, Kirk was definitely not being himself. Again, she noticed a different tone, or pitch, to his voice. Maybe he was coming down with strep?

She raised her gaze, only to find Tristan scowling.

Jameson cleared his throat and walked to the kitchen door. "I'm off to make a run to the market. I shall return in an hour or two." He stood there a moment, his gaze shifting from Tristan to her. Then he left.

Andi smiled hesitantly up at Tristan. "Well, I need to get back to work." With Kirk behaving so strangely, she felt she needed to keep busy. Maybe she could finish the final touches on the topsoil bones, bag them with the rest, and have the tree removed, then get to the leather-covered satchel containing the weapons. She scooted past him. She could wrap up her excavation log of the skeletal remains tonight, too.

"Umm, lady," Tristan said gruffly, clearing his throat a time or two. "I vow you've a look about you that sits ill with me." He moved closer. "Who were you speaking to that placed such an expression on your usually determined face?"

She smiled. "My boss. Usually, he's wonderful. I think he's having it rough with the students." She reached for the door.

"That's a poor excuse." He glanced at her and cleared his throat. "Would you care for a walk on the battlements?"

Andi's heart skipped a beat. She could go for a short walk with the Dragonhawk of Dreadmoor before delving into her work. A few minutes wouldn't hurt. "Would you finish more of your story?"

"I suppose I've no choice in the matter, for if I don't you will no doubt irritate me with your incessant questioning."

She flashed him a smile. "You're probably right."

"I know I'm right. Now hurry you up. I've not the time to see to each and every woman's whim you may have."

Andi shook her head, grinning. "I'm ready now. Let's go."

Tristan fell into step with her as they walked side by side, heading for the battlements. "I would offer you my arm, lady, but with regrets, I cannot."

"It's okay." She shoved her hands in her pockets. "But it is very chivalristic of you, though. No one has ever offered before."

"Aye, well," he mumbled. "Bloody fools."

She grinned, but kept silent.

As they crossed the great hall, Andi watched streams of late-afternoon light pour in through the tall windows. She slid a glance at Tristan and her breath caught. The beam of sun went straight through him. Outside in the light of day, he looked just as normal as the next person. Fascinating. When she looked up at him, he was staring at her.

" 'Tis an odd thing, aye?" he said.

"What?"

"You and I. Walking along as though normal."

Andi looked back down at the stone floor, trying to hide her blush. "It feels quite normal to me."

Tristan blinked. A lump formed in his throat, and this time it nearly choked him. As they reached the steps, he allowed her up first, stepping closely behind as they climbed to the upper floor. He could not stop himself from glancing at Andrea's long, lithe legs, clad in some form of hose cut off above the knees. Had he blood coursing through his body 'twould be nigh onto boiling at the sight. God help him, he wanted to touch her.

At last, they reached the top and made their way down the long passageway. Tristan watched her as they walked, her hand softly raking the walls as they went. 'Twas a habit he'd noticed before.

"Why do you do that?" he asked.

"Do what?"

"That thing you do." He pointed. "You touch the walls as you walk. I've noticed you do it often."

Andi smiled and shrugged. "I don't know. I guess maybe because I love how it feels under my fingers. I love thinking how long ago these walls were erected, and of the people who lived here, in a different century." She looked up at him. "It fascinates me."

" 'Twas quite a rough time to live in, lady." He held her gaze. "Warring and death, fighting and defending. Making sure the ones you cared about remained safe, had plenty to eat. Stayed warm. And remained alive."

They reached the small circular steps leading to the battlements. Andrea moved to climb ahead of Tristan. When she reached the platform, she turned and faced him. "Were you married? Before?"

Tristan stared down into her soft, hazel eyes. He noticed how they were light, with bits of green dashed about. "Nay, girl. I was not wed, nor had I sired any children."

She looked at him a moment before pushing the door open and stepping outside. The wind nearly knocked her back. Tristan passed her and moved ahead.

"Now, stay you behind me, Andrea of Virginia, for I'll

not have you becoming faint. Follow whilst I walk us to a spot that's not so treacherous."

Andi smiled. "Okay." If Tristan only knew the heights she'd been suspended in a harness, hovering for hours over a precarious excavation pit . . . But she wasn't about to let his chivalry go to waste. Nope, not her.

They walked a bit farther along the parapet before Tristan stopped. He turned and scowled. "Now, hold you those stones, lady, and do not let go. 'Tis a long fall to the bottom and I'll not have you making the trip."

Andi laughed, only to earn a fiercer scowl.

"Do you find my concern for you humorous, wench?" His brows furrowed. "A weaker man would be sorely bruised by your mirth."

"You have the most adorable accent." She covered her mouth with her fingertips. *Oops. Where did that come from?*

Tristan moved closer and stood with forearms stretched out before him, bracing his weightless weight on the stones of the walkway. "I vow you say the most damnable things at times, Andrea." He gave her a crooked smile. "You find my speech passing pleasant, then, aye?"

Andi shrugged and sighed. "Passing."

He laughed. "Cheeky wench."

Silence stretched between them for a few moments. "Tell me about Erik."

He sighed, his chest heaving with realistic effort. "Erik de Sabre. He'd been a friend of my sire's for years. When it was time for me to leave for knight training, he immediately offered to foster me."

"You don't have to tell me if you don't want to, Tristan." Andi didn't want to cause him any more grief.

He looked at her and shook his head. "Nay, 'tis best if you know. Mayhap it will help you in your excavations."

He looked out over the battlements and continued his story. "He fostered me and my men. Taught us astounding skills on horse and by blade." He turned, facing her. "My sire never suspected. Neither did we, until that fateful night in the dungeon."

She tilted her head. "You didn't notice a change in his behavior after his son was killed? Nothing at all?"

"He was grief-stricken, to be sure. He and his wife had borne their son late in life, and he'd lost his love during childbirth. He'd raised his son alone, with the help of the housemaids, and he'd never remarried." He rested his hand on the hilt of his sword. "I suppose he'd become a bit aloof, after we laid his boy to rest, and we hadn't seen him at all until my cousin's nuptials. Only his behavior in the dungeon enlightened us to the extent of his hatred." He was silent for a moment, remembering. "He claimed I'd stolen his life, that he'd given me everything and I'd killed him inside."

"It's actually quite sad," Andi said.

Tristan shook his head. " 'Tis why it shocked us so."

"And your family never knew what happened to you?"

"Nay. De Sabre hid it well, I'm sure. Me and the lads awoke two hundred years after our demise, my family long since having passed on." His face hardened. "No doubt Erik's end came, and while I regret the death of his boy, I cannot forgive the intentional murder of my men."

"So, he killed you with your own sword and cursed you to roam Dreadmoor Keep forever."

"Aye."

"And he managed to lure all fourteen of your knights into the dungeon, where he locked them in to die."

"Aye."

"Do you . . . remember them coming into the dungeon?" she asked.

He shook his head. "I remember their voices, faint, as though far, far away. Then there was nothing, until I came to."

How awful it must've been, experiencing all that Tristan and his men had. It made her brain ache, just thinking about it. "How old are you?" Andi gave a sheepish smile. "I mean, when you . . ."

"Aye, I know what you're asking, girl." Tristan raked a hand through his hair. "I was a score and twelve." He turned sideways against the parapet to face Andi. "And how old are you, Andrea Kinley Monroe?"

Tristan stared at her with such intensity, it made her skin tingle and her stomach do flips. It was as though he were touching her. And good Lord, if he said her name like that one more time, she knew she would melt on the spot, her body pooling in a big, waxy puddle on the floor.

"Andrea?"

She took a quick peek at the floor to see which part of her body had begun to melt first. Feet? Ankles? Knees? Everything blurred together.

"Look at me."

She couldn't. No way. Nope, she just couldn't look into those sapphire blue eyes and admit to herself she was attracted to a very dead Tristan de Barre.

Unfortunately, her head had a mind of its own.

Slowly, she lifted her gaze to his, and her breath crammed in her throat. The results were far worse than simple attraction.

Oh God. She was starting to fall for him.

Andi felt her heart swell with that revelation. And it scared the hell out of her. "I'm, uh, twenty-nine. I think."

He frowned. "You think?"

She nodded. "Before Aunt Mary adopted me, I was literally dropped off at St. Mary's Cathedral—no paperwork, no note with my birth information—nothing. So the hospital I was taken to approximated my date of birth, and that was that."

Intense blue eyes studied her, his dark brows pulled together. "You seem to have faired well. Not many can accomplish what you've done."

"Thank you. I've worked hard for it, believe me."

Tristan's eyes bored into hers, and her mouth went dry. He lifted his hand and traced the length of her hair. Her heart slammed in her chest, and she froze.

"By the saints, I could stare at you all eve. You're even more beautiful than you were all those years ago."

Andi could do nothing except stare into his hypnotizing eyes. Her breath hitched, as though he was going to kiss her. . . .

Just then, the alarm on her watch beeped and she jumped. Glancing down, she noted the time. "It's getting late. I'd better run if I'm going to get any work done today." She turned to leave, then stopped and gave him a grin. "You're not so bad, Dragonhawk."

He tipped his head and returned the smile. "Don't tell anyone. I vow I'd never live it down."

Andi punched the pillow and stared at the ceiling. She knew every stitch and variation in the thick, velvet canopy above her head. She'd lain there for hours, unable to sleep. So many things stormed her mind—Tristan, his ghostly men, Tristan, their murder, Tristan, the body and hoard in the bailey, the spooky presence that she was beginning to think existed only in her imagination . . .

And then there was Tristan.

They'd almost kissed. Well, it wouldn't have worked, but the chemistry was there. Had he been alive, he'd have laid a big one on her. No doubt about it.

No wonder she couldn't sleep.

After a full day's work, she'd eaten a light supper of sautéed chicken and vegetables, excused herself for the night, showered, and flopped into bed. She'd been tired the moment her head hit the pillow. Maybe, she'd even drifted for a bit. But thoughts of Tristan and ghosts filled her mind, and she hadn't been back to sleep since.

Tristan had asked that she keep it all a secret. As if she'd tell anyone. In a flash, Kirk would have her settled into the first sanatorium he could locate. Although he cherished the past and all its treasures, he constituted the epitome of reality and science. Besides, she couldn't betray Tristan.

She'd wanted to kiss him, too.

With a huff, she kicked out of her covers, her mind whirling around Tristan, his knights, and their unusual curse. Didn't they have an out? A way they could undo the curse? And even if they did, what would happen then?

Come on, Monroe, her inner voice scolded. *You can't undo the dead. It's final. Once there, you can't come back to life.* Once that sword found its way into Tristan's gut, the damage was done. Finite.

"Yeah, but you didn't believe in ghosts until now, did you?" she said aloud. Punching the pillow, she flipped over onto her stomach and buried her face, muffling her voice. "What am I going to do?"

Silence filled the room, only the faint ticking of her Indiglo watch making the slightest of sounds. *Tick. Tick. Tick. Tick . . .* Then it came.

It is here.

Like an icy fingernail dragging across her spine, the whisper raked over her, causing her body to shudder. Maybe, if she lay very still and pretended to be asleep, it would go away. Only seconds passed.

You are their only hope.

Leaping out of bed, she scanned the darkened room. There, in the corner of the room next to the hearth, a faint light began to glow. Similar to squinting against a hazy sunlight, it floated weightlessly above . . .

Andi blinked.

Above Tristan's shield.

Slowly, she crossed the floor.

The mist evaporated as soon as she drew close to the shield.

"Hello?" Andi checked every nook and cranny of the chamber, but the mist had truly disappeared. No whisper. No mist. Nothing.

Nothing, save the medieval shield.

"Lady? Is aught amiss?"

Her heart jumped to her throat as Jason of Corwick-on-the-Sea spoke through the door. Walking over, she flipped on the light and cracked the heavy oak. "Did you see anything?"

He shook his head. "All is quiet out in the corridor." He cocked his head. "Why? Did you encounter anything unusual?"

Andi nearly burst out laughing at the absurdity of a ghost knight asking her if *she'd* seen anything unusual. She turned and walked back to the shield. "Yes, I did. It—"

"It what, Andrea?"

She jumped again. Tristan appeared beside Jason as they both entered her room.

Lowering herself to her knees, she pulled the shield close and inspected its front. "The voice—whisper— whatever you want to call it. It got me out of bed." She turned the shield over. "It was a faint wisp of mist, hovering over this. The voice said, 'It is here,' and 'You're their only hope.'"

Tristan squatted down beside her, the chain mail groaning as he moved. "*What* is here?"

She shook her head. "I don't know." Lifting her eyes, she set her jaw. "Yet." Turning back to the shield, she began to examine it more closely. "The eye of Dragonhawk . . ."

"Mayhap a clue of sorts," Jason added, kneeling on the other side of Andi. "But to what, I wonder?"

Yellow-painted wood trimmed in black and banded with steel, notched by battles and cleaved with swords, the shield held a secret Andi was determined to uncover—especially if it meant breaking the curse for Tristan and his men. Running her fingers lightly over the surface, she traced the mystical rampant creature in its center. Drawing closer, she searched, staring hard, squinting at each variation. Half dragon, half hawk with a piercing blue eye, something about the black-and-green creature looked familiar.

"What see you, lady?" Jason asked.

Mystified, she again shook her head. "I swear, I don't know. There's something, but I can't seem to place it."

"'Tis the middle of the night, Andrea," Tristan said as he slowly rose. "You've plenty of time to gaze upon my shield and decipher the riddle. You need your rest."

Propping the shield in its place, she stood. "I suppose you're right." She slid him a sideways glance. "But sleep? After all this? You're nuts."

It was then Andi noticed the frown tightening Tristan's face. "What's wrong?"

"Jason!" Tristan shouted.

"Right here," Jason answered.

"Stand your post on the other side of the lady's door."

Jason threw Andi a grin before nodding. "As you wish." With that, he disappeared.

"You get more puzzling by the minute. Why did you just throw him out?"

Tristan's hot gaze simmered with way more than anger. "You've little on, woman, or did you notice?"

Andi glanced down at herself. Half shirt, shorts—her usual sleeping attire. Lifting one shoulder, she grinned. "Sorry. I was in bed, you know."

The muscles in Tristan's jaws tightened and his eyes turned a smoldering gray blue. "So you were."

"Um," she stammered, suddenly aware of the intense interest in the knight's even more intense stare. "I . . . guess I'll see you in the morning, right?"

It was a moment longer before he gave a slight bow. "Aye, then. Till the morn." Without another word, he disappeared.

Andi let a pent-up breath slip past her lips. Wow. That man reeked of sexuality. Raw, unleashed-for-centuries male sexuality.

With a final glance at his shield, Andi flipped off the lights, crept over to the bed, and slipped under the sheets.

Had Tristan de Barre of Dreadmoor been a flesh-and-blood live man, she'd hardly know what to do with all that raw maleness.

As her eyes grew heavy, a grin tipped her mouth. *Yeah, Monroe. You'd know exactly what to do with him.*

Chapter 15

A *woman.*
 A bloody, mortal woman. Tristan patted his ghostly steed's neck and sucked in a deep breath. A bloody beautiful mortal woman—one he could not keep his mind off, small, useless thing that it was. He thought back to the night before, when Andrea had stood in her chamber, barely garbed. Even dead, he'd felt the profound attraction. The lass fascinated him, intrigued him beyond belief. Intelligent, beautiful, a bit quirky. How his sire and brothers would roar at his compromising situation.

Tristan stiffened as his keen hearing picked up the slightest of sounds. Immediately, he knew who interrupted his thoughts. "Kail, you bumbling idiot. Even in death you lack stealth." He turned toward his captain. "What want you?"

"Damn, Tristan." Kail grinned. "You are a besotted whelp."

Tristan glared. His captain did indeed lack stealth; in life the man, who reached nigh onto seven feet in height, couldn't sneak up on a deaf man; size and strength alone had saved his sorry hide more than once. But the whoreson had intuition, damn him to hell.

Tristan's horse snorted and pawed the ground. He swung down, sending the ghostly steed running with a swat to the rump. A sharp crack of thunder sounded in the distance. Tristan inhaled, as though he might actually be able to smell the ensuing storm. If only he could. With a glare he turned to Kail. "I'm not a whelp, witless."

Kail stared at him for a moment, just before he broke out into laughter. The big man held his stomach as he continued his fit, until he gained a small amount of control. Kail wiped his teary eyes and smiled at Tristan. "She is beautiful, Tristan. You've chosen well."

Tristan frowned at the laughing idiot before him, then turned and strode across the bailey. "I've chosen nothing, fool. She is merely here to excavate the body and weapons. Nothing more."

Kail caught up to him. "I think you like her. My lord."

"Have you no men to oversee?" Tristan thumped him on the chest. "I vow you are powerfully close to irritating me already, Kail. Be gone."

"Pitiful, Dreadmoor. I'd expect a bit more out of you than a simple 'be gone.'"

Tristan stopped in his tracks and glared up at the giant. "You want more, captain? What do you care to hear? That I am unable to spend barely a waking moment without her in my thoughts? That I find myself seeking her out and watching her, but am too cowardly to present myself to her?" Tristan took a step toward his captain and frowned. He raked a hand through his hair and closed his eyes. "Do you want to hear how I would give anything to simply inhale her scent?"

Kail cleared his throat. "Nay, my friend. 'Tis no need." He slapped Tristan on the back, nearly sending him reeling. "But you should consider telling your lady, aye?"

Tristan rounded on him. "What mean you, tell my lady? She is definitely not mine to tell. For the saints' sake, man. She's alive. I'm . . . not. 'Twould be nothing more than heartache, for the both of us, in the end. You know that. Even if she accepted me in my sorry state, 'twould only end in misery."

Kail grinned at Tristan. "Mayhap, my lord. Mayhap not. Only you can choose the correct path. Now, think no more of it, for it pains me thusly. Come you with me, man. A bit of training with the blades will get your murky thoughts cleared."

Tristan shook his head. A good round with the swords might be the best thing for now. 'Twould certainly get his mind off Andrea for a spell. "Aye. Mayhap you've the right of it."

Kail smiled. "I usually do. Now come. I've a mind to best you this time."

Tristan strode toward the lists, ready to take his frustrations out on his captain. He feared an entire battle couldn't ease his thoughts of a certain brown-haired, hazel-eyed, beautiful archaeologist.

But it was worth a try.

Andi watched from her window as Tristan and Kail the giant—God, that man was huge—walked across the bailey, side by side. They stopped at the cutaway and stood, staring, Tristan pointing, Kail nodding his head. In a way it seemed perfectly normal, watching the two of them together, as though they were alive. But they were not. They were ghosts and Dreadmoor was full of them. Filled with an entire garrison of ghosts, carrying on as though they still had a castle, a home, a life to defend. It was nothing short of amazing.

And it confused the hell out of her.

The whispered message rushed into her thoughts. *It is here. You're their only hope.* What did it mean?

Walking back to the shield, she once more sat cross-legged on the floor and pulled it onto her lap. At least four feet in length, three feet in width, it was a thick, sturdy weapon that had saved Tristan from the sharp end of all sorts of medieval blades. *Too bad it hadn't saved him from the last one.*

She paused, that same, familiar feeling slipping over her. With eyes glued to the mystical creature, she stared until she was forced to blink, stared at the incredible, watching eye. The Dragonhawk's eye.

With a sigh, she set the shield upright, turned back to her bed, pulled on her sneakers, and set off to find something to eat. Jameson had promised her something delicious for breakfast, and if she had any luck at all it would be superrich and loaded with cholesterol. Lots of carbs, too. Maybe that would take her mind off a certain gallant knight whose incredible good looks and chivalristic ways made her sway just thinking about him.

She washed and dressed in a pair of faded jeans and tank top, then pulled her hair into a quick ponytail, and stepped out into the corridor. Jason jumped to avoid her passing right through him.

She blinked. "Ooh, sorry." How would she ever manage getting used to seeing so many ghostly knights?

After a charming grin, he gave her a low bow. "Good morn, lady. Did you manage any rest at all?"

Just talk to him, Monroe. You might as well face it. You're surrounded by spirits from the thirteenth century. They're not going away. She smiled. "Yes, I finally fell asleep." She made for the kitchen, the handsome young knight by her side.

Taller than her, he stood close to six foot, his brown hair pulled into a queue, a sword slapping his thigh as he walked. She'd never get over it. It was real, yet completely surreal. "Do you . . . stay by my door every night?"

"Oh, aye." He bent his head to meet her eyes. "You're my charge, you see. A most important task, given in faith by my master."

Light green eyes filled with determination and honesty stared at her; then he inclined his head. "Did you think any more on the shield?"

Taking the steps down to the hall, Andi nodded. "Yes. I woke up with it on my mind. I even inspected it again."

"And did the same familiar feeling grip you as it did last eve?"

What a cute guy. "Yes. And I still couldn't place it." She gave him an assuring smile. "But I will."

At the kitchen door, Jason stopped and bowed once more. " 'Tis with regret I cannot open the door for you, lady. Enjoy your meal and I shall be at your immediate call, should you need anything."

"Thanks, Jason."

"My most honored pleasure." With a roguish grin, he disappeared.

Nope. Never in a million years would she get used to that. She smiled and pushed through the door.

Jameson stood at the stove, flipping something delicious smelling in a pan. He didn't even grace her with a look as she walked over to the enormous oak table and sat down.

"I see young Jason has taken full charge of your stay here at Dreadmoor. A fine lad, that one. Hungry, Dr. Monroe?"

"Sure." A heavy sigh escaped her lips.

"Something amiss?"

Another sigh. "No, I guess not."

"I'm not convinced in the least. And I've a feeling you don't want me to be. " He cleared his throat and turned back to the stove. "I don't usually have the time for counsel, but you have caught me on a slow day. Tell me what is bothering you, my dear. No doubt you will anyway."

Andi couldn't help but smile. "Jameson, you're such a smooth talker."

"Yes, my lady, I know. Now proceed."

She blew a strand of hair from her eyes. "I wish Tristan wasn't dead."

Jameson choked on a gasp. "How's that?"

Walking over to the counter next to the stove, she eased up onto the surface and sat, legs dangling. "I wish things could be different, Jameson. He's so . . . nice."

This time Jameson did choke. Andi resisted the urge to slap him on the back to expel whatever had become lodged.

"Nice, you say? Promise me you won't make the mistake of allowing Himself to hear such an accusation. 'Twould make both of our lives much more difficult. Indeed."

She stared down at the floor. "I suppose it would be best if I tried to concentrate on my work, huh?"

Jameson rested a hand on Andi's shoulder. " 'Tisn't fair of me, lady, to advise one on such a delicate subject. It would, in my opinion, be best discussed with Lord Dreadmoor."

Andi rolled her eyes. "I knew you would say something like that."

Jameson swiftly lifted fried ham out of the pan and placed it on a plate. "If it is any consolation, young lady"—he turned and looked at her—"the master seems to have taken a fondness for you, as well."

"I like him, too."

Jameson, who looked decidedly uncomfortable at the tender moment, hastily retreated to the stiff, comforting, butlerish ways he was used to. "Now, if that's all the womanly drivel you have for me this morn, I shall see to your meal. 'Tis Thursday. Heath and Miss Kate will arrive in a few moments." He nodded. "My lady."

"Do they know? About Tristan and his men?"

Jameson's face blushed. "Aye, but were sworn to secrecy. Miss Kate adores the knights, and young Heath relishes the ground they walk on. No doubt the lad would live here, if his mum would allow it."

Andi smiled. "What about you?"

"What about me, lady?"

"I think you have the hots for Miss Kate."

Jameson coughed. "I've certainly no hots for anyone, young lady. 'Twouldn't be gentlemanly."

Andi leaned over and placed a quick peck on Jameson's cheek, then jumped down off the counter. "Whatever, Jameson. I'll see you later."

Jameson's white eyebrows shot skyward in surprise. "No doubt."

After an eye-watering breakfast of spicy ham and eggs, Andi rushed to her room, brushed her teeth, then set off to work. She had plans to recover the rest of the bones today and get the tree cut and hauled, so maybe by the end of the week, she'd be able to get to the hoard.

Thoughts of Tristan crowded her already crowded mind. It seemed like a hopeless situation. Never before had she been so indecisive. Then again, she'd never been placed in such a precarious predicament. Part of her wanted to resume digging in the dungeon to recover the rest of the chain mail—and whatever else lurked beneath the hard-packed dirt. Then again, she was hired as a

GAR employee to complete the excavation of the remains and hoard—of which Kirk, being the owner/investor of GAR, expected her to bring whatever weapons she unearthed with her when they met for dinner later in the week.

She supposed her priority should be the cutaway. Crossing the great hall at a trot, she missed the massive form leaning against the wall as she made for the door.

"A fine morn it has turned out to be, aye?"

With a squeal, she jerked to a stop. "Tristan, you scared me."

The grin he pasted to his face had the capability to curl the stockings off a nun. "I vow I did not mean to." He crossed his arms over his mailed chest. "Did you rest after last night's encounter with the mysterious voice? I must say, it concerns me to know you've encountered a spirit other than one of us."

First Jason, now Tristan. Never had she had so many concerned for her well-being. "I did sleep some, although my first thought was to jump up and check out your shield again." She smiled and answered before he asked. "No, I didn't recognize anything. But it'll come to me. I feel it. The eye of Dragonhawk."

It didn't seem as odd as before, Tristan walking beside her across the bailey to the cutaway. Yes, he was dressed in thirteenth-century chain mail and hose. But with each passing day, maybe it got a little easier to handle. Jameson certainly had no trouble, and neither did his ancestors before him. And, from what Jameson said, his son Thomas would take over one day. Then again, the Jameson family had been exposed to the fantastic situation for centuries.

"Lady? Where do your thoughts wander to? I wonder oft how you manage to keep your wits about you."

With a slight grin, she lifted a shoulder. "It's called multitasking."

"Ah, I see. You truly fascinate me."

The blush reached her ears in a matter of seconds. They were on fire. She didn't know how to react to him. Her natural instinct, as a female, felt so overwhelming.

Even as a ghost, Tristan had an abundance of magnetism. But the more she thought about the situation, the more it scared her. What if she really, *really* fell for this guy? This very handsome, very *dead* guy? God, what a disaster.

Reaching the cutaway, she flipped the lid on the large, plastic container holding her tools and busied herself. She didn't even flinch when Tristan spoke from behind.

"Lady, I—"

"Tristan, look." Andi turned to meet his gaze. "You've hired me to do a job, and you're making it very difficult for me to complete it in the short time that's allowed."

She didn't want him to leave her alone. She more than liked being around him; had found herself time and time again seeking his whereabouts. Even Jameson had advised her to speak to Tristan about her feelings. Being an enormous chicken had forced her to keep silent—at least that's what she told herself. She wiped her palms on her jeans and gathered her trowel. She looked down at her hands; they shook. Everyone in her life, save Kirk, had abandoned her. Facing another hurt didn't seem appealing, and she just didn't want to deal with it. She hated being a coward, but she had no choice.

Tristan stared at the lovely woman standing so rigid and stiff before him. He watched her slender hands, pale and elegant, tremble as she attempted to gather her digging tools. What could he say? He did not want her to leave. Swearing always gave him some form of comfort. Mayhap he'd try it.

"Merde." He began to pace, gathering up what pitiful strength he possessed to speak his feeble mind. "Is that what you truly wish of me, Andrea?" He walked in front of where she stood and stared. "To leave you to your work?"

She met his gaze. "What are you saying?"

"Lady." He prayed with a fervor his pitiful voice didn't crack. "'Tis a most—unusual—situation, I know. One I did not count on." He took another step closer. Barely a foot of space separated them. He ducked his head to catch her gaze. "I did not count on you, Andrea."

She shook her head, unable to believe his words. "I don't understand."

Tristan's stomach lurched. Saints, what if she bid him leave her? After seven hundred years he had found someone to care for. He'd never met a woman like her before, in life or unlife. He squeezed his eyes shut briefly, then gained a bit more courage and drew a deep breath. His hands clenched at his sides to keep from attempting something ridiculous, such as lifting her face to his.

"You intrigue me, Andrea. I find myself seeking you out at all times during the waking hours, and I pace endlessly during the night whilst you sleep, counting the minutes until you rise." He turned his back and looked up. " 'Tis a pitiful state I'm in, aye?"

The breath escaping her lungs barely reached his ears. "Nearly as pitiful as me, I guess."

Tristan smiled and slowly turned around to face her. "I—guess—as you say." He took a small step closer. He did not want to go too fast with his lady. "I think your digging could be put off for a while." He flashed her a grin. "If you can stand my constant company."

Andi's smile faded. "I'm sorry, I can't. Not today, anyway." She nodded toward the hoard. "I promised Kirk I'd excavate the weapons by the end of the week. He is anxious to inspect them."

Tristan frowned. "I didn't know he was coming here for dinner."

"He's not. I'm meeting him. In town."

Now, why did that sit so ill with him? "I see." He shifted his weight. "How old is this . . . Kirk?"

Andi grinned. "Over fifty."

Somehow, that didn't appease him enough.

Resting his hand on the hilt of his sword, Tristan nodded. "Very well. I suppose I can entertain myself for one eve without you."

"Sure you can."

"Saucy wench."

Andi laughed. "I do have to run what samples I have to the coroner's office in Northumberland this evening."

"I see."

She narrowed her eyes at him, then smiled. "I won't be out late. I plan on coming back and doing a bit more excavating in your dungeon." She shook her head. "I still have the rest of the mail to recover."

A smile tugged at his mouth. What a determined lass. And by the saints, he hadn't made the expression as much over the last few centuries. Until now. "Then I shall look forward to your return."

With the toe of her shoe, she pushed a small rock back and forth. "I've a lot of work to do today. Tedious, bone brushing, recovery. You could . . . hang around and tell me knightly tales. So I don't get bored here all by myself."

Stupid had never been a word used to describe any de Barre. *Never.*

Although he certainly had to wonder about the wisdom of embarking on this course with Andrea. Somehow, even the knowing of what could lie ahead didn't stop him.

"Aye, my lady. I wouldn't miss the chance."

Chapter 16

Now that the branches of the massive oak were barren of the entire skeleton, Andi concentrated on the hoard nestled at the bottom. After taking several more photos of the surrounding area, she focused on the large, wrapped bundle at the base of the sizeable hole. It was big enough for a Volkswagen. Andi climbed down the aluminum ladder and stepped off into the still-spongy black dirt. With a delicate touch, she fingered the bundle.

"Are you positive you don't want me to come down there?" Tristan called from above.

"No. You're way too big," she answered. Not that she wouldn't want him down there. "It's covered by a roll of leather, although some of it has rotted away." She fingered the binding. "It's tied together with some sort of vine—wait, it looks like yew, just like what was wrapped around the skull." She snapped another picture. "Very, very bizarre."

Tristan peered over the edge of the hole. "Can you see any of the weaponry within?"

Andi ducked her head and studied the aged leather satchel. "Yeah, I can, actually. Several blades, I think."

"It looks powerfully large, that sack. It's not possible for a wee maid like you to lift it out wholly."

Tristan was right. She ran her gloved hand over the bulging leather bag. "I'll have to loosen the twine and hoist out each piece separately."

"Have you ever held a thirteenth-century sword, lady? 'Tis heavier than you think."

Andi looked up and grinned. "Yeah, I have, and I can handle it. No problem."

"Hmm. We shall see."

God, there were those dimples again. How had he remained single for so long? "Okay." She blew out a heavy breath. "First, I'll have to cut this twining off and peel back the leather." Reaching into her tool belt, she grabbed her pocketknife and flipped open the blade. "Here goes."

Steadying her hand, she pushed the sharpened steel through the first twist of twine. Minutes later, she cut all the way through. The bundle heaved as the contents spread. Lifting the twine, she climbed the ladder and stepped out onto the ground.

She held the vine out for Tristan to inspect. "Just like the one around the skull."

"Bloody saints. 'Tis twisted yew." He bent his dark head over the braid, then quickly lifted his gaze to Andi's. "Witchery, Andrea." He inclined his head to the hole. "Whatever is in that satchel is cursed. As is the poor soul you dug out."

It sounded so absurd, yet proof of the black arts and witchery stood right before her, wearing chain mail made by a sweat-covered smithy over seven hundred years before. She shook her head. "I don't understand. What do you mean by witchery?"

Lifting a finger, he pointed at the braid. "Twisted yew is solely used by those practicing witchcraft. They think it holds some sort of ancient power useful in binding curses."

"Wow."

"Aye. Wow."

"If you two are through wowing, can we get on with the weapons? I'm passing curious to see what else lies within the bag."

Both Tristan and she turned to find Kail, Jason, and all twelve of the other knights slowly materializing at the dig site. They stood, arms crossed over mailed chests, legs spread wide.

Waiting.

Tristan pointed to the braid. "Twisted yew. I vow whatever lies within that satchel is cursed," he said to his men.

Sir Richard stepped forward and peered at the twining. "Aye, he's the right of it, just like that poor lad who was killed and buried. And I've a bad feeling in me gorge about what's in that bag."

Far be it from her to make a pack of curious thirteenth-century knights wait. Sidestepping two large men, she laid the twisted yew on the plastic tarp she'd set out earlier and quickly climbed back down the ladder. From the corner of her eye she saw fifteen male heads peering over the lip of the cutaway.

Talk about being under pressure.

Holding her breath, Andi gently opened one flap of leather, then the other. The breath swished from her lungs like she'd been hit in the chest.

As if an almost natural reaction, she began to count the pieces of black-tarnished, rusting armor.

Fourteen helmets.

She gulped.

Fourteen swords.

Wait. She counted again. Nope. Only fourteen.

"Merde."

Andi slowly lifted her gaze to the men staring down at her. She knew Tristan's thoughts without him uttering a single word—other than the swear. Glancing down at the sword lying on top of the bundle, she hefted it with a grunt.

"Be careful, Andrea," Tristan said.

"I will." It was heavy, but she'd expected it to be. Inching her way to the ladder, she climbed out, one hand holding the rungs, the other gripping the ancient sword. It seemed like minutes before she reached the top.

Before she laid the weapon on the tarp, a younger knight named Cameron stepped forward. " 'Tis mine."

Andi set the blade on the tarp and watched the blond-haired warrior kneel and study the piece of armor. She could see it in his face. It *was* his.

"A knight knows his blade, lady," Tristan said. He

moved closer to her and pushed a hand through his thick hair. Dark brows pulled close as he studied her face. "How many?"

She looked into eyes so blue, so intense, they nearly made her squint. "Fourteen helmets. Fourteen swords."

A muscle tightened at his jaw and he nodded, but said no words.

One by one, Andi lifted each piece of armor out of the cutaway and laid it on the protective plastic tarp. Although everything was tarnished and rusted, each knight claimed his blade, his helm.

Everyone, except Tristan.

The faces on fifteen ghostly knights were taut, tired, and each failed to hide the remorse of life lost, of all the events that led up to this point. Andi knew that, although the actual death experience remained a mystery, the realization that someone had snuffed all of their lives, then buried their most prized possessions in such a manner . . . she couldn't imagine what that felt like.

There she stood, gloved, covered in filthy orange and yellow GAR weatherproofs, in the midst of fifteen medieval knights, murdered centuries before.

And still with no answers.

But she did have a question.

Turning, she watched Tristan as he stood beside his men, staring at the weapons she'd laid out. The closer she got, the more her throat tightened. "Why only theirs?" she asked in a quiet voice.

He turned his head and looked down at her. The sight pulled the breath straight out of her lungs. Knowing it wasn't a true wind that blew his hair across a beard-studded jaw didn't distract from the illusion. He was magnificent—they all were. Tall, strong, and fiercely proud, they stood like dreamlike warriors. Actually, they were. And God, how she wanted to help them.

Tristan waved a hand toward his garrison. "They are here simply because they're my men. This was Erik's evil. Whether he was alone or with an accomplice, 'twas no doubt his work. Why he felt compelled to separate my effects from theirs, I have no clue other than his hatred toward me was twice as fierce." He glanced at the collection of swords and helmets. "Mayhap, 'tis why they can leave Dreadmoor land and I cannot."

That thought hadn't crossed her mind. "You can't leave the castle grounds?"

He shook his head. "Nay."

A gull screamed overhead, drawing her attention to the dark clouds moving in from the sea. A late afternoon sun turned everything in its path a hazy gold. She glanced over her shoulder; the castle loomed toward the heavens, dark, gray, foreboding.

Real, or not real?

Surreal.

The *beep-beep* of her wristwatch alarm broke the silence. Glancing at the face, she gasped. "Oh, crap."

A few chuckles erupted from the men, their sullen mood easing.

"What is it?" Tristan asked.

Oh, how she didn't want to, but she had no choice. "I've got to get ready to meet Kirk in the village. He is expecting me to bring the hoard for inspection—"

Fifteen "nays" sounded in unison.

Fifteen pairs of brows, all various shades of colors and shapes, pulled together for a disapproving frown.

Tristan spoke for his men. "Lady, you cannot take the weapons from Dreadmoor. 'Tis all they have left."

Andi nodded. "I know, and you're right. Besides"— she turned her eyes to Tristan's—"it is yours. I'm here simply to recover it for you."

The relief in all the knights' faces humbled her. No way would she even dream of taking what little they could call their own. No matter how upset Kirk became. He'd just have to fire her, or get over it. At least he'd have the pictures.

And no way would he fire her.

A low rumble of thunder sounded in the distance, an echoing of the storm making its way across the North Sea toward landfall. "I've got to get these inside before it rains. I don't trust the tarp system to keep them safe."

A litany of "ayes" sounded from the men.

"Jason!" Tristan shouted.

The young squire jumped to attention. "Right here, my lord."

"There you are. Hasten you to the gatehouse and inform Will he's needed here in the bailey." He scanned the knights. "Cameron, hasten to the larder and tell Jameson of the events. Tell him to clear the long table in the study for the weapons."

"Aye," Cameron said and disappeared to do Tristan's bidding.

"You others, busy yourselves for a bit. I've the lady to see to."

Without question, the rest of the knights vanished.

Leaving her alone with the Dragonhawk.

Tristan moved toward her, his big body crowding hers, broad shoulders and massive chest blocking any and all views. She couldn't see through him—he looked that solid. But his presence felt just as real as if he were alive and breathing. And God, how she wished he was.

One corner of his mouth lifted. "You've a dirt smudge on your nose, lady." He lifted his hand to her cheek, and with a forefinger rubbed at the spot above her nose, then to graze the line of her jaw. The mirth disappeared from his face and his jaw muscles flexed, making his expression more intense. He dropped his hand. "I vow, 'tis maddening."

Andi drew in a breath. "Strange, but I . . . feel you, somehow."

The ability to touch wasn't needed—she felt Tristan sink into every pore of her skin, sensed him with every breath drawn from her lungs. They stared in silence. She noted every sun line, every scar on his handsome face. . . .

His eyes darkened.

"My lord? Dr. Monroe?" Will said. "You called for me?"

Tristan's gaze dropped from her eyes to her mouth, where it lingered long enough to make her face grow warm and her skin tingle. Then he turned his attention to his mortal gatehouse guard.

"Aye. Dr. Monroe needs your assistance in loading these weapons into the hall. Drive you that cart from the greenery over here, posthaste. A storm is brewing and we've no time to wait."

With a nod, Will hastened to do Tristan's bidding.

"Thanks," Andi said, starting toward the hoard, slightly disappointed that their moment had passed. "I'll feel much better when these are inside. Plus, I still have to get ready—"

Tristan stepped beside her. "You're still going to meet Grey?"

Andi stopped and met his stare. "Yes. I have to. He's expecting me. Plus, I have the photo card of the hoard. He'll be anxious to see them."

Waving a hand in the air, he shrugged. "Call him and tell him you cannot come this eve. There's no need since the blades are remaining here."

Boy, how she'd love to do just that. Unfortunately, Kirk would not take no for an answer. "Trust me. It'll be better to tell him in person that the weaponry is remaining at Dreadmoor than to try and get through to him over the wire."

Tristan's gaze narrowed as he studied her. "Very well. I shall see you when you return."

"Wait!" Andi said as he started to fade. "Do you have to leave now?"

The corner of his mouth lifted. "Aye, for now I do. I've business to attend with my solicitor over the phone. Another land parcel sale. Boring, I assure you." He bowed, then winked. "Until later, my lady."

Then he vanished.

Andi stared at the space Tristan seconds before had occupied. Would she ever get used to being so fascinated by a ghost?

Chapter 17

The hum of the small crowd gathered at Dahlia's Gilded Shoe, the one and only village pub, died to something only a dog could hear once Andi stepped inside. Scanning the room for Kirk, she found him in a corner booth. Ten pairs of eyes, including the bartender's, watched her shuffle across the floor to the back. As she passed the bar, she recognized the cabby who'd brought her to Dreadmoor. "Hi, Gibbs." She winked. "Still alive."

That awarded her with several chuckles from the other patrons, including the wary cabdriver. They all resumed their chatter.

Kirk stood as she approached the table. He leaned over and kissed her cheek. "I apologize for such a common meeting place." He waved a hand in the air. "Not much to expect from a low-income fishing village." His eyes gleamed as she took her seat. "How many did you bring?"

Low-income fishing village? Common? What was wrong with Kirk? She'd never seen such a snobby side to his personality. Maybe she had, and had never noticed. And how on earth did he know what she had? She hadn't told him there were swords.

She forced a warm smile. Maybe he was still edgy about having to manage the other site? And maybe he was guessing about the swords. "This place is fine, Kirk. And the villagers are quite—"

"Andrea, the blades? Did you bring them?"

Leveling her gaze to his, she shook her head. "No."

A flush crept across his features, and his eyes hardened. "What? Why not?"

The sharp voice surprised her, made her flinch. Turning her head, she noticed everyone in the bar stared in their direction. "What is wrong with you?" she said quietly. The skin on her throat and face tingled as humiliation and hurt gripped her. Never had he spoken in such a way to her. It made her want to leave.

A calm expression replaced the seconds-before anger. Muscles ticked at his jaw, a sign he was still mad but trying to overcome it. Finally, he heaved a sigh. "I've no excuses, Andrea. Please, forgive me." He leaned back and stroked his pencil-thin beard. "You look as though you're about to burst into tears. Please. I'm sorry." He ducked his head when she didn't respond. "I'm begging now, Andrea. I couldn't stand for you to remain upset."

Andi blinked at the sudden change. "You've never been like this before, Kirk. Is it the hoard?" She shook her head. "If you're so fascinated by it I'm afraid you'll have to go to Dreadmoor to inspect it."

Something flashed in his gray eyes. A challenge? Wrath? Then he smiled. "And why is that?"

His smile stayed on his lips. And it bothered her.

"Andrea?"

Just as she opened her mouth to speak, a brown-haired woman in her forties stopped at their booth with a food-laden tray. " 'Ere's your order, sir."

Andi kept silent while the plates were set down. The woman flashed her a smile, wiped her hands on the yellow apron hanging from her waist, then left.

"I took the liberty of ordering for you, my dear." He smiled. "You do like fish, yes? Now. About why you've no hoard to show me this fine eve?"

Ignoring her irritability, she took a sip from her water. "The condition of the weapons is precarious at the moment, Kirk. They've only been out of the ground for a few hours—"

"I want details, Andrea. How were they placed? Describe each and every one."

For a reason unknown to her, she felt compelled to be vague. No, she felt compelled to leave. Maybe it was because of the way her mentor was acting? The word *jackass* came to mind. "They were wrapped in a stretch of leather, which had become partially rotted."

"Bound with twisted yew, no doubt?"

She nearly choked. "How did you know that?"

He ignored her question. "How many were there?"

She narrowed her gaze. "Fourteen."

Watchful gray eyes searched hers, without blinking. Then he leaned against the padded vinyl back of the booth. "Fourteen, you say?" He sipped his beer. "Interesting." Then, as if the whole ugly raising-of-the-voice thing hadn't happened, he dug into his meal of fried haddock and chips. In midbite, he stopped. "I assume you photographed?"

"Yes. I did."

A cool, wafting breath touched her neck. Turning, she looked behind her. No one was there.

"I suppose you didn't bring the digital?" Kirk glanced at her untouched plate. "Aren't you going to eat?"

Reaching into her purse, she pulled out the photo card and set it down by his plate. It would have been useless to lie about it. He knew how retentive she was about gathering all information at a dig.

A simple nod. "That's my girl." He promptly stuffed it in his pocket. After a long pull on his pint of beer, he wiped his mouth and glanced at his watch. "Christ, Andrea, I've got to run. I hate to make this such a hasty meeting." He stood and kissed her cheek. "I've fifteen undergrads awaiting me in Northumberland. I really do hate to leave them for long." He kissed her cheek. "You do understand, don't you?"

No. She didn't understand any of it. "You're leaving? I thought this was dinner as well as info-swap? If that's all you wanted, why didn't you just call?"

Kirk's eyes narrowed. "This is something we both love, Andrea. We've shared it since you were a young girl. I simply looked forward to it—the hoard *and* sharing it with my most prized student. Certainly, you understand my disappointment?"

Well, maybe she did. She'd wanted to excavate Dreadmoor forever. How would she have felt had it been snatched away from her? Or worse, had Kirk not given it to her to begin with?

After a deep breath, she stood. "I understand, and I'm sorry. It's just you've been so . . . demanding lately."

He chuckled. "I'm always demanding, love. That's not a new feature to my character."

She looked at the man who'd been the closest thing she'd ever had to a father. "It is with me."

Minutes later, Andi watched her mentor leave the small pub parking lot by cab and head south toward Northumberland. Maybe the undergrads were too much for him to handle? She knew how to, but Kirk rarely led such an inexperienced group without her.

Climbing into Jameson's Rover, she pushed her gloomy thoughts out of mind and pulled out onto the single-track road leading to Dreadmoor.

"What?"

Tristan's thunderous shout echoed across the bailey and probably reached the village. Not that he cared. He stared at the three knights before him. Pinching the bridge of his nose, he stopped and pushed a hand through his hair. "Why did you follow her? Did you show yourselves?"

Richard, Christopher, and Geoffrey shook their heads.

Richard cleared his throat. "Well, I believe the lady knew something was amiss."

After a few seconds of glaring, Tristan said, "You blew on her neck."

A quick nod. "Aye. I did blow on her neck."

Geoffrey shuffled his booted feet. " 'Twas only as a warning blow, Tristan. We feared she'd reveal too much."

That caught Tristan's attention. "Did she?"

Three "nays" sounded in unison.

"Bleedin' saints," Tristan muttered. He paused, then faced the three knights. "How went her meeting with Grey?"

All three knights glanced at one another. "Not very well, I'd warrant. He shouted at her thusly for not bringing any of our swords," Richard said.

"And the lady seemed quite taken aback by his behavior, as well," Christopher said. "Strange, but there was something oddly familiar about the man."

Tristan frowned. "What mean you?"

Christopher shook his head. "I vow I don't know. 'Twasn't his visage, but rather his—"

"Voice," said Geoffrey. "I recognized his bloody voice, but cannot place it." He scratched his head. "Daft but I think 'twas Erik. Bloody Erik de Sabre."

Chapter 18

Tristan followed Andrea down the stairs into the dungeon where she knelt to examine the links of chain mail. Quite a determined wench, he thought. A trait he rather liked in a woman.

Not any woman. *That woman.*

Gently, he cleared his throat. "I see you've made it back from the village unscathed." Saints, but he hated lying. Although not truly lying, keeping something a secret from her was lying enough. And it disgusted him to do the deed.

"Yes, although my boss was disappointed not to be able to examine the weapons firsthand."

"Aye. No doubt." Unavoidably, his gaze settled on Andi's mouth. How he'd love to wipe that forlorn expression from her lovely face. Forcing those lecherous thoughts from his mind, he met her eyes with his. A thought struck him. "I've got something to show you. Be you up for a bit of a climb? The North Tower has a powerfully grand view of the sea, and I've a notion to view it at once."

Andrea's smile nearly split her face. She nodded. "I'm up for anything." She glanced back down at the mail. "This is yours. Isn't it?"

"Do not fret overmuch about it, lady. More likely than not, aye, 'tis mine. But I don't see how that can help you solve this mystery. 'Tis only mail. Now, up the stairs you go and make haste, for I've not the patience to wait on you." More important things were at hand now. Like who Andrea's employer truly was.

Jumping the excavation pit, she turned back to Tristan, a knowing gleam in her eyes. "Oh yes, you do, Lord Dreadmoor." With that she raced up the stairs.

He watched her climb, his unchivalristic thoughts returning as he watched her long legs carry her to the chambers above. He cleared his throat. "You've the right of it, lass. More than you know."

Andi's stomach fluttered with excitement as they walked side by side. "Where are we going?"

"As I said, the North Tower. To my chambers."

Andi grinned. "You must like heights. First, a trip to the parapet. Now the North Tower." She shrugged. "Okay."

Tristan cocked his head. "You don't sound overly trusting, Dr. Monroe."

She laughed nervously. "Sorry. I trust you."

Tristan stopped and turned, his stare powerful and intense. "Do you in truth?"

Andi thought she would melt from the sheer heat radiating from Tristan's unfathomable gaze. His eyes were so acute, so blue—so knowing. He looked so *real*. A shiver moved over her spine. "Yes, I do trust you."

They stared at one another for what seemed like several minutes. A muscle flexed in Tristan's jaw as he studied her face, searching her eyes for something known only to him. "As you should, lady."

Andi smiled. Tristan tried so hard to be rough, but she sensed a big, overgrown teddy bear lurking beneath all that ghostly muscle and chain mail. That thought she would wisely keep to herself.

The two made their way through the keep, walking in comfortable silence. The lantern's flames danced on the walls, casting soft shadows that flickered at their passing—or rather, her passing. The thought saddened her. Her lone shadow moved against the aged stone. Tristan's shadow was a thing of the past, and it had been for more years than she could imagine. How had he endured it?

"Drag those gloomy thoughts of yours from your over-worked mind, wench." Tristan looked down at her. "I vow you will have lines embedded in your lovely forehead."

Andi smiled. "I guess you're right." She tucked her hair behind her ears and pushed her hands into her pockets.

As they reached the stairs leading to Tristan's chambers, he stepped to the side and allowed her to pass. "Andrea, I would open the bloody door for you if I could, but—"

"Tristan, honestly." She gave him a warm smile. "I know you would."

He cleared his throat. "Aye, well, then up you go."

Andi did as he asked and walked into his chambers.

Once in the room Tristan lit the lamps with a flick of his wrist. He strode to the far end of the chamber, where a wooden desk sat close to the hearth. Turning, he watched as she made her way across the floor.

Andi smiled and looked around, admiring the sheer masculinity of Tristan's chamber. Pure, raw male. Heavy brocade drapes surrounded the postered bed. The enormous fireplace took up the space of one entire wall. She looked up at Tristan, who stood by his desk, watching her every move. "This," she said, grinning, "is a great room." She walked to him, standing beside him as he leaned a mailed hip against his desk. "So, what do you have to show me?"

Tristan grinned and nodded to a small wooden box, perched on the desk. "Open it, Andrea."

Andi slid a cautious glance at Tristan, then picked up the box. It seemed quite old but well preserved. She lifted the lid and stared at its contents.

Nestled in the bottom of the box was a single silver and emerald earring—the very one she'd lost at Dread-moor twelve years ago, when she'd fallen through the stone steps of the kirk. She lifted her gaze. "How did you find this?"

Tristan shrugged his wide shoulders. "I suppose you intrigued me, even back then." He smiled at her, deep dimples pitting his cheeks. "You were a lovely thing, even at that age. All legs and arms, you were, and so fascinated with my home." He edged closer to her, his dark bangs boyishly falling across one sapphire-blue eye. "After you left, I visited the place where you'd fallen. When I found the bauble, I waited for Jameson's return and had him retrieve it for me." He smiled. "He was curious as to not only who it belonged to, but how it got there. I shrugged it off as though I had no clue and had him place it in a box for safekeeping." He shook his head, his gaze boring into hers. "I've kept it ever since, not knowing if I would ever see you again. 'Tis a day I shall never forget, the day you were here."

"Me neither. You saved my life."

Tristan snorted. "I did no such thing, lady. 'Tis more likely I almost talked you to death. I felt like an inadequate whelp that day, unable to physically help you. Saints, but you could have been terribly hurt." A brief flash of sadness crossed his features. " 'Twas a pitiful showing, to say the least. I even allowed your hand to fall through me. A fine knight I proved to be."

"That is a load of crap, de Barre," she said. "You saved my life that day, and I never stopped thinking of you. I wasn't sure what happened had even really happened, but I never stopped thinking of you."

He lowered his gaze and walked away. "What am I, Andrea? Naught but a spirit, capable of little more than having speech and entertaining you with a few unnatural tricks?" He flicked his wrist and a gust of wind sifted through her hair.

She stared at him until he met her gaze. She lifted her chin. "You became my knight."

He shifted his weight. "What am I now?"

She stared at Tristan, helpless to move. Her heart lurched at his words. What was he asking of her? How much of her extremely pitiful guts did he wish her to spill? She knew what he was. She also knew what he meant *to* her. And she almost kept that knowledge to herself.

If only he hadn't chosen that moment to stop and look up.

It proved to be her complete and utter undoing.

The bare vulnerability in Tristan's eyes stabbed at her heart. They were filled with aching, raw helplessness. A lonesome look of desperation—almost too much for Andi to bear. She moved closer to him, holding his gaze steady. "You are still my knight, Tristan de Barre."

Tristan stared in wonder. How it came to pass that he, a spirit, could possibly have difficulty breathing was beyond his comprehension. He had no bloody lungs, nor the ability to suck in air; yet as he looked into her wide, green-flecked eyes he could not draw a decent breath. Did he dare give voice to his foolish thoughts? His ghostly heart pounded against an equally ghostly chest and he squelched the urge to wipe sweaty palms against his thighs. Devil's horns, he was an idiot!

With what took every ounce of energy he could muster, he released his breath. Letting his eyes wander over the woman before him, he drank in every inch of her trusting face and wished heartily he could touch her, just to see if she was truly as soft as she looked. "Christ, Andrea," he whispered. "I find myself fiercely indebted to Erik de Sabre. 'Twas he who has placed us here, together. . . ."

"Oh, Tristan." Tears made her eyes glassy. "You can't mean that."

"Aye, I do." He moved closer. "I've waited more than seven centuries for you, Andrea Kinley Monroe." He stared at her and felt a prick of guilt for not telling her the truth, or at least the complete truth, of what his men suspected. He wasn't even sure how it could *be*. The men had voiced concerns over evil spirits embodying a live being, but how? And why now, after so many bloody centuries? Aye, it sounded daft, to be sure. For now, he would refrain from telling her. The moment they now drowned in was far too great to give up.

Saints, how he wished he could pull her to him and kiss her. He tasted her in his mind's eye, soft, supple lips moving softly beneath his own, his tongue tasting her sweetness . . .

Andrea lifted a timid hand to his jaw and stared at the place where she would have touched. Slim fingers moved from his cheek to, God help him, his lips, and he stood rigid-still, allowing her the motion. His ghostly heart pounded so hard, the place where it should have rested in his breast ached. He stared, mesmerized by her almost-touch.

"Christ, Andrea," he whispered. "I would give anything to taste you."

She looked at him, eyes darkened glassy, and gave him a wistful smile. "I think I'd let you."

But it could never be.

He sincerely hoped they both could survive the sheer torture about to be bestowed upon them.

Tristan smiled. "Come then, lady. Let us quit this chamber and go for a walk. I vow you need the fresh air."

Was it normal for her heart to feel like it would burst at any moment? Was he really hers? There he stood— tall, powerful, strength radiating, demanding. His broad shoulders corded with muscle, proving his physical strength from years of fighting. Long, dark hair draped in disarray down his back. His thighs were thick, his legs long and powerful, yet he moved with a grace that most men his size could never hope to accomplish.

Then there were his eyes, a blue so clear she felt sure he could read her innermost thoughts. He smiled, and roguish dimples pitted his cheeks, charming the Wellingtons right off her.

Yeah, he could be her knight. *Any old time.*

As they looked over the treetops from the tower, she wondered how it had been centuries before. Had Tristan looked from this same terrace, viewed the same sights as now? How utterly fascinating.

"How long have you known your employer, Andrea?" Tristan asked.

She gripped the cool stone of the terrace and stared

out into the waning light. "Since I was eighteen, I guess. He was my first internship." She looked at him. "Why?"

"Passing curious, is all. You seem powerfully fond of him."

"I am. He's the father I never had. When I began my understudies, he founded the institute, securing a job for me. I wouldn't have made it this far, had it not been for him. He paid my tuition and all university expenses."

The look he gave her sank clear to her bones. "Do you trust him?"

Without missing a beat, she nodded. "With my life."

Tristan paced before the hearth, the tidings still ringing in his head. "There has to be a mistake. Andrea's known him for years. She trusts him with her life, she says." He shoved a hand through his hair. "How could the spirit of Erik overtake a mortal? And why now? It doesn't seem possible."

Stephen, one of his first knights, answered, "How are *we* possible, Tristan? Is it ridiculous for us to reject the idea that Erik found a way to come back, when we ourselves are walking spirits?"

The orange flames filled his vision until it blurred. "Over seven hundred years, Stephen." Tristan turned and looked at his man. "And we've not heard one word uttered regarding Erik de Sabre. Not one." He lifted a shoulder. "So why now?"

"He's fearful your woman has unearthed something, mayhap?" Kail said.

"Or that he's *hopeful* she's unearthed something." Tristan rested his hand on the hilt of his sword.

"Bloody bastard."

Everyone turned their eyes on Marrok. Usually silent, the massive, seasoned knight, once thought by many to be a vicious loup-garou, pulled his brow into a fearsome frown. He turned his penetrating stare to Tristan. "I vow, if ever I'm granted substance, that foul neck of his will be snapped in twain. By me."

Tristan squeezed his loyal friend's shoulder. "Stand in queue, man. There'll be many others craving the like.

Including me." He eyed his men. "But only if it's truly him. We cannot be sure."

"How much do you trust this woman, Tristan? How do you know?"

"I trust her." Tristan turned to each of his men. "She's no part of this, that much I believe. Do not question her worthiness again."

"Aye, her actions proved thusly," said Richard. "You could see it on her face in the pub. She was just as baffled by Erik's behavior as the lot of you."

"How looked he?" asked Gareth, a tall, French-Norman knight whom Tristan had fought many battles with. "Still a woman?"

The men chuckled.

"Aye. He looks the same, other than he keeps his locks trimmed like a hedgehog."

More snickers, a few swears, then silence as Tristan addressed them once more. "If this theory proves truthful, remember that 'tis Erik's spirit who has taken over Andrea's mentor—'tis not Erik himself. And until we know further what is what, our suspicions of his identity shall remain silent to Lady Andrea. She looks upon him as a sire, and no doubt 'twould break her heart, should she know who, or what, we suspect."

A round of "ayes" sounded, and then Tristan made to leave. How he hated the deception, but 'twas unavoidable. "If it is Erik, then no doubt he is after something, and that something is here, at Dreadmoor. Andrea is not safe with him, even if it is just a spirit." He spared one last glance over his shoulder before seeking out his woman. "I vow, if it takes me another seven hundred years, I shall find out the truth of it all."

A few days later, Andi shifted on the hard-packed dirt and peered down at the five-by-five-meter square she'd dug in the dungeon. Having recovered Tristan's mail and helmet—which fascinated her beyond belief—she'd found nothing else except several animal bones and broken pieces of crockery, and a tarnished but stunning piece of jewelry, almost a charm that belonged on a necklace. All of the men disclaimed it, so Andi had determined it'd belonged to the remains.

What did it mean, that Tristan's mail had been buried down here, instead of with his men's? A clue? Or was the murderer just trying to cover up evidence?

With soft, even strokes she brushed the object wedged in the dirt, gently blowing as the hard-packed soil loosened. She knew it was probably just another chicken bone, but continued the excavation anyway, unable to walk away from an ancient object of any sort.

A feeling washed over her, a feeling that was becoming quite common of late. The hairs on her neck rose, and she froze.

"What have you there, lady?"

"Aye, might I see?"

"Not before I, dolt."

Andi slowly lifted her head and peered over the lip of the excavation pit. She swallowed her yelp of surprise as she gaped at three ghostly warriors, all bent over at the waist, watching her work. They looked at her, patiently waiting for an answer. She cleared her throat and smiled. This was definitely something she would have to get used to. "Hello, boys." She brushed the hair from her eyes. "Uh . . ." She glanced back at the object she was working on. "I'm not really sure what it is, actually. Probably just another chicken bone."

Kail, the biggest of the three and Tristan's captain, scratched his head, puzzled. "Why, lady, are you blowing on it?"

"Aye, and scratching at it with that small horse brush?" another said.

She grinned. "Well, it is very old and I have to work with it gently or else it will fall apart." She raised herself to her knees and glanced at the three knights. "Do you guys watch me all the time?"

"Aye, but mostly—" the younger of the knights began.

"Shut you up, lackwit!" Kail's face turned red. "If Tristan heard you he'd—"

"Kick your bloody, worthless arses into the afterlife." Tristan stood on the platform above, arms crossed over his mailed chest, scowling at the knights. Within seconds he stood before them, his expression thunderous. "Kail, you idiot." He jerked a thumb toward the door. "Get you gone from the lady's presence, and take those foul-smelling whelps with you."

Kail cast a sheepish glance at Andi, bowed low, then disappeared. The other two followed without a word.

She smiled up at Tristan. "They weren't hurting anything, you know."

Tristan grumbled. Loudly. "Aye, well, they need not be watching you day and night. 'Tis my duty."

"Oh, I get it." She threw him a saucy grin. "Watching me has now become a duty, has it?"

"Watch it, wench." He knelt down on one knee and peered closely at Andi. "God only knows what happens when I'm provoked." He leaned closer to her, sapphire-blue eyes studying every inch of her face. One corner of his mouth lifted. "You have another dirt smudge on your nose, Andrea."

Andi's heart slammed against her chest. She lifted her hand and rubbed the end of her nose with her forefinger and watched as Tristan's steadfast gaze followed her every move. She wiped her palms on her thighs and changed the subject. Pointing to the object in the dirt she smiled. "I've found something."

Tristan's gaze remained glued to her. "So have I."

Heat crept up her neck and burned her cheeks. "Are you interested?"

"Very."

Andi smiled up at the lord of Dreadmoor and rolled her eyes. "Flirt. I mean in that." She pointed to the object.

Several seconds passed before he dragged his gaze to the thing she pointed at. "And what is it?"

Resuming her position on her stomach, she brushed the edges of the object, a bit firmer this time. It loosened, as she hoped it would, and she brushed a bit more. "I'm not sure." She mumbled more to herself than to Tristan. Blowing softly on it, she gently lifted it for inspection. "Wow. Was I wrong!" She set it down.

Her insides reacted before her brain could register the thought. A huge knot formed in her stomach, just before her mouth went sandpaper dry. She slowly stood, easing out of the pit to stand before Tristan.

He frowned. "What is wrong with you, woman? Your face has gone pure white."

Andi pointed to the scapula in the pit. "A human shoulder blade. Is that," she began, her voice wavering. "It isn't you, is it?"

"Saints, nay."

Andi sighed with relief. "Good." She stared at him, her eyes narrowing. "Why not?"

Tristan barked out a loud, rumbling laugh and shook his head. "God's bones, wench. A moment ago you were nigh onto swooning, thinking 'twas me." He grinned as he took a step closer. "But to satisfy your curious mind, Dr. Monroe, when a soul is cursed, his earthly body does not lie about, waiting for its flesh to rot. It disappears, bones and all, until the curse is lifted." He shrugged. "So say the various and sundry other spirits who frequent my hall."

"I never thought of that, I guess." She glanced back down at the pit and tucked her hair behind her ears. "Then, who is that?"

Tristan stared down at the bone. "I don't know. I never allowed a body to stay in my dungeon. 'Twas always removed and given a Christian burial." He raked a hand through his hair. "But only God knows what de Sabre may have done before my sire arrived."

Andi looked at him, a brow raised in question. "Shall we find out?"

Tristan frowned, his eyes narrowed. "What mean you?"

"Well," Andi said, "no doubt the rest of the remains are down here. I'll finish the excavation and at least be able to sex the skeleton. Maybe find some personal effects you may recognize."

Tristan thought a moment, then took a step closer. He openly stared at Andi, from her feet to the top of her head. "Very well. But you've spent enough time in this drafty place this eve, Andrea." He looked at her, turning his head to the side and peering at her from the corner of his eye. "Proceed digging up the old bones, lady. And make haste. I've not the—"

"Patience nor the stomach for it." She grinned from ear to ear. "Somehow, I couldn't imagine you any other way."

Chapter 19

"Woman, what fascinates you so?"

Fastening the plastic container holding her tools, Andi covered the grid and wiped her hands on her thighs. Taking a step closer, she stared at Tristan's blade, strapped to his hip. "You said before that this looks exactly like your original sword?"

"Aye. In life it was never far from my person. 'Twas given to me by my uncle Killian."

Without thinking, Andi knelt in front of Tristan, pulling her head as close to the sword as she could, her eyes glued to the hilt.

"Um, lady?"

"Hmm?"

A loud, male whistle sounded in the bailey.

Tristan snorted. "I vow the men will tease me mercilessly, if you do not rise from that precarious position on your knees before me."

She looked up and blinked. It took a couple of good, solid seconds to realize just what sort of precarious position she appeared to be in. She fought the urge to flip the whistle-blower the bird. "Ha, ha. You'll just have to be teased." She pointed to the sapphire jewel in his hilt. "I don't know why, but this looks so . . . familiar."

"As well it should. 'Tis portrayed in every single tapestry my mother stitched now adorning the walls of Dreadmoor. 'Tis on my shield, as well. 'Tis the eye of the rampant creature."

"Hmm. Maybe that's it." She stared a bit longer, trying

to place the stone. She'd think on it. It had to be something else.

"Now, if you're through with your investigations for the day, I've much to show you, and I vow 'tis wearisome being out here in this soggy place."

"Well, then." Andi rose and brushed off her knees. "Be it far from me to make you weary." She turned and made for the keep. "Can a ghost run?" Without waiting for an answer, Andi took off, slipping and laughing all the way to the steps of the hall.

She burst through the door, breathless and excited. She pulled off her Wellies and rounded the corner into the kitchen, where she came to an abrupt halt.

Tristan stood against the far wall, arms crossed over his chest and a roguish smile plastered to his face. His dimples pitted his cheeks, giving him a boyish appearance.

He yawned. "What took you so long? I've waited more minutes than I could count." A wide, dimpled grin captured his features. One booted foot was casually crossed over his ankles.

"Cheater." She glanced at Jameson, who smothered a grin behind a kitchen mitt. Andi pointed and laughed out loud. "Jameson, you're smiling!"

Jameson resumed his manicured stance. "I most certainly am not."

"Yes, you are, too. Did you see him, Tristan?" She glanced his way.

Big mistake.

His acute stare shocked her to the bone.

Andi gulped and cleared her throat. "Tristan?"

He blinked, then grinned. "Aye, you smiled, Jameson. I saw it myself."

Miss Kate, who sat at the kitchen table, grinned. "I saw it too, Edgar. Lovely, I might add."

"Humph. I daresay all three of you have spent too much time in the wine cellars of late. Now, what will you have for dinner, Lady Andi? 'Tis getting on in the day and I am about to begin preparations."

"Got any microwave burritos?"

"Heavens, I should hope not."

Tristan cleared his throat in an authoritative manner. "Andrea, you must eat properly. I daresay the things you concoct cannot possibly be healthy for you. And by the saints, you are passing thin." He waved to Jameson, but kept his eyes on Andi. "Prepare her something powerfully healthy, Jameson. She shall need her strength over the next week, I'll warrant."

Andi gulped at that statement. The fact Tristan couldn't seem to take his eyes off her was something to be considered. Raw hunger blazed in his ethereal gaze, burning her insides. Heat rose from somewhere deep within her, straight to the skin covering her face and neck.

She shifted uncomfortably and crossed her arms over her chest. "What are you staring at?" No one had ever given her the time of day, yet Tristan stared at her with such . . . overwhelming desire. She swore she could feel his thoughts. It unnerved her.

She liked it.

Tristan cast a lazy smile. "Forgive my poor manners, lady. 'Tisn't often such loveliness favors the halls of Dreadmoor, such as you and Miss Kate. I vow to make all best efforts, due to my chivalristic training, mind you, to keep my poor eyes in their sockets whilst lecherously gandering at you. And I shall leave the gandering of Miss Kate to *Edgar* over there."

Andi stared at Tristan for a moment, then burst into laughter. "Dreadmoor, you're such a ham."

"Guilty as charged. Now let us be off. I vow you will enjoy an hour or two in the lists watching me joust. Aye?"

Andi crossed the floor to stand beside Jameson. "Anything you fix will be great." She leaned closer to his ear and whispered, "I think everything's going to be okay." With a quick peck to his weathered cheek, she turned to Tristan. "To the lists, then."

Tristan grinned at Jameson, who simply raised his gray eyebrows. "We'll be in the lists." He bowed. "Miss Kate, do try to keep my man in check."

She laughed and smoothed the front of her flowery tunic. "I'll do my best, sir."

Jameson watched the odd pair leave, and allowed an enormous grin to break his face.

"I see that, old man."

Jameson, unmoved by Tristan's stealth, didn't falter a bit. "I'm sure you do, my lord."

"Edgar, you are truly handsome when you smile."

Jameson blushed and gave Miss Kate a nod. "I'm sure I am, lady. Tea?"

Andi stood on the jousting field, surrounded by at least twenty-five to thirty heavily armed and mailed knights, watching as two equally armed and mailed jousters thundered toward one another. One of the jousters had been at the extreme sport for several hours now, and no one had yet unhorsed him. The training field of knights, from only God knew where, anxiously awaited a turn at the lances with the lord of the keep.

Tristan de Barre was, without a doubt, the best.

As Tristan and the other jouster, whom Kail named Stephen, shattered their lances against one another, Andi kept her eye trained on the one knight who captured her attention. Tristan, in one smooth motion, swung his leg over the ghostly horse's neck and landed in the dirt. He drew his sword and advanced onto his opponent. Stephen fought well, Andi had to give that much to him; but Tristan's size alone overwhelmed any challenger.

Tristan's and Stephen's swords clashed, and in a movement so quick Andi nearly missed it, Tristan efficiently knocked his opponent's sword to the ground. Stephen bent over at the waist, trying to catch his breath. Tristan removed his helm and, as he swaggered off, swatted a gasping Stephen on the backside with the flat of his blade.

" 'Twas a good showing, lad," Tristan said. A roguish grin spread across his face. "Mayhap on the morrow I'll let you win."

Stephen grumbled, "Nay, you won't, my lord."

Tristan's deep, rumbling laughter echoed across the

lists. "Aye, you're probably right." He stared at Andi as he made his way through the knights, glaring a time or two at anyone who happened into his path.

He looked determined.

Stopping just a few feet away, he looked up at his captain and glared. "Kail, I'll see to my lady from here. Be you about your business."

Kail winked at Andi and, with utmost respect, laughed out loud. "As you wish, Lord Dreadmoor. I promised young Heath a lesson in polishing armor." He walked off, shaking his head and bellowing at Heath, who was across the field, running in and out of the other knights.

Tristan scowled, then ignored him. "Have you been properly entertained this fine eve, Dr. Monroe?" He tucked his helm under one arm and shifted his weight. "I vow you'll not find a more satisfying bit of medieval sport to watch elsewhere."

Andi laughed. "I'm sure you're right on that one." She looked up and shaded her eyes with her hand against the bright late-afternoon sun. It glinted off the body of a jet as it passed over, just before it ducked behind a cloud. *Wow. Centuries colliding.* She let out a long sigh. "This is so great."

"Aye, it is."

She glanced back at Tristan. The feral stare made her shudder. His gaze lowered to her mouth and lingered there, and Andi had the sudden urge to grab him by the back of his thick neck and pull him to her, so that he could kiss her until she fainted dead away.

Instead, she cleared her throat. "I mean this"—she swept the lists with her hand—"and that." Pointing to the plane in the sky, Andi watched Tristan carefully, waiting for him to look. It was several seconds before he did.

He followed Andi's gaze to the plane, just before it disappeared behind another cloud. " 'Tis an aircraft, Andrea." He looked back down at her. "Even I ceased to be amazed some years ago."

Andi giggled. "No, silly. I mean, well, this!" She once again swept Dreadmoor's grounds with a wide arc. "Here

I am, standing on the training field of a medieval keep, surrounded by medieval knights while they clash swords, curse, scratch, spit, and wait for their turn on the jousting field." She walked a small distance away and was so entranced by her dreamy thoughts that she walked right through a knight, sitting casually on the ground, sharpening his blade. She looked down and smiled. "Sorry, Robert."

" 'Tis naught, lady."

Tristan stood and watched Andrea's enthusiastic amazement. A smile tugged at his mouth—an act that seemed to occur more and more frequent these days. The saucy wench had learned the names of his entire garrison—as well as a few extras who'd strayed in for sport. She drank in the sights and smells of his home. 'Twas vastly amazing. Saints, *she* was amazing.

Stopping short of the jousting field, she swung around. "And all the while a jet flies overhead, oblivious of all going on down here. Oblivious there are brave knights who fought bloody battles and saved and lost lives—centuries ago—making our world possible today. Oblivious that down here lives the most chivalristic and brave knight of all." She ran back over to Tristan, who stood with his arms crossed over his chest, the grin on his face unavoidable. She stopped in front of him. "I feel privileged." She panted as she grinned and bravely took a step closer to Tristan. "Thank you."

Thank you. Mayhap those simple words passed unnoticed by most, especially in the twenty-first century. But as he stared into the hazel depths of Andrea Monroe's eyes, he knew those words came from her heart. Damnation, he was becoming such a pitiful sap. " 'Tis naught, wench. But damn me if I wouldn't swing from the bloody battlements by my toes, just to get such a smile cast my way. You are most welcome, indeed. But 'tis I who should be thanking you."

"Me? Why?"

"For making me feel again." He openly drank in every

inch of her, from the top of her head to the sneakers she wore, lingering a bit longer on her mouth. "By the devil's horns, I want to kiss you. To feel your soft, full lips under mine, to taste you, smell you." He drew close, his mouth inches from hers. " 'Tis enough to make me bloody witless." He traced her jaw with a thumb, lingering on the air above her lips. "You, Dr. Monroe, are passing beautiful."

She gulped, her cheeks turning a bright shade of pink.

"And your blush is charming. I would kiss you soundly, right here in the lists, had I the substance to do so."

Andi could do nothing but stand and stare, caught in Tristan's spell. His deep, raspy voice washed over her in a way that caused her skin to heat, her lips to tremble, as though he were really touching her. They stood facing one another, right in the middle of the training field. Knightly ghosts surrounded them, some at swordplay, some in groups discussing whatever it was medieval knights discussed in the twenty-first century. Andi barely noticed any of them; only the one facing her now. No more than a foot of space separated them, and even that seemed like too much distance. She leaned her head back to look Tristan full in the face. Her knees wobbled.

His features weren't gentle; they were far from it. He'd been a seasoned warrior during his life, and it showed. Small nicks and scars, evidence of the brutality of his time, graced his skin. He had a strong jaw, shadowed with a day's growth of beard she doubted ever left, even if shaven. Full lips, straight white teeth, and the cutest hint of a cleft in his chin. His hair, black as night, rested in disarray well below his shoulders. God, even his Adam's apple was sexy. *Breathtaking* hardly described him.

But when he smiled—good Lord, that dimpled smile could melt her on the spot! His hardened features took on a boyishness when he grinned. No doubt he made sure not to smile during battle. Or maybe it didn't come across the same way to another man. . . .

"Lady?"

She blinked a time or two, then focused on the cause of her daydreams. "Yes?"

Tristan smiled lazily. "I can only hope those are thoughts of me causing such a tender look upon your face."

Andi's blush deepened. "You are conceited, Tristan de Barre."

"Aye." He leaned a bit closer to her. "I've been rumored as such."

"My point is," she began, then lost all conscious thought as Tristan smiled at her—again. "I'm hungry. Starved, even."

"So am I."

Andi tried to ignore that comment, but she felt her face flame. Tristan's satisfactory grin proved she could no more ignore anything he did than stop breathing. "Well, then, I'm going to go scrounge around in the kitchen to—"

"Your blush is passing lovely, Andrea."

Another impossible comment to ignore, to her way of thinking. "Well, you may take my blushes as a compliment, Lord Dreadmoor, for I can promise you no one else has ever coaxed them out of me before."

"You jest."

"Nope. You're the first."

He inclined his head as he studied her face, daring to lean closer; so close, in fact, she feared he might pass right through her. "Well, then." His voice deepened. "That is a compliment, in truth. And I dare another soul to try and wrench such a feat from me."

Andi sincerely doubted anyone ever would.

"Kate," Andi asked as she joined the older woman in front of the hearth in the great hall. "Can I ask you something?"

Kate smiled and patted her hand. "Of course you can, love. What's troubling you?"

Andi glanced to the corner, where Heath and Jameson sat across from one another, chess set between them, with Tristan and his knights in various stools surrounding the game.

"Ah, 'tis a heavy thing on your mind, eh?" Kate asked. "Go ahead, girl. After taking all this in, there's nothing you could say to shock me."

Andi smiled at the Scottish woman with the light and charming brogue. "It's strange, Kate."

Kate giggled before Andi could say anything else. "Aye, girl, 'tis strange all right. Look at that lot of ghostly hooligans playing board games with Edgar and Heath." She shook her head. "Who would ever have dreamed something as such existed?"

Andi nodded. "I know. I'm . . . stunned. Even more so that I'm falling for Tristan." She met Kate's puzzled gaze. "I can't seem to help it. I haven't known him long, but what I know, I like. Maybe even . . . more than like."

A warm smile split Kate's face. "Oy, girl, 'tis Lord Dreadmoor who you fancy, eh?" She nodded. "I can't say that I blame you. He's quite a dish."

Andi laughed. "Yeah, he's that all right." She turned her stare toward Tristan, who cursed as Jameson made a bad move on the game. "He's so much more than that, though. He's . . . not like other men."

"Nay, you can't say too many modern-day chaps can measure up to that one," Kate said. "Or the whole lot of Dragonhawk's knights, for that matter. So what worries you?"

Andi pushed the hair from her eyes. "You mean other than the fact he's dead?"

With a snort, Kate patted Andi's arm. "Pah! Only a minor setback, I'd say."

With a lowered voice, Andi blushed. "I can't stop thinking about him. He drives me crazy."

A knowing gleam lit Kate's wise eyes. "I'll bet he does, lass."

Laughing, Andi shook her head. "It is just . . . gosh, I can't even describe it. Natural? To be with him, that is. It doesn't seem all that strange to me. Me! The logical scientist."

Kate took both of Andi's hands in her own. "Let your

heart lead you, love, and don't let all that fancy education and book smarts change your course. If you've the strength to love him without all the usual . . . amenities, such as touching and sex, and bearing his children, then don't you hold back." She glanced at Tristan. "A woman who can call that man hers has a true champion by her side. Ghost or not."

Andi looked up to find Tristan's gaze fixed on her. It sent a wave of warmth through her.

God, she hoped she had the strength for it.

Christ, he hoped he had the strength for it.

Tristan watched as Andrea slept. Mayhap 'twasn't the most chivalristic of things, to be standing over the woman whilst she slumbered. Watching. But by the saints' robes, he could not seem to help himself.

Damnation, he wanted more.

Had he substance, no doubt chivalry would have long ago left him.

A painful need unlike any he'd experienced, even whilst alive, gripped him as he let his eyes roam over Andrea's sleeping form. Moonlight streamed in from the open shutters, throwing her barely garbed body in a myriad of shadows and glow. 'Twas enchanting. 'Twas . . . enticing.

He drew closer.

One arm rested above her head, the other draped easily against her exposed belly. Her breasts rose and fell with each breath, and Tristan found himself entranced by the movement as her sleeveless tunic pulled against her skin. He itched to touch her, to run his hands over every fair inch . . .

"Hi."

Tristan nearly jumped out of his ghostly skin. Andrea's voice, heavy with slumber, seared straight through him.

"Forgive me. I—"

"It's okay," she said, and sat up just enough to prop her head with her hand, which in turn lifted her tunic to expose more of her luscious belly. "I felt you beside me."

Tristan swiped a hand across his jaw. By the saints, he was a nervous whelp.

"Sit here," she said, patting the empty space beside her. "Beside me."

No mirth in her voice, and as a matter of fact, Tristan thought he caught a bit of shyness. He rather liked it. With no more than a thought, his sword and heavy mail disappeared, emerging on the floor in a heap, leaving him wearing his tunic, hose, and boots.

He sat down.

And noticed quite suddenly his thigh rested rather close to a scantily clad Andrea Monroe. Those plaid trews she seemed so powerfully fond of had ridden up her hip, exposing a goodly amount of long leg.

However the means, she took his breath away.

He could take it no longer.

Lowering himself, he rested on his elbow and stared with a boldness that even surprised him, given the situation. His eye roamed down those impossibly long legs, back up to linger at her flat midriff, and a bit higher to her breasts, which to his notion, were just right.

He slowly raised his gaze eye level to hers. "Don't mistake this for disrespect," he said, leaning closer to her. "I just can't seem to . . . help myself." He lifted one finger to her jaw, not touching but simply hovering over her skin. The shell of her ear fascinated him next, then the soft fall of her hair. Entranced, he traced her collarbone, then ran along the low-dipped collar of her tunic.

Then, God help him, lower.

Her breath hitched.

He watched the movement of his knuckles as they grazed the swell of Andrea's breast, rising and falling, a bit faster, with each breath. "Christ, if I could but touch you in truth."

Her hand skimmed over his thigh. "I'd give anything if you could."

Tristan's groin stirred, and he had to think twice about the sensation. He hadn't thought it could occur, him being naught but a spirit.

He was, to put it bluntly, dead wrong.

Andrea moved over, just slightly, a silent invitation for him. He took it, and lay on his side next to her, his weight braced by his elbow.

He moved his free hand to her hip, marveling at the lush curves. "You've awakened something powerfully fierce in me, Andrea." His eyes lifted to hers. "Were I a live man, I could not assure your reputation."

"Funny," she countered, her hand moving to his hand, "I was about to say the same thing to you."

Tristan gave a quiet laugh, then leaned closer, his eyes boring into the most lovely green-flecked orbs he'd ever seen. "Close your eyes, Andrea," he said.

Without hesitation, she did.

He ducked his head, bringing his lips to her ear. " 'Twould be a lie to say our joining would be slow and sensual," he whispered, raking the back of his knuckle over her cheek. "I would be fair overcome by you, the first time." He slid his fingers through her hair. "I vow the second time, though," he said, and she opened her eyes and met his gaze, "and the third, 'twould last until morn."

With a hesitant hand, Andrea, not more than a mere few inches away, skimmed her fingers over his lips, then licked her own.

Tristan nearly came undone.

"This actually hurts," she said.

He paused, wondering at the thunder of his own heart. "What mean you?"

Slowly, her hand traced his throat, then drifted across his chest, where it lingered before she lifted her gaze. "Wanting you so badly."

"Christ, woman," he said, his mouth hovering above hers. "I vow I can taste you. And were I able, there would not be a single inch left I wouldn't devour."

Tristan heard her gulp.

Then Andrea smiled, and the wistful look nearly knocked him off the bed. He could have sworn he saw her chest thumping beneath that painfully thin tunic.

"I've never been seduced before," she said. "I . . . like it."

Tristan felt his heart crack. Andrea's sincerity tore a hole in him he seriously doubted would ever close.

He placed a hand over hers, which rested just above the place where his heart would have been, had he been alive.

"I'll never be able to satisfy your body's cravings, Andrea. This is all I have to offer, and 'tis paltry, to my notion."

Her eyes darkened. "It's not paltry to me. It's actually pretty sexy."

He smiled and prayed she knew what she said. "Then I will forever endeavor to satisfy your desires." He slid his thumb across the air above her sweet lips. "But 'tis the most painful endeavor I've ever embarked upon."

Then she yawned a most unlady-like yawn, and her eyes drifted shut. "Stay tonight, will you? I like this."

Beasties couldn't drag him from her side.

Chapter 20

"Lady, if I may ask. What baffles you so about the markings?"

With a light touch, Andi traced the mystical dragonhawk on Tristan's shield. "I don't know, Jason. It seems odd, but when I look at it, I get a weird feeling in the pit of my stomach." She looked at him. "As if I've seen it before, but can't place it."

Having set up the downstairs study as a makeshift laboratory, Andi studied the displayed weapons now lying on protective coverings atop various folding tables, trying to concentrate on her job. Quite a difficult task, when she could think of nothing but Tristan and his sensual words and almost-touches. "I get the same feeling when examining a few other pieces, too."

"Which ones?"

She thought a minute. "The tapestries. Tristan's sword." She turned and met Jason's gaze. "And Tristan."

"By the saints," he said in a low voice. "What could that mean?"

"That's what I can't figure out." She pointed to the creature. "What do you make of it? I mean, I know you've looked at this same picture for centuries, but when you look at it"—she pointed to the dragonhawk—"the tapestries, and Tristan's sword, what do you think of?"

Jason drew his head close to the shield and studied it first. "I vow 'tis shaped like an eye of sorts, that stone.

No lashes, no brow, but an eye all the same. 'Tis the same color as Tristan's own eyes. Passing odd, I'll warrant."

A thought hit her, and she felt as if she'd been struck by a fastball.

"Oh my God."

Jason turned his head. "What is it, lady?"

"Jason, you're amazing. I can't believe I haven't picked up on it before." She swept the room with a final look, turning in a circle. "Where's Tristan?"

"Right. Well," Jason stammered. "He is having speech in the solar with his captain. He expects to be down, straightaway. I've been given the pleasure of occupying your time thusly."

"No, this can't wait." Without a backward glance, she rushed to the great hall and up the stairs.

"Lady! I beseech you! Wait!" Jason called after her.

Throwing a quick glance over her shoulder, she watched as Jason disappeared. *Wonder what's got into him.* Rounding the corner of the passageway, Andi hurried to Tristan's solar, where Jason materialized again.

"Lady!"

What a sweet kid, she thought. But she didn't have time to stop and give him assurance of her well-being. Not now. This might not be as big as she thought, but later couldn't wait. She needed to know. Now.

Pausing at the solar, Andi eased open the door. Richard's embittered voice stopped her.

"I care naught what that filth means to Andrea, nor whose mortal body he's claimed. He is a loathsome, foul idiot whom I mean to find a way to rid the world of."

Several "ayes" sounded, mixed with a few venomous curses.

Andi's heart nearly stopped. Who was Richard talking about?

"Sirs!" Jason pleaded from inside the chamber, but no one seemed to hear him over the heated discussion.

"She needs to know," Kail said. "We've got to tell—"

"Nay, we do not!" Tristan growled each word as a

threat. "We tell her nothing. 'Tis none of her concern. She's here to do a job, that is all. Naught more." Silence, then, "Swear it," he commanded.

"Sirs, I beg you, cease!"

Tears stung Andi's eyes as she stood at the door, stunned. Unsure what to do, she turned, only to find herself face-to-face with a woeful-looking Jason, who'd materialized once more before her. His big, sad brown eyes made her hesitate. She almost ran, ready to pretend the harsh words hadn't been heard.

Then she changed her mind.

The voices screeched to a deafening silence when Andi slipped inside the room. Fourteen medieval knights stared at her. Her gaze pierced only one.

"Andrea, I—"

She shook her head. "Don't. I want to know." She ticked off the numbers on one hand. "One, why 'tis none of my concern. Two, who the loathsome foul idiot is. And three, why I'm here." She lifted a shoulder. "Just to do a job." She paused, then mimicked Tristan, " 'Naught more.' "

Tristan rounded the desk and moved toward her, their eyes locked. "You know not what you say, lady."

"I know what I heard. I know poor Jason tried to warn you that I was right outside the door, but you guys were bickering so loud, none of you heard him."

After a long, exasperated sigh, Tristan pinched the bridge of his nose and shook his head. "Leave us," he ordered his men.

One by one, without meeting her gaze and without question to their lord, the knights left the chamber. Only Jason remained.

Tristan inclined his head to the door. "You too, lad."

Andi turned to the young knight. "I'll be fine. Go."

He gave her a somber nod, hesitated only a moment, then disappeared through the door.

"You do not understand what you heard," Tristan said.

Andi looked at him. A coldness settled within her insides, making her stomach feel shaky. Giving him the benefit of the doubt, she took a deep breath. "Yeah, and apparently I wasn't supposed to. So make me."

Moments passed before he answered. "Christ, this is passing difficult." A curse muttered from his mouth. " 'Twas not supposed to be this way."

"What way? What have you been keeping from me? God, I'm so stupid." Moving to the window, she gripped the sill and stared out at the gray clouds churning over the choppy North Sea. Without turning around, she pressed her forehead to the glass. "I trusted you."

A movement, more like a fine breeze, stroked her cheek. Tristan's voice dropped to a hoarse whisper against her ear. "You can trust me now, Andrea. I vow it."

Turning, she shuddered as she stared into piercing eyes. His body crowded her, caged her in, and although she knew it would take only the briefest of movements to pass through him, she remained locked in his ghostly hold. Breathless, she waited for him to continue.

"I've something to tell you, lass, and you won't like it. You may not even believe me. I'm not even sure I believe it myself. 'Tis why I've kept it from you this long."

Full, masculine lips formed each word, and Andi followed the movement with utter fascination. Small lines formed at the corners of his eyes, and a white, silvery scar nicked his chin. Her heart thumped wildly against her ribs, and breathing became difficult, pinching inside her lungs. "Tell me."

No hesitation, no loss of eye contact. "We believe your Kirk Grey is my murderer, Andrea. Erik de Sabre. Rather, his spirit."

The words sounded in her ears, chimed through her head, but they didn't quite seem to touch base. She frowned. "Excuse me?"

A muscle tightened in his jaw. "If 'tis true, he is dangerous, and I—"

Scooting past him, she stopped and turned. "What are you talking about, Tristan? Have you gone crazy? Kirk is just Kirk. I've known him nearly my whole life. He's like a father to me."

"Aye. As he was to us, as well."

Her head ached with the accusation. "It's crazy. There's no way he could be Erik de Sabre. That makes no sense at all."

Tristan moved toward her, his features set, determined. "And all this makes sense?" He swept his hand down his body. "You can accept that my men and I are spirits from the thirteenth century, but you can't fathom your man Kirk has been taken over by Erik's spirit?" He drew closer. "Truly?"

The air began to tighten in her lungs, trapping the normal route of breathing, forcing her to take short, gasping breaths. "It. Can't. Be." She glanced around the room, drew a lungful of air, then turned back to Tristan. "Why do you think this?"

He raked a big hand through his long black hair. "I had a few of my men follow you into the village when you met him for supper. They didn't identify him immediately, but recognized his voice, his mannerisms."

"That's insane. Couldn't they be mistaken?"

He shook his head. " 'Tis possible, I suppose. Mayhap he is an ancestor? But the men know his mannerisms, well and true. They had no second thoughts on the matter. Evil spirits have been known to possess mortals before, Andrea."

Silence jammed the room, the pressure of it squeezing her ears. Kirk had been the only person she'd considered family for all of her life. He loved her. No way was he this . . . thing Tristan and his men claimed. "I can't accept this, Tristan. Kirk loves me. He's real. My hand doesn't slip through him." She pleaded with her eyes. "So what does that make him, if I've done all those things?"

The harsh planes and beard-shaded angles of Tristan's handsome face tightened into a dangerous expression. "An abomination."

He might as well have hit her. Like a steel fist, it hit her square in the gut, robbing her of breath, of reasonable thought. With one last look, she moved closer, wishing she could grab Tristan by the collar of his tunic and shake him until he realized how wrong he was. "I've got to see for myself. He's the only family I have, Tristan. My only anchor."

Towering over her, he lowered his head, his mouth to her ear. "You've got me, Andrea. Do not forget it."

Had Tristan been alive, their bodies would be separated only by a whisper of air. Her heart raced, her mind twisted as she tried to distinguish fantasy from reality. Kirk was real. He'd been there for her all these past years. The only person who cared about her. She had to make Tristan understand that he and his men were mistaken. They were wrong.

Slowly, she lifted her hand to Tristan's chest. For a moment, she thought she felt his heart hammering under her fingertips.

Then, with the slightest effort, she pushed against him. And her hand passed through him.

Fantasy.

A tear slipped down her cheek. "I've got to go." Determined not to allow the imprint of his anguished face to pit her memory, she turned and made for the door.

Tristan pushed between her and the heavy oak, blocking her exit. "Do not, Andrea. I won't allow it. 'Tis dangerous." He drew his head closer. "De Sabre is dangerous. If he's inside your mentor, you will not be safe."

Hazel eyes challenged blue ones, frown against frown. "He is not de Sabre, he's not possessed by Erik's evil spirit, and he's not dangerous. He is a researcher, Tristan. Nothing more. And I'm going to prove it to you. Now please. Move."

He stared at her for a long time, his chest heaving, the veins in his throat standing out. Finally, he pushed off with a frustrated growl and walked off, without a word.

Andi cracked the door and slipped out.

By the saints, what had he done? Had he been such a fool to think he could keep this from her? Aye, he had. Damnation, she'd looked wounded. It'd nearly cracked his heart in twain, just to look at her fallen face.

Desolate. Aye, he had known the feeling, for longer than he would like to. But what to do now? She was determined to prove them wrong, and he didn't blame her. He wasn't even sure himself that her employer and de Sabre shared the mortal body. But how would he or any of his men persuade her? They had no proof, other than their own witness. If Erik had taken over Kirk Grey, how and when had it happened? The day he came to aid Andi? Even if that were so, no doubt the bloody bastard would lie through his immortal teeth, just to keep the secret.

He quit the solar, determined to follow her. Instead, he met his steward's disapproving glare, along with thirteen others.

"You heard, I suppose?" he asked Jameson. He knew his men had eavesdropped.

"I did, my lord."

"She's leaving."

"I gathered as much."

"Well, don't just stand there and glare at me, old man. What should I bloody do?" Tristan stared Jameson down, as if that might scare the man into revealing the secret to undo his drastic mistake.

It did not work.

"That, my young lord," Jameson said, "is something only you can remedy. Now, I've got to see to Dr. Monroe. She is terribly upset." With a slight nod he turned and left, leaving Tristan alone with his men.

"Well?" Kail asked. "Did she believe?"

Tristan shook his head. "Nay, she did not. And I've not a clue how to make her. Bloody hell, I don't want her to go, especially alone. 'Tis dangerous—more than she understands. Erik is responsible for not only my own death and yours, but more likely than not, countless others. Using Grey's mortal body, there's no telling what he will do." He pinched the bridge of his nose. "Christ."

"The whelp is already on her heels, Tristan."

Tristan nodded. "Good. Nine more of you go, as well. That way, we'll be able to know her whereabouts at all times, and make bloody damn sure she remains safe.

The constable shall be called at the first sign of disorder. Understood?"

"Aye," said all thirteen knights. They separated, ready to follow Andrea.

Hopefully, they would not have to keep vigil for long.

He wanted his woman home. And by the saints, he'd have it so.

"The ghosties chasin' ye off, I gather." Gibbs gave a knowing nod. "I figured as much, but ye lasted a bit longer than we—er, I thought." He pulled away from the gatehouse and turned his old, beat-up cab down the rocky path.

Andi ignored him and tried her best not to look back. She knew if she did, she'd bawl like a baby, or worse, throw herself from the cab and crawl back up to the castle.

Unfortunately, being hardheaded was one of her less desirable traits.

She turned around.

Tristan stood on the battlements, staring after her. There he stood, his bulky arms crossed over his bulkier chest, his long black hair whipping across his face as if the wind could actually touch him. He wore his usual black tunic over his mail, his sword strapped to his side. He looked just as real as any man. Only, he wasn't. He was a ghost.

And she'd hurt him by leaving. She knew it. She hadn't even been able to tell him about the connection she'd made. That would have to come later. This thing with Kirk . . . it needed to happen now. She had to know. Had to prove them all wrong.

She turned and looked at the road ahead.

The road leading away from Dreadmoor.

The same road leading away from Tristan.

Andi knew, at that very moment, she loved the man standing on the battlements. Lord of Dreadmoor. Tristan de Barre. Dragonhawk. Brave thirteenth-century knight.

A ghost.

Chapter 21

Foul did not even begin to describe his mood.

More like corpse-rotting, vermin-infested, a hundred disgusting flies swarming around an impaled, decaying . . .

Foul.

Tristan attacked his captain again, parrying and thrusting with a ferocity he hadn't used since he was alive and warring. The seven-foot giant finally begged off. Tristan swore in French-Norman, then spat on the ground and stormed away.

"Damnation, Tristan." Kail threw his arms up. "You're naught but ill to be around these days. What has befallen you?"

Tristan stopped in midstride and stared at Kail. "You know what damn well bloody sits ill with me, fool. Why ask?"

"Because there is not a soul left at Dreadmoor, living or not, that can put up with your poor humor a moment longer. Even Jameson has been heard murmuring about going on holiday, just to rid himself of your sourness." He glared, one eyebrow raised skyward. "What say you to that?"

Tristan strode back to his captain and soundly planted his fist in Kail's nose. "That's what I've got to say about it." 'Twas illusionary, the solid hit, but it felt good just the same. He turned and headed back the way he'd been going, which was absolutely nowhere.

Until he found a seven-foot, three-hundred-pound warrior on his back.

They hit the ground in a cloud of conjured-up dust, grunting and swearing until Kail straddled Tristan, pinning him to the ground with his oaklike arms.

"Get off me, you witless idiot." Tristan bucked and bared his teeth.

"Nay, I won't until I am passing sure you will end this ridiculous game." He grunted as Tristan thrashed to get free. "My lord."

Tristan lay there, beneath his captain who would surely pay later for his acts, breathing hard as if he actually had a pair of lungs to use the air around him. He closed his eyes and begrudgingly gave up. " 'Tis much easier to be foul than admit a wrong."

Kail gave Tristan a good push in the chest and got up. "Aye, 'tis a certainty, I'm sure. I'm not one to be wrong overmuch. Therefore I am less likely to know the feeling."

"Shut up, Kail."

Kail laughed. "Well?"

Tristan pulled his knees up and rested his arms against them. "I love her, dolt. And I'm passing weary of this waiting."

Kail snorted. "Then 'tis you who is the dolt, for if it were my lady, I would—"

"What? Just what would you do, oh mighty wise one on the matter of wenches?" Tristan grinned, the first time since Andi had left him.

"I would go after her. My lord."

Tristan cuffed Kail in one of his big ears. "Don't be stupid, man. You know I cannot leave the grounds."

"Aye, but you could call her, couldn't you? That is what I would do, were I you."

"And what?" Tristan jumped to his feet and began to pace. "She left because I deceived her. That is something that cannot be changed."

"She left to prove you, and us, wrong. The lads have been keeping an eye on her. It seems she's been unable to contact him. He's left for an important meeting of sorts. She is safe."

Tristan looked across the bailey as his remaining men trained. 'Twas more of a habit, and one of the few medieval things they enjoyed. Dust hung in the air at the jousting field, illusioned as it was. He turned back to his captain. "So?"

"So there's where you have something to decide on your own, little lad," he said, turning to leave. He stopped and glanced back. "By the by, friend, I am truly sorry I encouraged you to keep things secretive from the lady."

Tristan held up a hand. "Nay, Kail. There is no need for that, and you know it. Besides, you have groveled for two days solid. I cannot stomach it for another bloody moment. Now begone."

Kail grinned at Tristan. "You truly are a good friend. Now I'm off. I believe those pups at the lances need a bit of leadership." He slapped Tristan's shoulder as he passed. "Good luck, my lord. You, I do believe, shall need it." He walked away, shaking his head.

Tristan stared after him, unable to stop the smile spreading across his face. "Witless beast."

"I heard that, and I thank ye for such a fine compliment."

Tristan turned and made for the kitchens, where he knew Jameson would more than likely be.

Hopefully, near the phone.

He, Tristan de Barre of Dreadmoor, fearless knight of the thirteenth century, had a telephone call to make. And damn him, why hadn't he done the like sooner?

" 'Ere's ye check, missy."

Andi glanced at the waiter, checked her tab, and handed him five pounds. "Thanks." She rose to leave.

"Don't ye want to take that with ye?" He pointed to her half-eaten plate. "Ye've barely touched yer haddock."

Andi smiled. "No, thanks." She absently stepped out of the small chippy and into the bustling crowd of Berwick shoppers. She barely noticed any of them, or the rain splattering her blouse.

Although she had stormed from Dreadmoor to prove something, her mind habitually returned to one thing.

Actually, to one person.

Tristan.

She couldn't stop thinking of him. The first day hadn't been too bad. She was mad at him for deceiving her, and even more angry for accusing Kirk of being Erik de Sabre. She tried to stay mad, best she could. And it might have worked, had Tristan not sent her a personal guard of about ten big, burly, ghostly knights, in full battle gear. That made matters even more difficult.

They were posted outside her door. They were loitering in the lobby of the inn. They were stationed outside the inn. All in their invisible state, mind you, but there just the same. Jason had told her as much. In the evenings, they would take turns visiting her, sharing with her tales of Tristan's sorrow; how he moped around, missing her so. But she didn't want to hear it from them. She wanted to hear it from Tristan. So the garrison, even with their good intentions, was nothing but reminders of a particular overgrown lout of a knight whom she desperately missed.

To make matters worse, Kirk couldn't be reached. He'd left to inspect another find, this one close to Edinburgh. It ticked her off, really. He'd called in a senior intern from another research team to take over as site manager, and he hadn't even told her. She had run out to the dig, just to make sure things were being handled properly. They were, which made her feel somewhat better. Supposedly, though, Kirk had been interested in a medieval sword, or what was left of it, and took off. He wouldn't answer his mobile, either. So she'd decided to wait.

Not that waiting helped matters—any of them.

She'd eaten three tubes of cookie dough, to the horror of her guard, in an attempt to drown her sorrows and put the arrogant man out of her thoughts. It did nothing but hinder her appetite and give her a raging stomach-ache. That led to several parental scoldings from the garrison about how raw dough was not good for one's entrails. Finding a grocer who even sold a tube of cookie dough had been a miracle on its own.

It hadn't helped anyway. Tristan remained firmly imprinted in her mind, with or without the ghostly garrison to remind her, and he apparently wasn't budging.

She'd had a lot of time to think. It was unfathomable that Kirk Grey could be something as ridiculous as possessed. But she currently kept company with a handful of thirteenth-century knights. Who was she to say what was fathomable and what wasn't?

Still . . . it was Kirk. She'd known him nearly her whole life. She just couldn't wrap her brain around it.

Andi stepped to the curb to flag down a cab, then thought better of it and turned to walk the three miles to the quaint little inn she'd stayed at for two nights. Sneaking past her overprotective guardsmen earlier had been tricky, but she'd managed. Had it not been for the fire escape stairs off the balcony of her room, and the fact that she wasn't afraid of heights, she would never have managed it.

A short outing, alone, helped clear her thoughts—at least she'd thought it would. So she'd slipped out the back and disappeared into the crowd, walked for a while, then attempted a seminutritious meal.

Then she saw him.

Blending with the crowd, she endured being bumped and knocked about like a rag doll. A hundred people must have passed her, probably even brushed her. Then a flash of black silk caught her eye. Kirk? It couldn't be. He didn't wear chic, black attire. His baggy khakis and untucked cotton shirts were trademark and unmistakable. But so were his salt-and-pepper hair and goatee. She'd called out to him, but he hadn't heard over the crowd of shoppers.

Then, without realizing what she was doing, her feet, seemingly of their own will, turned to follow him.

He walked fast but graceful, with long, purposeful strides, knowing where he was going and apparently in a big hurry to get there. Kirk's normal pace was lanky and easygoing. Or was Tristan's talk of evil spirits inhabiting her mentor making her see things that really weren't there?

Why hadn't Kirk answered the mobile? Maybe he'd just gotten in?

A thought struck her. He could be meeting someone. A woman, perhaps. That had to be it. Kirk had found female company. Normal thing for a virile, healthy fiftyish year old man to do. That would explain the fancy clothes.

Andi dodged the passersby and started up the sidewalk. Seconds later, Kirk ducked into a street-side pub.

She toyed with the idea of following him in, but something held her back. Maybe the crazy ideas Tristan had put in her head caused her to hesitate? Either way, she paused. And that alone made her uncomfortable.

Posting herself in the bus stop cubby, she took a seat on the bench and waited. Only a few minutes, she thought, and then she'd go in after him—even if he did have a date. But one way or another she was going to get some answers.

Forty-five minutes later, Andi decided to enter the pub. What other option did she have? None. Her rain-soaked jeans clung to her skin, making her itch. Her hair was soaked, and she was just plain tired of sitting at the bus stop. Plus, it grew late and she had no desire to be on the streets of Berwick-upon-Tweed after dark. It was bad enough she'd have to explain herself to the garrison once she returned, and she didn't look forward to that at all. So instead she stood, weaved through the crowd, and took a deep breath before pushing the pub's door open.

Empty, save the bartender wiping the counter.

He looked up at her, expressionless. "Can I help ye?"

Andi cleared her throat and took a few hesitant steps in. "Uh, I'm not sure." She shifted her bag to her other hand and wiped her free hand on her thigh. Her eyes scanned the room. "Did a man dressed in black come in here a couple of hours ago? With a goatee?"

The bartender stopped wiping and stared at her. "Missy, do ye know how many folk come in and out of this place?" He continued to stare when Andi didn't answer. "Nay, girly, I don't remember no bearded man."

Andi swept the room again, then shrugged. "Sorry. I must have been mistaken. Thanks anyway." She turned and left the pub, puzzled.

An uneasiness crept over her as she hurried to her room at the inn.

Where had Kirk gone, and how, exactly, had he gotten past her? Ugh. It would drive her nuts until she spoke to him.

Moments later, Andi turned the corner and realized the magnitude of her big, fat, idiotic mistake.

Sneaking off from her ghostly guards was something she should have considered before doing it. Right out in plain sight, right by the inn's front door, stood Sir Richard, a six-and-a-half-foot bulging mass of medieval knight, arms crossed over his mailed chest, an enormous scowl plastered to his face.

Not a happy camper.

And only in Berwick would passersby completely ignore a giant man in medieval armor.

Sir Richard glared at Andi. "You, my lady, have some explaining to do."

Andi could do nothing but smile. He'd stood outside the inn and watched out for her, except for those times he'd convinced another of the garrison to switch places with him, and then he insisted on being at Andi's door. "I just needed a little break, Richard. That's all." She took a few steps to the inn's door, then turned back to him. "Are you mad at me?"

Richard looked quite uncomfortable at the question. He shifted his weight and shrugged, his mail creaking in protest. Then he gruffly cleared his throat a time or two. "Nay, of course not. Now get you upstairs and have a hot bath, before you catch your death out here in this bloody bog." He cast a glance down at her, and she smiled. He made another extreme effort to clear his throat, and then jerked a thumb to the stairs inside the inn, indicating for her to get moving. "Get you gone now, and make sure you allow us to follow you next time, aye?"

Andi grinned and tucked her hair behind her ear. "Sure. I'll see you later, Richard." Andi hurried past him and into the inn. She'd tell Richard later about seeing Kirk. Tell him now, and he and the others would harass her without mercy.

Andi rushed past the check-in desk, nodded to the clerk, then headed for the stairs. The plush carpeting muted her brisk footsteps; but even that didn't help. There were four more knights posted outside her room, arms crossed over their chests, some leaning against the wall, others sitting on the floor. She peeked around the corner at them.

"Lady!"

Jason was probably all of seventeen years old, but he proved to be the biggest mother hen of them all. The others all jumped at his cry, then rushed toward Andi like a pack of football players. "Where have you been, lass? We have been worried sick o'er ye!"

"I'm sorry, guys." She fumbled for the room key in her pocket, then opened the door. "I just needed to get out for a while. Besides." She flashed them a reassuring smile. "I'm all right." She looked up at Jason, whose unsure look of worry nearly broke her heart. "I promise. Really."

The giants grumbled but nodded their acceptance. Jason stepped into the room behind her, as was his usual routine. The hiss of his sword being drawn sounded so real to Andi's ears, she had to remind herself he forced the illusion. Once satisfied no one lurked in Andi's room, Jason sheathed his sword and came to stand before her. "I missed you today, lady." He avoided her eyes. "And those oafs out there are passing irritated. Please do not run off like that again, aye?"

Andi felt like a heel. "I promise, Jason. I won't leave again without taking a few of you with me."

Jason nodded and turned to leave, then stopped at the door and looked back at Andi. "His Lordship would be powerfully upset if we allowed anything to happen to you, Lady Andi." With that admission he turned and walked out the door.

Andi followed and softly closed the door behind him. Her heart lurched at the mere mention of Tristan. How she missed him! Walking over to the bed she threw herself down on it, stared up at the ceiling. She wanted to leave and go back to Dreadmoor. To Tristan. To unravel the mystery surrounding the estate. To see just what had happened to Kirk. And more than anything, she wanted to return with the proof that he had no part in any of it. But how would she accomplish that?

Reaching for her mobile, she punched in the speed-dial number to his phone. It went straight to voice mail.

"Kirk, it's me. Where are you?" She heaved a great sigh. "Please, call me as soon as you get this. Bye." Flipping the mobile cover, she tossed it on the mattress and continued staring at the ceiling.

She supposed she understood why Tristan had not told her about their suspicions of Kirk. Maybe she'd do the same thing, in his place. But his words to his men had hurt. Or was it because it was words not meant for her ears to hear? So frustrating.

In the next instant, the room phone rang, a shrill blast that filled the small room. Andi nearly fell off the bed. It was probably just Jameson, checking in on her, like he did every day. She rolled over to the nightstand and picked up the receiver.

"Hello?"

"Andrea, please come back."

Andi's heart swelled and her breath caught in her throat. "Tristan?"

"Who else would it bloody be?" He cleared his throat. "I vow if another ghost is seeking your attentions I shall soundly thrash him for it."

Andi smiled. "No, silly." She adjusted the receiver. "How is it you are talking to me?"

" 'Tis complicated to explain, to say the very least, and I've not the stomach or the patience to explain it to you at present. I throw my voice to you, is the best way to describe it." A heavy sigh pushed through the line. "I'm sorry, Andrea. I never meant to hurt you. I vow it."

Andi closed her eyes and imagined his face. "I know. And I am sorry for reacting so badly to it."

"I miss you fiercely, wench."

She laughed so loud Jason shouted at her from the other side of the door. "Is there aught amiss, lady?"

"It's okay, Jason. I'm just talking to Tristan on the phone."

"Does that mean we're going home soon?" Jason shouted back.

"Tell him aye, love." The sensual voice washed over her. " 'Tis been a miserable two days, at best."

Andi's heart skipped a beat. "What did you call me?" She knew the tag "love" in England could apply to anyone or anything—even one's pet goat. But Tristan did not use it. Ever. Fright choked the hope from her.

"Wench?"

"No," Andi said slowly. "The other one."

Tristan chuckled. "Ah." A knowing tone caught in his voice. "Love?"

"That's the one."

Tristan didn't even hesitate. "I love you, Andrea Kinley Monroe. Very much so."

A lump lodged in Andi's throat. "Really?"

"Of course really, wench. 'Tis a thing I would not jest with you about."

"I love you, too."

"Very much so?"

Andi could feel his grin through the phone. "Very much so." She felt like standing up and jumping up and down on the bed, she was so elated. He loved her!

"Andrea?" Tristan's deep voice called her back.

"Yes?"

"I don't hear you throwing your garments into your bag and readying yourself for departure. An 'I love you very much so' would include you hurrying home to me. Jameson is nigh onto making me daft. I need you here to control him and his henpecking ways. Even Kate cannot control him."

Andi laughed. "Is he right beside you?"

"Of course he is, and with a most ridiculous smirk on his face. He's holding the bloody phone for me. I vow I cannot say the intimate things I wish to, what with the busybody right beside me."

The breath escaped her lungs in a single sigh. "I love you, Mr. Dragonhawk."

Tristan laughed, then cleared his throat. "Say it again. This time, use my Christian name."

Andi closed her eyes and smiled as his deep voice warmed her. "I love you, Tristan."

"God, woman. Hurry you up and pack, so you might get here a bit faster. I vow I cannot stand another moment without you."

She hadn't been able to contact or find Kirk. And to be honest, she was tired of waiting around. When he got on a whim, especially one that included flying off to investigate a newfound artifact such as a medieval sword, he could be gone for days. Weeks, maybe. He'd call her. And then they'd arrange to meet. Maybe then she could see if he truly was possessed.

That sounded stupid.

"Lady?"

"I'll be home in three hours."

"I love you."

Andi smiled. "I love you, too."

Numerous grunts, hoots, hollers, and whistles, and battle cries, in more languages than Andi could name, hurtled through her door as her ghostly guardsmen eavesdropped on the words of endearment. She felt her cheeks heat with blush.

Tristan grunted. "I vow those are the nosiest old women Dreadmoor's ever housed. I cannot believe that sorry lot is guarding my woman. Hurry you home, wench."

"I will. Meet me at the gatehouse?"

"Aye, I will."

"Good. Bye, Tristan."

"Good eve to you, love. Hang up the bloody phone, Jameson, and make ready for my lady's return."

Andi smiled as she heard the phone click.

He loved her.

Tristan de Barre, mighty warrior and knight, loved her and only her. With lightning speed, she threw her things together as fast as she could grab them.

She had a knight to get home to.

Chapter 22

"Miss, ye 'ave a message at the desk."

Andi frowned. The innkeeper must have taken the day off. She didn't recognize this new voice. "From who?"

"I ain't at liberty to say. Ye'll 'ave to come get it and find out for yerself." The phone clicked as the messenger hung up.

Boy, how rude. Andi tossed her duffel bag, along with the couple of packages she had, back onto the bed and started for the front desk. It was already getting dark outside, and if the cab didn't hurry up it would be midnight before she got home.

Home. He called it home.

But was that what Dreadmoor was to her?

It sounded almost too good to be able to say those words.

Jason met Andi as she stepped out of the room. "Are ye not packed, lady?"

"Yeah, almost. But I've got a telegram at the front desk to pick up. It won't take but a minute, okay?"

"I shall follow you."

"No, that's okay. I'll be right back." Without waiting for him to argue, she turned and jogged down the corridor, then took the stairs two at a time. With a quick glance, she noticed the empty lobby. She walked up to the desk and looked around. "Hello?" No one answered. "That's strange." Turning, she started for the stairs.

She froze. The hair on the back of her neck rose.

She quickened her pace, but as she reached the foot of the stairs someone jerked her arm behind her, pulling her to a halt. A beefy, callused hand clamped over her mouth, muffling her surprise.

A strange voice whispered in her ear. "Goin' somewhere, missy?"

Andi recognized it as the desk clerk, the one who had just phoned her room about the telegram. The one who obviously wasn't the desk clerk at all.

Dumb, dumb, dumb, Monroe.

Wrenching around, she tried to pull free of her assailant but he twisted her arm up behind her, making her wince.

"No, ye don't, girly. Ye're comin' with us. Ye've got something someone wants very bad."

"Oh no, I'm not!" Andi mouthed the words against the man's hand as she slammed her heel down on his foot as hard as she could. He turned her loose with a shove.

"Bitch!" His face turned red. "Williams, grab 'er!"

Andi's heart raced. What could she possibly have that these guys wanted? As she rushed for the stairs, the second assailant brought her up short. Both looked to be in their mid-forties and as grungy as a body could possibly be. *Bleh.* And she'd put her mouth on his palm. Total mouth sterilization as soon as she was home.

Andi backed away, keeping them in her sights.

Then someone hit her from behind.

A blinding pain made her head swim. Pulling in a lungful of air, she pushed the yell out with all her might. "Ja-son!"

Hopefully, the knights hadn't headed back to Dreadmoor.

With a stifled cry of pain, Andi slumped to the floor.

She wasn't sure how long it'd been since hitting the floor, but by the grunts and foul medieval curses going on around her, it couldn't have been too long.

Several male voices swore in several languages. They yelled and made threats—promises of torture to various degrees. When the hiss of swords being drawn broke the air, she knew what was going on.

Her guardsmen had come to her rescue.

As she pushed herself up and opened her eyes, young Jason appeared before her. He bent down on one knee and gave her a stern look.

"Lady, are you hurt?" he asked.

"My head hurts a little, but I'm fine."

" 'Tis with many regrets you've had a mishap and I was not here to prevent it. But lay you still until we've control of the matter, if you will. I vow it won't take long."

Andi gave him a weak smile. "Okay."

With a nod, Jason rose and turned to join the others in their rescue.

The two thugs probably wouldn't be attacking anyone for quite some time. They scrambled around the room, trying to find an exit, to somehow get past the knights who had the pair caged in. There were ten warriors in all, and they ferociously met each attempt of escape with a drawn sword, accompanied by vows to use it in various morbid ways. Had Andi not known they were ghosts, she would never have been able to believe anything other than what she saw.

If they were this good dead, she could only imagine how they'd been in life.

Sir Richard charged the one named Williams, sword drawn and pointed at the man's neck. "What want you with the lass?" He took a step closer. "You had better be quicker about your answer if you wish to keep that vile tongue in your empty head."

The man dropped to the floor in a dead faint.

The look of disgust in Sir Richard's eyes almost made Andi laugh. She thought better of it, though, and kept quiet.

"Damned weakling would never have survived our time," Sir Richard growled to no one in particular, then stomped off to help the others terrorize the remaining assailant.

That thought alone brought Andi to her feet. "Jason!"

Jason met her gaze. "Aye?"

"Where's the other guy?"

He looked around. "What other guy, lady? 'Tis only these two witless dolts here."

Andy shook her head. "No, there were three. One hit me in the head from behind."

He looked around, startled. "Damnation." He stalked over to the other man and drew his sword. "Tell me now who hit the lady from behind."

The little man spat on the floor. "I ain't tellin' ye nothin', ye lil' shit!"

Jason frowned, then held his hand out. "Sir Richard, your head, if you please."

Andi watched as Sir Richard shrugged, then in one swift snap plucked his own head off and placed it, dripping with blood, in Jason's awaiting hand.

Her attacker's face turned a very nice, pasty shade of white. He gulped. "What the—"

"Now, dolt," Sir Richard's head said. "Tell the lad who hit the lady and why you idiots are after her. Now." Jason gave Sir Richard's head a toss or two, then threw it back where it landed, unfortunately backward, on Richard's neck.

The man hit the floor in a dead faint, his unbelieving eyes rolled back in his head.

Several growls of disgust erupted from the other knights; then Richard and Jason approached Andi.

Sir Richard bowed, then looked up. "Lady, you had best call Himself at once. He needs to know of the events before we depart, and I daresay he will not be happy with the news."

"Okay." Andi went to the other side of the desk to use the phone. When she rounded the corner, she stifled a scream.

"What is it?" Jason and Richard ran to her side.

She pointed. "It's the innkeeper. They must've knocked him out."

"Call Tristan immediately, lass."

Andi didn't waste another minute. She picked up the phone and dialed the keep. Jameson answered.

"Jameson, please put Tristan on the phone."

"Is something amiss?" Worry laced his voice.

"Kinda. Could you hurry?"

"Yes, lady. Just a moment. I'll place him on the speaker." She heard a muffled call for Tristan, and then his voice sounded in her ear.

"Andrea, what has befallen you? Jameson's as white as bed linens."

"Well," she said slowly, "there's been a little accident. But everything's—"

"What?"

Andi winced from his bellow. "I received a call in my room saying I had a telegram waiting for me at the desk. When I came down to get it, there were two men, well, actually three, if you count the one that hit me in the—"

"What?" Tristan bellowed again. "By the saints, Andrea! Are you hurt?"

"I'm fine, really. Just a knot on my head is all," she answered. She then listened as Tristan cursed viciously, and in at least two languages that Andi could tell, before returning to the phone. "Love, hold the phone up to Sir Richard, if you will. For just a moment."

"Okay." Andi waved to Richard, who came to her side. She held the phone out for him and he bent his head to reach the receiver.

"Aye," he answered.

Andi could hear Tristan bellowing where she stood. She watched poor Richard as he winced several times, managed a few "ayes," before bowing to her.

"Himself would speak to you again, lady," he said quietly.

She put the receiver to her ear. "Hi."

"I should have been there," Tristan said.

"Tristan, don't," she said. "It is no one's fault except the idiots who did it. Okay? I'm fine."

Tristan grunted. "Andrea, you could have been hurt badly, or worse—"

"But I wasn't. The guys managed just fine. No wonder Dragonhawk and his mighty knights are still so legendary. Wait till you hear what Jason and Richard did."

"Don't tell me. That ridiculous head prank they do, aye?"

"How'd you know?"

"Those two cannot seem to come up with anything new of late." He sighed. "If you call the constable it will take hours to leave. And how will you explain your guardsmen?" He was silent for a moment or two, then cleared his throat. "Have you called a cabby yet?"

"No."

"Call one, get in it, have Jason ride with you in the back, and come home. I can protect you at Dreadmoor. I shall call the constable and let him know what has happened. He can question you here."

"What about these guys?" Andi glanced at her assailants on the floor and pondered the urge to kick them.

"I vow I hate to ask this of you, but there is no other choice. Bind them, lady, as best you can. Once you are safely away I shall have Jameson ring the constable. The authorities can handle the matter from there." He chuckled softly. "Probably just a couple of ruffians who did not expect such a lovely, frail lass as yourself to be accompanied by a fierce lot of ghosts."

A thought struck her. Should she remind Tristan of the third assailant? She wasn't about to tell him she'd spotted Kirk. No way. She'd tell him once she made it home.

Andi cleared her throat. "Frail?"

"Aye. Now get you home, fair maid. I'll be the one waiting at the gatehouse. Mooning."

"All right. I'll see you in a bit."

"I love you."

Her heart seized. "I love you, Tristan."

Andi listened once again as Tristan shouted for Jameson to hang up the phone. She placed the receiver down and looked around the room. The knights all stared at her, grinning.

She put her hands on her hips. "What?"

"Naught, lass," said Sir Stephen. "We was just noticin' those sweet words ye have for Himself."

"Aye, an' no doubt he'll be wantin' ye home fairly quick," Sir Gareth said with a grin.

"Did ye call the cabby, girl?" Sir Richard said. "I vow 'twould be a long hike on foot, what with no mount."

"The cab!" Andi snatched the receiver up, dialed the number listed at the desk, then placed it back down. She glared at the knights, who were still smirking. "There." She started for the stairs. "Happy?" As she passed by one of the assailants, he groaned. Andi stepped on him, causing the man's breath to swoosh out of his lungs. The knights erupted into a raucous laughter.

"I need something to bind their hands." She glanced around the room. Finding a few pieces of twine behind the desk, she made quick work of tying the men up. The knights huddled around her as she completed the task. Finished, she stood and smiled. "There. I hope that will hold them." She couldn't resist one last kick to each of them, sending the knights into another round of laughter. "Now I'll go get my bag and we can leave."

Jason jumped to her side as she started up the stairs to her room. "Nay, lass. This time I stay by your side till we reach Dreadmoor. I daresay Sir Tristan will be livid enough with the lot of us for allowing you to face these scourges alone."

Andi studied the young knight beside her. Quite unlike any seventeen-year-old of today, no doubt. Warm brown eyes brimmed with more wisdom and bravery than any modern-day teenager she knew. His tall, lanky form had no trouble hefting the sword now sheathed in the scabbard. He was tough and unfearing and respectful. "You were wonderful, Jason. I would have no other guardsman watching my back."

"In truth?" he asked. "I daresay if those louts had known we couldn't really hurt them, there is no telling what they would have done."

"Well, we won't dwell on that. You saved me, and for that I'm grateful." She smiled at him just as she reached for the door. "Tristan thinks highly of you. I can see why." She threw open the door, ran over to the bed, and grabbed her bags, then followed Jason back down the stairs. After checking the innkeeper, she followed her ghostly garrison out the door, where the cab awaited to take her home. To Dreadmoor.

She couldn't get there quick enough.

Chapter 23

Andi's eyes nearly popped out of their sockets.

"My lady, your mouth is agape. And I vow 'tis time for me to leave you," Jason, in his invisible state, whispered in her ear.

"Uh-huh." Andi heard the mirth in Jason's voice as he left her. Her eyes remained glued to the man at the gatehouse.

Or, rather, the ghost at the gatehouse.

The infamous Dragonhawk stood just inside the gatehouse with a fierce frown, his bulky arms crossed over his wide chest. At six feet and six inches, *massive* and *intimidating* didn't even begin to describe him. And he knew it. Reveled in it.

Gone was his usual medieval garb. He looked like he did the first time they met—just as twenty-first centuryish as any gorgeous modern-day lord. No, much better.

The cab came to a halt and Andi slowly got out. The castle, lit in dim, flickering torchlight, shimmered against a black, star-dusted sky. She imagined it looked just as it had in the thirteenth century. And she just couldn't take her eyes off Tristan. Without much thought, she pulled her bags off the seat and walked up the steps to the gatehouse. Her stomach had a hundred butterflies beating their wings.

She felt like drooling.

"Pay the man." Tristan barked the order to Will, the gatehouse guard, then strode toward Andi. "I've got my lady to see to."

"Aye, my lord," Will answered. He ducked back into the gatehouse for the required funds.

Andi finally got hold of herself and closed her mouth. Tristan wore a pair of faded jeans, his sword strapped to his side, a black T-shirt, and a pair of hiking boots. His long dark hair nestled against his neck into a queue. She gulped. The T-shirt didn't hide one single muscle in that broad chest, nor did those jeans especially hide his thick, muscled thighs. God help her if she got a backside view.

Andi watched Tristan as he came closer.

And then watched as he stopped and turned to say something else to Will.

Whoa.

Perfect backside shot.

And it was well worth it.

Tristan turned and looked back down at her. His grin spread slowly, a wide, dimpling smile capable of knocking the wind from her lungs. *Breathtaking.*

She stared up at him as he stood before her. She smiled and took a deep breath. "Hi."

Tristan looked down into his lady's eyes and wished heartily that he could grab her, pull her small body against him, and kiss her until she begged him quit. He clenched his fists at his side, fighting the urge to touch her. He wanted to breathe in her scent, taste her lips, feel her slight arms wrapped around his neck. He stepped closer and shoved his hands into the imaginary pockets of his imaginary jeans, so he wouldn't be foolish and try the like. "I am glad you're home." He smiled down at her. "I've missed you sorely, girl." The desire to run his hands over her and check every inch over for injury pained him. He settled, instead, for query. "Are you hurt? How is your head?"

"I'm okay, really. Just a little headache." Andi stared openly, from his booted feet, to his long, jean-clad legs, and his black shirt. She finally met his eyes. "You," she said with a sigh, "look wonderful."

Tristan grinned. "I gathered as much, what with your mouth agape." He cast a bored look down at his attire. "Jameson's idea, bloody busybody."

Andi laughed, her nervousness slowly disappearing. She looked behind Tristan to the keep, to the drawbridge that was now down, waiting for her to pass. She knew there were ghosts littering the place, but making themselves scarce at the moment, probably at Tristan's command. She had an enormous headache, but right now it didn't matter. She looked at her knight, dressed in modern-day clothing, and felt her heart swell. He had an untamed, hungry look in his eyes. It made her feel wanted. Loved. *Desired.*

Before she knew what was happening Tristan had drawn close and her skin tingled. His stare was intense, searing, purposeful; she thought she'd drown in the deep depths of those blue sapphires. She couldn't help herself. She reached out and grazed his strong jaw with her knuckles, ran her thumb along his lips, tried to push back the dark lock of hair that kept falling in his eyes, but her fingers barely skimmed the lines of his face. God, she wanted him to kiss her so badly, she ached. She actually *hurt.* He must have read her thoughts, because his expression tightened.

"Andrea, don't." His deep voice washed over her. "Let us walk to the hall and sit by the fire. Jameson won't go to bed until he grovels at your feet and begs you never to leave again, and I aim to have you alone."

Had he ordered her to bungee-jump from the battlements, she would have tied the cord to her ankle and gleefully thrown herself over the wall, what with the way he looked at her that very moment. She had to snap out of it. Fast. She took a deep breath and smiled. "I guess I'm just a little nervous, Tristan." She smiled up at him. "I'm not used to being in love with someone, you know."

Tristan's jaw clenched. "You make my knees useless, wench, with such words." He frowned. "I vow you are the only one who can manage such a feat." He stopped in the middle of the barbican and looked down at her, brought his lips to the shell of her ear. "You humble me, Andrea Monroe. In truth." Then he continued leading the way.

Andi followed, unable to take her eyes from him. And

goodness, she couldn't hear that voice of his enough. The deep, strange accent melted her on the spot. She looked up to the starry sky. A bright, full moon bathed the bailey in a haunting glow. The sounds of the sea surrounded her, and the tang of salt twinged her tongue. Tristan walked beside her, just far enough away so she didn't pass through him. Everything about him shouted leadership, power, and strength. She found him impossibly beautiful.

Her very own knight.

He glanced down at her and smiled. "What form of mischief is combining in that lovely head of yours, Dr. Monroe?" he asked. "I vow I can see smoke rising from atop you."

Andi laughed. "No mischief, I promise." She searched the water in the moat and noticed how the moonlight gave it a silvery reflection. "Does it bother you to be here, Tristan?"

Tristan's answer came quick. "Since I met you, no." He slowed his pace as they passed over the drawbridge and started through the inner barbican. "Before, 'twasn't Dreadmoor I grew weary of." He looked up as they walked under the portcullis, then glanced down at Andi. "My mates keep me company, as does Jameson." He sighed and shoved his hands in his pockets. "I missed my family enough to wish passing, in truth. My mother and sire, along with my siblings, had all passed on by the time I came out of that well of nothingness, after Erik killed me. 'Twas nigh onto two centuries, at least."

Out of the corner of her eye, she watched him. "What are we going to do, Tristan?" She slowly shook her head, hoping maybe the motion of it would jar some sort of awe-inspiring brainstorm to occur, solving all their problems. It didn't happen.

"Let us go sit by the fire inside and get you something to eat. I vow Jameson's hopping up and down in anticipation of having you home, and cannot wait to smother you, no doubt." He smiled. "Once he is satisfied you are truly home and in one piece, I'll run his bothersome self off and we can spend the evening having speech. Or mayhap just gaping at one another. I vow I couldn't grow weary of either task."

"Let's try speech first," Andi said, laughing. "And then maybe we can gape a bit. I want to know everything about you."

Tristan grunted. " 'Tis a tale that could possibly take quite some time, lass."

"I've got the time."

Tristan gazed down at her. "Your hair gleams silver in the moonlight. 'Tis beautiful."

Those soft-spoken words nearly caused Andi to stumble. She saw white slash his face as he bared his teeth in a devilish grin. God, he looked so real. "What are you smiling at?"

"You, my lady," he answered, his voice deep and raspy, "are passing adorable."

Andi sighed. "Not so bad yourself, Dreadmoor."

He laughed, and the sound warmed her inside.

As they reached the doors, Tristan held up a hand to stop Andi from opening the door for them. "Nay, woman. I'll not have you opening doors for me this eve. 'Tis bad enough I cannot manage the task myself." He gazed down at her, raised one dark eyebrow, and then bellowed.

Loudly.

"Jameson! Open the door!"

Seconds later the door swung wide and a flustered Jameson stood in its opening, a crooked smile planted on his usually stoic face.

"My lady Andi!" He literally beamed. "I am ever so glad you've decided to come home."

Andi wasted no time in dropping her bag, throwing her arms around him, and kissing him soundly on the cheek. "It's good to be home, Jameson." She picked her pack up, slung it over her shoulder, and grinned. "What'cha got to eat in this place, anyway? I'm starved."

"Not anything you would prefer, I'd wager," Tristan said, chuckling. "Jameson, don't you have something nice and healthy prepared?"

Jameson stepped aside to allow them to pass, then

closed the heavy doors behind them. "Quite healthy, I am sure of it. None of those Pop-Tart concoctions she's so fond of."

For the second time in less than an hour, Andi's jaw nearly disconnected from her face as her mouth slacked open. She looked all about the great hall, completely amazed. She looked up at Tristan, who leaned against the wall and crossed his arms over his chest. He grinned.

"There were too many of them to fight off, I'm afraid." He pushed off the wall and bowed. "I'm not the only mooning fool at Dreadmoor, you know."

As Andi looked around her she easily counted at least fifty chain-mailed knights littering the great hall. Dragonhawk's knights were there, all fifteen, including Tristan. But there were more. They sat on the floor. They perched on the steps. They waited in chairs.

And they all stared at her.

Grinning.

"They are powerful glad you have returned, lady." Tristan's whisper brushed her ear. "You see, you won their hearts the day you traipsed out to the lists in those, those—"

"Pj's, my lord," one knowing knight called out.

"Thank you, Graves. Aye, those pj's." He grinned. "They've been besotted idiots ever since."

Andi blushed. "You guys are crazy," she said, "but very sweet."

That gained several grunts and grumbles from the ghostly garrison, and a few blushes, as well.

"Now, you moon-faced dolts have had your look, you see she is fine—now begone. Get to your posts and make sure no one passes onto Dreadmoor's land without my knowledge of it." He scanned the room, glaring. "Keep her safe, or answer to me. Now go, and make haste." He turned his gaze to Andi, and his frown disappeared. "I've a mind to have her to myself for quite some time."

Andi didn't doubt for a second he would succeed, either.

Her heart already belonged to him.

* * *

Erik watched as the two buffoons lumbered down the darkened alley, laughing loudly and slapping one another on the back as they told witless jokes. Odd, how the mortal body he'd taken molded with his spirit, giving him powers he'd not known existed. His keen sense of smell alerted him to their overwhelming scent of ale. Even at a hundred paces he could smell their stench. Disgusting excuses for human beings, the both of them.

Which is why he'd decided to give fate a helping hand.

Erik stepped out of the shadows as the pair made their way up the alley.

"Bloody saints," the one called Sonny murmured.

The other just stood, gaping.

But even in a drunken stupor the pair gasped as recognition set in.

"Well, well, my boys." The man spoke with a crooning calm. "You seem a bit jumpy this fine eve." He took another step closer, causing the men to back against the wall. "Are you not glad to see me?"

"Uh, aye, boss," Sonny said. He shifted his beady black eyes to his partner. "Was it ye who bailed us from the jailhouse?"

The man smiled, content with the reactions he caused in the two useless idiots. "Technically, yes, it was. I could not afford for you two babbling fools to tell the constable too much information, now, could I?" He smiled. "And why was it that you felt the need to approach Dr. Monroe, when I had clearly instructed you to merely follow her to the inn and alert me to her arrival?" He watched as the men shifted their weight. Their eyes were clear now, the haze of liquor snuffed by fear. He took another step. "Now, what to do?"

Without another word, Sonny bolted. In one swift motion, Erik calmly reached his arm out and snatched the running man by the throat, lifting him soundly off the ground. He allowed the man to dangle helplessly while pinning the other with a glare. "You're next, you know." With a quick snap of his wrist, the man dropped the lifeless body of Sonny to the ground.

The other drunken man opened his mouth to scream, his eyes wide with terror.

His scream died on his lips.

Smiling, Erik flung the second man to the ground. "Useless, witless fools." He brushed his trousers off, straightened his jacket, and left the alley.

He thought briefly that he couldn't have found a more spectacular mortal host.

Chapter 24

Only after Andi had devoured one and a half peanut butter and jelly sandwiches, which she had to practically force Jameson to prepare, were she and Tristan finally left alone.

Heaven help her.

She wasn't used to such attention.

And she most definitely wasn't at all used to being on the receiving end of such heated, ravenous looks such as the ones Tristan de Barre of Dreadmoor now cast her way. Except, of course, for the one night, not too long ago, when she'd opened her eyes and he'd been standing over her, staring. *Starved.* The memory of his near-touches and stark-honest confessions made her heart race.

Andi pulled her legs up under her bottom on the soft, leather sofa that had conveniently been added to the great hall furniture. It now sat facing the fireplace, and the low fire burning gave the room a gentle radiance, casting just enough heat for a mid-August night.

Tristan sat beside her, turned comfortably to the side, his long, jean-clad legs stretched out and perched on one of the matching ottomans. He'd kicked off his illusioned hiking boots and socks and now sported his bare feet, his sword propped against the stone hearth. He watched her with a predatory gaze that unnerved her. Her stomach flip-flopped. God help her had he been able to actually put his hands on her.

"You've a bit of that mixed concoction on the corner of your mouth, love."

Great. He wasn't staring at her with uncontrolled lust. He gandered at the remnants of her PB&J, which obviously plastered her face. An awfully big ego she'd developed of late, it seemed, and a fat lot of good it did her.

Andi quickly found out it wasn't the PB&J Tristan seemed so fascinated with. Once she removed the concoction with the end of her tongue, his ghostly gaze remained glued to her mouth. She gulped.

"It's not polite to stare, Tristan."

Tristan took his time dragging his gaze from her mouth to her eyes. "I vow I do not remember taking an oath to be polite when entering knighthood."

Andi couldn't help but grin. "You're not very shy, are you, de Barre?"

He slid closer, proving that he really wasn't. With one arm braced behind her, he leaned forward, his mouth inches from her own. "Were I alive, this conversation would not be taking place." He moved to her ear and echoed the request he'd asked nights before. "Close your eyes, Andrea."

Her eyes closed on their own, so fierce were the emotions his voice and nearness caused. Her breathing became rapid, and she gripped the side of the sofa in a tight clutch. "What are you doing?"

"Can you feel me, Andrea?" His voice spoke softly against her neck.

The slightest bit of static, or a slight breeze, grazed her skin and she shivered. "I . . . think so." Her stomach knotted, and she itched to reach out to him. "Tristan . . ."

His breathing, while not stirring any air, sounded harsh against her throat, as though he were actually devouring her. "Ever since the night I lay beside you, I've thought of nothing else, save touching you." The staticky, sensual feeling moved to her mouth. "Tasting you."

She slowly opened her eyes to find Tristan's heated gaze fixed on hers, his mouth hovering close to her lips.

With a steady hand, he lifted his thumb to trace her bottom lip.

"I would kiss you senseless, woman," he said, his voice low, erotic, "and I vow 'twould be burned into your memory forever."

What he was doing now was burned into her memory.

Andi lifted her hand and fingered his stubbled jaw, traced the sexy Adam's apple, the hollow, and the so-real-looking vein in his throat. "I've thought of nothing else except what it'd be truly like to be with you," she said.

"Aye, and I, you." His ghostly touch moved down her throat, caressing her collarbone. "Unfasten your buttons, Andrea."

With her heart pounding, Andi kept her eyes trained on Tristan as, one by one, she undid the first few buttons of her shirt, revealing the laced edges of her bra. Her skin grew warm as those beautiful eyes darkened, watching her every move.

Fascination lit those darkened eyes as he moved his forefinger along the edge of that lace, over the rise of her breast above the material. It left a simmering warmth in its wake, one that made her shift, trying to get closer, trying to ease the ache that burned low in her abdomen.

So close they were, in fact, that their bodies all but melded into one another.

She watched his hand, strong with thick, roping veins, move over her stomach, across her hip, and down her thigh.

She shifted some more.

A bit of Tristan's hair loosened from the queue and fell over his shoulder, and it looked so tangible, she couldn't stop herself from reaching out to slide her fingers through it.

And they did.

Then he stopped.

They stared at each other for a long, long time. Andi drank in every small detail of his face, every small knick and scar, every line, until her eyes collided with his, and they stared some more.

"I vow, we'd best cease," he said, his voice hoarse. "You drive me witless, woman. Painfully witless."

Catching her breath, she nodded, but continued to stare. She just couldn't help herself. He was the most beautiful man she'd ever seen.

And to crave his touch yet be unable to have it nearly killed her. And that's how it would be . . . forever.

She forced a smile and buttoned her shirt. "Okay, then. Tell me about your family. Did you have brothers or sisters?"

Tristan heaved a gusty sigh and leaned back, his gaze turning serious. "I could pretend all night to touch you, and to whisper things I've dreamed of doing to you. Indeed, I vow I cannot promise not to. But for now, we'll have speech. And just so you'll know, I am not in the least bit finished with you concerning your attack. I had Jameson phone the constable as soon as you left the inn, and I daresay he will be calling you first thing in the morn."

"You did?"

"Aye. But for now, so we can catch our breath, I'll tell you of my family, beginning with my sire first, since you're near bursting with curiosity. And aye, I had three brothers who tormented me for many years."

"You probably loved every minute of it. Do you look like your father?" Andi pulled one leg up onto the sofa and rested her chin on her knee. She waited for him to answer, glad of the diversion to take her mind off how it felt to have his ghostly mouth slide over her skin.

"Aye, it has been said I am the spitting image, the same eye color, same hair, same height. Big, strappin' lads, the lot of us."

"The lot of you?" Andi asked.

"Aye. My sire, my uncles, my brothers, and I. All a bit rather—"

"Enormous?"

Tristan chuckled. "Enormous it is, then. My sire's younger brother, Killian, jesting oaf that he was, looked enough like my sire to be his twin. 'Twas unnerving at times. The only thing telling the two apart, save their personalities, was my sire's scar and eye."

"Scar and eye? What happened to him?"

"He was wounded while at war, and 'twas quite fierce looking, I assure you. He wore a patch over the eye, for the most part. 'Twas macabre to some, although my mother quite loved it." He reached out his hand and held his finger close to Andi's temple, the skin tingling in its wake. "The scar ran from here," he said, drawing an imaginary line down her face, then across her eye, "all the way to here." He finished tracing the imaginary scar, ending it across Andi's lips. A second went by before he withdrew his hand, and she immediately missed the sensation. "The sword blinded that eye, turning it nearly white. I remember my mother telling him how roguish she thought it made him appear. And I remember my grandmother constantly begging him to remove 'that bloody patch.' "

Andi smiled. "I bet your mother thought him to be the most handsome man in all of England."

Tristan laughed. "My mother was a full-blooded Scot, as was my grandmother. They both hated all things English, until they met their loves. They liked each other immensely. And aye"—his gaze bored into hers—"my mother and sire were very much in love. But 'tis an amusing tale of how they came to be."

"What were their names?"

Tristan stared into the fire. How he missed them. "Gage and Kaila."

"Gage and Kaila," Andi repeated. "How lovely."

Tristan laughed. "My sire would scowl at you, had he heard you refer to his name as 'lovely.' But he would have enjoyed it—secretly, mind you."

Andi yawned. "Tell me."

"Tell you what, sleepy one?"

"Gage and Kaila's story."

"Nay, love," he said. "You need to rest."

"Please?" She stifled another yawn and lay over onto the sofa, near Tristan's lap.

Tristan took a deep breath. Having Andi lie so close to him, and him unable to do a damn bloody thing about it, was nigh onto making him a daft idiot. The fact she did not realize what she did caused him even more discomfort. "Saints, woman." He sighed. "All right, if it will please you, I shall tell you just a bit." He shifted on the sofa to give Andi some room, stretched one arm over his head; the other he draped close to Andi's head, tracing the length of her hair, and began. "It all started when my mother highwayed my sire and held him for ransom in her dungeon."

"Oh, I like her already."

"I'm sure you do, wench. Now rest and I'll tell you a bit more . . ."

Tristan glanced down at Andi and smiled.

Gage and Kaila's tale would have to wait.

His lady was already fast asleep.

He watched his finger glide along the lines of her brown tresses. They looked powerfully soft, and he could nearly imagine what they must feel like between his fingers. He continued, tracing the soft bones in her wrist, the long fingers, and, God help him and his lecherous self, the shape of her hip. She stirred him in ways he never thought possible. He felt almost mortal again.

Almost, but not quite.

Andi cracked open an eye and stretched. A good-sized fire blazed in the hearth. A soft fleece blanket had been draped over her. A hazy darkness lingered in the room, waiting for daybreak. She blinked, suddenly aware she wasn't in her room. Confused, she sat up and looked around.

"Settle down, love."

Andi turned to see Tristan, stretched out and in the same place on the sofa as he was when she fell asleep.

Monroe. MON-ROE! You were being entertained, not to mentioned fondled, by the most handsome, chivalristic medieval knight in the entire world, and you fell asleep? Dumb, dumb, dumb.

"How long have I been dozing?" She stifled a yawn. "Have you been here the whole time?"

"Aye."

"You're sweet, Tristan de Barre."

"Have a care not to let such a tale get around the garrison, if you will." He winked. " 'Twould be unbearable."

Then it hit her.

Again.

"Your eyes."

Tristan frowned. "What's that?"

She pulled closer and stared. "Your eyes."

One side of Tristan's mouth slowly lifted. "What about my eyes, love?" He lowered his head, coming within an inch of her face.

The breath in her lungs stilled for an instant. She jumped up and tried to calm her jittery nerves caused by his pure, raw maleness. At the hearth, she turned back. "That's why I came to your solar the other day in the first place. I made a connection."

Crossing his arms over his chest, he inclined his head. "Go on."

Pacing, she spoke her thoughts aloud. "Well, Jason actually made the connection. Your eyes are the first thing that caught my attention all those years ago. Stunning. I never forgot them."

"Aye, I've been told they're rather comely."

She shot him a glare. "Stop that, you conceited man. Now listen."

Holding up his hands in defense, he nodded. "I apologize. Proceed, woman."

"Thank you." She began to pace again. "When I arrived at Dreadmoor, the next thing I noticed were the amazing tapestries covering the walls. The scene depicts the same knight in all of them." She met his gaze. "You. The legendary Dragonhawk."

Another smile. "Guilty. My mother and grandmother stitched them."

Andi nodded and resumed her pacing. "Then Jameson took me to my chambers, where I noticed your shield." Pushing her hair back, she continued. "Even then a familiarity came over me, but I couldn't place it."

"Place what?"

"Then," she continued, ignoring his question, "that voice, or presence, or whatever you want to call it led me to the dungeon, where I dug up your mail. Now I've discovered bones. Bones that do not belong to you."

Tristan rose and crossed to the hearth. She stopped pacing and stared at him. "Jason and I were in the study going over all these items—the shield, the tapestries—and then we discussed your sword, and that's when it hit me."

"Saints, woman, tell me. My patience, as you know, is very short."

"It's the eye, Tristan. Your eyes. The eye of that mystical rampant creature on the front of your tunic, your shield, your crest. The stone in your sword. They're all the same. That amazing, stunning shade of sapphire."

Rubbing a hand over his jaw, he stared into the dying flames in the hearth. "So you've made this . . . connection. With the eyes." He turned to her. "What do they mean?"

She shook her head. "I believe the answer is in the hilt of your sword. In the Dragonhawk's eye. See? The presence is trying to tell me something. I know it." She rubbed her temples. "But without your sword, how can we figure it out? I feel positive if we can locate it, it would be huge. Important. Phenomenal."

Those stunning, piercing blue eyes studied her, searched her, grew hungry and dark. "Then you may just have to remain at Dreadmoor until you piece the puzzle together, aye?"

A smile pulled at her mouth. "I'm serious, Tristan."

"So am I."

Oh, there went her breath again. Escaping her. God, she'd never seen a more intense look on a man's face before. At least, never directed at her. "You don't mind me staying past the original contract date?" She batted her eyes.

"You're passing tolerable. I suppose you can stay."

"Ha, ha. Then I'd better get busy figuring this out." She stretched her arms above her head, and several bones cracked. "I've got to earn my keep, you know."

"Indeed. Tell me you are still intact after that snapping."

"Just getting rusty, I guess," Andi said, sighing. "I'm getting old, you know."

"Hmm. I seriously doubt you could catch up to me, even if you tried." He looked at her, one eyebrow raised. "When is your birthday?"

"It's in two weeks."

Tristan stared, then laughed. "Truly. By the saints, woman. We shall celebrate it."

"Really, Tristan," she said. "It's just another day—not even my real birthday. Not that big of a deal."

He threw her a scowl. "Well, it is now." He stood, paced a time or two in front of Andi, then stilled before her. "As much as I detest leaving your charming company, there is a matter of utmost importance I must see to. It cannot be delayed for another moment." He cocked his head to the side and grinned. "Might you amuse yourself this morn? Or should I have Jameson fetch young Heath to give you company? The pup adores you, you know."

"What are you up to?"

Tristan had the decency to look shocked. "Business, and none of it yours at the moment. Now, will it be Heath or Jameson? Perhaps one of the knights can divert you for a bit?"

Andi laughed and shook her head. No one ever made a big deal about her birthday. *Ever.* Well, Kirk always took her out to dinner. Her aunt Mary hadn't been too big on celebrations of any kind, actually. She'd sort of gotten used to it.

Andi had a sneaking suspicion this would be a birthday unlike any other.

"Will you force me to choose your companion?" Tristan crossed his arms across his chest. "I've not the time to stand here and wait for your thoughts to gather."

"I promised Heath a day. Or I could spend it with Kail." She grinned at Tristan. "Yeah, I think I'd better have them both for the day."

Tristan frowned. "Very well. Young Heath and Kail

the lackwit it shall be." He glared for a moment or two, then broke into a grin. "I'll have my captain fetched posthaste, and Jameson can send Heath over once he arrives. And behave yourself, if you can muster up the strength." He took a step closer and stared down at her. "Jameson will alert you to the constable's call today. I want to be present whilst you speak to him, as I shall have my own queries. Until then," he said, his deep voice graveled and sexy, "I shall moon over you immensely until I can have you to myself once again, lady." He stepped back and made her a low bow. "Good morn to you, then." With a dimpled grin he turned and strode from the hall.

Andi stared after him. He had a confident, raw male swagger of a walk that made her throat go dry. Cocky. Arrogant. And she liked it. A lot.

He was going to plan something for her birthday. Exactly what that something would be was another question entirely. With a thirteenth-century knight behind the project, she could do nothing more but wait. Ooh, and she hated waiting. Two whole weeks of it, too.

In the meanwhile, she'd try and get Kirk to answer his mobile. And she had the dungeon to finish.

Just as she entered her chamber, her own cell phone began to chirp. The screen flashed PRIVATE, indicating it was an unknown caller. She flipped the cover and answered. "Hello?"

"It's good to hear your voice again, Andrea."

"Kirk! Where have you been? I've been trying to—"

"I know, I know. I skipped the dig in Northumberland for a few days to investigate an artifact further north. Not to worry, though. There's a responsible intern there in my stead. Dreadfully bad weather most days, I'm sorry to report. I lost my mobile in the process. I'm sorry, love."

"It's okay." The past few days crashed over her, and yet she hesitated to tell him anything. Why? Because it sounded nuts, that's why. How do you tell a person you've known all your life he may possibly be harboring the spirit of a thirteenth-century murderer in his body?

Right. She just couldn't bring herself to do it. The closer it got to her lips, the more absurd it sounded. One thing she did want to know. "I could have sworn I saw you in Berwick."

"You were in Berwick? When?"

"Yesterday. I followed you into a pub but—"

"I wasn't in Berwick yesterday, Andrea. I only just arrived from Edinburgh an hour ago. Clearly, you are mistaken." He chuckled. "Who would have thought there'd be another as dashing as me walking the streets of England, hmm?"

Andi smiled. "You're right. It must've been someone else." The person had looked just like Kirk. How uncanny.

She felt as though she should tell him of the attack at the inn. But he'd worry, maybe even pull her from Dreadmoor. And she just wasn't ready for that yet. She'd wait, tell him about it later.

"Have you taken the photo card in for developing?" she asked.

"Right. Quite a nice lot of blades, to be sure, as were the helms. None of them extraordinary, though, I'm afraid."

Andi blinked. "What do you mean?" That certainly didn't sound like something Kirk would say. He loved all relics, no matter what condition they were in.

"I was hoping to find one in particular. That's all." He cleared his throat. "Maybe the stress of a solo excavation has you edgy? I think you should start jogging again. Remember how much you used to like it?"

A smile pulled at her mouth. Kirk remembered everything. "Yes, but back then I had more time."

"Well." He cleared his throat, his tone becoming more parental. "You've plenty of sand to jog on there at Dreadmoor, love. You're right by the sea. I insist you do it. It will make you feel loads better. Now. I've a dig to oversee. And after this is all over with, we shall celebrate your birthday. A nice big steak dinner." He paused. "It's in two weeks, right?"

"So they say."

"Tsk-tsk, Andrea. You've always been a party pooper when your birthday comes round. We'll have fun, I promise."

Andi smiled. "I'll hold you to that, boss."

An hour and a long, hot shower later, Andi felt refreshed and ready for the day. Her thoughts returned to her earlier phone conversation. Kirk seemed more like himself, and it comforted her beyond belief. No way could he be the things Tristan accused him of. But neither could she dismiss the knight's accusations.

Maybe Kirk looked like Erik de Sabre? Or, like Tristan mentioned, maybe he was even a descendent? Crazier things had happened. Either way, she wasn't going to argue with Tristan and the garrison about it anymore. They'd dropped the subject, and so would she. She'd focus on figuring out the mystery of the unknown soul whose bones were buried with the hoard, the one buried in the dungeon, and enjoy her time at Dreadmoor. Not to mention her newfound love.

That thought gave her pause. What if figuring out the mystery meant releasing Tristan and his men from the curse? Could that even be done? What would happen if the curse was lifted? She shuddered at the many possibilities. It was a topic neither she nor Tristan had approached yet. Among others.

Minutes later she found herself being escorted across the great hall by Kail, Tristan's captain. He was huge and intimidating—to the average ghostly medieval passerby, perhaps.

Andi, on the other hand, knew him to be a big, overgrown puppy.

Just as they were about to leave the hall, Jameson stepped from the kitchen.

"Lady? The constable would like to speak with you."

"Just a minute, Kail. I'll be right back." She trotted over to the kitchen and Jameson handed her the cordless. "Hello?"

"Yes, Dr. Monroe? This is Constable Hurley in Berwick. Do you have a moment?"

Andi put her hand over the receiver. "It's the constable," she whispered to Jameson. He turned and left, probably to get Tristan.

"Yes, Constable, I can talk."

"Right. First, let me apologize for your mishap at the inn. Usually a fairly friendly place, Berwick."

"Thank you."

Tristan walked through the door and stopped by her side. Andi placed a finger over her lips to keep him silent. He frowned, then lowered his head close to hers to listen.

"Can you tell me what happened?" the constable asked.

Andi told him, minus the part about her ghost knights.

"I see. The men were questioned immediately, but it seems they feel you had a bit of . . . help. Say, ten or so big, broad lads?"

Tristan shook his head. She gave a soft laugh. "I wish I'd had ten big lads. It would have made things a lot easier."

Tristan grinned and nodded, his eyes fastened on hers. It made her knees wobble.

"Yes, it seems they would have had a bruise or two. They did make bail, though. Barely a couple of hours after their arrest."

Tristan frowned and motioned for her to let him speak. "Constable, Lord Dreadmoor wishes to speak with you."

Andi held the phone while Tristan bellowed, "What do you mean, they made bail? Who posted it?"

Andi leaned in and listened.

"I wasn't there, but the jailer described a woman as being the one. Posted the bail with cash, as well. Four hundred pounds for each," Constable Hurley said. "Not to worry, Lord Dreadmoor. I've a man already posted at their flat. They apparently share it. I'll let you know if anything turns up."

"What of the third man? The one who escaped?" Tristan said. "He thrashed the back of Dr. Monroe's head. I want him caught."

"So far, we've turned up nothing solid. I am on it, sir."

Tristan's voice dropped to a deadly growl. "Notify me

as soon as you have him in custody. I want to get to the bottom of this."

"Aye. Consider it done."

Andi clicked off the phone and stared at Tristan, who hadn't budged. Not more than a few inches separated them. "Thank you. I'm, uh, not used to having someone worry so much over me."

He studied her face with such concentration, such intensity, that it took every effort to keep her eyes trained on his. Placing a hand on either side of her head on the wall behind her, he caged her in and lowered his head. "Get used to it, Andrea. I take care of what's mine. And you"—his gaze dropped to her lips before returning to her eyes—"are mine."

Chapter 25

A brisk breeze caught Andi in the face as she walked beside Tristan's captain, observing the stone structures. They completely fascinated her. And she needed something good to take her mind off Tristan. That rat had nearly melted her into a pool of mush with those endearing words and heated ghostly touches. And dear Lord, what a sexy look. He'd hovered so close to her, his lips a breath away, it'd taken all her strength not to lay one on him. "What year was Dreadmoor built, Kail? The buildings are wonderfully preserved."

Kail scratched his head and gazed skyward. " 'Twas the Year o' our Lord 1287 when the job was complete. Tristan constructed the plans himself, and worked on most every building with the men till finished."

"Tristan drew the plans for Dreadmoor?"

"Aye."

"He never told me." Andi looked around as they walked. It was still early morning, and a light mist had blown in from the sea, whispering an eerie haze over Dreadmoor. She looked each building over as they passed, finding it thrilled her to know Tristan not only had drawn the plans for the castle, but had physically worked on it. His very real and mortal hands had touched the stones that lay mortared together. The thought of it caused her to shiver. "Are these all the original buildings?"

"All but the kirk."

"What happened to the original one?"

Kail rested his large hand on the hilt of his sword and looked down at Andi. "As you know, Himself, along with the lot of us, was in a state of being in between places for nearly two centuries. When Tristan came to and presented himself to the Jamesons, they didn't know what had happened to the old building. The one standing was the only one they knew."

Andi stopped. Another breeze sifted her hair, catching a few strands on her lips. She brushed them back, turned a complete circle, then looked up at Kail. "Where was the old kirk?"

Kail turned and pointed behind them. "See you the lists, lady?" His voice came out as a rumble. " 'Twas there, when once we were living, that the kirk stood."

Andi's gaze followed Kail's finger to the lists. Ghostly knights milled about, some at the blades, others waiting their turn to joust. Some were in pairs, wrestling ferociously in the dirt, grunting and cursing in several medieval languages, while others stood back and cheered them on. Andi looked up at Kail. "Over there? In the middle of all that?"

Kail straightened and drew his brows together. "You, my lady, are up to something." He glared, one eyebrow raised skyward. "What be it?"

She shook her head. "I don't know. I feel as if what I search for is right under my nose." She met his gaze. "But I'm just too blind to see it."

He stopped and inclined his head. "You're far from blind, woman. You've accepted the fact that fifteen knights from the thirteenth century were murdered and cursed, presented before you. You speak now with a dead man." He smiled. "Your lovely eyes need only stretch a bit further. Then you'll find what you're looking for." He winked. "I'll warrant."

Andi sighed. "I hope you're right." She paused and looked at the big man. "Kail, what would happen if the curse was lifted?"

He peered off into the distance for a few seconds, then scrubbed his jaw and met her gaze. "I cannot be certain, my lady, but I fear we would all just pass onward."

"Onward?" Andi asked.

"Aye. To the other side." He shrugged. "Wherever that may be."

Somehow, that thought made Andi's stomach ache.

Two weeks flew by, faster than it ever had in her entire life. And she'd had amazing luck with her work. So far, she'd recovered all of Tristan's chain mail, his helm, and several bones from whomever the unfortunate soul was in the dungeon. It was enough to determine the sex and approximate age.

Female. Between the ages of thirty and seventy.

It'd baffled everyone. Never had Dreadmoor's dungeon housed a female. And yet the bones didn't lie. Terrance Daughtry had the state pathologist looking in on it for her. Privately. Just the way Tristan wanted. No questions asked. Not even Kirk knew. She'd begged Terrance to keep it confidential. And he had.

What she couldn't figure out was why the presence had led her to the dungeon in the first place. Simply to find the mail? Or was it the bones? If anything, it complicated an already complicated mystery.

That, of course, made her much more determined to solve it.

Dragonhawk and his missing knights. Right at her fingertips. Right under the world's nose. It still amazed her. Every time he stared at her with that . . . smoky look, she knew he was just as real as any man alive. Maybe even more so. He wasn't like twenty-first-century men. He was . . . different. They just didn't grow them like Tristan anymore. Or the rest of his knights, for that matter.

And who would've believed that she, Andrea Kinley Monroe, would be caught sitting in a thirteenth-century haunted castle, watching the National Rugby League's quarter finals with fifteen seasoned medieval warriors?

She wouldn't trade it for the world.

Many things bothered her, but one nagged her even in sleep.

What was to become of her and Tristan?

The avoided subject worried her. Up to now, she'd fallen back on the excuse that the recovery wasn't finished. But what happened when it *was*? Long-term as well as short-term concerns flooded her mind, such as how on earth could it possibly work between a mortal and a ghost? And try as she might to push the concerns aside, they kept surfacing. She knew she'd have to speak to Tristan about them. He probably sensed the same things, but hadn't said anything. If they decided to be together, what would it be like to be celibate for the rest of her life? No children? Never having him hold her?

Her getting old while he stayed young and virile?

And the whole thing with Kirk perplexed her. She'd asked him vague questions about Dreadmoor's haunted past, but he always claimed not to know much. The fact that he'd known about the blades and twisted yew vines bothered her for a while, but after she'd asked several villagers about curses and witchery, more than one volunteered information on twisted yew.

In other words, she was stuck.

Pushing those gloomy worries aside, she thought of Tristan. One thing was for sure. The Dragonhawk of Dreadmoor had a medieval trick up his sleeve for her birthday. And for the first time in her life, she couldn't stand the wait.

"Damnation, old man," Tristan bellowed, "can you not fix the bloody concoction?" He leaned over Jameson's shoulder and scowled. "I vow 'tis giving me a raging headache just watching you."

Jameson raised his silvery eyebrows. "No doubt, my lord. Perhaps you would be more suited pacing by the fire in the great hall?"

"I would be more suited if you'd just get on with it, man. Should there not be a bit more sprigs over to the left?"

Jameson heaved a sigh and arranged a few more sprigs of small silk poppy buds on top of the two-tier birthday cake. "Is that satisfactory, Lord Dreadmoor?"

Tristan scowled at his man. "Your tongue has become

slithery and loose of late, Jameson. Just decorate the bloody cake. And where, by the devil's horns, is that witless Stanley? Did you not say he was of a reliable sort? So far he is one half hour late."

Jameson rolled his eyes and used what Tristan perceived as extreme effort to smother a grin. "One would nearly believe you might be anxious over all this, my young lord." After a quick smirk, he avoided Tristan's glare.

"It is not anxiousness." Tristan cleared his throat. "I love the wench, and no one has ever bothered to rejoice in her day of birth. If she will permit me, I shall rejoice in it every year for the rest of her life."

Jameson, whose usual calm and collected manner radiated from every pore of his sixty-eight-year-old body, gaped in not-so-much surprise. His mouth curved up, ever so slightly, into a pleased grin. "Are you about what I think you are about, Lord Tristan?"

"Bloody right I am."

Jameson beamed. "Well done, lad!" He cleared his throat. "I couldn't be more pleased."

Tristan grunted, but he couldn't stop the smile from spreading across his face. "Aye, neither could I. And now that I have accomplished making you eternally happy, could you please finish the bloody cake?" His head snapped up. "I do believe your young cousin Stan has arrived at the gates. Call down to the barbican and have Will send him up." He smiled at Jameson. "I've got some last-minute illusions to concoct. Is my chamber ready?"

"Aye, my lord."

"And the battlements?"

Jameson inclined his head. "Exactly as you ordered."

For the hundredth time in less than an hour, a smile pulled at Tristan's mouth. "Perfect."

She could stand it no more.

Andi pulled on her sneakers and a pair of shorts, pulled her ponytail through the hole in the back of her Braves cap, and made for the hall. If she didn't get rid of some of the anxious energy rapidly building in her system, she'd explode. Her muscles would become toxic. Not a pretty sight.

Tristan de Barre was up to no good, and Jameson had told her to be ready by eight o'clock sharp. Four more hours to wait on the date of her life. A date with a thirteenth-century medieval ghost knight. The legendary Dragonhawk.

She just couldn't sit by and wait on that.

Instead, she decided to take Kirk's advice and go for a jog on the beach. It would soothe her jittery nerves to run along the surf until her lungs burned, until she had to stop and bend over at the waist, sucking in as much air as necessary. Maybe.

No one was about. Jameson remained in his sanctuary—the kitchen—probably preparing something delicious. Tristan and the guys couldn't be found—and there was no telling what they were up to. Even Heath busied himself, doing odd jobs for Tristan.

Slipping out the main door, she crossed the courtyard and made it to the path behind the keep, which led down to the surf. The wind, always blustery at Dreadmoor, whipped her ponytail this way and that as she crept down the steep, rocky path. Within minutes, she reached the pebbled beach.

Whitecaps dotted the blue-gray water of the tumultuous North Sea. The sun, which had been fairly bright a few hours earlier, dipped in and out of swirling gray clouds. The heavy scent of salty sea life clung to her palate with each breath. Behind her, Dreadmoor rose from the massive hunk of volcanic rock serving as its base. How dramatically beautiful, she thought. Wild. Powerful. Dangerous.

Just like its owner.

After stretching her muscles, Andi turned and began to run, a slow, easy pace, allowing the scents and sounds of the sea to wash over her, soothe her, seep into her skin. The farther she ran, the longer her strides became. Faster, harder, a half mile, then one. Soon, Dreadmoor disappeared behind her.

Go back.

In full stride, Andi turned her head. The forceful sea wind whistled past. With a shake, she pushed forward, pumping her arms to make her legs go faster.

Go back now!

Sand fanned in an arc at her sudden halt. Now, she'd heard something that time. Breathing hard, she scanned the beach. No mist, no ghost. Empty.

Hurry home.

Too late.

A vicious force shoved her to the ground. Someone straddled her, pinning her facedown in the sand. A heavy hand anchored her head so she couldn't move, sharp pebbles biting into the flesh of her stomach, her cheek.

"Let me up," she yelled.

"Shut up if you want to live."

A man. A heavy man. Her lungs, already exhausted from her fast-paced run, burned from his weight. She gasped for air.

"I want the swords. All of them. If I don't get them, more than just your pitiful self will pay."

His hand forced her face into the sand and rock, pushing until she couldn't breathe. Panicked, she began to writhe and buck, fighting for air. Oh God, she was going to die. . . .

"Do you hear me?" he said gruffly in her ear.

"Get you off her, or you will wish for a fast death."

In one fluid motion, the man rolled, taking her with him. He used her body for a shield as they stood. Andi sucked in great gulps of air as her lungs expanded, then sporadically coughed until her eyes watered. The man dragged her up.

Tristan, dressed in full battle regalia and accompanied by Dreadmoor's other fourteen knights, stood, slowly moving toward them. The hiss of fifteen swords being drawn broke the air.

The man grabbed her ponytail and yanked hard, forcing her head back. He pushed his mouth to her ear. "Tell your boyfriends to put away their toys, bitch." He pulled her hair harder. "Now!"

"Tristan!" she sputtered.

All knights froze. Their expressions were murderous. But not nearly as much as Tristan's.

"Jameson!" Tristan yelled.

A gunshot rang out over their heads. Jameson stood several feet away, a rifle shouldered and aimed.

The man pulled Andi's arms behind her until she thought they'd snap in half. "You tell your man to lower that bloody firearm or I will break her in two," the man threatened. He tightened his arm around her head and she gasped, her fingers trying to loosen his viselike grip around her throat. "Do it!" he yelled.

Slowly, he began backing up toward the dunes, dragging Andi with him. She trained her eyes on Tristan's. His face was thunderous. Never had she seen him seem so enraged. His body shook, as though ready to explode at any second.

"Lower it," Tristan said to Jameson.

Jameson pointed the rifle down. Instead of running, the man stood statue still for what seemed like minutes. His hand tightened around her throat; then he shoved Andi hard and disappeared into the dunes behind them. She fell to her knees, coughing and trying to drag in a decent breath.

"Follow him," Tristan ordered his men. Slowly, they disappeared. "Andrea, come here."

She raised her head. He hadn't moved, just stood there, shaking, the power within him seemingly ready to burst into flames.

Jameson walked over, rifle over his shoulder, and knelt beside her. "You're beyond Dreadmoor's border, lady. Himself is unable to cross the boundaries like the others. Here, now. I'll help you. Master Tristan is most anxious to check you over." Gently, he pulled on her elbow.

As soon as she rose, her feet began to move. They didn't stop until she stood before Tristan. God, how badly she wanted to throw herself into his arms, press against his broad chest, feel his powerful arms protective, comforting. Instead, she wrapped her own arms around herself and stood as close to him as possible.

He leaned, lowered his head, and whispered against her ear. " 'Tis all right, love. Would that I had substance, I would hold you and try my damned bloody best not to squeeze you too tightly. It would be powerfully hard to let you go. . . ."

The more words he spoke, the more fierce her lungs burned, her chest tightened. She couldn't help it. Tried real hard not to. She wasn't a baby. But tears formed faster than her brain could refuse, and they spilled over onto her cheeks.

"Christ. Tilt your head up, Andrea, so I can have a look."

Sniffing, she did as he asked. Sapphire eyes searched her face, and she watched his expression harden as he took in every inch.

"Jameson. I want the constable out here tonight."

The aged butler, with rifle in tow, walked up beside them. "My thoughts exactly. I'm on my way now." He left, walking ahead to do Tristan's bidding.

Tristan ducked his head to catch her gaze. "I'm sorry, Andrea. I should have been here."

The look of anguish in his face made her heart ache. "Tristan, really. No one could have guessed—"

"I should have been here."

Drawing a deep breath, she lifted her chin and gave him a brave smile. "You're here now. You brought Jameson and you saved me." She lifted her hand, close to his jaw, and held it there as if she stroked it. "That's all that matters to me."

They stood there, staring at each other, for what seemed like forever. Finally, Tristan cleared his throat. "My men are following him as we speak, so I've no choice but to leave that matter to them." He drew closer, his brows drawn into a frown. "You've scrapes on your face. Come on, love. Let us get back to the keep."

Together they walked side by side, but Andi knew—felt a change in Tristan, a shift in his mood. One she hadn't felt yet. It scared her, gave her a sick feeling in the pit of her stomach. Somehow, she sensed things were about to drastically change.

*   *   *

Never, in life or in death, had he wanted to kill another human being more than the one who'd had his woman's face pushed into the sand. It made his insides burn, made skin that had no nerves tingle with building, blinding rage. To have to stand by, like a bleeding idiot, and watch.

Watch, without being able to do a damned bloody thing.

Worse, how could he ever protect her? Even within Dreadmoor's walls, 'twould be nigh impossible. If someone wanted to harm her, they could if determined enough. He'd have to rely on Jameson. Or mayhap he could employ more mortals. . . .

Either way, he couldn't perform the deed himself.

He watched but kept silent as Jameson doctored Andrea's scraped flesh. How he wished he could do it. Those lovely eyes of hers remained on him, followed him whilst he'd paced. The sight nearly buckled him.

"How did you know?" she asked.

He stopped and turned. "I heard you. I heard . . . him." He didn't mention that the man had stood, staring at him, just before fleeing. As if he knew him. Recognized him, mayhap?

Jameson gave a nod. "Good as new, my lady. I shall return once the constable arrives. Jason? Would you accompany me?"

Jason, who'd remained behind, had not left Andi's side since returning to the hall. He gave her a warm smile. "Should you need anything, you've only just to say it." With a nod at Tristan, he left the hall with Jameson.

"Hey, Dreadmoor," Andi said. "Come here."

He almost smiled. Such a cheeky wench. In two steps he stood before her.

"It's over now. You can get that scowl off your face." She smiled, trying to look brave, no doubt. "I'm fine. Really. Someone obviously heard about the hoard and wanted to get their hands on it. It is a wealthy stash, you know. Probably worth quite a lot. Rivaling the queen's bank account, even."

"Aye. Mayhap you've the right of it." But he doubted it. Searching her face, he stared at the small red scrapes marring her skin from the sand and pebbles. The skin on her throat had a perfect imprint of the bastard's fingers where he'd squeezed. Saints, the scene flashed before him again and made his insides flame. He wished the man's throat was beneath his own fingers. . . .

"Tristan."

Again, they stared. He felt as though she could read his every thought. Hazel eyes explored his face, begged him to relent, but he could not. Not now. Not ever.

He could *never* protect her. And truly, that was the beginning of it. She'd stood there, with her own arms wrapped about herself, and he'd wanted nothing more than to be able to take her in his embrace. But he couldn't. Never could he.

"Constable Hurley is at the gates," Jameson announced.

Without breaking their locked stare, Tristan answered, "Send him to the study. We'll await him in there. No doubt he'll want to see the blades and helms."

Within minutes, Jameson ushered the constable into the large, book-lined room. Tristan, stationed behind a rectangular oak desk, rose but did not extend a hand. "Constable. Thank you for making the journey."

A tall fellow, Hurley appeared to be in his late forties, short-cropped dark brown hair shot with gray at the temples, and wearing a dark gray suit and black tie. He looked at Andi. "Are you all right, Dr. Monroe?"

Andrea brushed a scrape on her cheek. "Yes. I'm fine."

"Can you tell me what happened?" Hurley readied himself with pen and paper. "Try not to miss any details."

"I'll tell you the details," Tristan said, trying to keep his voice calm. He felt as though he wanted to shout every word falling out of his mouth. "The bastard was completely dressed in black, including a mask of sorts. He pushed her face into the sand so she could not draw a decent breath. He choked her with his bare hand, and

threatened her life if she did not produce the swords."
He pinned the constable with a hot stare. "What else do
you need to know?"

Constable Hurley met his stare with a brave one of his
own. "I realize you're upset, Lord Dreadmoor. But—"

"Upset? Not even close." He leaned over the desk,
balancing his weight with his arms. "I want the man
caught, Constable. I'll have no one threatening my—
Dr. Monroe."

After a moment, the constable nodded, then turned to
Andrea. "You didn't recognize the man, did you? His
voice, perhaps?"

Andrea shook her head. "I'm sorry. No, I didn't. He
took me completely by surprise."

"Was he British?" he asked.

Andi nodded. "Yes."

Hurley inclined his head to the table centered in the
room. "Are those the weapons?"

Andrea gave Tristan a short smile before answering
the constable. "Yes. Fourteen swords, fourteen helmets."
She looked up at him. "Worth quite a nice sum, I should
say. Anyone who knows medieval weaponry would know
their monetary value."

"No doubt." Hurley returned to the desk, his attention
on Tristan. "I assure you, Lord Dreadmoor, that I will
personally be on this case. I'll notify you of any changes.
Meanwhile, I'll send a few men to post at various points
along Dreadmoor's border, if you like."

Tristan nodded. "Very well. Will, my guard at the barbican, will show them to their posts."

As Hurley shifted away from the desk, he bumped it
with his hip. "Oh, beg pardon—"

Tristan could only watch as the pewter pencil holder
flew toward him.

Then through him.

Hurley's face drained of all color. He glanced from
Andrea to Tristan, then down at the pencil holder on
the floor. It took several moments before he cleared his
throat and straightened his suit coat.

Tristan lowered his voice and stared directly at him.

"Thank you for your discretion, and cooperation, Constable. As always, it is more than appreciated."

Hurley stared for a long time, more likely than not trying to collect his disrupted thoughts. He'd seen, and he knew, but wasn't letting on. Finally, he smiled and gave a nod. "Right. I'll see myself out." He glanced at Andrea. "Dr. Monroe." With that, the constable turned and left—and noticeably faster than when he arrived.

Tristan moved toward Andrea. Saints, how he wished he could hold her. "Well. This is a night the constable will never forget, aye?" He eyed her. "You should rest, Andrea. The day's events have been barbarous. You look tired."

The hurt in her eyes made him feel like a bloody idiot. It could not be helped. Yet he found it passing difficult to crush her poor heart—especially after having been attacked. Instead, he gave her a smile. "Come, I'll walk you to your chambers. You'll have a good rest, and we'll have your birthday supper tomorrow night. Aye?"

With a slight nod, she moved toward the stairs. "I can see myself up, thanks. I'll see you in the morning." Without another word, she turned and mounted the steps.

He watched until she rounded the top stair and disappeared into the passageway.

"Pitiful, Dreadmoor. Truly pitiful."

Tristan shoved his hand through his hair and turned around. Kail, Richard, and Stephen stood, arms crossed over their chests, frowns on their faces. As if he needed a scolding. "Aye, I know. What did you find?"

"We followed him to Berwick," Kail said. "Not once did he remove his mask, Tristan. Kept the bloody thing on the entire time. Passing odd."

"Aye," Richard said, pacing before the hearth. " 'Twas as though he knew we were there and didn't want us to see his face. Even in private."

Tristan waited. "And?"

"And," Stephen said, "he dodged into a pub—the very same one your Andrea followed her mentor into. We couldn't . . ."

"You couldn't do what?" Tristan said.

Kail grabbed his shoulder. "We couldn't follow him into the bloody pub. 'Twas a force keeping us out. Just like you cannot leave Dreadmoor."

Tristan slammed his fist against the wall. "It has to be Erik. Bloody witch."

"We waited, but he never came out," Kail continued. "I watched him disappear through a door—"

"You what?" Tristan's eyes narrowed.

Stephen waved a hand. "Nay, not *disappeared*. Disappeared. He opened a door, slipped through, and closed it behind him."

Scrubbing his face with both hands, Tristan walked to the hearth. With a flick of his wrist, the flames jumped to life. "De Sabre wants the swords. Why?" He shook his head. "What could it mean?"

"They were bundled in twisted yew, Tristan," Richard reminded him. "Cursed."

"We're cursed!" Tristan said. "And he's a spirit living in a mortal body. Still Erik's spirit all the same. Who knows why he wants the bloody things?"

"Mayhap," Kail said, walking to his side, "he's after only one. Yours."

Tristan trained his gaze on the fire. "Mine is the only one not in the bundle."

"Aye, but does he know that?"

"Yes, he knows. I think."

All three men turned. Andrea, dressed in a rather large sweatshirt and those drawstring pants she was so fond of, stood behind them.

She smiled and lifted one shoulder. "Your voices carry. I've got an uncanny hearing ability, too. And I'm starved."

Tristan walked to her. "I know you choose not to believe that Erik and your Kirk are sharing the same body. But they are. It's the only thing that makes sense."

"Something did happen, the day I began the bone retrieval."

Tristan nodded. "Aye, your mentor became ill. What of it?"

Andi began to pace. "It doesn't make sense, yet it's so . . . bizarre. I can't stop thinking about it."

"Go on, lass," Kail said. "We're all ears."

"Well," she began, "Kirk jumped into the grid pit and was going to start the retrieval, and I was going to bag. Then we were going to switch. Up until that point, I hadn't noticed him acting differently. But he lifted the skull first, and it was wrapped in yew vines—"

"Bloody witch's curse," Gareth said.

"Well, as soon as he loosened the vines, he almost immediately dropped it, started to shake, then threw up."

"Damn me, Andrea. Why didn't you tell us sooner?" Tristan said.

"I'm sorry. At the time I didn't know I was employed by a thirteenth-century ghost."

That won several snickers from the guys.

"Besides, I thought he'd just had bad food." She shook her head. "I'm really trying to get a grip on this, guys. I can't wrap my brain around this whole thing. Can't Kirk fight this spirit? God, he was like a father to me."

"Aye," Tristan said, with more vehemence than he planned. "And Erik was like one to me, as well." He arced his hand toward the men. "To all of us. We squired under him. We battled with him. He taught us everything as young knights."

She folded her arms across her chest. "So murdering all of you was his revenge for his son's death?"

"Aye."

All was silent for a few moments.

"He gave Tristan his name, you know."

They all turned to find the rest of the knights, except for two who were still watching the pub in Berwick. Gareth, who'd spoken, inclined his head. "Fearless. Vigilant. Powerful."

Andi looked at Tristan. "Dragonhawk." She walked over to the hearth, where mounted on the stone above was the mystical symbol belonging solely to him. She stared at it. "It's amazing. That eye, it holds a secret that's driving me nuts." She shook her head, mumbling to herself. "What is it?"

Tristan glanced at his men. They all wore the same

baffled expression. "If anyone can figure out the mystery, Dr. Monroe, 'twould no doubt be you."

She looked at him and the corners of her mouth tipped up. She snapped her fingers. "I've an idea."

"Saints, Tristan," Richard said. "She's that wicked glint in her eye again. I've seen it before, in Berwick." He shuddered. "A bad sign, that."

She began to pace, weaving in and out of the knights as she spoke. "None of you have heard the same voice I hear, nor have you seen the weird collection of mist. Right?"

A round of "ayes" filled the hall.

"Right." She nodded. "I don't know who this is, but I know I'm not crazy. It's chosen me for some reason. Now, I've been doing a lot of thinking about the bones under the oak tree."

Tristan studied her as she voiced her theories aloud, to no one in particular. Just out loud. She astounded him, what with her wit and cleverness.

"Okay, bear with me, guys, I'm just throwing things out here. We twenty-first centurians call it brainstorming." She rubbed her chin. "The first night I arrived, the presence made itself known when I went out to check the cutaway. Later, as I began the excavation, it led me to the dungeon, where I found Tristan's mail and the mysterious set of bones." She looked at everyone. "Follow me so far?"

Another round of "ayes."

"Good." She resumed her pacing. "Now, I've heard some strange warnings from that presence. It warned me on the beach, but I heard it too late." She walked in a circle. "What if the presence belongs to that of the woman's bones in the dungeon? What if those remains belonged to someone who knew about all of you?" She shook her head again. "I feel as though I'm being led around, being given clues—no, being fed clues. And although I've made a slight connection, I still can't figure out what the heck I'm supposed to be doing. But why me? Why haven't any of you been given clues? What about Jameson? His family has been here forever." She turned and fixed her eyes directly on Tristan. "Why me?"

Tristan returned her stare. "Mayhap because you're a woman."

"Aye, and mayhap the remains are those of a woman, like you say," said Kail.

"There haven't been many wenches here at Dreadmoor," Gareth pointed out. "Not since before."

Andi turned and looked at him. "Before what?"

"Before they all died, love," Tristan said quietly.

"Oh," she said, rubbing her brow in heavy concentration. "Who was the woman who was here before?"

To think so many centuries had passed since his thoughts had searched through so many minor details of his life before. "We had several serving maids. Most lived in the village, though. And one older woman. Our cook."

Silence filled the room, spanning several seconds at best. Then every knight in the hall cursed.

Andi's puzzled look touched everyone. "What?"

"Christ," Tristan said. "It didn't even occur to me."

"What?" she said, growing impatient.

He looked down at her. "My cook came with me from Greykirk—my father's home. She was more like family than anything. She'd been kicked out of her own hall, supposedly for witchery, and my sire took her in. I'd been around her since I was a lad."

Andi's eyes widened. "So?"

Tristan met her gaze. "She was Erik's mother."

Chapter 26

For at least the hundredth time that night Andi rolled over, punched her pillow several times, and tried to fall asleep.

What a useless effort it had been.

She jumped up, padded barefoot to the window, and threw it open. Crisp, salty air engulfed her as it swirled into the room and manipulated her senses. It soothed her, comforted her. But it did nothing to solve her problem.

She stared out into the night and listened to the waves of the North Sea crash against the rocks. The full moon bathed the entire bailey in a pale glow. It was beautiful here. Peaceful. And it felt *right*.

Tristan felt right.

As right as being in love with a ghost can be, anyway.

She'd felt him withdraw after the attack on the beach. Just because he couldn't physically help her, he'd withdrawn. She knew it without even having him admit it. And this thing with Erik/Kirk. It was an invisible barrier between them. It seemed impossible that Kirk could be anyone other than who he'd claimed.

Had the spirit of Tristan's killer taken over Kirk's body when he freed the skull from the yew? But that would mean the remains were Erik's. Who would have killed him? And cursed him?

She pressed her forehead to the glass. Could it be? God, it sounded insane. *As if staying with a spirit for the rest of your life isn't? Come on, Monroe. Think. Use your brain.*

What *had* she really been thinking? That she and Tristan could have a chance together? Not that it wouldn't be unusual, but she felt safe with him. He was strong and protective and had an abundance of chivalry. And she had never felt so wanted by anyone in all her life.

She squeezed her eyes shut to block the memory. It didn't help. He was everything she'd ever secretly dreamed of having, save the little annoyance of him being dead.

She sighed and rubbed her eyes. She wasn't fashionable and flirty like a lot of women. She taught medieval archaeology, dug around in the dirt, and rarely dated. If men noticed her at all, they treated her more like a friend. Or a sister.

But God, the way Tristan looked at her made her shiver—more of a caress than a casual glance. She'd felt it clear to her toes. He made her feel beautiful, womanly, *desired* beyond belief.

Come.

Andi's heart jumped. After a second, she chuckled out loud. "Oh no. Let me guess. The voice." Pushing away from the window, she plopped down on the bed. "What do you want? Who are you? Are you trying to drive me insane? Because I'm already halfway there."

Silence drifted within the room for several seconds. Maybe even minutes.

Come now.

"Okay. You did try to warn me earlier on the beach. I heard you." She blinked in the dark. "Thank you. But . . . but I just don't know what you're trying to tell me here." Waiting, she stared into the darkness. "Come on. Give me something more than a wisp of mist and a whisper." She waited. "Please?"

A slip of air brushed the skin on her neck, the whisper close to her ear. *Now.*

A silvery sheen of mist appeared before her chamber door. What did she have to lose? It could very well be that she was totally nuts, imagining the whisper, the mist, the breeze on her neck that made her shiver. But whatever it was, she felt it had something to do with Tristan and his knights—and the curse.

Hurry.

"Okay, I'm coming." Shoving her feet into her sneakers, she eased out of her chamber.

Jason was, of course, there at the ready. Andi put her fingers to her lips, then whispered, "The presence. Don't follow me, you might scare it away. But tell Tristan and keep an eye out."

Jason nodded and disappeared.

Andi crept along the passageway, down the steps, and across the great hall. The lamps flickered across the enormous room, casting long shadows that danced at the slightest urging of a draft. She made no sound as she followed the strange mist out the front door.

The moon loomed over the bailey like a great, white ball, casting the landscape in an eerie luster. The air wafted with the scent of seaweed and salt water, and she could taste it with every breath.

Situated on the rocky coast of the North Sea, Dreadmoor was brutally beautiful. She shivered as a brisk breeze washed over her, and she rubbed her arms vigorously to ward off the chill. The temperature felt warm during the day, being mid-August; nighttime was a different story altogether.

As she neared the cutaway, she felt silly, talking to a waft of mist, but she did it anyway. "I've already excavated and recovered that entire area. I found nothing more." The mist moved past the churned soil where the giant oak had overturned the bones and weapons. "Okay, not going to the cutaway." Farther she went, past the arc of the spotlight perched on Dreadmoor's rooftop, to the edge of the bailey. Finally, the mist stopped, hovering in the air like a wraithlike cloud.

Andi turned a circle, staring into the moonlit night. They were in the dead-center of the lists. "Are you Erik's mother?"

The mist hung in the air, becoming very still. Minutes ticked by. The presence didn't answer.

Kneel.

The air around Andi calmed. "What?"

Pray.

"Kneel. Pray. What's that supposed to mean?"

Silence, then one last whisper.

Behind his eye.

Tristan watched, in his invisible form, a safe distance away, as Andi talked to the wind. She twirled in a circle, threw up her arms, then stomped over to a large rock at the edge of the lists and lay back. God's bones, she must be battling deep thoughts. He knew he was responsible for the forlorn expression she wore, with her eyes screwed shut like they were.

He loved her, and it pained him to see her in such distress. He'd thought the task of closing his heart to her would be easily done. How wrong he was. But was it fair to keep her?

With resignation, he materialized behind the rock and spoke as softly as his deep voice would allow. "Andrea?"

She squealed and darted away from the boulder, turning to face Tristan as she covered her heart with her hand. "Tristan!" Her breath came out in a gasp. "You scared me!"

Tristan dragged a hand through his hair and rubbed the back of his neck. "I vow 'twas not my intention, lady. Jason told me you sent for me." He couldn't stop the frown from crossing his face. "What, by the blessed saints, are you doing out here at this hour? And who are you having speech with? 'Tis a bloody good thing that the moon is high, or I'd see naught but your shadow. Now, why are you out of bed? What is this about the presence?"

She stared at the lists. "Kneel. Pray. Behind his eye."

Tristan blinked. "What?"

She shook her head. "That presence. You know, the voice I keep hearing and no one else can hear it? It led me out here." She pointed to the center of the lists. "Right there, actually. It said those three things. Kneel. Pray. Behind his eye."

" 'Tis passing strange."

She looked at him. "It makes no sense."

"Neither does a lot of things," he mumbled.

"What?"

An aggravated sigh tore from his lungs. " 'Tis naught. Come sit you on this rock as you were before and try to keep quiet for once." He stared at her. "I have something I wish to discuss with you."

"You want me to leave. Right? I knew it."

Tristan rubbed the bridge of his nose. "Saints, nay." He pointed to the rock. "Sit."

Andi resumed her position.

By the devil, he felt like a bumbling whelp of nine in her presence. How could he even bring himself to spout the witless words from his mouth?

Somehow, they came.

"You've no idea what it does to a man, Andrea, when he feels—he knows he cannot protect the woman he loves." He looked at her. "And I cannot protect you. Not alone. Not without mortal help."

"Tristan, don't."

"Please, Andrea. If I don't say these words now, they may never come forth again."

She quieted and settled back against the rock.

"After you were attacked, I felt the only way to keep you safe was to send you away. Although my knights and I are a fearsome-looking lot, we're ghosts, Andrea." He started pacing. " 'Tis more than that, and we've yet to discuss it." He rounded on her and drew close. "What sort of life would you have here, with me? Have you thought of that? No intimacy, Andrea. No touching, other than my ghostly attempts. No real sex. No children. Have these things not crossed your mind?" He stared into her eyes. "I'm a ghost, woman. I'm quite well and used to not having substance. But how adjusted are you to never having a man's touch?" He began to pace once more. "Never have I felt so helpless. And yet—" He stopped and looked at her. "The more I thought on the matter, the more I knew I couldn't simply send you off, never to see you again. I'm much more selfish than that."

He ducked his head. "Did you know that about me? How bloody selfish I am?"

She pushed herself off the rock and stood up straight, wrapping her arms around herself as she spoke, staring up at the moon. "I'd always thought of you as my knight. Only mine. I shared my vision of you with no one." A small, tight laugh escaped her. "It's childish, I know. Completely illogical." She shook her head. "I snuck out here twelve years ago, fascinated by the legend of Dragonhawk and his missing knights. Little did I know then that I'd met the infamous Lord Dreadmoor." The quiver in her voice belied her bravery. "Now I know everything about you. And I can't stop thinking of you, thinking of our intimate times together, even if they are ghostly."

"God, Andrea." Tristan couldn't believe his ears. "Look at me." He watched as she lifted her gaze. He couldn't see the bright color of her eyes, just the glassy softness of the moonlight's reflection in her tears. His heart felt as though it would burst, and yet he knew his ghostly form possessed no heart at all. His senses overwhelmed him; skin that could no longer tingle became alive with the long-forgotten sensation.

He glanced down at his tunic, for he was quite positive he could see his heart thumping against it. And a bloody annoying lump had formed in his throat. The urge to touch her swept over him, and he clenched his hands at his sides to prevent himself from trying the like again. They stood no more than a foot apart, and not for the first time, his ghostly body reacted to her nearness.

" 'Tisn't childish. Nor illogical." His voice sounded ragged, even to his own ears. "Strange, but for us, it seems rather normal."

He took a step forward, his eyes never leaving hers. She stepped back until her shoulders met the boulder at her back. Tristan loomed over her, wanting to be closer still. He stared into her eyes, so soft yet so alert, so painfully deep he thought his poor knees would fail him at any moment. He braced his hands on the rock, one on each side of her head as he bent closer. "Saints, Andrea." It took every effort to keep his voice from cracking. "You are so beautiful." He moved his head closer still, his lips a slip away from hers. His gaze moved to her mouth, then back to her eyes. "Christ, I want to kiss you."

Her chest heaved with every breath. "You look so real," she said, and reached to touch his chin. They stared at one another without saying a word. Each breath became ragged, her chest heaving with each intake of air as she watched him. "You know? When I look at you, it actually hurts to breathe." She closed her eyes. "I crave your touch, your scent, your taste. Kiss me, Tristan. However you can, just please." She gazed at his lips as they drew closer to hers. "Please don't stop what you're doing."

"Andrea." He lowered his head to her hair and inhaled. "I vow I can imagine what you smell like." His head dipped until his lips hovered just above hers, his gaze caught with hers. He moved closer still and slanted his mouth over hers. Their lips met, not physically touching but emotionally entwining, their essence mingling.

"I swear I can taste you." His words whispered against her cheek. He pulled back and stared at her. "What does it feel like, Andrea? Can you feel me?"

Andi looked up into his eyes and smiled through a haze of tears. "More than you know." She reached out to touch his cheek, but went too far. Her hand passed through it as though it were a shadow. Hesitantly she lifted her eyes to his, blinking in surprise.

"I vow it won't be enough, Andrea Kinley Monroe," he said, her name meant to be a caress on his lips. "It won't ever be enough. Were I alive, it still would not be enough."

Chapter 27

"Wake up, my birthday wench. I vow you sleep longer than any live being I know."

Andi cracked open an eye. Tristan perched on the side of her bed, a thick arm on either side of her head, staring at her.

She'd overslept.

"Tristan, let me up," she said.

He didn't budge.

One side of his sensuous mouth lifted into a sexy grin. "Were I alive, you wouldn't leave this bed for a fortnight, at least." His grin grew more devilish as his head lowered to hers. "Unless, of course, it would be to move to the floor. . . ."

Scooting under his arm, she slid off the side of the bed. "You're a naughty man, Dragonhawk." She threw him a saucy grin of her own. "Tease."

Walking to the window, she pressed her face to the pane. The sun peeked in and out of gray clouds. "What are the guys doing?"

Tristan walked up behind her and peered over her head. "Training. Jousting. Fighting. The usual. I've two watching the pub where the masked man was seen entering. All the other knights are here."

She didn't turn around. "I asked the presence last night, in the lists, if she was Erik's mother."

He paused. "And?"

Andi sighed. "No answer. Only kneel, pray, behind his eye."

She turned around, leaned her bottom against the sill, and stared into his incredible eyes. "I've said those three things in my mind all night long. Kneel. Pray. Behind his eye. Over and over again." She pinched the bridge of her nose, then looked up. "I want to figure this thing out so badly."

Long, thick black hair fell over one broad shoulder as Tristan lowered his head. "If anyone can, 'tis you. I've no doubt about it. But I want you to put it aside for today, Andrea. It's your birthday, and I've a mind to woo you properly."

The smile on her face spread slowly. "Oh, you do?"

His mouth hovered over hers. "Aye."

"I love it when you say 'aye.' Very sexy."

That made his eyes churn a dark, dangerous blue gray. "Aye, then I shall remember to say it often. Aye? Aye, aye, aye . . ."

She laughed, and it took solid strength to look away. Another stream of curses made her peer out the window. "Are they waiting for you?" A line of jousters stretched for what seemed at least a mile. "Jason told me in his day, there wasn't a soul around who could best the Dragonhawk, save his sire and Uncle Killian.

He snorted. "Even they had difficulty."

She smiled. "Ooh, you conceited man. Let's go. I want to watch for a minute before I start on my work."

"Ahem."

Glancing over her shoulder, she raised her eyebrows. "Just a little. I'm working on a theory. I just want to go over the blueprints." She smiled. "You can come, too."

"You are a most determined, tenacious wench, Andrea Kinley Monroe. Very well. You can watch me make a few passes, and then we'll go over the blueprints together." He ducked his head, his mouth positioned over hers. "We'll be in close quarters then. You'll have no chance of escape."

Pushing away from the window, she raised one eyebrow. "As if I'd want one."

Andi shielded her eyes. Tristan's horse tossed his head, ready to go again. Flipping his visor up, the big knight flashed the whites of his teeth as he grinned. She couldn't see his dimples, but she knew they were there, pitting his beard-scruffed cheeks. She smiled and waved, and he nodded in return. With a flick of his visor he trotted off, back to his side of the field to ready for his next opponent.

Earlier, she'd whispered *I love you* to him from across the field; big fat mistake. She'd forgotten Tristan wasn't the only ghost around Dreadmoor who had an uncanny hearing ability. The bailey had erupted in shrill whistles and male voices shouting, "I love you, too, Tristan." He'd planted his fist in more than one nose for the teasing he'd received. So she'd refrained from whispering words of affection while there were other ghosts about.

She'd gladly reserve those words for later.

She shook her head and watched Tristan prepare for another pass. One more, and she'd head to the study and go over the blueprints of Dreadmoor's original building structures.

The wind caught her hair and tossed it across her cheek. Strange, to think they jousted right in the middle of where the original kirk used to be. She guessed they were running their mounts right over the altar. She stared, fixated.

She blinked.

Altar.

Kneel. Pray.

Behind his eye.

Her heart lurched. Oh God. Why hadn't she realized it before?

Leaping out of the chair, she ran toward the lists. "Tristan! Stop!"

A powerful and very sweaty Tristan pulled his mount to a halt and turned in his saddle, his eyes following her as she ran. She waved at him. "Hurry! Come here!"

He flung his helmet to the ground and slid off his horse, landing in a run. He didn't stop until they'd met in the middle.

"What's wrong with you, woman?" His face hovered

less than a foot from her own, worry creasing his brow. "Andrea, for the saints' sake. What is wrong?"

God, he looked so real, standing there, sweating, his hair plastered to his head. It was so easy to forget he was a ghost.

But he *was* a ghost. And she just figured out what to do about it. She hoped.

"I need to dig up your lists."

An hour later, fifteen ghostly knights surrounded Andi in the study as she pored over the original blueprints of Dreadmoor.

The ones drawn by Tristan's very own live hands.

She lightly touched the pane of lead glass covering the aging parchment, dragging her fingertip from one corner to the other. "It's been right here all this time, staring me in the face. I didn't even see it." She peered at the fading ink indicating the area of the original kirk. "Kneel. Pray." Her eyes lifted to Tristan's, who stood across the table from her. "The presence wants me to search the spot where you would have knelt for Mass."

"Whatever are you looking for there, lady?" Jason asked. The other knights waited for her to answer.

Andi shook her head. "I'm not exactly sure. The other part of the message is 'behind his eye.'" Shrugging, she held Tristan's unusual gaze. "Whatever it is, it has to do with you."

"What about her birthday?" asked Richard. The others mumbled their concern.

"Listen," she said, addressing Tristan more than anyone. "This *is* my birthday—to figure out this crazy mystery. And to help you guys any way I can." She smiled. "It's *passing* important to me."

The corner of Tristan's mouth lifted, the dimples pitting his cheeks. An intense look crossed his face. "I shall put my well-designed birthday plans off a bit longer, if you wish."

Their eyes met, and Andi gave him a knowing smile. "I do wish it."

The big knight gave a nod. "Then let's get at it, lady."

Andi lifted a ruler from her site kit, took a few measurements from the prints, and scribbled them down on her notepad. When she looked up, the knights had their stares fixed on her. With an encouraging smile, she inclined her head. "Okay, boys. Let's go."

"My lord, a phone call," Jameson announced. " 'Tis Constable Hurley."

Andi glanced over her shoulder at Tristan. "Do you need me?"

"Nay. Jameson can hold the receiver. I'll be only a moment." He turned and followed his man back into the hall. Once in the kitchen, he positioned his ear and mouth to the piece and spoke. "Aye, Constable. What is it?"

Constable Hurley cleared his throat. "Right. I'm afraid I've a bit of disturbing news, sir. I wanted to inform you first."

Tristan's stomach knotted. "What is it?"

Hurley cleared his throat. "The woman who paid bail on the two who jumped Dr. Monroe? She's been found in a car behind a pub, the Infidel. Dead."

Tristan's mouth tightened. "Christ."

"That's not all, I'm afraid. Just this morning, we found the bodies of the two men, along with a third, who happened to be dressed in all black, in an alley no more than three blocks from the Infidel." He heaved a sigh. "Their bloody necks had been snapped."

Tristan took a breath to keep his anger at bay. "Thank you for the information, Constable Hurley. If you will, keep me informed."

"Well," Hurley continued, "that's still not quite all of it."

"Oh?" Tristan sent a glance at Jameson, who raised his white eyebrows.

"The third man had a slip of paper in the pocket of his trousers." The line went silent for a moment. "It had Dr. Monroe's name, address, and contact number in the States, as well as your address, Lord Dreadmoor. Her mobile, as well. I'm guessing it was the chap who attacked her on the beach."

Tristan cursed under his breath. "Bleeding saints."

Again, Hurley cleared his throat. Tristan saw it was a habit the policeman had. "I realize you've quite a . . . unique situation there at Dreadmoor. I suggest you have Dr. Monroe stay close at hand. At least until I've a better handle on this. No leads have been found so far. The crime scene was clean as a whistle—save Dr. Monroe's name. Whoever did this knew what they were doing."

Tristan agreed. "So it seems. Thank you, Constable. We'll be careful."

"Very well, then. I'll keep you posted."

The line went dead, and Tristan paced the kitchen. "Bloody saints, Jameson. She could have been killed."

Jameson calmly lifted the lid off a pot and stirred its contents. "Had he wanted to harm your lady, he could have done so by now. 'Tisn't the lady he wants. 'Tis something else."

"Mayhap." He walked over to the door and glanced over his shoulder. "I'm not giving him the chance."

Halfway across the hall, Kail stopped him. "She's found something. Digging like a madwoman, that one." He gave Tristan a grin. "She's determined."

"Don't I know it?"

Kail paused and turned his head. "What's wrong?"

Tristan continued through the great hall and out the door. "That was the constable on the phone. There's been four killings and Erik is responsible, I'll warrant." He cut his gaze briefly to Kail. "No matter that he's taken over her mentor's body, he'll not get to her. I vow it. I've not a good feeling about this, Kail. Not at all."

As they walked up to the old kirk site, Tristan paused and stared. His Andrea was on hands and knees, her lovely little rump high in the air whilst she plundered the soil.

"Quite a sight, aye?" Kail said.

"Hmm. Quite." He gave his captain a warning glance. "Put your eyes back in your head, man, lest you want to lose them."

Kail laughed and slapped his shoulder. "I'll keep them, if it's all the same to you, little lad."

"Tristan!"

He ran to Andrea. "What is it?"

Shaking her head, she set her trowel down, pushed up, and sat back on her heels. She dragged her arm across her forehead. "Another leather tarp. Wrapped in twisted yew." She looked over her shoulder and met his stare. "It's a single sword. I can feel the outline of it."

Tristan's heart plummeted. Centuries ago, he didn't believe in curses. After having lived one for over seven hundred years, he was anxious to see what the tarp enclosed. "Christ, Andrea. Open it."

Lying on her stomach, she leaned over in the freshly dug earth and withdrew a large, leather-wrapped object. She scooted backward in the soil until the thing leveled to the ground. First to her knees, then to her feet she rose, holding the satchel as though her very own babe.

"Bleedin' saints, Tristan. Could it be so?" Stephen asked at his side.

Tristan looked around. All fourteen of his knights encircled him, just as anxious as he to see what the leather pouch revealed.

"Merde," mumbled Jason. "More twisted yew." He crossed himself. Twice.

Andrea lifted her face to Tristan's. "Let's go inside."

Moments later, everyone, Jameson included, huddled around the table while Andrea flicked open a knife and cut the yew vine. Slowly, she lifted the edges of the leather.

Fifteen gasps, followed by fifteen curses, filled the study.

"Damnation, Tristan," Richard said. " 'Tis yours."

"Why was it separated from ours?" Jason asked.

Tristan shook his head. "I vow I don't know." He turned his eyes to meet his love's. "Is there aught wrapped with it?"

Andi's mind spun in a hundred different directions. She heard Tristan ask the question, she heard the medieval male curses in the room. Even Jameson had uttered a soft "merde." But in her own mind, she could hear only one voice. *Kneel. Pray. Behind his eye.*

As she ran her fingers lightly over the weapon, it

struck her that centuries before, Tristan had gripped the leather-wrapped hilt, had sharpened the steel blade. It made her tingle inside just thinking of it. With ease, she stroked the sapphire stone set inside the hilt.

She gasped. Then she cursed.

Every male in the room snapped his head up.

"What is it?" Tristan asked. He moved to stand beside her, so close she could feel the hair on her arms go rigid from his energy. "Andrea!"

Taking the knife, she carefully wedged the blade tip where the stone met its steel casing. "Behind his eye . . ."

Another round of curses filled the room as she worked the sapphire stone from the hilt. It popped out with ease, as though it'd been removed before. As she looked down, she realized why.

Beneath the stone lay a tiny, folded piece of parchment. Her heart slammed against her ribs and her fingers shook.

"Go ahead, love," Tristan urged, leaning his head closer. His lips seemed to brush the skin on her neck. "See what it is."

With a slow, deep breath, Andi opened the ancient parchment. She stared, unblinking, at the crude ink markings. "It's French-Norman," she whispered, scanning the words. The breath in her lungs left in a rush. "Oh God."

She looked up. Every knight in the room stood no more than a foot or two away. They crowded around her, staring, waiting.

"What is it, woman?" Gareth said. "I vow 'tis torture, the waiting."

"Aye, lady, please," Jason said next to her. "I cannot stand it."

She pushed her hair behind her ear. "I . . . I can't be sure." She met Tristan's gaze. "It looks like a verse."

"A verse? What sort of verse?" said Richard.

Tristan's dark head bent over the parchment. After a moment, he lifted his eyes to hers. "Read it."

Andi shook her head. "I can read the words, but I can't translate all the words—"

"It matters naught. Just read it," he said in a low voice.

With a deep breath, she nodded. "Okay. Here goes." The room fell silent as she formed the strange, French-Norman words. Five sentences in all. And out of those, only six words were familiar.

Pray. Kneel. Fate. Befall. Silent. Forever.

Andi raised her gaze and looked around, then stared into Tristan's eyes. "What did it mean?"

A look of total defeat fell upon his handsome face. " 'Twas a release from the curse. 'Tis obvious that it does not work."

She blinked. "What do you mean, doesn't work?"

Sweeping the room with his hand, he raised his voice. "Look at my knights, Andrea. Look at me. We're all still the same." He swiped his arm through hers. "See? We're all still spirits."

Her eyes fell to the old verse. Who'd penned it? God, how bizarre it all was. A month ago, she would have laughed at anyone who'd suggested she believed in curses. How different things had become.

Kneel. Pray.

Andi's head snapped up and she searched Tristan's face. "This is wrong."

He inclined his head. "What?"

Without waiting to explain, she turned, grabbed the sword, and fled the study. "This is all wrong," she called over her shoulder. "This has to be read exactly where it was found. Where it was buried. On purpose."

Tristan ran beside her. "The kirk?"

Fifteen ghostly knights ran beside her as she made her way across the bailey. "The old kirk site."

With a silent prayer, she hoped she was right.

Chapter 28

Andi stood on the old kirk site, Tristan on her right, Jameson on her left. Once more, she read the words scribbled on the aged parchment.

Thunder cracked and roared overhead. The sea waves bashed Dreadmoor's base, loud, threatening, deafening. The wind picked up, so brisk that she had to turn her back to the brunt of it. Shielding her eyes, Andi looked first at Jameson, then at Tristan.

"What's happening?" she yelled, searching his face for answers.

His mouth moved, but no words came forth.

Then, as fast as the wind whipped up, it completely died.

Tristan's lips kept moving, forming words with no sound. His face hardened as he looked around. The other knights all tried to speak, but their voices remained silent.

"Jameson? What's going on?" she asked.

His face paled as he looked from one man to the next. "My lady, I do believe you've reversed the curse."

Before Andi's eyes, the knights, one by one, slowly began to fade into the waning afternoon light.

Her stomach tightened to a painful knot, a queasy feeling settling in, rising to her throat. She didn't think they'd just disappear. "Oh God. No."

Looking from one knight to the other, she helplessly watched as they slowly vanished. Her eyes clashed with Jason, a smile tipping the corner of his boyish mouth.

Sir Richard gave her a low bow. Tears stung her eyes. "Please, no."

Tristan moved closer to her, his big body looming over her like a sheltering tree. Their eyes locked, and she watched as he searched every inch of her face. His hungry gaze lingered on her lips for just a fraction, then moved up with a painful slowness. His face tightened, his jaw clenched, and his silent lips mouthed words she would never get to hear, but would be burned into her memory forever.

Do not forget me.

His body began to blur, the edges dimming, until she could see clear through him. Just before he faded away, he lifted his hand to her jaw, a caress she'd feel only in her dreams.

Then he was gone.

They were all gone.

Turning a slow circle, Andi looked at Dreadmoor's empty bailey in astonishment. It'd happened so fast, she couldn't grasp it, couldn't force herself to believe it. It just couldn't be.

A salty breeze wafted in from the shore, catching on her tongue and lingering there. Seagulls shrieked overhead, echoing like a crying child. She wanted to slump to the ground, but couldn't find the energy to move.

Jameson placed a gentle hand on her shoulder. "My lady, please don't weep so. Come now. I'll fix you a nice pot of tea and we'll sit by the fire."

Andi turned her head and stared into Jameson's clear blue eyes. Wrinkles gathered at their corners, but warmth settled onto his aging features. She sniffed. When had she started crying? She hadn't even felt the stream trailing down her cheeks.

Until now.

The tears clung to the back of her throat, burning and making the breath catch in her lungs, forming that eternal lump that no matter how hard you try, you just can't swallow past. Words escaped her, so she nodded and allowed Jameson to grasp her elbow and guide her across the grounds.

Moments later, Jameson had Andi settled in front of

the hearth on the sofa, a fire blazing, a pot of tea on the side table. He sat beside her, watching the flames. Neither said a word.

Jameson had to be even more saddened than her, she thought. He'd grown from a toddler to adulthood knowing Tristan. She'd known him for only a short time, and already her heart was breaking in two. She could only imagine how Jameson felt.

Just then, the phone rang. Jameson gave her a grave look. "Drink your tea, lady. I shall return in a moment." With a nod, he excused himself and quit the hall.

A sigh escaped her, and she pulled her knees up and stared into the orange embers. Thoughts of the past several weeks stormed through her mind, of Tristan, his men, and how a terrible crime had been committed over seven centuries before. Fifteen men had lost their lives.

And the killer had gotten completely away with it.

"Miss Kate is on her way over straightaway," Jameson said. He returned to his place beside her. " 'Tis . . . overwhelming, my lady."

"Oh, Jameson," she said, her voice cracking. He pulled her to him, and Andi buried her face in his stiff butler's collar and cried. He patted her on the back, but she felt his chest shake, too.

God, in the space of a minute, she'd lost her soul mate. Her heart ached as though being squeezed in a vise. The tears wouldn't stop flowing, and poor Jameson took the brunt of it on the face of his jacket. Still, the sweet man tried his best to console her.

Moments later, Kate walked through the kitchen entrance. She hurried to the sofa. "Oh dear, is it true?" She sat on one side of Andi, her hand giving a comforting squeeze. "There, there, loves, I know it hurts."

Together they sat, quiet at first, until Andi's tears subsided. Kate gave her a warm smile. "Why don't you rest a bit, love? I'll help Edgar whip up a quick supper."

Andi heaved a sigh and nodded. "Are you sure I can't help?" She really didn't feel like doing much of anything, except . . . nothing. Her heart was broken. And it hurt like hell.

"Nay, sweet, you go rest. I'll have me daughter bring Heath round in a bit. He'll want to be here, for sure."

With a thankful smile, Andi rose from the sofa. "If you change your mind and need me, just call." With that, she left Kate and Jameson together and crossed the great hall.

Every step was a painful memory. Across floors Tristan not only grew up on, but roamed as a spirit. Tapestries his mother and grandmother had stitched reminded her of the great warrior he was. What a sincere and loyal man he was.

He'd been hers for a while. . . .

At her door, tears began anew. Jason no longer stood guard at her door, Kail would never bellow up the corridor, looking for Tristan. . . .

Quickly, Andi slipped into her chamber, crawled up on the bed, and cried herself to sleep.

She had no idea how long she slept before a voice pulled her from her dreams.

"Andrea?"

Her eyes flew open. What was Kirk doing here? And was it really Kirk? He stood there, a smile crossing his striking features.

"Hello, Andrea. Surprised?"

She nodded. "A little. This is the first time you've come out since you got sick on the first day of retrieval." She studied him. "Where's Jameson? Did he let you in?"

Kirk moved into the hall. He turned, his gaze missing nothing. "Yes, he told me to come straightaway and get you. And everything is actually quite perfect." He gave her a smile. "I want you to pack your belongings right away. I've another job for you." He cocked his head. "Why, darling, you look pale. Are you feeling ill?"

That nearly knocked the breath from her. Inwardly, she staggered. She wasn't ready to leave Dreadmoor. Not yet. "I'm not finished here, Kirk." Technically, she was, and she knew it. She couldn't just stay on. Yet she hadn't had time to adjust.

Adjust to life without Tristan.

He inclined his head and stroked his goatee. "What is

wrong with you, girl? You look as though someone's just run over your favorite puppy." He tilted his head to the side and studied her face. "Come now, Andrea. You're not still nursing the notion of Dragonhawk, are you?" He looked around, then back to her. " 'Tis a daunting place, Dreadmoor. I can see how you've become attached—quite a nice chamber you have here. But the job is complete and you can't stay on forever. You've excavated the remains and recovered the hoard." He glanced around. "By the way. Where's Dreadmoor?"

The lump in her throat came back. He was talking so fast, she could barely keep up with what he was saying. "He's . . . not here. Business, I suppose."

A smile lit Kirk's face. "Right. Business." The glint in his eyes danced. "I would truly love to view the hoard. The pictures, I'm sure, didn't do it justice. Direct me and I'll take a look whilst you gather your things."

She looked at her boss and mentor. She was in no state to show him the swords that had belonged to Tristan's men. But what could she say? "Sorry, I've just lost the love of my life and can't deal with you right now"? Perhaps Tristan and his men had been wrong about Kirk, perhaps not. How was she to tell? She knew the longer she remained at Dreadmoor, the longer her heart continued to ache, yet she couldn't bring herself to leave.

Nodding, she inclined her head toward the hall. "I'll show you the weapons, Kirk, but I'm not leaving here tonight. I'm . . . too tired. I'll be right down."

He shrugged and flashed her a smile. "Perfect. I'll wait downstairs."

Andi washed her face and made her way to the great hall. She wondered where Jameson was. He'd known of Tristan's concerns over the odd belief that Erik's spirit might have been released and overpowered Kirk, yet here Kirk was, inside Dreadmoor.

Every footstep through the halls hurt. Every room, every inch of space reminded her of Tristan. How strange, to be in love with a man you've never even touched before. And never would be able to touch.

Dragonhawk. How the name fit him. Fierce and powerful, he'd fought his way into her heart and anchored down.

But the anchor had come loose, thanks to her.

Kirk met her in the hall, a long satchel slung over his shoulder.

"What's that?" she asked.

"A souvenir," he said. "Come. Show me the grid site. I'd like to see the remnants."

"A souvenir? What is it?" she asked. "And wait, I've got to go speak to Jameson for a second."

"That won't be necessary," Kirk told her, taking her by the elbow. "He gave me the souvenir—to us, on Dreadmoor's behalf, for your doing such a wonderful job. He asked me to bid you farewell as he had to leave unexpectedly for the village."

Jameson had left without saying good-bye? No way. And what did Kirk have in the bag? Something definitely felt *wrong*.

"What sort of souvenir?" she asked again. "Kirk, wait a minute—"

"Come on, Andrea. The souvenir is a surprise. You'll love it. I promise. Come along now, to the cutaway."

In an instant, her employer grabbed her by the arm.

"Kirk, you're hurting me," Andi said. "Stop!"

"Oh, come on, love. Humor me," he said, steadily leading her out of Dreadmoor Castle. His strength overpowered hers, and all the doubts she had smacked her square in the face.

Jesus, Tristan and his men had been right.

As they crossed the bailey, Kirk pulled her to a halt beside the first cutaway. He shoved her in front of him.

He smiled. "Ah, where it all began. Tell me about it, won't you? On second thought, don't. I grow weary of waiting. Read this, won't you? And hurry. I've not much time left."

Andi turned and watched, stricken as Kirk thrust a slip of parchment into her hand. A burning sensation started in her throat. Kirk stood behind her, Tristan's sword leveled at her. "Kirk? What are you—what is going on?"

A smile lifted the corner of his mouth. "Oh, come

now. Don't look so hurt. They were just a lifeless lot of spirits." He inclined his head toward the note. "You must know by now who I really am? I'm sure your mentor wasn't too keen on the idea, but he's the one who loosened my garrote. Now read."

Her hands began to shake as she glanced at the paper. Inked in bold slashes and in the same French-Norman language were six sentences. Another verse.

Another curse.

She looked up. "Why do I have to read it? What is going on?"

Kirk heaved a weary sigh. "Because. You read the other one. How do I know, you ask?" He smiled again, stroking his beard. "I felt it the moment it happened. 'Twas like a jolt of energy shooting through my body." His gaze penetrated her. "I knew, because when I tried to step onto Dreadmoor land, I could. Before, I couldn't."

Andi glanced over her shoulder, toward the castle. Maybe Jameson would see what was going on and call the—

"Nay, my dear. He won't be calling anyone," Kirk, or whoever he was, said.

Tears of anger, frustration, and hurt filled her eyes. "What's happened to Kirk? How did you—"

He slid his eyes to the cutaway, then back to her. "I've been trapped beneath that bloody tree for centuries, and all I needed was someone to release me. Nature's fate was responsible. Had that tree not been tossed by the storm, I'd still be below it, bound by the yew. But once your mentor released me, it gave me the chance I thought would never come."

"But what did that have to do with the Dragonhawk's sword?"

He laughed, an ugly sound that crawled up Andi's spine. "You see, my job wasn't finished, all those years ago. Someone . . . stopped me."

"Erik de Sabre," she accused, even before he admitted it out loud.

With a low bow, he shrugged. "The very one. And

aye, I did kill de Barre, along with his entire garrison. Those stupid lads followed him around like he was a king." A cynical smile curved his mouth. "And when I called to them, they came running to see what had happened to their beloved comrade. They were still drunken from their carousing, so quite useless. 'Twas a simple thing to lock the dungeon behind them." He stared off for a moment. "I gave him that name, you know. Dragonhawk." He shook his head. "Before he killed my son."

She shook her head, confused, disbelieving. "He didn't kill your son—"

"Stop driveling, girl, and read the damn verse!" he shouted.

Andi felt her face drain of color. Tristan had tried to tell her, but she wouldn't believe him. Not fully, anyway.

The fear gripping her receded, just a bit. She looked up and stared him in the eye. "The bones in the cutaway belonged to you."

"My beloved mother. The sneaky old witch. Still had a few tricks up her sleeve, I suppose. She must have overheard me curse de Barre, then seal the others in the dungeon." He sneered. "She always did have a soft spot for the bloody whoresons."

"So it was she who wrapped the twisted yew around the satchels?"

"Aye. 'Twas a protective curse. And 'tis why we're at these odds right now." He narrowed his gaze. "She lured me to that hole, you see. The one I'd dug for the armor. Unfortunately, it also became my grave." The smile faded. "I'd just laid the bundle in the hole when she walloped me over the head—damn near whacked it clean off. I didn't know it at the time, but by wrapping that cursed twisted yew about my head and neck, she bound my spirit—until your Kirk Grey released me."

Andi had a hard time staying focused. This was not Kirk talking, this was Erik. And even though she was on information overload, if she kept him talking, maybe Jameson could call for help, although she seriously doubted anyone could help her now.

"What about the remains in the dungeon?" she asked, trying to buy time. Jameson and Miss Kate had to be somewhere. *God, please let them be safe.*

"Insignificant. An old serving maid, I believe. She heard the ruckus and ventured too close to the dungeon." He smiled. "I couldn't let her take word back to de Barre's sire."

She kept her gaze fixed on his. "What are you going to do with me? With Kirk?"

He sighed. "Well, it's apparent your work here is over. And your mentor won't remember a thing, although he may have to take the blame for those pesky vermin I had to take care of." Moving closer, he lifted the ancient blade to the level of her heart. "So I guess you'll join your ghostly love in the grave. I can't very well have you running about, trying to bring awareness to my well-being, not that anyone would believe you." He shrugged. "Who knows?" He studied her with flat, lifeless eyes, and when he spoke, his voice held a lethal threat. He pushed the blade, just enough to pierce her skin. "Read."

She winced at the pain and lifted her gaze to his. "Your son's death was an accident. But you're nothing more than a pathetic murderer."

He gave the blade another push. *"Read!"*

The fleeting thought that it was Tristan's blade piercing her skin skimmed her mind, and she bit back a cry, lifted the paper, and read. The strange words tumbled out, and when the last word was spoken, it happened.

Kirk began to tremble and lowered the sword. He gasped for air, and bent over at the waist, coughing profusely. Throwing down Tristan's sword, he fell to his knees.

Andi froze, unsure what to do. God, what was happening?

As she stared on, a slight mist swirled around Kirk, enveloping him at first, then slowly drifting toward Andi. Kirk began to vomit, retching over and over until, spent, he fell to his side.

The mist wafted around Andi, and her heart whammed against her ribs. Fear choked her, a scream dying in her throat.

The mist shifted away, and then began to take form. The image, blurry at first, quickly took the shape of a man. It solidified, turning to flesh, bone, hair.

Andi had no doubt who it was. "Oh God," she whispered.

The man looked at her and laughed. "Close, but no, even I can't claim that title." His gaze leveled with hers. "Yet."

Andi glanced around, her heart beating wildly. She ran toward Kirk, still lying on the ground.

Tristan's sword lay next to him.

Erik must have guessed her move, and he beat her to it. With a forceful shove, he knocked her out of the way and grabbed the sword. He leveled the tip at her throat.

"Feisty wench, eh?" His eyes hardened. "Get up."

Chapter 29

"Were I you, I'd lower that rusty blade, Erik."

Andi froze. It was her imagination. Had to be. The air lodged in her lungs, making it impossible to draw a decent breath. She began to shake, refusing to look behind her, refusing to *believe*.

"Dragonhawk. Rather, Dragonhawk's useless spirit. Back so soon?"

Erik's amused voice reached her ears. Slowly, she turned around.

Her knees weakened and it took every ounce of strength she had to keep herself upright and not slide to the ground.

Tristan stood no more than three feet away, barechested, his sword drawn. Jameson stood to his left, his expression unreadable. All fourteen Dragonhawk knights formed an arc around him. They drew their blades all at once, the hiss echoing throughout the bailey.

"Andrea, move away from the swine. Now," Tristan ordered her.

As she began to move, Erik pushed the sword into the skin of her throat and laughed. "What are you going to do, Dreadmoor? Hmmm? Certainly, you don't think you can defend your woman? Last time I heard, you were all a useless lot of spirits." His look swept the other knights. "You're pathetic, de Barre. Truly." His eyes bored into hers. "You can't protect her and you know it. Now you can watch her die. A just reward, I think, for allowing my boy to die."

In two strides, Tristan stood facing Erik. In one swift motion, he cut the air with the blade of his sword, nicking Erik's chin. Andi watched in fascination as a line of blood trickled down his throat.

"Andrea, move!" Tristan shouted.

As if in a dream, she dove to the left. Jameson grabbed her elbow and pulled her aside. Her mouth went dry and her breath caught as realization pulled at her, sinking its teeth into her mind's flesh.

Tristan was alive!

She wondered if the others were, too, but when Jason moved to stand next to her, then slid his hand down and grabbed hers, her heart swelled. He looked at her and winked, then gave her a reassuring squeeze. His very real hand held hers.

Somehow, the verse she'd read aloud had reversed the curse Erik had placed on them. They were all alive!

Jason lowered his head and whispered against her ear, "Stand steady, Lady Andi. What you're about to lay witness to may very well steal your breath."

With a weighty sigh, she braced herself and leaned into the very solid body of Jason. Hardly able to comprehend that he, alive and breathing, held her hand, she watched as an even more disbelieving thought gripped her. Tristan readied himself to fight a very real Erik de Sabre from the thirteenth century. Alive now, no longer residing in Kirk's body. With real swords and real blood.

With a quick glance at Kirk, who now sat a safe distance away beside Jameson, Andi turned her full and disbelieving gaze at Tristan and his foster father.

Tristan tried to rid his mind of everything save the idiot before him. Quite a difficult task, knowing his woman, whom he'd never been able to so much as kiss, stood no more than twenty paces away. That would soon change.

He breathed a steady, even rate, keeping his stare fixed as he slowly walked a predatory circle around Erik. Damnation, he could barely believe it. "What does it feel like to come back after all these centuries? After lying beneath that oak with twisted yew about your neck? To be a traitor? To take the lives of those you welcomed into your hall? Gaining the trust of their fathers? Treating us like sons? Being our leader? Tell me, Erik." He all but growled. "I want to know."

Erik, smooth and agile as ever, countercircled. "Feels bloody wonderful, to be truthful. I gave you everything, de Barre. My knowledge, my training skills—everything." The cynical smile curving his lips made his face appear sinister. He thrust with a vicious strike. "What did you do for me in return?" He charged this time, and Tristan deflected the blade with his own. "You took my only child," Erik said calmly. He paused, his face blank. "You took my life."

"Is that what you truly believe, Erik? That we killed your son?" Tristan said, blade outstretched. " 'Twas an accident, and you well know it."

The pain on Erik's face proved he did not. "Fifteen trained knights, and you couldn't protect one small boy? Nay," he said, his voice cracking. " 'Twas no accident. You allowed it." He arced his blade. "Even seven centuries of being a damned soul isn't enough of a repayment for what you took from me." A smile touched his mouth. "Mayhap your life. Again."

The sickness his foster father suffered pained Tristan, but at the same time, he knew there would be no saving Erik. His mind had turned evil from hatred. But Tristan wanted to know everything, questions answered. He owed it to his men. He continued to circle. "Why Andrea?"

Erik laughed. "Right place, right time. For me, anyway." He jabbed at Tristan. "Her unfortunate employer happened to be the one to free me from that cursed yew, which allowed me to escape my tormented prison. One, I might add, my own sweet mother placed me in."

Tristan continued to circle, Erik following his lead. "How did you get their swords and helms?"

Erik's face hardened as he followed Tristan's lead. "I gathered them after your men died in the dungeon. I'd already cursed them, you see, but their deaths came more slowly than yours." He smiled. "I'd bound the armor and planned to bury them so no one would find them, but I hadn't realized my own mother's fealty rested elsewhere until . . . later." He thrust the blade at Tristan, who sidestepped. "She followed me out to the hole I'd dug and all but took my bloody head off. Next thing I know, I'm here."

Tristan tapped his blade to Erik's. "You didn't know she'd placed a protective curse on the weapons herself, or that she'd taken my sword, penned a rather useful verse on it, and buried it?" He charged Erik. "Or that your mother's spirit would contact Andi and lead her to it?"

Erik returned the charge. "It doesn't matter now, does it?" He held up the blade in his hand, turning it side to side. *Tristan's blade.* "Isn't it odd, Dreadmoor, that you're about to die a second death at the tip of your very own sword?" A smile slid to his mouth. "Even if your knights survive, you will not. And thanks to Dr. Monroe, I have my life back. And more."

"Nay, you don't." Tristan moved toward Erik, the arc of his blade swiping the air.

Erik attacked full force, anger turning his face blood-red. With vehemence, he charged.

Tristan waited for Erik to advance, coming within a few inches of Tristan's neck. In a move the Dragonhawk had made famous, he deflected the steel and used his elbow to hammer a stunning blow to Erik's jaw.

Erik stumbled back, shook his head as if to gather his wits, then charged Tristan with a bloodcurdling yell. "I will not yield!"

Tristan remembered the same words in the dungeon, more than seven centuries before. Except this time, they were reversed.

Ducking and missing the sword's blow, Tristan fell to his knees and plunged the blade into Erik's stomach. "Aye," he said. "You will."

Their gaze locked, and Tristan watched the pupils in Erik's eyes grow large until he staggered back and fell to the ground.

Dead.

Tristan's breath came hard and fast. Slowly, he rose and walked over to retrieve his sword. As he bent over, Erik's body began to shake violently.

"Tristan, leave it and move back!" Kail shouted.

They all watched in horror as Erik, being the abomination that he was, convulsed faster and faster, his flesh peeling from bones, his bones turning to dust. Back to where he belonged.

The bailey fell silent. Tristan raised his head and stared at his men. His knights.

Kicking his sword aside, he picked it up and glanced at what used to be Erik de Sabre. "Someone remove that rotting pile of dust from my keep."

All fourteen knights let out a battle cry worthy of a thousand men. No doubt the village heard.

Then his eyes fell on Andrea. Taking powerful strides, he came to stand nose to nose with her, so close a whisper couldn't pass. Her eyes widened, but before she could catch her breath Tristan dropped his sword and swept her up, their lips nearly touching. His body shook, and he briefly wondered if he would fall over with pure joy.

Andrea stared at him, breathless and, for the first time to his notion, unable to speak.

Tristan, on the other hand, had no trouble at all.

"I love you, wench. I vow you feel powerfully fair in my arms."

She tried to make her mouth move, but nothing came forth. Her tear ducts, on the other hand, worked just fine. Tears slid down her face. She lifted a hand and hesitantly touched first his cheek, traced his eyebrows, then ran her fingers through his hair. The sensation nearly made him drop her. She looked back up, and still found her tongue lacking the muscle to speak. Tristan found better uses for it.

He stared down at the woman in his arms. *His woman.* Her warmth spread across his bare chest, making his muscles quiver. Her trembling rocked him to the bone, even as he held her tight. He had dreamed of this moment for what seemed like eternity, and never did he believe it could possibly ever happen.

And yet he felt the weighty proof in his arms.

He searched her face with his eyes, not wanting to miss a single line, a single freckle—wanting to miss nothing. His own hand shook as he took his glove off with his teeth and threw it down. Lifting his hand to her cheek, he grazed it with the back of his knuckles. He tried to speak again, but found a solid lump in his throat nigh onto robbing his breath. He swallowed past it. "Damnation, Andrea, you're powerfully soft." He drew a deep breath and his words flowed out on the exhale. "I vow I could hold you here and stare at your beautiful face for the rest of my days."

He watched tear after tear slide down her cheek as she stared up at him with those warm, hazel eyes. He could wait no more. He bent his head close, his gaze trained on hers as his mouth settled comfortably over quivering lips. So warm and soft, he found himself craving more. He brushed his lips across hers several times, then with strained control deepened the kiss. When her hand grasped the back of his neck and pulled him closer, it sent him over the edge. He tasted her, deeper and deeper, swallowing her gasp of surprise.

Tristan lifted his head from Andi's, but didn't break eye contact. Their lips were a whisper apart, and he could do nothing save stare and thank God and the saints above he had been given such a gift. His breathing panted with the effort of having to maintain control. He wanted her so badly, his insides shook. Suddenly, a loud snort sounded in the bailey. Only when a brave soul tapped him on the shoulder did he remember where he was, and who was about.

Tristan turned and glared at the snorter.

His entire garrison formed a half circle around him. Jameson, Miss Kate, who'd joined them, and Kirk Grey huddled with them. They all stood by, devilish grins plastered to their faces, although Kirk looked a bit on the pale side. No doubt he was having a bit of trouble taking it all in.

As was he.

Tristan smiled down at Andi and set her back on the ground. He kept his arm tightly about her shoulder. She teetered a bit and he gripped her tighter still. She stood, staring, eyes wide. Her lips moved and something came out, but damn him, he couldn't understand a word. Saints, but he missed his uncanny hearing ability.

Lowering his head, he leaned toward her mouth. Her warm breath caressed his ear and neck, and he all but hit the floor from the impact of it. Shaking his head, he focused on her words.

Her question floated out on a whisper. "How?"

With a smile, he tapped her nose. "Nay, love. We've got time for questions such as that later." His grin widened. "I have another question for you, and by the saints I must ask it now before my nerve deserts me."

Her gaze remained fixed on his, following him all the way down as he knelt on bended knee. He cleared his throat and grasped Andi's hand, unsure if the trembling came from hers or his own. More likely than not, 'twas both.

"Andrea Kinley Monroe." His voice came out hoarse and scratchy. He hoped she didn't care. "I beg you, wed me. I vow you'll not regret it."

He watched several more tears streak her reddened cheeks. A smile began in the corners of her mouth and crept into her eyes.

"Yes." So soft, he could barely hear her at first, but then she threw her arms about his neck and squeezed. "Yes! I'll marry you!"

Whistles and bellowing cheers from his knights erupted across the bailey, drifting on a North Sea breeze. Tristan looked into his love's eyes and smiled, then stopped whatever words were about to make their escape from her lovely mouth. He, without a doubt in his medieval mind, kissed her good and sound, leaving no question as to how much he loved her.

And would do the like. Forever.

Chapter 30

Andi grasped the edges of the sill and leaned out of her window. She filled her lungs with crisp, sea air, then let it slowly escape. The cool night wind bit through her thin cotton shirt. A crescent moon hung low, filtering the dark and bathing the grounds below in a soft glow.

Dreadmoor's very live sentries moved about on their watch, dark shadows of souls who'd lived centuries ago, and who'd been given another chance to live now. It amazed her. And it had changed her, too. In the way she thought, her beliefs, her dire requirement for scientific proof. Would she ever get used to it?

As difficult as the concept was to grasp, Erik de Sabre had obtained bewitching powers and enough knowledge to use them to cast impossible curses. His spirit had taken over poor Kirk, who reeled with the knowledge of it. He remembered everything, and yet had not been able to stop Erik's spirit from doing the evil that he'd done. By Erik's hand, he'd murdered the woman and the three thugs from Berwick, and would no doubt have difficulty coming to terms with it. The police had no witnesses, no evidence or fingerprints—nothing to prove Kirk had done it. Which, in reality, he hadn't. But no one would ever believe the circumstances. Kirk had flown back to the States to be with his wife and family, and Andi could only hope he'd heal.

The ever-so-slight sound of the tide lapping at the rocks soothed her. Thousands of stars littered the sky, and she'd counted at least four shooting ones over the past hour. She remembered a time when there wasn't a shooting star around that would go unwished upon—but her dreams had come true, and she honestly couldn't find a single solitary thing she'd rather have.

Today being her wedding day and all.

She was marrying a thirteenth-century knight and moving into a castle garrisoned by fourteen medieval warriors. Amazing.

Remembering their trip back to America to gather her belongings and settle her affairs made her grin. Himself had been so preoccupied with flying for the first time, he'd just held her hand and stared out the window the entire time.

Not so with the flight home.

After devouring close to three trays of food at each meal, to the chagrin of the flight attendant, Tristan had two brawls with the ornery eleven-year-old twins seated in front of them, walked around inspecting everything allowed, and had finally resigned himself to simply staring at Andi.

Until he fell asleep.

Andi grinned. Seven hundred years of roaming could cause one to be in desperate need of a nap, she supposed. Unfortunately, his snores were so loud even the twins stopped giggling and turned to scowl. Tristan had cracked open an eye and winked, then repositioned his long legs, which even in the spacious comfort of first class, had no other place to go except out in the aisle. Then he'd drifted back off to sleep. God, she'd watched him for hours.

Pushing away from the window, Andi moved to the bed and lay down. One single moonbeam streamed through, shooting a shaft of light across her bedcovers. Staring up at the canopy she realized there was no way in burning Hades she'd get one ounce of sleep.

She kept seeing Tristan's face before her, saw how his eyes burned with such fierce desire, such admiration—she thought she'd faint dead away from the sheer force of it. He'd been pretty chivalristic about the whole thing, though. After blatantly informing her of his powerful desire in detail, which had turned her cheeks several shades of red and her brain to mush, he'd proceeded to tell her they would indeed wait until after their nuptials before sleeping together. He'd then kissed her completely senseless and left her at her chamber's door. She sighed.

Sometimes chivalry stunk.

A rough rap on the door made her jump. A deep murmuring, followed by a few French-Norman curses and a rough clearing of throat, left no doubt who bellowed on the other side of the oak.

She hurried across the cool wood floor and flung open the door. The love of her life stood with his arms crossed over his chest, scowling at her guard. Jason bravely returned Tristan's glare, then straightened and gave Andi a bright smile.

"My lady, I am sorry for this disturbance, but Himself would not listen. I informed him of your wishes, but 'twas no use."

Andi smiled up at Tristan. He stood not three feet away, wearing a navy blue and white rugby shirt and sweatpants. His sword, as usual, rested against his side.

He frowned at Andi. "Do not grin at me so, woman. What kind of rot is this, anyway? I cannot see my very own betrothed before we wed?" He turned to Jason and thumped him in the chest. "And you, pup. You forget your place in this hall, do you not?"

Jason had the good grace to blush. "Nay, my lord."

"Begone. I'll tend to this wench on my own."

Jason peered at Andi. "My lady?"

She burst out laughing and waved the young knight away. "I'll yell if I need you."

Jason bowed low, turned, and sauntered up the passageway.

Andi grinned at her husband-to-be. "Lord Dreadmoor, do you know what time it is?"

Tristan took one step, which brought them nearly nose to nose. The dim light of the corridor shadowed every sharp plane and angle of his handsome face. His eyes burned a bright sapphire that scorched her clear to the bone.

The roguish grin he gave her lit up his features. "Aye, but from the looks of your lovely face you were not exactly hard sleeping, love." He opened his arms for her, and Andi wasted no time at all in sinking against the hard wall of his chest. His strong arms folded around her, his chin resting on top of her head. " 'Tis a ridiculous custom you Americans have. I vow I won't tolerate it."

Andi smiled against his shirt. "That's quite apparent, my lord." She sighed and snuggled closer.

"Something is bothering you, love. I can sense it." His deep and raspy voice, with that ever-present sexy accent, made her shiver.

She lifted a shoulder. "I guess I'm the only bride not to have a bridesmaid. Do you think Jameson will be my maid of honor?"

Tristan's laugh rumbled through the passageway. "You have that insufferable man in the palm of your hand, Lady Dreadmoor. You could talk him into anything, I'd wager. But," he said, his voice low, "I understand completely how he feels." He stilled, a tenseness so rigid Andi could feel every muscle in his broad chest tighten. He cleared his throat, tilted her head up with one finger, and held her gaze with very little effort. "We are betrothed, Andrea. In my day, by truth and by law, we'd be legally wed."

She couldn't look away, or even blink. A smoldering blue gaze burned into hers. His eyes remained open as he lowered his head and settled his mouth against her lips. After a moment they nudged hers open and demanded more. His tongue tasted her, swept the inside of her mouth, traced her teeth. He sucked her lower lip and she all but pooled to the floor from the sensations washing over her. She didn't know if the quivering came from her or him.

What she did know, though, is she definitely didn't want him to stop.

One large hand held her tight at the small of her back, the other buried in her hair, kneading her scalp and neck. Tristan deepened his kiss even more, and Andi thought she would die from the wave of emotion. Her heart pounded as he robbed her of breath. All at once he pulled away, letting his forehead rest against hers.

"Saints, woman, but I love you." He kissed her nose. "You know not how long I have dreamed of holding you this way." His mouth moved to her ear. "Of feeling you beneath me . . ." Tracing the curve of her jaw, he ran his thumb across her lips. Drawing closer, he lowered his head and inhaled. A callused knuckle grazed her skin as he pushed her hair aside, settling his mouth against her neck. Firm, demanding lips mouthed against her ear, "I want you powerfully bad. Was it me that said we should wait?"

"Uh-huh." What with the tiny amount of brain function still remaining, Andi knew, for a certainty and without a doubt, just how badly he *did* want her.

It was, she noticed as Tristan leaned into her, quite obvious.

A loud, annoyed grumble interrupted any betrothed thoughts she and Tristan might have had. They both turned to the annoyed grumble-maker.

Jameson stood in the corridor, back stiff as a metal rod, draped in an old-fashioned nightgown and slippers. A disapproving frown crinkled his face. One graceful gray eyebrow shot up and disappeared into his impeccable gray hair, and he tapped a slippered foot against the floor. Andi smothered a grin, thinking he looked as though he had stepped out of the pages of a Charles Dickens novel.

"Master Tristan, I do believe 'tis time to allow Herself to retire for what remains of the night. Surely you don't wish her to have dark moons under her eyes for the ceremony?" Jameson glared at Tristan.

"Go back to bed, Jameson. I don't recall asking your permission to seek out my betrothed. Besides, we're doing naught but . . . visiting." Tristan pulled her tighter against his chest. She nearly wheezed from the loss of air.

"Nay, my young lord, you did not. But I am here to remind you of your vast amount of patience and chivalry." Jameson took one step closer. "You *do* remember those charming qualities you possess, aye?"

Andi watched as Tristan and Jameson had a stare-down. In the end, Jameson, of course, won.

Tristan mumbled a curse under his breath. "Begone, you meddling old man. I never go back on my word. Allow me to say my good-nights without your bother-some presence."

Andi could have sworn she'd seen the corner of Jameson's mouth lift in a smile of victory. He bowed low to her and Tristan. "Good-night, then, my lord and lady." He straightened, turned, and strode back up the corridor.

Forcing her chin up with his knuckles, Tristan sighed. "I've waited over seven hundred years to have you, wench." He groaned and pulled her mouth to his. "I can wait a few more bothersome bloody hours." He kissed her long and deep, his hungry lips claiming every inch. The stone wall dug into her back as Tristan leaned into her, kissing her jaw, her neck, her collarbone. His breath rushed against her ear and she shivered.

A loud clearing of throat snapped them both back to reality. Tristan jumped so hard, he knocked his head on the wall above Andi's head. He cursed, gave her a quick peck on the nose, then turned and stormed up the corridor. Andi lost count of the medieval curses that poured from his mouth.

As if after that kiss she could actually walk. Andi pushed away from the wall and felt her knees sway. She caught Jameson, the throat-clearer, out of the corner of her eye. He gave a slight nod, then turned and disappeared into the darkness.

Andi smiled and turned to go back to bed. Just before she closed her door she saw Jason step into place by her door. He grinned and gave her a low bow. What an adorable guy he was.

It could have been minutes, or it could have been hours, she was unsure. Sleep had claimed her, the ebb and flow of the tide lapping at the base of Dreadmoor lulling her into slumber.

Then something woke her up.

Cracking open first one eye, then another, Andi peered into the darkness. The skin on her neck went icy, and she knew immediately that someone was in the room with her.

"Hello?" she whispered. "Who's there?"

As she stared, the soft, flimsy waft of familiar mist gathered and formed, suspending in midair. Although she'd encountered it several times since arriving at Dreadmoor, it never failed to unnerve her. She continued to stare, as her mouth had once again locked up.

This time, though, things were different.

The mist shifted, focused, blurred, then shifted again, right before Andi's eyes. Slowly, it began to take shape. Within seconds, the form of a woman shimmered before her. Dressed in a long-sleeved dress, a simple shift covering it, her hair pulled back and covered with a small cap, she folded her hands in front of her and simply stared.

Andi swallowed past the lump of uncertainty and astonishment in her throat and attempted to speak. "You're Erik's mother. Aren't you?"

The woman gave a simple nod.

Breathing deeply, Andi tried to get her erratic nerves under control. "Thank you for what you've done. Without your help, this mystery would never have been solved, and Tristan and his men would still be cursed."

The woman smiled and nodded again.

"I'm sorry about your son—about what he was and all you had to go through," Andi said. "Tristan never meant for your grandson to die, and would have done anything to save him. They didn't know he was there." She paused when the ghostly figure simply stared. "Tristan and his men were—are very fond of you."

Another smile touched her lips, and then she began to slowly fade. She inclined her head and spoke, a soft, feathery whisper. "Thank you. Love him forever. . . ."

Then she was gone.

Andi smiled. Two days before, she, Tristan, and the entire garrison had not only buried the skeletal remains from the dungeon, who according to Erik was one of Tristan's housemaids, but erected a gravestone in honor of Erik's mother, in the village cemetery. Her true death unknown, her true final resting place unfound, Tristan wanted a formal Christian burial for the old woman he'd been so fond of. At last, the ghost who'd helped rescue Dragonhawk and his knights from an eternity of roaming as spirits, who'd known they'd suffered at the hands of her own demented son, finally found peace.

Epilogue

Good Lord, her nerves pulsed. Andi couldn't remember when she'd been more fidgety. More than the time she had to give her oral book report in front of the entire seventh grade. More nervous than the time she'd lectured her first class of 120 students at the university. Even more nervous than the time she had to do a television interview with *60 Minutes*.

Andi chanced a peek, and not for the first time that hour, into the large, oval mirror standing in the corner of her room. She couldn't believe the image staring back at her was, well, *her*.

The long, cream-colored gown she wore had been handsewn, according to Tristan's explicit instructions. Trimmed in gold braid and thread, the delicate stitching adorned the bodice, and sewn into one of the sleeves was a small embroidered mystical creature—Dragonhawk. Kate, the sweet woman, had done a wonderful job. She'd even helped Andi with her hair. With a masterful touch, she'd swept Andi's straight, shoulder-length hair up into an elegant twist, adding pearled pins and sprigs of baby's breath. She actually felt . . . beautiful.

Jameson had said all brides were beautiful on their wedding day. What a sweetheart. She'd made the skin under his white eyebrows turn beet red from the giant kiss she'd given him.

A soft knock at the door interrupted her thoughts. With a final glance she turned and crossed the floor. When she opened the door she faced Jameson, whose mouth literally fell open. An unlikely response from him, to be sure. She quickly scanned downward, hoping to find everything in order. Just her luck the hem of her gown would be caught up in the waistband of her hose, exposing God-knew-what to God-knew-who.

A slow grin crossed his weathered and usually stoic face, and he lifted his gaze. "My lady Andi, you look absolutely breathtaking. I daresay Himself will be pleased beyond words."

Andi's skin flamed from the compliment. "Thanks, Jameson. Is it time?"

Jameson nodded briefly. "Aye, 'tis time." He held out his arm for her to take, which she gratefully did, then started down the corridor.

A very small number of people attended the celebration. Live people, that is. Jameson, his son Thomas, who looked just like Jameson, Miss Kate, her daughter, and Heath, the priest, to name a few. Tristan and his knights, of course. Even Constable Hurley showed up. Dread-moor had quite a haunted reputation, but there were a few who put their fears behind and dared to come forth.

The remainder of the guests were restless spirits, ghosts from all corners of England, Scotland, and France. They had poured in through the front gates in droves, just to see the arrogant Dragonhawk and his lady wed. The news had apparently traveled fast, because there were knights and warriors of all shapes and ages, littering the bailey, the lists, the great hall, and the chapel—ghosts Andi had not once even laid eyes on. And they'd been there all week. From what she heard, they'd planned on staying.

That was to be expected, she guessed.

She was marrying a fierce and, apparently, notorious battle-seasoned thirteenth-century knight.

By the time the sun began its descent and the sky turned various shades of purple, gray, and orange, Tristan had threatened to toss her over his massive shoulders and haul her to the kirk. She wouldn't have minded, really. Not one little bit.

As Jameson led her to the staircase her heart began

to pound. That is, until her eyes landed on Tristan. Dragonhawk.

Then her poor heart nearly stopped.

The groom-to-be stood at the foot of the stairs, speaking with his captain. Kail must have announced her, because Tristan's head turned. He stared, a feral glint lighting his eyes, a muscle tightening in his cheek. It almost made her turn and flee.

Almost, but not quite.

Jameson led her down the stairs, and it was a darn good thing, too. She would surely have tripped had he not been holding her steady.

Jameson approached Tristan, gently placed her hand on his arm, then stepped aside and gave Andi a low bow.

The lord of Dreadmoor all but robbed her of breath. He was so big, she thought. His very presence demanded respect and authority and power, reeking of self-confidence. It lingered in each and every knight's eye, whether live or ghostly.

She, on the other hand, thought him a deliciously dreamy and chivalristic hottie.

He wore his mail, new of course, as was the other knights', and a teeny bit less creaky. Dark hose strained to cover his massive calves and thighs, followed by boots and a black surcoat. The mystical Dragonhawk, same as the one on his shield, was stitched on the front, its head thrown back as though issuing a mighty command. Its eye eerily glowed the same shade of sapphire as Tristan's. More of Kate's beautiful handiwork. His sword, now polished and gleaming, hung low on his lean, narrow hips. Then she noticed something odd.

The sapphire stone was missing from the hilt. It'd been filled in with a black stone. Onyx?

But before she could think further on that, a voice, deep and raspy, growled in her ear.

"Lady, you're gaping. I vow 'tis immensely satisfying."

The corner of her mouth lifted. "No doubt."

He caught and held her gaze, and the impact alone nearly knocked her over. Love and desire shone bright and intense in his eyes. She couldn't have torn her gaze away had she tried.

Not that she would want to try, of course.

"You are passing beautiful, Andrea. I vow I am the luckiest man in the entire world—dead or alive." He grinned, gave her a quick peck on the tip of her nose, and then lifted his gloved hand to her chin. Tilting her head, he lowered and whispered words meant for her only. Warm breath caressed her ear. "God, I love you." He stared a moment longer, then straightened and tucked her hand in the crook of his arm. "Let's be off to the kirk, wench. I vow I am ready to wed you."

Andi grinned and looked up—and noticed for the first time just how many ghostly medieval knights could actually fill a great hall. They all stared at her and Tristan, some more fierce looking, a few no more than fifteen or sixteen years old.

Jason, bless his sweet soul, stood close by. He grinned at the pair and led them through the gathering of men. "This way, my lord and lady. Move, you men there, and make way."

Jameson awaited across the great hall, door open and lanterns lighting the path outside to the kirk. They passed through the doorway, followed by Tristan's garrison and no less than one hundred ghostly knights.

A slight salty breeze wafted across the bailey. Andi lifted the hem of her gown with the one free hand she had, praying she wouldn't stumble over anything. At the rate of speed in which Tristan pulled her, it was a miracle her feet even managed to light on the ground.

Maybe, he was in a big hurry.

Standing now at the front of the small chapel, Andi turned her attention to the priest waiting for them. He opened a large, leather-bound ledger and began to scribble. She forced herself to breathe. A quick glance around the room proved all this was still happening—it really wasn't a dream.

Jameson stood to her left and behind her. Jason took a place beside Jameson. Kail stood on Tristan's right side. The rest of the Dragonhawk knights stood in a line behind them. Kate and her small family lined the wall on Andi's left. The small kirk was literally filled to the brim with the remaining ghostly knights and warriors who'd traveled to Dreadmoor.

The plain, weathered stone kirk suited Andi just fine. Torches lit the room, their flickering flames casting a warm glow. Tristan had her hand tucked safely within his own as they faced the priest. She held on to him so tight, she felt his mail pressing into her skin. Then, before she knew it, the priest started saying his part of the ceremony, in Latin. He turned to her and Tristan, repeating the words in English.

"Tristan de Barre, Dragonhawk of Dreadmoor, how take ye this woman, Andrea Kinley Monroe?"

Tristan cleared his throat, turned, and stared down at her. The dimples pitted deeply into his cheeks, although he didn't smile. There was that intense look, the very one that made her completely senseless. Her knees swayed a bit.

"I take this woman as my own, in the name of our Father." His deep voice washed over her like a wave. "Forever."

The priest nodded, then turned his dancing blue gaze to her. "And you, Andrea Kinley Monroe of Virginia, how take ye this man?"

Andi turned to Tristan, and as soon as she looked into his blue eyes, so full of love, the tears started to roll down her cheeks. "I take this man as my own, in the name of our Father." She sniffed. "Forever."

Tristan reached a gloved hand and caught the trail of tears with his finger. When he lifted it to his lips she knew she'd experienced only one thing more emotional, and that was when Tristan came back to life. Her heart filled with joy.

The priest turned the ledger around on the table before them and nodded. Tristan took the pen, dipped it in ink, and signed his name. He dipped it once more and handed the pen to Andi. She watched her own hands tremble as she signed.

The priest nodded. "In the name of our Holy Father, and before these witnessing souls, 'tis done." He turned to Tristan. "You, my lord, may now kiss—"

"I know that." Tristan grinned at the priest, then pulled Andi into a tight embrace, lowered his head, and captured her lips—then proceeded to kiss her senseless, right in front of the entire garrison and gathered ghosts. Shouts and cheers erupted around the small ancient chapel, but Andi barely noticed.

What girl in her right mind would have, while at the mercy of a chivalrous knight such as Tristan de Barre? The renowned Dragonhawk.

Her husband.

Somewhere in the back of her mushed mind, Andi felt something tugging at her finger. Tristan broke the kiss, gave her a quick peck on the nose, and grinned. She looked down at her hand.

On her finger sat the most beautiful wedding ring she'd ever seen in her life. A wide, silver band, with a lovely sapphire setting in the center. Her head snapped up. "This is from your sword."

"Aye." Tristan produced another ring, much larger than the one on her finger. "I had this one fashioned, as well." One corner of his mouth lifted in a charming grin. "So we would match."

Andi smiled, took the ring from his palm, and tugged off Tristan's glove. She pushed the ring into place and stared up at her husband. "It's beautiful."

"You, my love, are beautiful."

Before she could still her racing heart, Tristan swept her up into his strong arms and took off down the short aisle of the kirk, heading for the doorway.

Jameson hurried after them, Kate by his side, grinning and waving at the same time. "My lord and lady, wait!" He panted as he ran. "A feast has been prepared!"

"Well done, Jameson," Tristan shouted over his shoulder. "Have it sent up to my chambers, posthaste."

Andi turned and glanced behind her as they left the kirk. Jason laughed, a broad smile lighting up his face. Kail slapped Sir Richard on the back, sending him sprawling. Jameson simply stood in the aisle, grinning. Andi waved and held on to her husband for dear life.

He had a purpose; that much she knew. And she knew it, as he carried her across the bailey and through the great hall, without a shadow of a doubt.

Even as Tristan held the treasured bundle in his arms he could scarce believe his good fortune. Andi stared up at him with wide eyes as he climbed the staircase. He flashed her a quick grin.

"Lady Dragonhawk, I vow you'll force me to lose my footing if you do not cease looking at me with such affection. 'Tis unnerving."

Andi giggled. "You're full of it, Dreadmoor."

"Aye, for a certainty. Moon away, love." Tristan reached the top of the stairs and stopped. He studied every inch of his bride's lovely face, from her greenish-flecked eyes to her full, inviting lips. When her hand snaked around his neck and pulled him closer, 'twas nearly his undoing.

He bent his head and brushed her lips with his. Her sweet mouth trembled, and his poor knees wanted to buckle from the emotions it ignited within him. His throat tightened, so he swallowed. Twice. It did no good. Damn bothersome lump.

With long strides he started up the passageway and pulled to a halt just before plowing into his young knight.

Tristan glared. "Damnation, Jason. How'd you manage to get here first? Move you away."

Jason smiled at Andi and blushed. "Shall I guard your door, my lord?"

Tristan walked past the boy and opened his chamber door. "Aye, and guard it with enthusiasm, pup." He kicked the door shut with his foot.

"Aye, my lord!" Jason shouted from the other side.

Tristan glanced down at his lady, who gave him a bright smile. "He is very sweet," she said.

Tristan shook his head. "That sweet lad," he said, tossing his head in the direction of the door, "has killed more men in battle than you could fathom. I daresay 'tis best he knows you now, instead of when he was alive in the thirteenth century. The pup blushes at the mere sight of you." He grinned. "You would have been the death of him, lady." He brought his head closer. "As you would have me."

Andi's breath rushed from her lungs. The hungered look in Tristan's eyes stirred her insides and warmed her skin. A shiver tickled her spine, her heart skipping several beats in its wake. She couldn't speak—she could do nothing but stare into the blue depths of his gaze and watch with anticipation as he brought his lips down to hers.

"Do not close your eyes, Andrea of Dreadmoor." His command whispered against her mouth. "I want you to see what you do to me."

She forced her eyes to remain open as Tristan brushed his lips across hers, their eyes locked. He pulled back, then softly brushed them again. Arms of steel tightened around her, his muscles tense. He slowly set her on her feet, his eyes never leaving hers. Large calloused hands skimmed her skin as he framed her face. Her heart raced out of control.

Her head held captive, Tristan lowered his mouth and kissed her, brushing his lips across hers over and over, his fingers kneading her scalp, tracing the shell of her ear as he deepened the kiss. Her breath escaped as he tasted her lips with his tongue, softly at first, then possessive, demanding. Reaching up, she entwined her fingers in his long, silky hair and pulled him closer.

A low moan escaped him, his breathing harsh. "Help me out of this mail, woman, for I vow I cannot do it alone."

With trembling fingers, Andi helped him out of the heavy-gauge steel. Once free, he stepped toward her and in one swift move scooped Andi back into his arms. In two strides he stood at their bed, and he claimed her mouth once more.

Following her down to the softness of the duvet, he kissed her neck, her ears, her throat, her jaw. Nerves she didn't even know existed tingled with sensation.

Tristan, breathless, lifted his head and held her gaze. "God, Andrea." A rush of warm breath sent a shiver across her skin as his deep, accented voice whispered against her ear. "I cannot get enough of you. I want to touch every place on your body that I've only dreamed of touching."

Andi stared back, unable to utter a sound. The truth of his words glowed in his eyes. For a moment his entire soul gaped, open and vulnerable, just for her, and she drowned in the depths of the love he offered.

And love he most certainly did offer.

Tristan's large hands shook as he unlaced her gown and pushed it aside. The fire in his eyes smoldered as he slowly removed each layer of lace. When not a stitch remained, he touched her with his eyes first, and the heat radiating from his smoky look made her skin warm, in some places scorched as she ached for him to touch her. A deep breath escaped him as his gaze moved from her face, to linger on her breasts, where he muttered something in French-Norman that Andi didn't quite catch. His eyes moved over her stomach . . . and below, lingering again. Strong hands, roughened from swordplay, followed the same path, the pads of his fingers and thumbs grazing the skin over her hips, her ribs, and slowly up to her sensitive breasts. She couldn't help but close her eyes. . . .

"Open your eyes, wife. I want you to watch everything I do to you."

Andi looked, and Tristan's gaze bored into hers, dark and stormy and filled with anticipation. Her breath lodged in her throat.

"Thread your fingers through my hair and pull me close," he said, his voice heavy. "And breathe, for the saints' sake."

A smile touched his lips, and Andi took in a breath and did as he asked, just before Tristan's mouth teased the side of her breast, kissing every inch, his tongue as warm and erotic as the groan that escaped him. Or was that her?

"Tristan, now," she said. She didn't think she could stand another second.

He stood without a word and shed his own clothes, never once dropping his gaze. He came to her, stretched out above her, held her head between his hands, and kissed her until she couldn't breathe.

Scars and muscles covered Tristan's massive back as she ran her hands over him, felt his body tense beneath her fingers. His hands never stopped moving, touching every bit of her as though a newly discovered treasure. Skin to skin, body to body they moved, and then he shifted his mouth to her ear.

"Take me inside you, love," he said, his accent thick, his voice hoarse. "Christ, I want you now."

Andi thought she'd drown in the love she felt for Tristan at those desperate words, and she wrapped her legs around his waist and gasped as he claimed her, filling her completely, heart and body. His gaze never faltered, not once, watching her intently as he moved with a desperation and fierceness Andi had never known. Possessive.

Just as spears of light burst behind Andi's eyes from the intense climax, Tristan groaned and covered her mouth with his and shuddered as intense pleasure crashed over him. Then he kissed her, erotically slow. Gently, he nipped her bottom lip with his teeth, then lifted his head. The look of his own wonder of discovery turned his eyes a dark, tumultuous blue-gray.

With her heart beating wildly out of control, tears spilled over Andi's lids, and Tristan brushed them away with his thumb. Kissing first her jaw, then the tip of her nose, he whispered against her mouth, his voice gruff with emotion.

"I would gladly wait another seven hundred years for your love, Lady Dreadmoor." He caressed her jaw with his callused knuckles. "I love you, Andrea de Barre." He rested his forehead against hers. "I will love you forever."

Andi's heart seized with joy and emotion. Her dreams

had come true after all. She had her knight, who loved her and only her.

And boy, did she ever love him back!

Wrapping her arms around him, she smiled. "I will love you forever, too." She kissed him, deep and long. "My very own fierce Dragonhawk."

Read on for a sneak peek at
Cindy Miles's next ghost story, due out
in November 2007. . . .

Northern England, Castle Grimm
Present Day

Gawan studied Ellie, scrubbed a hand over his chin, then gave her a nod. "Aye. If it will ease your mind a bit, I'll tell you what I can." He closed the door. "Mayhap you should sit."

Sit? Nothing good ever happened after the suggestion to sit before the Telling of Whatever. But since she'd asked for it, and she really didn't have a clue what was happening, or how she kept appearing in this man's bedroom, Ellie found a comfy window seat and sat.

And waited.

Meanwhile, this guy she didn't even know—Gawan Conwyk—paced with his hands clasped behind his back and his dark brows drawn close, as though he were in deep, deep thought.

Somehow, she felt as though she were in deep, deep doo-doo.

Gawan stopped, grabbed a straight-backed chair, pulled it up, and sat across from her. He leaned forward, his muscles pulling his shirt taut. "What do you recall about last night? When I found you?"

Ellie thought about it. And thought some more. Was

it just last night? It seemed a lot longer than that. "I remember being wet and sitting on the road." She focused. "Wet and cold. Lights, I think. Really bright ones, and then . . ." She looked at Gawan. "You. I only remember you." She took a hearty breath in and studied the room. "I remember getting into your truck, then coming here." She snapped her fingers. "I remember Nicklesby."

A smile lifted the corner of Gawan's mouth. Cute smile, she thought. Cute and . . . comforting. Nice lips. *Really* nice lips.

"Nicklesby leaves a grand impression on everyone, I'll warrant." He gave a stern look. "Do you know how you came to be in the lane?"

The lane. How *did* she end up on the lane? For that matter, how'd she end up in the north of England? "I just can't remember."

" 'Tis fine, girl." He studied her, those deep brown eyes boring into her as if he could will the information from her brain. She wished he could.

"Can you recall your family? Do you have siblings? Your mother and sire, mayhap?"

Ellie thought hard. Certainly a normal person would remember their own family? She closed her eyes, thinking for some stupid reason it would help her concentrate. Maybe help her focus better. *Sire? Who said sire anymore?*

Then it came. First pitch-blackness, then a flash of light. Yellowed light, foggy and dim. It illuminated a scene, almost as though she watched an old movie. It faded just as fast as it had appeared.

"What is it?"

Ellie opened her eyes and stared at Gawan. "Not much. A young girl, maybe eight or nine years old, sitting on a wooden dock."

Gawan cocked his head. "A wooden dock?"

Ellie nodded. "Yeah. A dock floating over the water. Maybe a river?" She recalled the scene again. "I think it was me."

"Nothing more?" he asked, his voice calm, soothing.

"No."

Gawan frowned, scratched his jaw, then sighed. "I've something to tell you that may frighten you, but there's no sense in putting the matter off." He reached out a hand, large and callused, she noticed, with thick veins, and squeezed her own hand. "I beg you, don't be afraid."

The pit of Ellie's stomach lurched. "What?"

He inhaled a deep breath, then released it. "I suppose I should have told you from the first, but you kept disappearing." He shifted in his chair. "I have a rather . . . unconventional occupation."

She stared. What did his occupation have to do with her situation? Certainly, he had a good reason. "So . . . what is it?"

Those soulful brown eyes rimmed by dark lashes blinked; then Gawan leaned closer. His soapy scent wafted toward her nose. "I sort of . . . see the unliving."

Silence.

Without moving her head, Ellie glanced around. She scanned each corner of the expansive room, looking for a hidden camera, or who-knew-what, then locked eyes with Gawan.

"You what?" she asked. She scooted closer to the edge of her seat.

He shoved a hand through his hair. "I know it sounds ridiculous, unfathomable, mayhap, but 'tis the truth. I vow it." He cleared his throat. "I see"—he coughed—"spirits."

Ellie peeked over the very broad shoulder of Gawan Conwyk and eyed the door. The one she'd be going out of at any second. Good Lord, how could someone *that* cute be *that* delusional? Oh, his poor mother.

"Ellie?"

Her eyes darted back to Gawan, who had the look of a wounded puppy. Too bad. Didn't matter how cute and sexy he was—he had *issues*. Major ones. Ones she felt sure she couldn't help him with. And here she sat . . . in his bedroom—trapped! Poor guy. Almost made her own situation seem trivial. Her muscles bunched as she got ready to make a break for the door—

"She's going to bolt!" a gravelly voice barked from behind the large oak door. "Grab her!"

"Hush, Sir Godfrey! You'll frighten the poor lamb—"

"Move over, woman! I cannot see a bloody thing—"

Ellie froze in her tracks as two . . . images? . . . sifted through the closed door. She blinked, rubbed her eyes with her knuckles, and stared.

A strange word grumbled from Gawan's throat. Ellie suspected it wasn't nice.

The images—a man and a woman, slightly transparent and wispy and looking as though they'd stepped out of another century—slowly erected themselves. The woman covered her red lips with two fingers and gasped. The man coughed.

The woman had a big bird on her head.

"Now, Ellie," Gawan said. His voice, while deep and a bit raspy, resonated in a low, soothing tone. Sexy, she'd think, if the situation wasn't so damn bizarre-o. "Mayhap you should sit? Come." He touched her elbow. "Sit back down. I'll explain—"

Ellie looked at the man and woman, who simply stood stiff and stared back at her. Blinking.

They'd just stumbled through a closed, solid-oak door.

That just wasn't possible.

She slid a glance at Gawan—whose eyes pleaded with her to do . . . something. Sit? No, she couldn't sit. Definitely not sit. Run, maybe. How she loathed being a coward, though. What else was she to do? Gawan claimed to see ghosts, for God's sake, and then . . .

She chanced another peek at the two by the door. The woman with the big bird on her head gave a sheepish grin and a hesitant wave. The man just frowned.

She could nearly see through both of them.

She could see them?

Ellie closed her eyes and squeezed her temples. "Not real. Not real. Not re-al—"

"What in heavens!" Nicklesby—who reminded Ellie of an older version of Ichabod Crane but dressed in a long, striped sleeping gown and a hat—stormed through the door . . . and right through the bird lady and the man.

"Beg pardon," Nicklesby threw over his shoulder. Then he scowled at Gawan and made a beeline for Ellie.

"My dear," he cooed, grasping her hand and giving it a gentle pat, " 'tis all right." He tugged her gently. "Come away from this chamber of madness and let me settle you into another." He scowled at everyone in the room. "One where you may gain a spot of peace."

Ellie's mind whirled, but she focused in and studied Nicklesby. He felt . . . safe. Maybe a blend of Ichabod Crane and Ebenezer Scrooge. Yeah, that was it—especially in his old-fashioned nightclothes. And that silly long hat. But if he thought she was about to bunk *here* for the night, he was crazy, too. . . .

Gawan gave a hearty sigh and shoved a hand through his hair. "Nicklesby, let me. I'll settle her just as comfortably as yourself, I vow it."

The two by the door stared on, watching the exchange, but remained silent. Maybe they couldn't speak? No, they'd certainly spoken earlier. Or was that her imagination?

In a way, it all struck her as pretty hilarious. She couldn't recall her own name, or where she was even from, but she felt pretty sure she'd never had two guys—even if one did look like Ichabod Scrooge—fight over who would do the honors of *settling* her into bed. Ha, ha! Ho, ho! What a riot!

In a swirl of mist her mind drifted, away from the room with all its strange people. Nicklesby's hand remained on her elbow, so she knew she hadn't left. Very, very bizarre.

Who *was* she? And how in the heck had she ended up in northern England? God, her brain hurt from all the deep, heavy thinking she'd been doing. And none of it had helped.

Except for the small, fragmented flashes she'd had. But they'd been too quick for her to make any sense of them. So far, they'd all been nothing more than miniature scenes of who she could only assume was herself, either sitting on a wide, shady front porch with big, wispy ferns, or a sunny floating dock on the salt marsh—always alone. And none of it meant anything to her. Could be, it wasn't her at all. Then who?

And this guy—Gawan. Even in the midst of her weird situation, she couldn't help but be drawn to him. Silent yet strong, emanating a sense of security and power unlike anything she'd ever experienced—save the small fact that he claimed to see dead people. His voice, while a bit raspy, wasn't too deep, definitely not too high, but just right. Calming, even. And that strange Welsh accent made it all the more intriguing, not to mention he was cute as hell.

Wait—how did she know she'd never experienced anything like that? She couldn't even remember her own name, or where she'd bought the clothes she had on, or jeez—she didn't even remember getting on a 747 and jetting across the Pond.

Gawan claimed to see spirits. And she could see them, too.

The headache started to return.

As did the voices. . . .

"Honestly, Godfrey, I can handle this—wait, she's coming back round." Gawan leaned close to her. "Ellie? Are you well?"

Ellie blinked and focused on the handsome face of Gawan Conwyk. His soft, fathomless—ancient?—eyes studied her. "Are you?" he said. "Okay?"

Godfrey? Who was Godfrey?

Again, Ellie scanned the room. The man and woman had moved closer, now only a few feet away and curiously studying her. Nicklesby had stepped back, and Gawan had taken his place at her elbow. Everyone seemed genuinely concerned over her well-being. So why did it all seem so . . . surreal?

"Do not worry overmuch, Ellie," Gawan said, his voice low. " 'Twill be easier deciphered come the morn—"

It was at that exact moment—the one where she'd

almost felt a little calm—when a figure burst through the thick stone wall. A child—a young boy, rather, maybe nine or ten years old—dressed in dark knickers and socks, scruffy ankle-high boots, and a long-sleeved white shirt with dark suspenders, came hurtling toward her. He pulled up short just a few inches away, out of breath. He, too, was nearly transparent.

Not only that, but the outfit he wore made him look like a paperboy announcing the sinking of the *Titanic*.

He stared hard, and then his nose screwed up and he cocked his head. "Blimey, she doesn't look much like she's dead," he said in a thick, nearly incoherent British accent. He leaned close. "Sir Godfrey, I thought you said she was dead."

The man, Godfrey, coughed.

"Oy, young Davy," Nicklesby said. "Be you quiet!"

Ellie blinked. Too much weird stuff was happening, and cowardly or not, she figured the best thing to do would be to Run Like Hell.

Dead?

"She's going to bolt!" Godfrey cried.

Just as she bolted.

Jerking out of Gawan's grasp, Ellie ran—straight through young Davy, slammed into the very narrow and bony shoulder of poor Nicklesby, then right through the flimsy forms of Godfrey and the bird lady . . . and straight out the door.

Down the passageway she flew, the hiss of gaslights throwing a pale yellow streak over the stone, reminding her of an old Frankenstein movie. She'd watched that before, right? Good Lord, at least she remembered something.

Down the winding stairs and across the oversized great room, Ellie dashed for the double front doors, voices arguing and seemingly right on her heels. Her heart thumped in her chest and her lungs burned, but by God, she was leaving this madhouse—cute guy or not.

Then her body grew light and wispy, and an eerie feeling of her feet not actually touching the ground stole over her. Her vision became very, very blurry.

Gawan called to her, above the ruckus of the others as they quibbled and argued over . . . something, but his voice began to fade, as well.

All just before her body sifted through those thick, ancient double doors . . .

. . . and vanished.

HIGHLANDER IN HER BED

Allie Mackay

She's fallen in love with an antique bed.
But the ghostly Highlander it comes with is
more than she bargained for...

Tour guide Mara MacDougall stops at a London
antique shop, and spots perhaps the handsomest bed
ever. Then she bumps into the handsomest man ever.
Soon Mara can't forget the irresistible—if haughty—
Highlander. Not even when she learns that she's
inherited a Scottish castle.

Spectral Sir Alexander Douglas has hated the Clan
MacDougall since he was a medieval knight and they
tricked him into a curse...the curse of forever haunting
the bed (the very one that Mara now owns) that was
once intended for his would-be bride. But Mara makes
him feel what no other MacDougall has—a passion that
he never knew he'd missed.

0-451-21981-3

**Available wherever books are sold or at
penguin.com**